Praise for the Hercynian Forest Series

The Wolf You Feed (Book Three)

"Quirky and engaging characters, plot twists, adventure and fantasy, humor and thrills, all put together flawlessly " ~**Carolyn Weathers, author of *Crazy* and *Leaving Texas***

"The settings are vivid and real and the characters loveable. The plots interesting and contemporary. Highly recommended for those who want a true "beach read"—especially a Long Beach one!" ~**Marie Cartier, author of *Baby, You Are my Religion: Women, Gay Bars and Theology Before Stonewall***

"I dare to add Reba Birmingham's name to the distinguished list of fantasy writers who use magic, myth, and mystery to discover new meaning in old truths. It was truly inspiring to see lesbians, a Native American, and fantastical forest creatures join together to defeat an evil that is as ancient as the Bible and as modern as today's headlines." ~**Mel White, author of *Stranger at the Gate: To be Gay and Christian in America* and *Holy Terror: Lies the Christian Right Tells Us to Deny Gay Equality***

Words on a Plate (Book Two)

"Tired of fantasy that features the same old wizards and dragons and knights on a quest? Reba Birmingham has just the antidote for you. *Words on a Plate* introduces us to an enchanting mix of magical powers, elves, mysterious happenings in a Peruvian jungle, ravens delivering messages via thumb drives, a horticultural society and its politics—and a main character who is a tax preparer. Not your usual Tolkien clone! Funny and suspenseful by turn, this delightful fantasy brings new life to an old genre. I enjoyed it. You will too." ~**Sheila Finch, author of *A Villa Far From Rome***

"An exciting adventure with unique characters navigating their way through fantasy and reality…[*Words on a Plate* is an] easy read, writing is crisp, and the mystical characters are interesting with creative powers." ~**Katie Cotter, former news editor,** *The Advocate*

Floodlight (Book One)

"As an avid reader and writer of YA Fantasy, *Floodlight* hit so many of those elements that I love about fantasy—the mysterious heritage, the unseen world that parallels the one we know, the amazing characters and creatures that we encounter, the adventure, the impending doom, and the fun. But I loved getting to enjoy all those elements with a fully established relationship. I love Panda, the hard facts-and-figures person, and her free-spirited. kind wife, Mitzi. These two balance each other completely. Panda is joined by their friends, Juniper and Val, as they whisk away to another country to save Mitzi...oh, and maybe the world while they're at it! ~**Debbie McQueen, author of The Dragon King Series**

"In this first novel in a projected fantasy series, debut novelist Birmingham's LGBTQ representation among the cast is refreshing. She parallels the fictional cult with the patriarchy, and she compares inter-species relationships in the fantasy world with LGBTQ relationships in ours." ~**Kirkus Reviews**

"I love me some wacky plots and characters, and between the thrills and chills in *Floodlight*, this book has a lot of humorous stuff in it. Besides, there are elves and griffins and dwarves—oh, my!— who could ask for anything more? If you like the funny urban fantasies of Charlaine Harris or Jim Butcher's Dresden Files, you'll likely enjoy Birmingham's new series." ~**Jessie Chandler, award-winning author of The Shay O'Hanlon Caper Series**

"Likable main characters…(and) sweet elf characters. Having two lesbian married couples was refreshing to read. The balance between supportive and not supportive of lesbian relationships (was) realistic." ~**Bookloverblogs.com**

Circle of Stones

Book Four
The Hercynian Forest Series

Reba Birmingham

Launch Point Press
Portland, Oregon

The Hercynian Forest series

Floodlight

Word on a Plate

The Wolf You Feed

Dedication

To Librarians Everywhere, in recognition of the Good they do.

You are hereby deemed Citizens of the Hercynian Garden

By the Eternal Order of Free Creatures

s/Ehrenhardt Winter, Leader

"The secret of life is in the shadows and not in the open sun; to see anything at all, you must look deeply into the shadow of a living thing." Ute saying

People, Places, and Terms USED

Ali Badawi—Agent of the Hercynian Garden from Egypt, and master herbalist.

Aurora Brown—Ralph's wife.

Bill Miller—Long-suffering husband of Hortense Miller.

Bonnie Bruce-Pippin, a/k/a as Bon Bon—Janet Bruce-Pippin's daughter.

Brad Butler—Mayor Reed's campaign advisor.

Bridgette McGreggor—Of French descent, wife of socially prominent Denise McGreggor.

Brooke Fowler—Panda's stockbroker brother in New York.

Brutus—Panda & Mitzi's beloved Bengal cat.

Charlotte Windingle—Socialite and patron of the arts and of the Merryville Horticultural Society.

Constance Sliwa—Professor from Merida University in Merryville.

Denise McGreggor—Socialite, daughter of the late Agnes McGreggor, and a Legacy member of the Merryville Horticultural Society.

Doug Harker—On the Mayor's Planning Commission.

Ehren—Mitzi's father, leader of the Free Creatures (aka Ehrenhardt Winter).

Ekk—Panda and Mitzi's guardian elf. (aka Ekkehard Schmidt) Husband of Elsa.

Elsa—Panda and Mitzi's guardian elf and wife of Ekk.

Florence Dinwitter, a/k/a Flo—Board member of Merryville Horticultural Society, married to Judge Dinwitter.

Francisco Gonzalez—Candidate for Mayor.

Free Creature—Used to refer to any being free of *Lupus Imperium*, an umbrella for all things evil.

Gary Smithers—Former Merryville City Councilman.

Grunzueg or Gunzweig—German, translates to "Green Stuff," has magical properties used to build things in the Hercynian Garden.

Hercynian Forest/Garden—The Hercynian Forest is the Black forest in Germany; the Hercynian Garden is a magical place within that forest (aka "The Garden").

Hortense Miller—English woman, married to Bill Miller, former president of the Merryville Horticultural Society.

Jack Johnson—Husband of Sally, financial supporter of the Horticultural Society.

Janet Bruce-Pippin—Board member of the Merryville Horticultural Society.

Jay—Former barista at "Not Your Mother's Coffee House." Ehren's partner.

Jeremy Dapp—Mayor Reed's campaign advisor.

Juniper Gooden—Curator at Merryville Museum, wife of Valerie Gooden.

Lidia—Merryville Horticultural Society member, retired schoolteacher.

Lulu Tuigamala—Merryville pólice officer and security guard at Merry Hearts Memory Care.

Margaret—Mayor Reed's secretary.

Merry Hearts Memory Care—Where Aurora Brown lives.

Mitzi Fowler—Panda's free-spirited wife, sometimes travel agent/tour guide, half-human and half-griffin, apt to sprout wings in times of grave danger.

Monte Hunt—On the Mayor's Planning Commission.

Panda Fowler—Our accidental hero, married to Mitzi Fowler.

Puddle Fowler—Panda's sister, prone to wander the world.

Ralph Brown—Proprietor of Taggart's Emporium.

Sally Johnson—Merryville Horticultural Society member, airy-fairy wife of Jack Johnson, who owns a large landscaping company.

Schwartzwald—German, translates to "The Black Forest."

Scott and Mary Day—the Fowlers' next-door neighbors.

Sister Lucia Reya—Mitzi's long-distance therapist and a Peruvian Nun associated with *Las Hermanas del Sol* (Sisters of the Sun).

Sylvia Arviso—President of the Merryville Horticultural Society.

Taggart's Emporium—Established 1956, only independent hardware and gift shop in town.

Tom Reed—Mayor of Merryville.

Twyla – Guardian Fairy sent from the Hercynian Garden to assist Panda and Mitzi.

Valerie Gooden—Native American from the Ute Tribe, a nurse, Juniper's wife, and one of the Fowlers' best friends.

Wolfrum—Cult Leader of *Lupus Imperium*, formerly known as the Wolf Raven Religion.

Zauberbuch—A grimoire or magical book containing spells and knowledge.

PROLOGUE

THE FOWLERS' KITCHEN

I sat in our newly restored kitchen, in the middle of a conversation with my friend and protector, Elsa, a German elf. My cat, Brutus, slept fitfully in his bed on the floor near my feet. I surveyed the new paint and flooring while Elsa cleaned the counter. A mere month before in this very kitchen, Wolfrum, the leader of an evil sect of monks, had attacked me and Brutus.

The surprise attack happened after a showdown at St. Olaf's, where Wolfrum blamed me for ruining his plans to "purify" Merryville for his creepy cult, *Lupus Imperium*. Talk about accidental heroes. My wife, Mitzi Fowler, and I, Panda Fowler, never asked to be part of a fight that spanned parallel universes and determined the balance of good and evil for all free and unfree creatures.

It made me shiver, thinking about our nemesis standing mere feet from where I now sat and using lightning-like energy to try to kill us. My ankle twitched at the memory. I wouldn't be surprised if Brutus was dreaming about the sizzling charge that deflected off my GPS ankle bracelet and torched him. We were both recovering.

When these unwelcome memories invaded my mind, my mood darkened, and a shiver ran down my spine. It wasn't just these memories, I sensed something bad was about to happen and my insecurities kicked in. It wasn't easy living in the midst of magical beings and feeling so inadequate.

"Teach me magic." The words rushed out of my mouth before I even had a chance to think about them.

Elsa must have felt my change in mood and responded kindly. "We don't have much call for magic in Merryville—and you have Ekk"—I pictured her little blond husband—"and me for spells and such, if and when trouble happens. And you know, *Liebchen*, you're not supposed to use magic outside of the Hercynian Garden because you happen to be bored."

"I know." I sighed and twirled my unruly brown hair. It was harder to stay home and heal than I'd imagined. A new thought zinged through my mind. *Spells.* "Are you a witch?"

Elsa's response was sharp. "Panda, drop it."

I wouldn't have been so frustrated if I weren't stuck at home. My ankle injury was stubbornly refusing to heal completely. I did get to work a little with tax clients on Zoom, but I missed sitting across the desk from them at Fowler Tax Service. Truth be told, though, they didn't really need me right now. My relief tax preparer from a temp agency was doing fine. Ekk also popped in to check on the business when he wasn't at Taggart's Emporium. I was in self-pity mode due to being out of my routine. The living room grandmother clock ticked as I traced the patterns on the Formica tabletop with my index finger.

"Elsa, if you teach me magic, I'll show you how to do taxes." My eyes flashed with emphasis, and I leaned back in the aluminum-framed chair, which creaked.

Elsa chuckled and responded, "Panda, knowing how to do taxes is not the selling point you think it is. Besides, Ekk already knows taxes." She paused as if struck by an idea. "In fact, maybe that's why I married him."

It took me a second to realize she was joking. Elsa didn't usually joke. She was actually quite funny with her German deadpan delivery. We both cackled.

"You should do stand up." I tipped the chair back dangerously, then leaned forward, not wanting to add another injury.

Elsa returned to cleaning off the kitchen countertop, standing on a little stool to reach the new granite. A light brown lock of hair escaped her braid, and I watched her brush the strands back with her free hand. I didn't know Elsa's true age, and it seemed rude now to ask her after all this time together. Sometimes she seemed so young, and other times, like now, her rosy face held a certain maturity giving off a motherly vibe. *How long do elves live anyway?* I asked myself.

As if she heard my nonstop thoughts, Elsa faced me again. Her white teeth sparkled as she grinned, gesturing to me with a dishtowel in hand. "And don't forget, you already have your own magic. Work on that."

"You hear Elsa, Brutus?" I scoffed. "I have my own magic. Sure didn't feel like it when we got attacked." I ticked off bullet points on my fingers. "I don't fly like my wife, had no lightning coming from *my* hands like you know who. Me and Brutus here were just lucky the ravens came and chased Wolfrum off." Elsa appeared to have stopped listening. I drummed my fingers again on the Formica table and felt sorry for myself.

Elsa continued to clean and shine the new granite countertop. I didn't think it looked dirty at all. "Is your coping mechanism cleaning?" I asked sarcastically.

In her sweet German accent, she replied simply, "Cleanliness is good." The cupboards and appliances on the counter shone from her polishing. "I'm coping fine."

"Uh-huh." She wasn't fooling me. Ekk and Elsa may be expert guardians, but they were affected by the constant trouble too.

Brutus made a squeaky, yawning sound and stretched. Ever since his brush with death, he was acting like an old man and sleeping a lot. A beam of sunlight bathed his golden spotted fur, which had mostly grown back after his courageous defense of his mama. We all loved him so much. He was a beefy Bengal cat, but he'd lost some weight and still sported a worrisome spot on his chest that hadn't healed. The warm sunbeam coming through the window and onto him and his soft bed must have felt soothing. The kitchen was a tad chilly. My heart melted as he rolled on his back, four paws up, curling toward the light. I wished I could crawl in his bed with him. My jeans and T-shirt weren't warm enough. I reached down to scratch Brutus' ears and was rewarded with a weak head butt before he closed his eyes again. A cool fall breeze blew through the open top of the Dutch door, and I saw leaves in the backyard spin in a circle due to the whirly gust. It made me shiver from the temperature drop, and I thought about going upstairs for a sweatshirt. "Sure is a cold fall."

Bugging Elsa about magic wasn't new. After our many adventures together, it was clear my own magical abilities paled next to Elsa's and others in our immediate circle. Along with some impressive cooking skills, Elsa had flower magic. She could fill a room with certain floral scents and actually influence people's moods. She also did this mumbling incantation that could pause a combatant mid-attack. It came in handy this year more than once. Most recently, however, she had used her healing magic to save Brutus and me after Wolfrum attacked us. Impressive. But my wife, Mitzi, as a half-griffin, had the coolest skill of all. She could fly.

Now Elsa was polishing the toaster and still had her back to the dinette. "Panda, things have settled down now. My *Zauberbuch* stays in the treehouse, under lock and key. You aren't completely well yet either. And your magic may be stronger than you think. It was you who completed the compass pattern at St. Olaf's during our showdown against *Lupus Imperium*." She turned to me. "Hang onto that. We still haven't figured out how ravens knew to come to our kitchen and chase Wolfrum out. You were the only one here. Ekk thinks you may have somehow summoned the ravens."

I exhaled. "Or maybe they're simply fickle. Haven't they changed sides before?"

She paused. "They did split from the wolf side of the cult, but I would describe them more as independent than on our side. Ravens take care of ravens. No more talk of this right now. We should be talking about Mitzi's birthday." Elsa folded the damp dish towel and hung it on the oven handle, a sign she was done cleaning and talking about magic. She smoothed out her apron and sweetly inquired, "Now, would you like some lavender lemonade?"

I was thirsty, and lemonade would be absolutely wonderful. I wagged my finger at her. "You're changing the subject."

Elsa went to the refrigerator and pulled out a frosted metal pitcher. "You are observant. I am, and I want some lemonade. With Mitzi and Ekk at the hardware store, this is the perfect time to plan for Mitzi's birthday. Do you think she wants a big party?"

I stretched and yawned. "We've been through so much. She probably would like to spend it with our usual friends, Val and Juniper, and a couple friends from the Horticultural Society."

Elsa set a frosty glass in front of me. "And Scott and Mary Day."

"Oh yeah." I cast a glance sideways and winced. Of course, the next-door neighbors. "It may be time to fill them in a bit on what's been going on over here, but every time I mean to, they're off on another trip."

"They've been good to you both."

"I know," I said. "Or maybe we don't stay here for her birthday. Any elf-holes around we can use to travel to some exotic place for the day? Someplace beautiful or famous. Mitzi would love that. I—"

"Panda," Elsa said sharply.

I put up my hands in surrender. "Okay, I—"

Elsa was staring at Brutus. "Panda, look at Brutus."

"What?" My beloved pet was gasping for breath. Immediately, my ankle started hurting too. Our twin injury. "Oh my god, Brutus!"

Elsa went to Brutus' side and put her hand on his chest. "Grab him and come on." She ran to the back door.

I reached down and gently picked up the whole bed, wrapping up the cat, as tears sprang from my eyes. "Call the vet. I'll—" By the time I stood with the bed, Elsa was already out the Dutch door leading to her treehouse.

"Where are you going?"

Over her shoulder Elsa yelled, "Just follow me. Hurry."

Clutching Brutus and his bed to my chest, I whispered, "Hold on, baby." I didn't think. I followed Elsa at a fast limp and wondered how I would navigate the ladder that led up to Elsa and Ekk's treehouse with my bum ankle and leg. Instead of climbing the ladder, Elsa went to the right of the tree trunk and disappeared into the thistle bushes. This immediately sparked a memory of being in the Black Forest of Germany months ago. Elsa had led Juniper and me to a magically concealed entrance to the Hercynian Garden. Was this another one of those? The old oak tree predated our home on Thistle Drive by almost a hundred years. Did Elsa and Ekk hollow out the trunk to make an entrance? It was a brilliant place for a camouflaged door, as the base of the tree was wide and gnarly. The thistle bushes were planted close around the base like a collar on a shirt, and the sight of them alone kept folks from walking up to the tree directly. Yes, this must be a magical entrance. The wind picked up, and I adjusted my hold on the bed to keep Brutus warm.

Even though somewhat panicked, I had to hand it to Ekk and Elsa for being so clever. I was amazed neither Mitzi nor I had any idea we had an elf hole literally in our own backyard. Brutus' whole body shivered against my chest, which focused me. *Was that a seizure?* Elsa's head appeared through the bushes, and she said urgently, "Enter here and watch your step. There are stairs." She disappeared again, leaving unbroken, Scottish thistles swaying in the breeze.

CHAPTER ONE

THE HARDWARE EMPORIUM

A bell over the entrance door to Taggart's Hardware Emporium tinkled. Mitzi Fowler and Ekkhard Schmidt entered, followed by a cold breeze. Mitzi stamped her feet as if she were shaking off snow and took her hands out of her puffy pockets to blow on them. "This weather's crazy."

Ekk, a German elf, commented, "It's not Black Forest cold." He had a windbreaker on over his collared shirt, but the snaps weren't fastened.

She hugged herself. "It's all relative. You seem to have adapted to California. When you got here, you wouldn't have worn a jacket like you are now."

He held out his sleeves and harrumphed. "It was March not September when I got here. And it's only a windbreaker." Ekk, fond of his homeland, sometimes romanticized it and the creatures there. "You have to be tough in my country. We used to walk patrols through the snow in my village. Sometimes our feet got numb. And Christmas—"

Not wanting him to go too far into this, Mitzi said with a loud voice, "Okay," and changed the subject, bringing him back to the here and now. "Now, what do we need?"

"I need some things for the treehouse. We're thinking of insulating it better. Hey, maybe you'll find something here you want for your birthday."

She laughed and gestured around her. "At a hardware store? Not likely." Mitzi did love the store, a staple in downtown Merryville, but her idea of a birthday gift was more along the lines of a spa day at a five-star hotel. The warehouse-like space was part of an old sawmill, now chopped up into retail stores and restaurants. Taggart's was lucky enough to include the working potbelly stove from the old mill that now sat in a corner with chairs around it. Mitzi suspected this was the reason Panda liked to come here with Ekk, to sit and drink coffee while he shopped. It made her grin, thinking of her wife and her predictability. Mitzi inhaled the delicious aroma of brewing coffee and thought sitting with a cup right now might be nice. She fancied she could still faintly smell cut wood, although the notion was silly since the mill had been gone for decades. Ekk pulled a small flip notebook out of a pocket to review his shopping list. He was an organized elf.

Mitzi, hands in her jeans back pockets, turned her attention to the man in a shop apron behind the counter. "Good morning, Ralph." The counter was heavy glass in a wood frame, and an antique cash register sat upon it, the metal decorated with swirls. The surface of the counter was cluttered with boxes of maps, small items, and impulse buys, such as keyrings and flashlights, gizmos and doohickeys—all which almost hid the proprietor.

A wizened, black face beamed a smile and greeted them. "Mornin,' Mitzi. Who you got with you today?" Ralph, who'd been cleaning his lenses, put on his glasses and squinted. He was in his eighties and from somewhere in the southern US. His accent and manners were distinctive, and Mitzi had never seen him wear anything other than Levi's jeans, a blue apron, and a crisply starched, ironed work shirt. He squinted at Ekk. "Oh, if it isn't my favorite tax man. Still workin' on your kitchen?" Ralph was a talkative sort, once he got started. "I could have sworn without my glasses—well, never mind. What can I do you folks for?"

Ekk's face lit up. "Kitchen is finally done, thank you. Got a new project."

Mitzi studied him. "I wondered why you were always going to Mr. Taggart's store."

"It's Ralph Brown," the old man corrected Mitzi. "Me and Aurora bought this place from old man Taggart."

"Now I remember. Hey, I've been meaning to ask about your accent. What state are you from?"

Ralph pointed to a red pennant on the wall with a white A on it. "I'm from Bama."

"I don't recall a state named Bama." Ekk seemed puzzled with finger and thumb on his chin.

Ralph laughed, showing long white teeth. "Alabama to you, sir. Home of the Crimson Tide. Best football team in the country." He mimicked throwing the pigskin.

Ekk tilted his head and said, "Alabama. Football, although we call it foosball in my hometown near Baden-Baden, Germany." He stroked his chin. "I just saw *To Kill a Mockingbird* and think it was filmed in Alabama."

"It was," Ralph confirmed with his deep voice.

"I haven't had a chance to travel in the South but would like to see Bama sometime. My wife and I haven't seen much of the United States other than California."

Mitzi listened with interest.

Ralph paused. "You should go. Alabama's changed since the 1930s when the *Mockingbird* film was set, but there's still a piece to go."

"What do you mean?" Ekk's blue eyes were sincere.

Ralph smiled sadly. "My wife is white."

Ekk seemed puzzled. "Okay?"

"Er, racism, Ekk." Mitzi put a fine point on it for her German friend.

Ekk shook his head and put a hand over his mouth. "Oh, of course."

Ralph brightened up, not one to dwell. "That's why we're here in California now." His smile was contagious. "Aurora's sister lives, well lived, here. She died a few years back. I guess you want to be near your kin when you get old. Anyway. I'd go back to Bama. Still got some cousins in Mobile I'd like to see. Sometimes I miss the cookin' in the South. You can take the old boy out of the country but…"

Ekk adopted his version of a Southern accent and made a gun with his fingers. "Ya cain't take the country out of the old boy."

Mitzi cringed at the corny humor, but she was greatly relieved when Ralph issued a true belly laugh. Ekk and Ralph couldn't be more different, but they connected. *Must be a man thing,* she thought.

"*Herr* Schmidt, *ver* are your papers," Ralph said with an awful German accent, and he and Ekk both cracked up again. Mitzi rolled her eyes.

He went on. "My wife's family lived in Wulfen for a bit when her dad was in the British Forces."

"No kidding? My Elsa spent some time in the UK, and Germany, of course. But we're here now. So much to see. I'd love to see the Grand Canyon and Yellowstone too."

Ekk was about to say more when Mitzi interjected, "I can book the trip." As a part-time tour guide, she didn't need much encouragement to plan a tour. Both men turned to her. "What?" Ekk asked. He and Ralph grinned.

"I'm a travel agent. You let me know when you and Elsa are ready to go see the rest of the United States, and I'll put a trip together." She grinned broadly.

Ralph pointed at her with a crooked arthritic index finger and said, "She can. This pretty girl sent me and my wife on a cruise one year. We had the best time."

This was the first time Mitzi had heard Ekk say he would like to see the rest of the United States. During their adventures over the last few months, she had never thought about what they wanted for themselves.

So far, Ekk and Elsa had devoted themselves entirely to their mission of protecting Panda and her. She tucked this bit of information away to discuss later with her wife.

Ralph drummed on the counter. "Whatcha' looking for today?"

"Doing some more woodwork. I'm thinking of a small hutch with little cubicles."

"I saw a mighty fine piece of German furniture in town, a great big hutch at Merryville's Horticultural House—" Ralph was about to say more when his phone rang. "'Scuse me," he said, and turned to pick up the wall-mounted phone.

Mitzi took off down an aisle to browse and left the men to talk some more. It was probably good for Ekk, who lived in a house filled with estrogen. At least Brutus, their cat, was a boy.

Meandering down the aisle, she realized she did love Taggart's, although she didn't think about it much. Located in downtown Merryville off Main Street, the shelves at Taggart's were stuffed with not only tools, wires, batteries, nuts, and screws, but also with gifts and kitschy signs and other novelty items as well. Maybe she did need something from here.

Ekk caught up with her as she studied a household repair kit with shiny red tools. "Shall I suggest to Panda she buy you tools for your birthday? I think those are good German tools too—WOLF-Garten brand. See the logo?" Seeing Mitzi's astonished expression, he said, "I kid you not."

Mitzi had been handling the tool kit absentmindedly. She now noticed the red wolf head in a circle logo and put the thing down as if it were hot. "Um, no. And certainly not WOLF-Garten." Anything to do with wolves reminded her of *Lupus Imperium*—translated as "wolf authority." "No more wolf anything, please. Besides, Panda and I are not 'do it yourself' lesbians."

"DIY lesbians?" Ekk was getting quite good at colloquialisms.

"Oh yes, that's one of the stereotypes for lesbians. It's been around for ages."

"Oh? Any others?"

She ticked off on her fingers each one. "Well, some people think we hate men and always wear Pendleton shirts and comfortable shoes." She pointed at the tools. "We're supposedly really good at building and fixing things with power tools."

Ekk slapped his knee. "Ha. Well, that one's not true. Remember when Panda tried to fix the dishwasher?" They both snickered, thinking of all the water on the floor.

"Let's see, you don't seem to hate men." Ekk pointed at himself. His wire-framed glasses and sharply pressed shirt gave off the impression of a professor giving a lecture. "I've never seen you in lumberjack clothes, and Panda's always complaining about the number of shoes you buy." He put four fingers together over his lips. "Oops."

Mitzi walked on and waved her hand. "Forget it. The stereotypes are stupid, Ekk."

But once on a subject, he had to finish it. He kept talking about it to himself as they climbed the stairs to the loft in Taggart's. "Twyla built the treehouse, very DIY. As far as I know, she's not a lesbian, but who knows with fairies."

Mitzi stopped and turned. "How ironic. In this world some people call gay men fairies." She continued climbing to the second level.

Ekk got serious, following her. "Why would people call a human a fairy? In the Hercynian Garden, we call a unicorn a unicorn, not a donkey. I sure miss the Black Forest sometimes. But until this threat passes, I'm ready to stay in my treehouse."

Right before reaching the top of the stairs Mitzi said, "Actually, I'm happy to be home right now too. I've missed our regular life."

Ekk lifted his hand from the mucky banister and wiped the dust on his pants. "Running off to Peru and Germany weren't in your plans, I'm sure. It's been a busy year." They stepped onto the landing.

"No kidding," Mitzi responded. Busy was the understatement of the century to describe searching for magical portals, facing down their enemy, and fighting Wolfrum. "Panda's bored, but once she's better, we're committed to helping the Merryville Horticultural Society with their community garden. We'll be busy again. In a good way. We owe Denise McGreggor big time since she paid for Panda's house-arrest monitoring."

Ekk ran his fingers lightly over the shelves, searching through tangled lights. "This place is so disorganized," he said. "Is Denise the president of the flower club?"

"No, Sylvia Arviso is. Denise McGreggor is the legacy blueblood whose family owns the home-monitoring company for people on house arrest, among other companies. Her mother, Agnes, was a charter member and past president of the Horticultural Society."

"You studied its history." He stroked his chin, thoughtful. "That club is important to you?"

"This community garden project is very important to Denise. So guess what? It's going to be our new favorite project too. We owe her. Panda will probably rope you into it. She's the new, free, official bookkeeper."

He laughed. "She did say something about bookkeeping for a nonprofit." Ekk made hang loose hands and shook them, cracking Mitzi up. "Easy-peasy, as they say."

It surprised Mitzi that this elf from another world was so up to date on colloquialisms and their local drama. In a way, Ekk reminded her of her father, Ehrenhardt, whom family and friends just called Ehren. Her father visited Merryville recently and, even though he was the leader of all free creatures and had the Hercynian Garden to run, he enjoyed gossip about her local community. "You sound like Ehren."

"Your father is smart. As a temporary leader of the Hercynian Garden, I learned it's very valuable to pay attention to what's talked about in the keep, even if it seems trivial. Makes for less surprises."

"I guess Merryville is our "keep." Panda had a closer connection with Ekk than Mitzi, so she enjoyed this chance to talk one-on-one with him. Panda's connection with Ekk was understandable since they both did taxes and loved watching old movies on TV, but it was time to form her own bond with him. Since they were the only ones upstairs in the loft area of Taggart's, she chanced the real question she'd wanted to ask him. "Do you think Ehren will ever come back to Merryville?"

Ekk was still and gave the question proper attention as dust motes swirled. "Your father really likes it here. It's a vacation from his responsibilities in the Hercynian Garden. But even if he wanted to, Immigration and Customs probably have a flag on his passport after this last visit. He has to travel as a man now, and I think his new relationship has made it impossible to go back to being a full-time griffin."

"Oh. That makes sense."

He tilted his head and shrugged. "So the answer is I don't know."

Ekk wasn't stupid. He was actually very sensitive to his charges. He scrunched up his face. "Mitzi, I know how important it is to you whether or not your father comes back, even if you asked it casually. I think the answer is maybe. He loved having you back in his life and seeing your world, and I'm sure you'd like to get to know him better." Ekk sat on a barrel. "But he does have the Hercynian Forest to run.

From my short time in charge, I can tell you, it's a never-ending thing. He's got the keep full of citizens, nine provinces, a magical moat, and now with the Wolfrum part of the war over, he's rebuilding and enlarging the Hercynian Garden. Plus, the new boyfriend, Jay, has given him a new lease on life."

Mitzi was curious. "So what's Jay, a barista, going to do in the Garden?"

"Make coffee, I guess." He hopped off the barrel and put an arm around her waist. "Come on. Let's shop."

She felt deflated, hardly like the half-griffin child of the King of All Free Creatures. She wiped her eyes.

"Now, what is it you wanted to find up here?" Ekk asked.

"I want some shelves. My home office is so cramped. I don't have places to put everything." She smiled sadly. "When you said you were coming here, I was thinking I could build something for the office. What a laugh." Her fingers trailed over the do-it-yourself shelf packages. "Like I said, we're not Home Depot lesbians."

He stood up straight as if reporting to duty. "Well, it's a good thing we're in Ralph's Emporium then." Ekk peered at her and saw her tears as she turned away. "Hey, hey." He put his hand on her arm. "I've been so busy making sure you survived, I didn't think about what you did for a living or if you were happy doing it. Since I do taxes, I've gotten to know Panda's work world but not yours. I have time now and could build you some shelves, but the room you're using for your travel business is, as you say, cramped. Have you considered renting an office?"

She laughed derisively. "Seriously? Fowler Travel Services can be done in a phone booth, so not really."

Ekk kept probing. "Are you happy doing your tours?"

She leaned against a wooden beam. "I don't know. Mostly I guess, but this year everything had to be canceled. Maybe it's time for something new." She changed the subject. Mitzi didn't let anyone see her inner self easily. "Do you need anything else?"

"Yes. Come help me pick out some lights for the treehouse ladder. It'll make it safer at night for people to climb."

Her face brightened. "I have a perfect idea. They have some wonderful little lights shaped like stars, and a string of lights in the shape of tiny trailers, and one—"

Ekk sighed comically and held up his hands in a stop motion. "I want to make climbing at night safe, not decorate, but let's go see what they have." Mitzi and Ekk moved through aisles of toy trains and coffee makers, fly catchers and bathroom fixtures, and found the lights. As they considered options, the bell over the front door tinkled, and they heard a loud female voice with a British accent speak. "Mr. Brown, I hope you're going to tell me my sprinkler heads have finally arrived."

"Good day, Mrs. Miller," Ralph said with a friendly tone. "I'll go take a gander at what we got."

The imperious voice continued, and followed him to the back of the store. "I'm in charge of transforming five acres, and I don't have any help. When I was president of the Horticultural Society, things ran like a well-oiled machine. We had no shortage of volunteers. Honestly, the new board is a nightmare."

"It's Hortense," Ekk whispered to Mitzi. "Didn't she sue the Horticultural Society? How is she working on a project for them?"

Mitzi put her finger to her lips and listened to the conversation below. She whispered, "She's back in the Society."

"No." He was scandalized.

"Shhhh. Her coming back was a part of the settlement when she dropped the lawsuit." At his astonished expression she said, "I know, awkward."

Down below in the store, Ralph responded to her with his Southern drawl. "Mrs. Miller, you want so many. I got you some, but not all of them. Like you said, five acres is substantial."

"Well, when are the rest coming in?"

"They're on back order. Perhaps a week is all."

During the pause, Mitzi and Ekk crept closer and eavesdropped shamelessly.

Hortense was not happy. "You know, I've been coming here for two decades." She shook her head and peered down her nose at the old proprietor. "I'm tempted to take the club's business to Handy's Hardware, as soon as it's built. Putting up with these inconveniences calls for a discount, don't you think?"

Mitzi and Ekk snuck a peek, all in on the drama, and saw Ralph frown as he rubbed a spot on the counter glass with his weathered thumb. "Hortense, my prices are fair, and I got a business to run." He tried to lighten the moment and put a hand on his hip. "And where else are you going to get the Windingle purple paint?"

Hortense pulled herself up to her full height of 5' 11" and said imperiously, "You know someday, Ralph, National Paint & Tool or someone else like them will figure out the exact shade." She harrumphed. She was a great harrumpher, but she conceded for now. "Send the bill to this address on the flyer." She tossed a paper on the counter.

Mitzi shook her head at the woman's cheapness and arrogance. Independent stores like Taggart's were becoming rare and faced a real threat from the big corporate chains. She whispered to Ekk, "She might save a dollar a can for the Society, but so what?"

Ekk grinned. "Doesn't this mean you and Panda are going to be working with her on the community garden project?"

Mitzi flipped her two beaded braids back over her shoulder, distractedly noting they were getting long. "Not if I can help it. We kind of have to volunteer after Denise McGreggor paid for Panda's leg monitor, but I didn't sign up to work with Hortense. You know she was in with the weird pastor in the park where the fire happened, although now she says she had no idea they were linked with *Lupus Imperium*." She was getting mad as she talked, recalling her friend Valerie Gooden telling her about the garden club drama. "Valerie told me they only approved to let Hortense back in the club by one vote. It was part of a settlement when she dropped her lawsuit against the Society."

"Wow."

"It wouldn't have been financially smart not to do it, so they all held their noses and took her back."

Ekk shook his head. "That club. Your father loved hiding in their clubhouse while he was on the lam. He does love beautiful things." He was referring to Victoria Merry's old mansion that she left in her will to the nonprofit. It was where Ehren had hidden after escaping Wolfrum's clutches. The club was currently being tented for termites.

This made Mitzi grin. "On the lam? You've been watching Bonnie and Clyde with Panda again, haven't you?"

Ekk posed like he was about to do the fifty-yard dash and quoted more from the movie in a Chicago accent, "If we run, we can make it."

Mitzi stood with her hands on her hips. "I won't run from Hortense. Denise's mother was a founder of the Merryville Mavens, and the culture is changing. She's the one who needs to deal. Denise rocked those old biddies on their butts after returning from Europe with her beautiful French wife." She used her arms to make a model-like pose. "They sure didn't see that coming. So Panda and I will be part of the change."

They heard voices getting louder downstairs. Out of curiosity, they crept to the area of the loft closest to the register and spied over the rail to see Hortense in high dudgeon and Ralph wearing a pained smile. "Well, they're not going to get in my trunk by themselves. Put them in the car for me, will you, Ralph?"

While she tutted, Ralph scribbled something on his order pad, probably to give himself time to count to ten.

Hortense departed through the open door without waiting for an answer and pressed her key fob to open the trunk of her Mercedes. Ralph stretched his back and moved toward the pile of boxes.

Ekk's gallantry would not allow the eighty-year-old man to carry heavy boxes full of brass sprinkler heads alone. He raced down the stairs and said, "Let me help you, Ralph." Mitzi sighed and trailed along behind him.

Hortense heard the clatter and spied Mitzi through the open door. She immediately took a few steps back into the store and shouted, "Missy."

Mitzi froze on the stairs halfway down. Hortense called again. "Missy. Aren't you one of our volunteers?" The grin on her face was downright scary. "At the club."

"Yes, it's Mitzi. With a z. Yes, I—"

"Good. Like Liza with a Z. I need people on my committee. Do you know I handled the entire rose rejuvenation at city hall? The mayor loved it. You're just the right age too. These younger people don't understand how many pairs of hands it takes to accomplish literal gardening magic." She beamed a smile at Mitzi, who suddenly felt as old as Methuselah. "Can you come with me now? I could really use some help, and Denise McGreggor and I aren't on the best of terms— ahem, she's nothing like her mother."

Mitzi wanted to say, "Well, after you sued her club and Denise personally, I can see why," but she buttoned her lips. The project was very worthwhile, and she had promised Denise to help. Wouldn't it be a big help to Denise if she kept an eye on Hortense? With her outside voice she asked her companion, "Ekk? Do you mind?"

He appeared surprised but said, "No, you go ahead. Call me if you need a ride." His eyes were merry.

"I'll be there in a minute," Mitzi said to Hortense. "Let me help get these boxes in the car."

"Good. No time like the present to get started." Hortense was positively cheerful and clapped her hands. Mitzi winced. It was easy to see how she'd been in charge before.

Ralph moved slowly, grateful for some help. Ekk took one end of the first box of sprinklers and Ralph the other, and they soon moved six heavy packages to the waiting trunk while Hortense sat behind the wheel of her Mercedes, watching them in her rearview mirror. Mitzi helped organize the trunk, and Ralph was appreciative of her work.

"Thank you, Mitzi. I bet you're good at puzzles."

"She is," Ekk said.

Mitzi said to Ralph, "My wife and I will be working on the big garden project she got those sprinkler heads for."

Ralph shook his head. "Then you have my sympathy. She's a mean one. Aurora never took to her, and there ain't hardly a soul she don't like." He turned to Ekk as if an idea had struck him. "Ekk, are you interested in any part-time work? I could sure use a good man on Sunday afternoons. That's when I go see my wife."

"You know, I think I'd like working here," Ekk replied. "Where's your wife?" Ralph closed the trunk.

Hortense honked and Mitzi said, "Later guys. Duty calls." Mitzi opened the car door and got in with a sigh.

Without a tip to Ralph or a thank you, Hortense pulled away.

CHAPTER TWO

PANDA IN THE ELF HOLE

Even though I knew it was an illusion, I winced as we dove straight into the Scottish thistle bush. I'd recently been the recipient of a thistle sting, so plunging through the reddish-purple flower heads was very brave for me. Thistle stings hurt for hours. Plus, while clutching Brutus to my chest, I didn't want to injure him. The pet bed was our shield, however, so we confidently entered where Elsa's head disappeared.

I didn't feel a sting. Instead, warm air greeted us. I saw a glow ahead, as my foot found the first stair step. I emerged past the illusion and saw a cave-like room, lit by flickering light from a lantern hooked on a root growing out of the wall. I carefully felt for each step until reaching a hard-packed dirt floor. Once fully in the room, I almost dropped Brutus while trying to keep my balance and take in the sight.

The space had roughly hewn walls covered with what I knew to be magical *grunzueg*, which translated from German as "green stuff." Lots of things in the Hercynian Garden were made from it. Various tools hung on protruding roots, as were bunches of dried herbs, mushrooms, and the aforementioned lantern. The space appeared to have grown organically, although without magic, this was not possible. The ceiling was the bottom side of the trunk, and the floor and walls were dirt, as one would expect under a giant oak tree. They had used the *grunzueg* like paint, and it gave strength to the cavity. This made me wonder how permanent it was. I knew the magical properties of *grunzueg* decayed over time in the human world. For now, it seemed to magically keep the place from caving in.

Elsa was flipping through pages of her *Zauberbuch* frantically with a yellow cat we called Blondie. She first appeared when Brutus and I were injured and glued herself to our boy. I wondered again if Elsa was a witch. Didn't they have cats as familiars? Was Blondie Elsa's familiar? Without looking up, Elsa pointed to a wooden table near the far wall. "Put Brutus on the tabletop."

I carefully placed him, still in his bed, at the center of the wooden table, and Blondie immediately leaped upon the table to join him, making an odd trilling sound. The table was apparently one of the things Ekk had worked on with all those trips to Taggart's. *How long have they kept this secret?* I wondered.

Elsa chattered in German to the cat, who started licking Brutus' head. Sick with worry, I inquired, "What's she doing?"

Blondie appraised me with such intelligence, I knew she was offended at having her actions questioned, so I smoothed my windblown hair and spoke directly to her. "Never mind. I'm sure you're helping." The cat went back to her duties, mollified.

I turned my attention back to Elsa, who wore a serious expression. Book open, she had a finger on a particular sentence in her *Zauberbuch*. She appeared pretty witchy in this underground space, her face defined by lamplight and shadow. "Panda, leave us. I need all my energy right now. You need to go."

"But Brutus—"

Elsa reached with her free hand and actually gave me a gentle push. "Sorry, but leave Brutus to me. Go. Tell no one about this place. Not even Mitzi." Elsa turned back to her work. As I left, I finally noticed a dank odor of roots and earth, which didn't seem overly healthful. The last thing I heard on my way up the stairs was Elsa's soft voice, mumbling in German, and more trilling noises from the new cat. My ankle was burning, and I was worried about Brutus. Once free of the hidden space, I became cold again and decided to get a sweatshirt before returning to the outside table near the tree. Once settled, I pulled up my pant leg and worked the compression sock down. Crap. My wound appeared red and angry. I wanted to go back in the elf hole and ask Elsa about it, but she had her hands full. I would only get in her way since the hidden room was so small. Mitzi would know what to do. Needing to connect with someone, I decided to call Puddle, who was still in Peru.

It took a minute. The electrical impulses had to travel far to reach South America. My sister's distinctive voice answered, "Panda Bear. What's up, sis?"

I sighed. "So much to tell, and I really can't get into specifics right now. I needed to hear your voice and something normal. How's Peru?"

"You called me for normal?" Puddle snickered. "Me and Dieter are staying in a village at the foot of Machu Picchu. He's been trying to find relatives but has only found a second cousin, once removed. Remember when our aunt drilled the family tree chart into our heads?"

Remembering our rather OCD aunt I said, "Yes, she was always trying to teach us something. Hey, have you talked to our brother lately? I haven't."

"Brooke? We see him all the time. I saw him about a week ago back at the convent. It's so funny." She snorted. "He's got a thing for Mitzi's therapist."

This was news. "He's in Peru? I never thought he'd leave New York. Good for him. I wondered if he was interested in Sister Lucia. He was so attentive when around her, Does she like him back?"

"Sister Lucia made it clear she's married to the church. So, no. But he's still sticking around, working with the nuns to bring money in for their orphanage. He's probably hoping he can change her mind over time."

"Wait, Wall Street Brooke Fowler? Helping for free? Isn't he the dude who made us pay interest if we borrowed a couple of dollars from him as kids? Wow."

Puddle giggled. "The Lord moves in mysterious ways."

"Look at you, quoting scripture. Are you converting from Hinduism?" Panda hoisted her aching leg up on a chair. "How are you, sis?"

She was silent for a minute. "You know me. I'm about done here."

Puddle was known for her itchy feet, never staying in one place for long. "You're always welcome here, sissy. We have some amazing stories to tell you, but not on the phone." I stared at the illusion around the base of the oak tree.

"Gotcha. You never know who's listening. I've got some things to tell you too." Puddle sounded serious. She was prone to conspiracy theories, so I didn't give the comment much weight. "By the way, Twyla doesn't like the heat in South America. She came down here with Brooke but left already."

"Where did she go?" I remembered what Ekk said about fairies being unpredictable.

"Dunno. It's probably good they went their separate ways. Brooke was pretty pissed at her 'cuz right after they got here, she was already trying to use, uh, other means to raise funds for the nunnery. I guess things got pretty messed up. You know, he's a control freak, and she's, um, not."

"She means well. Ha. I wondered about that pairing. From what I gather, messed up is probably an understatement." We both giggled, remembering how awry things went when Twyla watched my house.

Puddle went on. "So Twyla left for parts unknown, maybe back to the Garden. As for the convent, things have pretty much calmed down here, if you know what I mean. In fact, it got boring after Juju went back to whatever he did before guarding us. I miss him. Dieter is busy with his search for family, and I'm pretty much on my own. You can only watch so many hummingbirds, ya know? I might visit you."

"Okay, sis. I hope you do." I thought of our cat, suffering. "By the way, say a little prayer for Brutus. He got injured recently, and his prognosis isn't great."

"Brutie? Oh no. So that's what's going on? I figured something happened. Do whatever you need to so he gets better. I love your little dude." I knew she meant it. Puddle was a huge animal fan.

"Elsa's on it. She's ah, working on something now to fix him. Well, keep in touch." Panda focused her eyes on the thistles around the oak tree base, aware of the fragility of life. "I love you, Puddle."

A beat. "Seriously. You okay, weirdo?"

"Yeah."

"Take care then. And Panda Bear? I can't think of a better person than Elsa to care for Brutie, and don't forget, cats have their own higher power, ya know. Love you too. Say hi to Mitzi." She ended the call.

Puddle's last comment about a "higher power" made me smile. My sister was a chronic pot smoker, but during one period when she was trying to stop, had picked up the concept of a "higher power" at some Twelve Steps meetings. Puddle had also dabbled in Buddhism, Hinduism, and other philosophies, anything but the Episcopalian church we were raised in. But in any spiritual tradition, I knew I wasn't in charge of whether Brutus lived or died. As our Ute friend Valerie would say, Great Goddess Spirit in the sky had this. Even with this acceptance, waiting was still hard. Even though Mitzi and Ekk were due back soon, I gave into telephonitis and called my wife. As the phone rang a couple of times, I went inside to find a snack, holding the phone to my ear. I was an emotional eater.

Mitzi sounded breathless when she answered. "Hi, honey. Can I call you back in a little bit?" In the background, I heard Hortense Miller's distinctive British voice giving instructions of some sort.

I sat up. "Wait, weren't you going to the hardware store? Where are you? I thought you'd be back by now. Did I hear Horse Face?" Horse Face was my immature nickname for Hortense.

"I got hijacked. I'm being trained right now on how to open a bag of mulch."

"Did I hear correctly? You're with Hortense Miller? Where are you?"

"The garden project, downtown."

"Oh." *Not Taggart's.* "Anyway, Mitz, something's happened with Brutus. Elsa is treating him now with Blondie."

Mitzi was suddenly focused on the call. "Brutus? Oh my god, what happened?"

Given the events of the past year, I understood her reaction. "We weren't attacked. Nothing that dramatic, but his injury is getting worse."

Her voice raised a notch. "I thought Elsa figured out how to reverse…can you get me? I need to wash up and then tell the ladies I need to leave." In a whisper she said, "Hortense just left for her meeting. What a B."

"You need to tell me more about your hijacking for sure. I'm on my way."

***

MERRYVILLE HORTICULTURAL SOCIETY "THE PROJECT"

Charlotte Windingle's family was the biggest developer in Merryville. They donated the land and provided use of the Horticultural Society office trailer. The single wide was powder-coated their special trademarked purple, of course, and situated dead center in the community garden project. A couple of four-seater golf carts were parked out front, since five acres was, literally, a lot of ground to cover. Charlotte had never been much of a gardener, but she was a well-known ambassador for her family company's philanthropy in Merryville. She dearly loved to be in the middle of trends, and right now, the community garden project was in the news. As developers, Windingle money was responsible for transforming much of downtown, and almost every block contained a building sporting their distinctive purple art deco colors. Charlotte's grandmother had chosen the shade, and now they were part of the Windingle brand.

Sylvia Arviso stood with some of the other horticulture board members, Denise McGreggor and Valerie Gooden, waiting for their meeting to begin. Sylvia noted how Sally Johnson wandered around nearby, digging her hands into a bag and smelling the coconut mulch in it.

Charlotte wore brand new stretch jeans with a matching jacket and impossibly white tennis shoes with little rhinestones on them. She was obviously having fun dressing "gardeny" for this new project with her family name all over it. The fifty-something's eyes were bright, as she was engaged in gossip, a guilty pleasure. "I knew Hortense was coming because of the settlement, of course, but actually seeing her car when I pulled up really rattled me."

Denise said, "Come now, Charlotte. My lawyer said it was the cheapest way out of the lawsuit and honestly, what damage can she do? Sylvia's assigned her to the sandpit in the far corner." This made Charlotte cover her mouth and cough. Even with her own lack of a green thumb, she knew sand wasn't ideal for a garden. Sylvia hummed as she checked off items on the clipboard she held, pretending she didn't hear Charlotte and Denise being catty.

Valerie, blue-black hair blowing in the breeze, leaned against a shovel, worn leather gardening gloves on her brown hands. She, out of all of them, was most at home in the earthy environment. Raised on a Ute reservation in Colorado and familiar with sand, Valerie chimed in. "The sandpit could actually be a great place for the succulents. We just need to work it a bit."

"Thank you, Valerie. That's why we put you in charge of choosing the plant locations." Sylvia nodded approvingly. She eyed the other board members. "We all need to work together to make this work. Remember, it's about the underserved community getting access to fruits and vegetables."

"You're such a good person." Denise gave Valerie a half-hug, still mischievous.

"Better than us," Charlotte said, and they both laughed heartily.

Sally wandered back over. "Do you like the golf carts? Jack ordered them especially for us." The ladies all turned to admire the carts, red four-seater, electric vehicles with Johnson Roofing stenciled neatly on every flat surface.

"They're beautiful," Denise said. "Thank you both so much for what you do for us." She was a social butterfly and always knew what to say.

"My painters will make them match the trailer, if it's okay," Charlotte said.

Sally responded, "I'll ask Jack." They all knew Jack would do anything for his wife.

"Can they put in a heater too?" Charlotte asked. The ladies chuckled at the joke. The open-air carts were a bit chilly during the unseasonably cold fall they were having.

"All we need now is more electricity to plug in the carts." Sylvia glanced at her watch and after a beat said, "I'm going in to check on the presentation." She was wearing an Alice & Olivia jean jumpsuit from Nieman Marcus and silver sandals. Even though she stepped carefully up the metal stairs to the construction trailer, they still made a clatter.

As Sylvia climbed the steps, she heard someone behind her say, "Those shoes are not very practical." Hortense's distinctive voice made her jump. As she turned around, she saw everyone staring at the new arrival.

"Hi, Hortense," they unenthusiastically chorused.

Even though Sylvia was now president, Hortense still had a way of making her feel like an incompetent child. She turned toward the tall English woman, dressed in pedal pushers with a flower-print tunic and gardening clogs. "Hortense, today is merely the board meeting. These are fine for sitting in the trailer." She was immediately mad at herself for explaining.

Hortense twisted her lips into a semblance of a smile. "I've been surveying my, ah, plot area. Sand? Really? Well," she laughed merrily, "Hortense does mean gardener in Latin." She pinned Sylvia with a meaningful gaze. "I love a challenge." She whistled as she went around the back of the trailer where a series of potting benches and sinks had been installed.

Charlotte pantomimed throwing up, and Denise stifled a laugh. "This is going to be fun," Charlotte said. "Come on, girls. Let's go inside and get warm." Gossip session ended, they tromped up the metal stairs and into the rather snug interior. Janet was waiting for them in front of a wall with "Garden Project" and an image of the garden goddess, Antheia, projected on it.

Janet Bruce-Pippin was a whiz with PowerPoint, and therefore the official maker of these presentations for the board. She was more suited to the administrative tasks of the Horticultural Club than the actual digging part. Her own garden at home was decent, but everyone knew she hired someone to do it. Janet brightened as the board members entered. "Ladies, take your seats. We have some coffee brewed." She pointed, and her daughter Bonnie, wedged in behind a metal cart, motioned like Vanna White at the rather elaborate setup for such a small surface. Three pots—one decaf, one leaded, and one with hot water for tea, were on a tray, crowded with china, cream, sugar, and cookies. Sally Johnson went straight for the shortbread cookies.

Sally, somewhat of an enigma, appeared simple on the surface, but she could come up with the deepest observations on occasion. Today she had dressed in button-up Levi's, a pink cowgirl shirt with yellow piping and pearl buttons, and gardening Crocs. Without any makeup, Sally appeared younger than her forty years. Everyone knew she didn't drink coffee, and, as she stood scanning the tray, Bonnie pulled out a bottle of Nehi Grape Soda for her from the second shelf.

Sylvia picked up her pointer and nodded to Janet to start the presentation. "Shall we?" She surveyed the ladies around the table: Valerie, slender and relaxed with her herbal tea, Charlotte, with the patience of a small child, scarfing cookies, and Denise, adding the gravitas of being a legacy member. "Oh, where's Hortense?"

With perfect timing, Hortense, former president of the club, entered the room, floor creaking. She took the last available seat. Bonnie asked, "Would you like a beverage?" in her best teenage imitation of a butler.

"I brought my drink, thank you." Hortense put a reusable water bottle on the table. "I highly recommend these. Very eco-friendly." On her water bottle "Seeds of Transformation" was printed down one side in red letters and "New Spirit" down the other. "In fact, I have several of these if you ladies want one."

Sylvia frowned. This was very "in your face" considering recent events involving New Spirit that had ended with a lawsuit over the club.

Only Sally said, "I want one," obviously missing the significance, as even Bonnie made a face. Seeds of Transformation was the name of the gardening mission Hortense had set up with New Spirit, the tent church in the park. It was New Spirit that had invited some religious cult leader to Merryville from Germany, and it had been a big scandal in town. Sylvia didn't know the whole story, but some of the society's members had been involved. Panda Fowler had even been arrested.

Denise McGreggor, one of the women sued by Hortense, lifted her eyebrows and fixed her eyes on the slide projected on the wall. The atmosphere was tense.

Charlotte, in an attempt to lighten things, lifted her cup and saucer as she said, "I don't want one. Those bottles are a pain in the butt. God wouldn't have invented china if we weren't supposed to use it."

Bonnie appeared confused. "God invented china?" She had never heard such a thing at St. John's Episcopal.

Denise, unable to remain silent any longer, shook her head. "Of course not, Bonnie. Josiah Spode did."

Hortense put down her water bottle. "Bonnie, you are so innocent. You should probably run along now. This is definitely not the place to learn about god."

Denise glared at Hortense.

"I thought this was a Horticultural Society meeting. That's not anti-god," Charlotte said.

Bonnie slunk down on a box of announcements behind her beverage tray as the sparks began to fly.

Hortense surveyed the ladies' faces around the table. "Well, this club is certainly a lot, um, gayer than it was when Agnes McGreggor and I joined."

"Ladies—" Sylvia started.

"How dare you," Denise said, outrage showing on her face and in her tone. "Leave my mother out of this."

Hortense raised her eyebrows almost to her hairline, yet appeared amused. "You did slip into the organization on your mother's coattails, and this club has changed."

"What does that have to do with tea in China?" Charlotte was being funny again.

"With all this…diversity…well, we're hardly likely to be asked to decorate the Southern Baptist Convention next month." Hortense shrugged. "Let's go on."

"Hortense," Denise put her napkin to her mouth, as if to remind herself not to say something she would later regret. She didn't like a public spectacle. After a breath she said, "The bylaws are what govern this club, not the Bible."

"I'm not saying the Bible should be our guide," Hortense said. "Charlotte asked what does that have to do with tea in China, and I simply pointed out how this change has affected our work in the community." She said this with a flip of the wrist.

Charlotte put down her coffee cup, which made her saucer rattle. "You old horse's ass. I was joking." She was on a roll. "You're only here because our lawyer said we had to take you back."

"Point of order. Point—" Janet said weakly.

"I can see your diversity doesn't extend to Christians." Hortense stood and began to collect her things.

Sylvia turned to Janet, who was the club parliamentarian.

Janet finally shouted, "Point of order. We are not a religious 501c3 or a church. We are a gardening club for fuck's sake."

Everyone shut up, and they all turned to the normally quiet Janet in surprise. Bonnie's eyes widened.

Sylvia rapped the gavel on the table and said forcefully, "Thank you, Janet. Now, we have much work to do, ladies." She fixed her dark brown eyes on each one. 'Charlotte?"

Charlotte exhaled. "I'm sorry for calling you a horse's ass, Hortense."

"Denise," Sylvia's tone was flat.

Denise hesitated a moment before she lifted her well-manicured hands in surrender. "Okay, I'm sorry for the distraction." She added provocatively with the sweep of a hand, "Period."

"Apology accepted." Hortense loved stirring up trouble, and she seemed quite pleased as she sipped on her Seeds of Change bottle. "You may continue."

Sylvia wasn't letting her off the hook. "Hortense, you were part of this too."

After a dramatic breath, Hortense said in an almost sing-song voice, "I'm sorry this club has chosen the path it has, but the community needs voices like mine. I will stay."

The hackles on the back of Sylvia's neck prickled. For not the first time, Sylvia realized having Hortense back was going to be a challenge. She cleared her throat and dialed it down a notch. "Okay. You've all received your paperwork. You know the plants we've chosen and where they're going to go. Thank you, Valerie."

Valerie nodded silently, taking it all in.

Sylvia addressed Hortense next. "Did the sprinkler heads come in?"

Hortense raised her eyes to the ceiling and shook her head. "I have some, but not all in my trunk. These small independent places can't keep up with a project of this size. I can't wait until a new home improvement store comes into town."

Denise spoke up again with a firm tone of voice. "We're sticking with Taggart's. We have to support small businesses. They've been around since before the club started." She gave Hortense the gimlet eye and gestured toward the agenda. "My mother started the account for the club with Ralph and Aurora Brown back in the seventies."

Hortense couldn't let it go. "With all due respect to your mother, Agnes, time marches on." She brushed imaginary lint off her blouse. "I thought you of all people wouldn't care about silly things like tradition." She grinned, but the gleam in her eye was positively malicious. Everyone knew she was doing a back-handed swipe at Denise returning from Europe married to a woman.

The expression on Denise's face warned Sylvia another fight was coming. She needed to cut off this train of conversation. "Ladies, new rule. If it's not on the agenda, we aren't discussing it." She tapped her pointer at the makeshift screen a couple of times. "Today we must make decisions on the design. I have Juniper Gooden coming in to—"

She was interrupted by clamoring outside, and Mitzi Fowler stuck her head in. "Oops. Sorry, I've got to go. Something's happened to my cat."

Valerie's head jerked up. She was a close friend of the Fowlers and loved Brutus.

Seeing she had just interrupted the meeting, Mitzi apologized again and mimicked making a call to Valerie. Then she was gone.

Denise leaned forward. "That reminds me. I want Mitzi Fowler on my committee. We're going to—"

"Sorry, dear, I didn't know," Hortense said with syrupy sweetness. "She already joined mine."

Denise appealed to Sylvia. "When did we choose committee members?"

Before Sylvia could answer, Hortense said quickly, "I ran into Missy at the hardware store. We really need to do something about Mr. Brown—"

The door Mitzi left open smacked shut loudly due to a sudden gust of wind. Everyone jumped, but at least it cut off Hortense's tirade. Sylvia couldn't help but think this project was going to be one long nightmare.

CHAPTER THREE

MERRYVILLE CITY HALL–MAYOR'S RACE

Mayor Tom Reed was at his wit's end. The primary election was coming up in June, and his numbers weren't great after the last few months. Two challengers had already filed papers to run against him. He stood behind his desk, wearing his Merryville windbreaker over his golf clothes, peering out the window at downtown. "Thank God the feral cat and homeless thing died down," he said. "Those screaming meemies are an easily stirred-up bunch. What's next?"

His campaign consultants sat in the visitor chairs. Brad Butler said, "We've got the community garden ribbon cutting, but uh," he studied a calendar in front of him, "not until March." He peered at the papers spread over Tom's planning table. "I can go over the demographics for you."

Tom's instincts were pretty good and, truth be told, he hated the detail stuff. "Not right now. We're a few months away. Let's focus on the fundraiser. Did you get me a celebrity?"

Jeremy Dap, hunched over computer printouts, winced. "Well, yes and no. We couldn't get a Hollywood celebrity, but we did get Mona Martin."

Tom smiled. Mona was from Merryville and was popular in the local Shakespeare productions every summer. She was also rumored to be the face of the new big box coming into town. "Good. I like her. What else?"

Brad and Jeremy appeared nervous. They'd been somewhat subdued.

"Well? I'm paying you guys a lot per minute. What?"

"Tom, I guess I'm the one who should tell you because I used to work for Gary Smithers," Brad said.

Tom frowned. Gary Smithers, the former city councilman of his political party, was arrested after a major scandal. He put his index finger forcefully down on the maps and statistics. "This is political poison, Brad. Why bring that up? What happened wasn't my fault. Who could have known he was mentally unstable?"

Jeremy responded innocently. "It was pretty spectacular, sir. I mean, a sitting city council person goes to one of your citizen's homes with a machete and tries to chop up a couple of domestic workers. You had to know your opponent would use it."

"Thank you, Jeremy, for your piercing insight," Tom said sarcastically. "I know what happened." He paced the posh office like a caged animal. "This is old news. It's over. He's in a mental institution, right?" He threw these words out hopefully. "Aren't we all supposed to be sympathetic? Mental illness and all?"

Jeremy cleared his throat. "Not right now. People are terrified. This morning Gary Smithers escaped from Merryville State Mental Hospital. It's all over the news." He picked up the TV remote control and clicked to Channel Five.

"What?" Tom grabbed a golf club and pointed it at the wall-mounted TV where the chyron now rolled the words BREAKING NEWS. He shouted, "Turn it up."

Sure enough, perennial talking head Jessica Walters stood in front of Merryville State Mental Hospital with a serious expression. "The police chief has issued an all-points bulletin for Gary Smithers, who is believed to be, if not armed, extremely dangerous." Jessica swiveled her head dramatically left and right as if expecting him to come flying at her, then stated directly into the camera, "For those who don't know, Gary Smithers used to be a highly regarded city council member in Merryville. He was the founder of the "Bring Back our Family Values" annual picnic and a part of the mayor's "Make Merryville Beautiful" campaign. It was a shock to the local community when he went to a constituent's home with a machete and allegedly threatened two immigrant domestic workers. After his arrest for attempted murder, he was placed at the Merryville State Mental Hospital, pending trial after a psychiatric evaluation." Jessica touched her left ear as if getting a message. "Wait, we have—" she gave her trademark smile—"we're going to cut to Bob Dawson, who is with Francisco Gonzalez, candidate for mayor. Mr. Gonzalez is commenting on the situation."

Tom exploded at Brad and Jeremy, who cringed. "Dammit. Couldn't you get ahead of this?"

Jeremy said, his voice weak, "Gary's timing to escape is bad, but Brad and I—"

The TV cut to a storefront downtown next to Fowler Tax Services. "Hi. Bob Dawson here, and I'm down at the Francisco Gonzalez Campaign Headquarters for the hotly contested mayor's race."

Tom glowered at his re-election team. "You should have seen this coming. And his campaign office is next door to those women where, well, you know. I'm sure his choice of location wasn't an accident."

Tom lifted his eyes to the ceiling and counted to ten, a habit of his when trying to calm down. He heard Jeremy whisper to Brad, "Seen which, the escape? The campaign office?" He saw Brad pull his head back and put his index finger in front of his lips to keep Jeremy from commenting further. It didn't surprise Tom. Brad knew him better than Jeremy did. He knew how irrational he could be when upset. It was wiser not to argue with him when he got like this.

The TV interview showed a close-up of candidate Francisco Gonzalez, young, handsome and serious, making a statement. "The threat is real. Mayor Reed chose Gary Smithers, handpicked him as a candidate to run a council district in Merida, what we now call Merryville. Even before Smithers picked up a machete and threatened to behead two of our citizens, one of whom works next door to our headquarters, Gary was racist, homophobic, and like this"—he crossed his index and middle fingers—"with the mayor. It makes you wonder how many of those views Tom Reed espouses." He lowered his voice, sounding more like a politician than an activist. "I have sympathy for anyone whose family is struggling with mental illness. See my web page for my policies. My point here is, we need a mayor with good judgment. I mean, what's he going to do now with his man on the loose?" He angled his handsome face toward the camera, as if he could see those on the other side watching, and asked in his lightly accented voice, "I mean, where are you, Mayor Reed, the golf course?"

Muttering "his man" under his breath, Tom marched out the door to the reception area where his secretary sat. "Margaret, cancel my game with the boys. I can't be seen playing golf when the police are tracking down my former city councilman."

Margaret silently nodded and picked up the phone at the same time. She appeared trained to ride out his temper tantrums by doing his bidding.

Somewhat appeased, Tom returned to his office where the two advisors seemed a bit less glum. "What now?"

"Mayor, we do have a plan to make everyone forget this. You know those lesbians, the Fowlers?" Brad asked.

The switch was so sudden, Tom stopped in his tracks. "Who? Lesbians? There was the one at the museum and her wife."

"No, the curator at the museum is Juniper Gooden. It's her wife Valerie you're thinking of. It was their friends, the Fowlers, who owned the house where Gary Smithers, well, you know, went crazy. and they own the tax business Gonzalez used in his TV spot." Brad said.

"Brad fought me on this at first," Jeremy said, "but I think you need something LGBTQ to show you're not homophobic like Gary was. Also, if the Fowlers don't hold what Gary tried to do to their housekeepers against you."

Tom glared at him. "I don't follow."

"We're thinking, if they don't hold a grudge, why should the general public? Makes it a non-issue," Brad said. "Then we can talk about projects like your new community garden." Brad stood and waited for the idea to take hold, exuding prep school manners. "You know the old saying—two birds with one stone. Just be careful it doesn't backfire. These people—LGBTQ, whatever, can weigh down your platform."

"I'm not a fool." Tom rubbed his strong chin. "And it's LGBTQ plus, Brad. Don't forget the plus. Ha! So, Jeremy, what's the plan?"

Jeremy added the kicker. "Make them a part of one of your community teams, maybe even a commissioner."

"I like it." Tom's mood brightened considerably. "That would sure change the conversation." This strategy could get him re-elected.

"Do you have a commission you can name them to?" Jeremy asked.

Brad jumped in. "If you're sure you want to do this. Putting one or all of these folks on a commission is one part of dismantling the other side's argument about how your former city council person was so anti-gay. Let's face it. The poor man was simply…unbalanced."

"Save your sympathy for my campaign." Tom stroked his chin. "Isn't that a bit obvious to put them all on commissions?"

"True," Jeremy responded. "But if we can find the right commission and pick one from the bunch, the right person, it could be gold. Worth a try, don't you think?"

The mayor put his golf club back in the bag and stowed it in the closet. "What's available?"

Brad was prepared and pulled out a list. "Open commissions. Okay. We've got Vector Control—"

Tom snorted and swatted at the air. "Mosquitos. Nobody even knows what vector means." He took a swig of coffee, as he sat down behind his desk, getting back into work mode. "Something related to that," he moved his hands in circles while making a disgusted face, "whole lifestyle. Do we have a diversity commission?"

Brad ran his finger down the list. "No," he said dismissively. "Maybe we need one."

The more liberal Jeremy offered, "Good idea, but we need an ongoing committee so we have, ah, people who can guide and teach whomever we pick. You did create a community plan to follow." Community plan was code for whatever Tom wanted to see happen in his town. "We've been good at getting our people spread throughout."

After a beat, Tom said, "Pick only one. Do me a favor, though, and don't pick the curator—Juniper whatever. She's a pain in the ass and gets too much press. Because of her Floodlight exhibit, we had to pour money into the homeless and feral cats, and I wasn't able to redo the parking lot at our old mall. Nobody knows her wife. I think the best bang for our buck is to get one of the girls who lived at that house where, ah, Gary went."

"Agreed," Jeremy said. I'll get right on it. Panda Fowler is a tax preparer. The other one, I'm not sure."

Tom finally grinned. "We can't pick somebody who was arrested recently, so not the tax girl. Get her, ah, wife."

"But Panda Fowler was completely exonerated…"

Tom liked feminine women, and Panda was androgenous. He said, "She doesn't present as well as the other one. Mitzi's a looker. Give her something easy. What about the environment? That's pretty airy fairy."

Brad tilted his head, thinking. "That could work, but no openings."

Tom returned to the closet and pulled out his driver. "I think, as head of local government, I just decided to make our environment more of a concern in Merryville. The community garden is part of the environment, right? We need to expand the planning commission." He took a swing at an imaginary ball.

"You want her on the city planning group? Are you sure?" Brad said. Tom stared at him.

"Right then," Jeremy said. "Brilliant. I'll get right on it."

"I didn't fall off the turnip truck yesterday." Tom returned to his chair and spun it toward the window. "Call Mrs. Hortense Miller, who's so obsessed with roses. Let her ask the lesbian so it doesn't come from us. I will publicly announce it once it's a done deal." All three men had a laugh together. "It's gonna be funny because this Jose has to come out more pro-gay and environmentally concerned than me, ha."

Jeremy exhaled loudly. "Sir, please don't call Francisco Gonzales, or any Hispanic people, Jose."

Tom barked his famous laugh. "Don't be a little snowflake, Jeremy. Just having some fun."

***

Our two-story house on Thistle Drive had become, since March, a compound. Ekk and Elsa lived in the backyard treehouse while Mitzi and I remained in the regular, human-people house. Everyone used the kitchen and other common areas, and it worked quite well—until now. I was upset an entire magical workshop had been built on our property and Ekk and Elsa had kept it from us. It especially frosted me because Elsa wouldn't even let me touch her spell book. This was my mood when Ekk came through the back door from the yard, clutching a brown paper bag.

Pointing at the bag, I asked, "Lunch? I thought you went shopping."

"No. Copper brads for a, uh, project."

Not trusting anything now, I echoed his words. "A project." I pressed my lips together, and I held my car keys in one hand while holding the front doorknob with the other. "I'm going to get Mitzi. Oh, how did she end up with Hortense? Didn't you go to the hardware emporium together?"

Ekk probably sensed these were not innocent questions and truthfully answered. "Hortense showed up at the hardware store and asked Mitzi to come volunteer at the garden project."

"Oh." I crossed my arms. "I see. I wasn't sure you were telling me the whole story."

"Why?" Ekk asked, and took a few steps forward. "What's wrong?"

Unable to hold in my resentment, I said, "Brutus is really sick, and Elsa's down in your secret hidey-hole I'm not supposed to know or talk about. How come you didn't tell us about it? How many other things don't we know? This is our house, you know." I was breathing heavily.

Ekk made an "o" with his mouth and replied softly, "I'm sorry, but it was necessary for your safety."

I was ready to argue, but he cut me off at the pass. "Here was our thinking, Panda. What you don't know, you can't reveal to anyone else accidentally," he paused, "or if put…under pressure. Elsa's workshop contains some powerful magic."

Fair point. I thought, but remained stubborn, arms folded.

He went on. "Remember when you were arrested, and the house was searched with a warrant? Even if you didn't mean to, you may have given it away."

My eyes got watery. It was in our backyard during the time the house was searched?

"I'm sorry, Panda, truly," he said with a rush of words. "Can we talk about it more later? You get Mitzi, and I'll help Elsa with Brutus."

"Yes, we'll talk then." I knew I was acting like a twelve-year-old and stomped out the front, as Ekk made a beeline for the backyard. The stomping made my leg hurt.

I appreciated the explanation, but I wasn't ready to let Ekk off the hook quite yet. We would definitely talk about secrets later. I hated secrets. This train of thought was derailed as I lifted my leg to climb into the driver's seat and said out loud, "Ouch." My own wound was really bad today. Was it the cold weather or something worse? Brutus and I were injured by the same evil magic from Wolfrum. The thought wouldn't leave me alone, as I drove through town fast. Mitzi was probably already waiting on the curb to be picked up.

I'll never forget how I'd been getting ready to feed Brutus when Wolfrum, who we all thought was gone from our world or dead, called out from behind me. He stood on our bright, happy kitchen linoleum, wearing his monk's robes again, which covered much of his body. He wore a suit the last time we'd seen him, in an attempt to pass himself off as "Pastor Wolfrum." His widow's peak was white, and his pale face was full of cuts from being carried by ravens through a broken window at the Lutheran Church. His words still sent a chill down my spine.

"Strangely, you have proven hard to kill. I was almost rid of you in jail, but this will be better." His lips twisted into a malicious smile, and his energy and weird eyes made me believe this was the last thing I would ever see. He shouted "Enough," and raised his hands theatrically.

The lightning bolt-like thing that emanated from Wolfrum's hands sent some magical electric charge at me that was mostly deflected by my ankle bracelet. Brutus sprang at Wolfrum and got a pretty good frying from the metal bracelet's ricochet. It flung him across the room. No matter how many times I played it over in my mind, I couldn't have done anything differently. Brutus and I were almost killed.

Now we shared a wound since the rest of the energy was absorbed into my leg that now throbbed. With the kitchen nearly destroyed during the attack, Ekk spent lots of time at Taggart's Hardware Emporium. In the pit of my stomach, I sensed whatever made *Lupus*

Imperium try to kill us all was far from over. Thank goodness the ravens had come and carried Wolfrum away, an event I still didn't understand.

Traffic was light. As I drove the last block, I thought about how to explain everything about Brutus to Mitzi without mentioning the elf hole.

***

After Panda left in a snit, Ekk dropped his bag with hardware purchases on the dining room table with a metal clunk and hurried to the base of the big tree in the backyard. He scanned the backyard for prying eyes before he entered the space he and Elsa had created to handle emergency issues.

Elsa wiped her hands on her apron and ran to Ekk as soon as she saw him.

Ekk stood on the last stair and hugged his beloved to his chest as he kissed the top of her head. "How is he?"

It was Blondie who answered with a series of meows. "I know, honey. I'm worried too," Elsa replied to her. "You just keep him warm." She turned to Ekk, her cherubic face tear-stained. "He has lost some vitality, but I'm keeping it at bay, although how long that will last…" She let her words trail off. "I called Valerie. She suggested an indigenous ritual called a sweat. A *heilung hutte*." Elsa often reverted to German when speaking privately with Ekk.

"A healing hut? Huh." Ekk let her go and stepped down onto the dirt floor. "Good idea. I'm glad you called her. Many cultures have cleansing rituals, but Native American ones may be the best." He crossed three steps to where Brutus lay. "Hello, Brutus." He reached down to pet the big kitty and gave one to Blondie, too, for good measure. "Panda went to get Mitzi. I noticed she was limping."

Elsa's worry was evident. "That's another thing. Panda's injury also has a seed of something in it, some evil Wolfrum planted when he attacked her. I'm missing something, some element we need." She went back to her *Zauberbuch* and said over her shoulder, "Valerie and I are going out to find fresh wolfbane."

Ekk nodded. "We can trust her."

Elsa was still a bit possessive about her spell work. "I felt something from her after her grandmother died. She's got some strong healing energy in her, but it's not garden magic."

Ekk looked at Brutus, who was lying still with thready breathing. "Healing, magic," Ekk said. "Call it what you want. We need everything we can get."

CHAPTER FOUR

I pulled our new-to-us Land Rover to the curb in front of a large, wooden sign announcing, "MERRYVILLE GENTRIFICATION PROJECT." Underneath the words were two different colorful renderings of the area. One showed a picture of the old tire plant and the other a computerized vision of the same land with neat rows of garden plots surrounding a modest building. Someone had vandalized the sign—the word "MERIDA" printed over MERRYVILLE with a thick, black magic marker. A neat line was drawn through MERRYVILLE.

Mitzi opened the door and jumped inside the Rover.

"Hi, babe." When she leaned over to give me a kiss, I smelled some type of lotion. "*Bain de Solis?*"

Mitzi smelled her hands. "Sunscreen Hortense had. Kind of greasy." She searched for a tissue. "Now, what happened to Brutus?" Mitzi's focus was like a laser beam.

"I'll fill you in but—" A shooting pain made me rub my thigh. "Ow. Do you mind driving?"

"Oh, honey. Of course."

I said truthfully, "Brutus is with Elsa in a place she told me not to tell anyone about, even you." There was no way I wasn't going to tell Mitzi.

Mitzi gave me an incredulous stare. "What kind of place? And does anyone include the wife? Of course not. What's happening? And what's going on with your ankle and leg anyway? Seems like it's getting worse."

A realization I'd been actively avoiding hit me like a ton of bricks. "I think it's related to Brutus getting worse. Switch with me, and I'll tell you what happened."

With Mitzi's help, I hobbled around to the passenger side of the car. It was difficult getting all the way up in the seat, but between Mitzi helping and a strategically placed handhold, I made it. My ankle felt like it was on fire, the pain radiating up my left leg.

Mitzi climbed into the driver's seat and put the car into drive. Before pulling away, she noticed the defaced sign. "Oh wow, did you see the sign?" She pointed.

"Yeah. It's always something in Merryville. Didn't it used to be called Merida?"

"A long time ago. Now. Cat."

I clicked my seatbelt into its slot. "Okay. This morning Brutus seemed weak and was sleeping in his bed. Elsa and I were talking in the kitchen when Elsa told me to look at Brutus. He was," my breath caught, "gasping for air."

We stopped at a light, and Mitzi reached out to put her hand on mine. "What secret place is he in? I need to see him."

Any qualms I felt about keeping the secret disappeared immediately. I hadn't actually promised. "Okay, okay." First, I turned off our cell phones and tossed them in the back. "Do you remember the entrance to the Hercynian Forest? How it appeared to be a rock, but that was an illusion?"

"Yes. It was an entrance to the Hercynian Garden at the Black Forest in Germany." Mitzi straightened up and turned her head to me before refocusing on the road. "Where is this portal?" Tears welled in her eyes. "Is Brutus in the Black Forest? And what's with the cell phone business? I don't think anyone monitors our cell phones other than ad agencies." She put one beaded braid behind her ear. "You're starting to sound paranoid like Puddle." She was upset.

Trying to calm her, I said, "I did talk to Puddle today, and she may come visit—"

Mitzi took her eyes off the road for a second. "Portal. Cat."

"Anyway, the elves created a disguised entrance," I leaned over, watching Mitzi's astonished reaction. "Like that one in the Black Forest but *in our backyard.*"

Mitzi shook her head. "What? Where in our backyard? And why didn't they tell us about it? It's our house." As we stopped at another light, Mitzi paused and said, "We don't have any big rocks like the one in the Black Forest."

I spoke softly, as this was top secret information. "Not a rock this time. It's thistle bushes at the base of the oak tree. Ekk said if we didn't know about it, we couldn't tell anyone else, and it has some powerful magic inside. Remember that search warrant? Anyway, after Brutus began breathing badly, Elsa said to follow her, and we ran through the fake bushes into this secret room under the tree."

"What?"

"She's probably in the room right now with Brutus and that Blondie. She told me to get out and not tell anyone. That's when I called you. Oh, I did call Puddle first, but then when you didn't come right home, I called you. Now we're up to date."

"Did you tell Puddle?" Mitzi was getting mad.

"No, heavens no. You saw how much trouble I had telling you."

After a few silent blocks we were home. Mitzi apparently used the time to calm herself. After she pulled into our driveway and turned off the engine, she took my hand and said, "I hate surprises, but we need to trust them. Ekk and Elsa are our guardians and haven't let us down yet. If you're still in danger, Elsa needs to do whatever is necessary to fix your leg injury too. In fact, I'm calling in the cavalry. Valerie is a home health nurse. Let's get you inside."

Once my wife made up her mind, things happened. I felt no need to respond verbally, so I nodded. Sometimes that was the key to a happy marriage.

As Mitzi jumped out and came around to help me down, I had another shooting pain and groaned as I swung my leg out the door. Since leaving the house, my lower leg had visibly swollen. I pointed at it. "Valerie won't know how to fix this."

Helping me down, Mitzi said, "You don't know that."

I got into the living room with my arm around Mitzi and fell heavily on the couch. Ekk rushed in and asked, "Do we have any Epsom salt?" He saw my condition and said, "Uh-oh."

Ekk and I locked eyes.

"It's happening again, isn't it?" Mitzi said.

Elsa came into the house with Brutus wrapped in a blanket. "How's he doing?" Mitzi asked her. "Panda's injury is acting up too. Please check it out. Is this ever going to stop?"

Ekk took Brutus from Elsa, placed him into my arms, and sat beside me. Elsa tried to quickly exit, but Mitzi stopped her with a sharp question. "What is it you say in Germany? Halt. We need to have a wee chat."

Elsa opened her mouth, as if to defend herself, but seemed to crumple. "I'm sure Panda told you about the, you know." She flipped her head back and motioned to the tree in the backyard with her eyes.

Mitzi was in command mode. "She certainly did. I'm not mad, but you better show me like, right now."

After a sigh, everyone left me, no doubt to examine the elf hole.

***

After the meeting, Sylvia said goodbye to her board. She felt pretty good that they finally got through it with no bloodshed. Sally left first with her husband, Jack, who pulled up in a shiny, red crew cab with

Johnson Roofing stenciled on the side. She imagined them with matching pajamas that said Johnson Roofing, and chuckled. Sally waved generally in the direction of the group and let Jack help her onto the high seat.

"Bye, Sally. Bye, Jack," the women called.

Jack, a man of few words, gave a little wave before he climbed in the driver's seat and took off down the dirt road, leaving a slight dust trail.

Charlotte waved her hand at the dust in front of her heavily made-up face, as if it were a much bigger deal than it was. "We need to get some asphalt laid soon."

Sylvia lifted her clipboard and made a note, then headed for the trailer. "It's on the list."

Janet handed her laptop to her daughter, Bonnie, who made a beeline for her mother's Buick. "I'll be right there," Janet said and followed Sylvia inside the trailer. "How's everything going with the city? We didn't talk much about it at our meeting."

Sylvia fairly beamed. "Well in hand, Janet."

Hortense, still inside, apparently couldn't resist responding, while stuffing her agenda into a plastic bag. "Under my leadership, we forged quite a strong bond with city hall. You're all benefitting from this now."

"Yes, you did, Aunt Hortense," Janet said. As a member of the old board under Hortense, as well as a member of the current board, she was the bridge between old and new society memberships. "And Sylvia is keeping it going."

Hortense didn't respond. The comment had to chafe, so she switched to another topic. "Your uncle could use a call from you now and again."

This stopped Janet cold. Hortense was Bill Miller's second wife, and she stood by him while he'd gone through the criminal justice system for destroying Valerie Gooden's Rothchild orchids and braining a cop with a frying pan. Janet hadn't seen him in a while.

Janet's gaze flicked to Sylvia. "I'll call him."

As Sylvia ambled outside again, she heard Janet say to Hortense, "Please don't keep bringing up the past. It's already awkward."

Hortense's retort, "Facts are facts," rang in Sylvia's ears as she walked down the steps to the women outside.

It wasn't long before she saw Janet rush out of the trailer with Hortense hot on her heels. They joined the group, as a black luxury vehicle carefully drove down the make-shift road.

"That's me," Denise McGreggor said brightly, as Fergus pulled up in her Bentley and opened the back seat door so she could get in. "*Ciao, bellas.*"

"*Ciao*, Denise," the women called back in the same spirit.

Hortense pointed to one of the carts and said to Sylvia, "Well, that's me."

"Didn't you drive here?" Sylvia asked.

"A neighbor brought Bill to pick up the car. He needed it for a doctor's appointment. He…hasn't been well. Surely you can't expect a seventy-four year-old woman to walk home. That is, unless my niece will drive me."

"I would take you, but we'll be late to Bonnie's piano lesson," Janet said hurriedly. At that exact moment Bonnie called out the window, "Mom."

"I hear you, got to grab my purse." Janet rushed back to the trailer.

The remaining women avoided eye contact, aware Hortense and Janet were at odds. Finally, Valerie said, "I'll drop you, Hortense. We need to talk about succulents anyway for the—"

"Sandpit," Hortense completed. The comment had a definite edge.

Knowing how Valerie hated social politics, Sylvia wasn't surprised to see her tent her fingers over her chest, silver rings sparkling on her long brown fingers, as she said, "Sandy area, I was going to say."

Sylvia decided to try flattery. "Hortense, you of all people can make that plot work. But if it's too much of a challenge—"

"Of course it isn't," Hortense snapped. "Just making sure you all appreciate how much of a challenge it is." She climbed into the passenger seat of the cart, waiting to be chauffeured by Valerie.

Sylvia stayed professional. "I do, Hortense. And thanks, Valerie. Charlotte and I are meeting with someone, or I would do it. Put the keys through the mail slot when you return the cart. Thank you both for making this project work. I'm glad we're all coming together for the good of the community."

Valerie was hard to read. Hortense made a tight smile and nodded once, curtly, before Valerie started the golf cart.

Hortense said over her shoulder, "I'm starting on my plot right away. It obviously needs a bit more tending than the rest of the site."

Sylvia met her gaze. "I know you'll work miracles. You've got my number, so call me if you need anything." She turned back to Charlotte, who had watched the tense exchange with interest.

Valerie pulled out a scrunchie and tamed her hair before driving off with Hortense, who was already pointing and giving directions.

"Poor Val," Sylvia said under her breath, as she shook her head and watched them drive away.

Charlotte took a deep breath, hands on her hips. "So. This is actually happening. I promised to keep the Windingle tradition of community philanthropy alive. This may be my greatest triumph." She shaded her eyes in the late afternoon sun and surveyed the cleared area. "It was such an eyesore before. Even dug up like it is, it looks better."

"I agree." Sylvia threw the clipboard in the back of another golf cart. She was tired. "Let's go. We're going to make this a showplace."

Janet returned with her purse and hugged Sylvia one more time. "Hortense will settle in. She does love gardening. Thank you for letting her come back."

Bonnie honked the horn. "Mom."

"Thank you for all you do," Sylvia said to Janet. It'll all be fine. Let's give it time."

"Mo-ther."

"Coming, Bon-Bon." Janet jogged to the car.

After Janet drove away, Sylvia felt energized. "Charlotte, this is going to be amazing. The university metal shop is working on the gates. I wish we could afford to put the design on the walls surrounding the entire area, but we could do an annual fundraiser to add one section at a time."

Charlotte laughed and put on a golf visor. "Let's call it "Build That Wall." Both ladies laughed. "Your chariot awaits."

"Seriously though, the club has to be Switzerland when it comes to politics," Sylvia said. "I've been talking to Mayor Reed. He's the one who wanted Hortense in the, uh, sand area."

"Huh. Wonder why."

Sylvia shrugged. "I wondered, too, but he's supporting the new board. Maybe that's punishment to Hortense for being so difficult. It surprised me he even knew we had a sandy area. Anyway, I'm thrilled he's going to kick in some money and give us a grand old party for the opening."

Charlotte's eyes glittered. "You know I love a good party."

Not taking her eyes off the newly graded road, Sylvia asked, "When does the reporter get here?"

Charlotte hung on to the roof strap. "Any minute. He's going to meet us over by the water tower in the back." She pointed.

Sylvia drove the cart toward one of the only structures left standing after the tire factory buildings were razed. "Did he call you or did you call him?"

"He called me," Charlotte said, her voice bubbly. "Said it was a small follow-up to the main story." She regarded Sylvia's concerned facial expression. "There's no such thing as bad publicity."

"It could help us get more donations," Sylvia said. She liked to keep her eye on the bottom line. "Maybe we'll get enough to do another section of fence."

They hit a pothole. "Bumpy." Charlotte loved action and surprises. She still grinned broadly. Sylvia knew Charlotte was the face of Windingle Developers and wanted to contribute. Charlotte was at every gala and did all the media, but sometimes Sylvia wondered what her actual authority was. "Did you run this interview by Windingle corporate?"

"I didn't. This is just a fluff piece."

"Who, other than you, should we ask for more fence money?"

"Boris Hunt handles those things." Charlotte rolled her eyes. "Boring Boris."

Sylvia parked next to the old water tower, and Charlotte gasped. Vandals had been at work. Sylvia shook her head like she didn't see what she knew she saw. Phillip Pen, in scruffy jeans, high tops, and an NPR T-shirt, was already there. The photographer he brought, a young man with a professional camera, snapped pictures wildly. Phillip called out, "I have some questions for you, Mrs. Windingle."

The ladies walked around to get a better view of what the reporter and photographer were photographing. On the far side of the water tower, someone had painted a large skull and crossbones—the universal symbol for poison. Charlotte paled and said, "I don't, I mean. Shit, Sylvia."

Sylvia quipped. "You were saying about publicity?"

"I'd better call Boris."

CHAPTER FIVE

AN OLD ENEMY RETURNS

At six p.m., Ralph moved to the front of his shop, turned the OPEN sign to CLOSED, and locked the door. He took the till out of the cash register and carried the drawer with arthritic hands to the back of the store through aisles of whatzits and thingamabobs. It was getting dark early, so he flipped on the overhead bulb in his office, which smelled of dust and paper. The safe in the corner was huge and painted green, in the style of the old West, with gold filigree framing the giant box. It was this ritual each night, executed like clockwork, which would be his undoing.

His cat, Ratter, lay atop the store safe and watched Ralph turn the large silver dial. Ratter stood and hissed, his fur fluffed out in alarm.

"What is it, boy?"

Ralph felt a cool breeze that could only be coming from the door to the alley behind the Emporium—the door, which he never left open or unlocked.

"Finish what you're doing," a man's voice said flatly.

Startled, Ralph jumped and turned in a move that belied his eighty years. "What the—?"

A man, about fifty years old, trim, but with wild, unkempt hair, stared back at him. He wore hospital scrubs and those paper shoes often seen in hospitals. Ralph adjusted his eyes in the semi-dark, and his right hand pressed his glasses closer as he kicked himself mentally for not getting his new prescription yet. "Gary?"

"Hello, Ralph. Need a permit? How about a ribbon-cutting for a grand reopening?" Gary Smithers' eyes sparkled, and he appeared preternaturally elated. In a split second, his face turned into a mask of sadness. "Oh, sorry, it won't be so easy since I'm not a city councilman anymore."

Ralph stayed calm. The man was clearly unstable. "What do you want?" The air felt condensed as if before an explosion. Ratter made a low, extended growl in his throat.

"You can start by giving me the money in your safe. Yeah. I know your routines. We used to have a pretty good system going." His expression was calm, and he smoothed down his longish hair. "I bet you've saved up a lot since I've been away."

"Things have changed, Gary, you know…"

"I know everything. Your wife is in Merry Hearts getting Alzheimer's care, right? And next door the owners of the work/live space are from Bulgaria. Did you know they paid me a hundred thousand dollars to make sure their applications went through? Their work visas weren't exactly in order." He laughed merrily, pivoting to anger a second later. "Unfortunately, I had to give all that back when the city turned on me, so I'm a little short."

Ralph had heard about Gary's fall from grace, of course. Who hadn't? After the mad city councilman went to Mitzi's house and threatened someone with a machete, his business dealings were revealed during the fallout. It concerned him, how Gary had moved from corruption to violence.

He was dangerous. Ralph wasn't afraid for himself—his only thought was for his wife. He needed to keep the situation from escalating. Having lived through much discrimination as a black man in the South, he resolved that one more crazy, white man wasn't going to be the end of him. He said with a calm voice, "I'm sure money changes hands all the time, Gary. Let me get you some more, friend." He gestured to the till on his desk. "You can have that now." He painfully knelt down to open the safe.

Gary made a move toward the till near Ralph, and Ratter hissed again. This set Gary off, and he lunged for the cat, who scratched his hand. Ralph became alarmed. Although he'd felt he could calm the situation as long as he gave Gary what he asked for, things changed fast.

"Fucking cat!" That's when a flashlight beam hit the scene. Gary was sucking on a bleeding scratch on his knuckle when a uniformed cop entered. "Mr. Brown, you okay?"

Gary laughed and spoke first, appearing relieved to see the policeman. "Thank God for rescuing us from this wild cat. Maybe we should call animal control." He was such a good actor.

The officer relaxed. "Okay, glad to hear it." He switched his attention to Ralph. "Mr. Brown, the door from the alley—"

He dropped like a sack of sand when Gary Smithers brained him with a wrench taken from a nearby shelf. The officer landed on the floor hard. Gary reached for the till. "I'll take this for now, but I'll be back. Gimme some work pants and a shirt. Got any shoes?"

Ralph shook his head. "No shoes, what size pants?"

"Thirty-four long and a large shirt. No tricks."

Ralph pushed an unopened box toward Gary. "Shirts are in the box. I'll get the pants." Ralph went into the store to Taggart's work clothing shelves, selected a pair, and brought them back to his office.

"Good." Gary put them under his arm. "And, Ralph," he said, as if with sympathy, "I'd hate for anything to happen to your precious Aurora. Let's agree to keep this between ourselves." Gary took the cop's shoes and stuffed the cash in his pocket. "Oh, and I almost forgot." He held up his hands to reflect the symbol on the side of a family crest. "*Lupus Sanctorum Lupus Infectio.*" He pointed at Ralph's arthritic hands and ran out, giggling.

Ralph's hands were seized with pain, but he immediately went to the officer on the floor, who was waking from being momentarily knocked out. "He's gone out the back door." His hands were curled like claws, but he did his best to point.

Officer Dittle was mad. He tried to get up but was still dizzy. "I thought he was a friend of yours. Who was he?"

Ralph didn't answer. He was surprised Officer Dittle didn't recognize the former city councilman, but he was young and new. Much skinnier and with wild hair, Gary bore little resemblance to his official photo that used to appear regularly in the *Merryville Bee*. "Let me call an ambulance, officer." Ratter darted out the back door into the alley, as if he were going after the intruder himself.

Officer Dittle sat up, one hand feeling the bump on his head. "No, I'll call it in." He studied the safe that was still locked, and felt for his radio. "At least he didn't get in your safe. I'm sorry I didn't get here sooner. Do you have any idea who he was?"

"No," Ralph lied. He swallowed and rubbed his one rheumatic hand with the other. Man, they were smarting. "I'm just glad you got here. Let me help you up. You really need to have someone see to that bump on your head, son."

The cop spoke into his shoulder radio. "Met 22, officer needs assistance at Taggart's Emporium. Reporting an armed burglar on the loose."

"On the way, 22. What's the weapon?"

Ralph helped Officer Dittle off the floor and sat him on the stool. He whispered, "Pipe wrench."

Dittle repeated it into the radio. "The weapon's a pipe wrench. Perp is 50s, medium build, about six feet tall, wearing green hospital scrubs and…my shoes."

The dispatcher's voice raised a notch. "We already have an APB out right now for Gary Smithers. He escaped from County Hospital. Stay at your location 'til the watch commander arrives."

Ralph went to the back door to close it, intending to put down the bar to keep it secure. First, he stuck his head out and called for the cat. "Ratter. Come on back in here."

The cat was nowhere to be found, and his heart sank. Then what he didn't see hit him in the face. He turned back to Officer Dittle and asked, "Did you drive here?"

The shoeless cop ran to the door. He slugged the door frame before getting back on his radio. "Met 22, find my car. The perp took my cruiser."

***

After he had his treatment, Elsa placed Brutus on a beach towel next to me on the couch. I petted him, and tears sprang to my eyes. "Is he on something? He seems dopey."

Elsa's apron was wet in spots, and her hair had escaped its braid. She nodded. "A concoction. You're probably going to get the same. Let me see your leg."

I used both hands to help lift my ankle and lower leg onto the ottoman. "It's the injury that almost killed me, right? What's happening? I had trouble driving today."

Elsa gently lifted my sweatpants and inspected the swelling. "I think so. You and Brutus will be okay if we treat it now and stay on it."

"I don't know. Brutus isn't any better."

"He's a cat and considerably smaller. He also got quite a blast of dark magic."

Ekk entered, wearing Elsa's pink, rubber dishwashing gloves. He carried a steaming pot of water that gave off a scent of something vaguely medicinal. After setting it carefully on the coffee table, he pulled out a steaming rag and began to wring it, deftly moving it out of my reach. "No, it's poisonous," he said. "See these rubber gloves?"

I was frustrated. "And you're putting it on me? Thanks a bunch." To lighten my comment, I said, "Nice gloves, pink is your color."

Ekk made a face in return and carefully laid the hot rag over my ankle.

It felt lava hot. "Yow. Wait. That does feel better."

Mitzi came out of the bathroom, sat down, and put her arm around me. "What's happening, folks? I think it's time we talked about this stuff again. Why are Brutus and Panda having these issues? And I really wish you'd tell us more about the elf hole. Panda and I were blown away that we didn't know."

Elsa glanced at Ekk before refocusing on us. Her tone was soft. "When we took our vacation to Mexico, we'd planned to talk about all the things that you girls had been through, to explain everything. But when we got to that beautiful place, it was so easy not to."

I offered possible reasons. "We were all tired, burnt out, suffering from PTSD—pick one."

Ekk took off the rubber gloves and put his hand on Elsa's shoulder. "This is my fault. I suggested we let things settle before we talked to you. We just…never got around to it."

"I get it," I said. "Once we felt the warm sun and weren't in Merryville anymore, we all wanted a break." The two of them appeared bedraggled, which made me want to defend them. "And it was your honeymoon."

Ekk studied my leg. "It was. Watching the ocean and sleeping in was so pleasant. Elsa and I never experienced surf and sand in Germany."

"Okay, so we all pretended our lives were normal, and we all needed a break," Mitzi said, snapping everyone out of their glassy-eyed reverie about the vacation. "Unfortunately, we're still on Wolf Raven's radar."

"Now known as *Lupus Imperium*," Ekk said.

"Wolf Raven, Lupus, the bad guys, whatever." Mitzi stared at my leg and her brow furrowed.

"Okay," I said, "let's do it now. Nine months ago, we didn't know you. I was doing taxes and Miss Darling here," I patted Mitzi's thigh, "was helping me out in between her planning trips for people." I pointed at Ekk. "You were in the bushes, hiding, and Lulu, the security guard, and I caught you."

Ekk tilted his head. "Oh, you want to go way back. Those were very different days. We had no idea how you would take the news that you two were part of a global, actually extra-global, reality."

I grinned at Ekk affectionately. "You were so cute, and you told me my name was weird."

He appeared embarrassed at the memory. "I was delirious. If you recall. We disappear when starved, and I hadn't eaten. That was disorienting."

I moved my leg. "Ow! It stings and throbs at the same time, almost like it's alive."

"Your leg isn't alive, other than being attached to you, but Mitzi's right. This isn't over." Elsa sank into a chair, exhausted. "Panda, when you were hit with that dark magic energy stream, something was injected into you, like a germ. We need to figure out a cure. All I've been able to do is slow it down."

"You will cure her though, right?" Mitzi sounded alarmed. "I mean, I almost lost her to this." Her alarm grew. "Make more of that goop you used at the hospital." She hugged me tighter.

Ekk conferred with Elsa, who supervised his adjustment of the rag on my left ankle. She mumbled a bit, and the scent of eucalyptus filled the room.

I inhaled. "I've never smelled that scent before. Usually, you do lavender or roses or citrus or something." Brutus' nose twitched.

Elsa blew a stray wisp of her hair away from her face. "The scent is specific for this situation. The 'goop' as Mitzi says, is not a permanent solution. I don't have all the answers yet, but we will find them." Her expression was determined.

I decided to continue with the chronology of events. "Anyway, so the next thing we know, Mitzi is kidnapped by Wolfrum's sister, Odelia, and taken to Germany. Juniper and I rescued her."

"With a little help," Mitzi said, "from Lily and her warrior wife, Heloisa."

"I'm telling the story, so you get my version. By the way, first question. What ever happened to Odelia? She turned against *Lupus Imperium*, like changed sides, and now she's good."

Ekk sat and crossed his legs. "Odelia? Not much is known, and I wouldn't count on her being *good* simply because she no longer follows her brother's cult. She might even be dead. When Wolfrum got back to Schwartzwald Castle, I bet heads rolled." We were silent for a moment, staring at the living room coffee table, which was full of medicinal items on top of the magazines. The fireplace hearth held Brutus' empty bed, blanket, and toys.

I spoke first. "Do we even know whether Wolfrum went to the Black Forest? Isn't it possible he's dead? Do you think he'll come back here?" I was worried. After all, it was me who last had an up close and personal encounter with him.

Ekk scratched his chin. "Ehrenhardt has his seers and spies working on it. Let's concentrate on the here and now and leave that to them."

"But no more secrets," Mitzi said.

"The Garden has spies?" I asked.

Ekk and Elsa nodded.

Brutus woke and stretched.

"Hey, handsome boy. How ya doing?" Mitzi reached over me to pet the big spotted kitty.

"Meow. Meooow."

We swiveled our heads to Ekk and Elsa, who understood the cat language.

"What did he say?" I asked.

Ekk cocked his head, concentrating. With mischief in his blue eyes, he answered, "He said, 'Meow.'"

"Come on." I wanted to know.

Ekk sighed. "He said he's hurting, and he's a little cranky about it." To the cat, as if answering a question, he said, "Brutus, Blondie is working on your healing in the special place."

Elsa started to get up, and Ekk made a patting down air motion and rose instead. "Rest, Elsa. I'll get him," he said to us. "Brutus wants to be in his bed. I think he's doing a little better. Complaining is not always a bad thing. He also loves the extra attention."

"Well that's good, right?" Mitzi asked. "What's next? What about my Panda Bear? She complains a lot. She likes attention."

Elsa had fallen asleep in the chair, her apron crumpled. Sleeping in her apron with rosy cheeks, she could have been a life-sized German doll. Ekk placed Brutus in his bed on the floor near the hearth and picked up a throw to cover Elsa. The temperature was dropping, and the house was a bit chilly. "Panda's at the top of the list. We'll figure it out. Now, let me tell you about the elf hole."

"Finally at the top of the list," I said. "I would love a fire for this story. Would you mind, Ekk?"

"Watch this." He tossed a log on the andiron and said, "*Ignis.*" A small flame appeared in the center, soon consuming the log's surface on the way to becoming a cozy fire. This got a smile out of me, and even Mitzi appeared impressed.

"Wow, that's the first time I've seen you do magic like that, Ekk. Isn't that forbidden?"

It sure got my attention. "How much else can you do? Can you teach me that?"

Elsa opened her eyes, and in a warning tone drew out his name. "Ekk." That was all she said, but he appeared sheepish.

"Just trying to distract the girls. Listen." He sat next to the exhausted Elsa and put his arm around her. "It wouldn't hurt to teach them a few things—Wolfrum was in this very house. We don't know if he went back to the Black Forest or if he is still here. They may need to protect themselves again."

"Ekk, he's gone, and it appears Panda has some raven friends," Elsa said.

It was rare for them to disagree in front of us, and we watched with interest.

He went on. "I asked the Garden about that. This is twice now ravens have come to help Panda."

I piped up. "Three times if you count when I was actually in the garden outside Schwartzwald Castle and that raven didn't give me away."

"That's right, but we still don't know if they have joined the fight on our side. Maybe they're fickle. The danger isn't far away in Germany. Ladies, Wolfrum probably infected people's hearts when he was here. You saw how he controlled that New Spirit Church leader. Elsa, you and I can't be everywhere. That's why," he swept his arms out like one might to present a gift, "full circle, we made the elf hole. It's for safety." He made one more argument. "We didn't tell you because it's best things like that are kept a secret in case—"

"In case what? We get tortured?" I really wanted to know.

Ekk avoided my gaze and glanced at Elsa.

Elsa closed her eyes again. "I need a nap."

Mitzi got up. "I'm so sorry, you two. Here we are thinking about ourselves and look at you. Thank you for all you do for us. Now go. Rest. I'll start dinner in a bit."

Elsa nodded, and Ekk helped her up. They were so cute together. Since their recent marriage, they were even more cuddly. When they were out of earshot, I said, "They remind me of little German salt and pepper shakers." I turned on the TV.

Mitzi snuggled up to me. "Now, find us a good show."

CHAPTER SIX

HORTENSE'S SECRET TEA PARTY

The previous day, Hortense had left the meeting in the trailer feeling smug. Those women had no idea with whom they were dealing. Sandpit, indeed. After the hired help put up her little "Sandpit Shed," as she thought of it, Valerie had dropped Hortense at home. Since Bill was back from his appointment, Hortense drove her Mercedes over to Lidia's house. She knew the others in the horticultural group talked behind her back, but she didn't care. She had her own group comprised of former board members. With any luck, they would be reinstalled to replace the board of the Horticultural Society when the time was right. She pulled up in front of Lidia's modest home and strolled inside to join her like-minded friends for an early evening meeting. Florence, Judge Dinwitter's wife, was already seated in the living room with Lidia, their hostess.

"Tea, Hortense?" Lidia had old china. Some cups had hairline cracks, but the women present were too polite to appear to notice. Her housekeeping was nothing to brag about either, but she was loyal. They knew her income had diminished after her husband died years ago. Hortense sniffed. Lidia really could use fewer house cats as well.

"Certainly, dear. Milk and two sugars, please." She appeared horrified as Lidia reached for the tea. "Milk in first, Lidia, milk in first."

Florence asked, "How was the board meeting?"

Hortense dusted an imaginary piece of lint from her tunic. "You wouldn't believe the plan they have for this community garden. They still have that horrible woman from the museum in charge of the design."

Lidia made a disgusted face. "Juniper Gooden? Remember when she showed up to the club wearing that T-shirt with "Feminist" in silver sparkles on it?" She poured tea over the milk. "Do you think the club will ever recover?" She reached over and handed her the milky tea, the cup rattling a little on the saucer as she shook her head. "Hortense, that community garden project was your idea."

Florence was so upset she stood and paced around the room. "Maybe we should start a new club. My husband—"

"Sit down, dear," Hortense said, interrupting Florence before she got going. "Keep your eyes on the prize. We will win the day. Don't I always have a plan?"

"But—" A knock on the door cut Florence off. Lidia got up and shuffled to the front door. Florence asked, "Who's that?"

Hortense lifted her eyebrows. "You'll see."

Lidia stepped back and let her visitor in. "Mr. Butler, come on in."

The former staff member for Council Member Gary Smithers stood in the doorway, full of boyish charm. "Hello, ladies."

Hortense patted the loveseat next to her. "Bradley, come sit by me. We have a lot to talk about."

Florence shook his hand and flipped into social mode. "Bradley, I'm so glad to see you. It's been ages. How's your mother?"

"The same. She's still at Merry Hearts." He sat and put an overflowing leather bag full of papers on the floor by his feet. "I drove here from the mayor's office."

Lidia was like a hawk on its prey. "Is he on board? That's what we need to know." She was direct and to the point.

"Lidia, manners," Hortense said in a chiding tone. "Please, tell us about the meeting."

"It's okay, Mrs. Miller. It's all but done and dusted. Tom is upset about Francisco making Gary Smithers' escape a campaign issue. He wholeheartedly supports the community garden project and is glad to have you ladies in his corner."

Hortense watched him with a gimlet eye as he said this. "Thank you for the public service announcement. Now, what specifically is he going to do for us? I've heard rumblings about Ring leaving the property in poor condition. I won't have the Miller name associated with another scandal."

Brad leaned forward confidentially. "Don't worry. Our city attorney vetted this report personally. It's solid. We're now working on public perception. The mayor chose Mitzi Fowler to serve on the environmental committee—"

Hortense cut him off. "What? Why that Fowler woman? Why not me? I've been involved in all his beautification projects since he was elected. Why I—"

Brad held up his hands protectively. "You said it yourself, Hortense. You can't be involved with another scandal. It's a win-win. Keep your friends close and your enemies closer, and all that. We don't know of a problem with the property, but if things do go south, your name's not on it. In the meantime, we need to get the mayor re-elected. He's got a number of opponents this time around."

"Well, what about that Missy? She's a lesbian, you know, and her so-called wife, Panda, was thrown in jail for burning down our tents when I was doing Seeds of Change for New Spirit Church. That's pretty scandalous. I don't see how that helps Tom."

"Mitzi. Her name is Mitzi." Brad turned sideways and shook his head. "Hortense, with all due respect, your husband Bill was arrested for beating one of our decorated detectives, Charlie Potts, with a frying pan. He got off with community service because he had no prior record, and Potts didn't push it. The mayor's office helped a great deal."

"How is that any different than this Panda Fowler's acquittal?"

Florence chimed in. "And she went to federal prison."

Brad sighed. "For a few weeks, and that turned out to be based on a false arrest. She has no criminal record. All arson charges against Panda Fowler were dropped when Bud somebody or other—that homeless guy from the church—confessed. The city is lucky she and her wife didn't sue us. And remember Gary Smithers went insane and tried to kill their housekeepers, or whatever they are. They got a lot of public sympathy for that. After the press conference on their lawn, then Panda Fowler's arrest for arson, people thought we were picking on them. The other side of this city council race, Francisco Gonzalez, is using these facts as proof we discriminate against the LGBTQ community. That's why Mayor Reed—"

Lidia's eyes lit up. "Oooh, I get it. By appointing one of those lezzies, he's in good with that community for the votes." She put down her teacup, rattling all the way. "But how does that help Hortense and our project?" Lidia would never be accused of having too much tact, but she did get to the point.

Florence jumped in. "Lidia, they don't call them lezzies anymore. They're legal now." Florence loved to reference legality, as if being married to a judge made her a lawyer by osmosis. "But, Brad, I'm at a loss as well. How does that help us? What does this Mitzi Fowler know about the environment? My husband, the *judge*, says that scientific men have it all figured out. They did an environmental impact report or something before the project was approved. It's called an E-I-R." She pronounced each letter triumphantly, as if laying down a full house in poker. She loved knowing things.

In a more normal tone, Brad said, "That's what I said earlier. They did do an EIR, and everything's fine." He hesitated. "I hope this Mitzi

Fowler won't be too active on the committee. There's not much for her to do other than be on it and go to the meetings. Mayor Reed talked to Doug Harker and the guys, and they'll play nice. What he's hoping is that Hortense will be the one to invite her on." He said this last part with a big grin and a comical fluttering of eyelashes. His words hit their mark.

Time stood still for a moment. Florence held her teacup frozen, as they waited for a response from Hortense, who jumped to her feet and let out an uncharacteristically explosive, "Ha! This could actually work."

The energy in the room picked up considerably as Lidia and Florence shared a nod.

Hortense practically purred her next words. "Let me guide her, Brad. This is perfect. She's already on my committee for the garden project. The mayor knows I'm always happy to help."

***

With Merryville elections on the horizon, silly season was in full swing. Monday morning Mayor Tom Reed had barely cleared his office door when confronted by election shenanigans on the way to the elevator.

A familiar voice called, "Sir." Tom automatically grinned and turned around, willing himself not to show displeasure when he confirmed it was Phillip from the *Merryville Bee*. Phillip was a burr in his hide. He had authored an award-winning story about the disappearance of Mitzi Fowler that had turned into a murder investigation. Tom was front and center with the police chief when he announced an international warrant was about to be issued for Mitzi's wife, Panda, the main suspect. Unfortunately for them, Panda and Mitzi awkwardly arrived at precisely the same time a press conference was being held on their lawn. Clearly, Mitzi was very much alive. This debacle didn't reflect well on Reed's leadership, and the opinion pieces that resulted were merciless. Since that time, he avoided Phillip at all costs.

He acknowledged Phillip with a tight smile, as he pushed the button, willing the elevator to come quickly. "I'm on my way to a meeting," he said. "How did you get on this floor?"

Instead of answering, Phillip tried to put the mayor at ease. "This isn't about Mitzi Fowler or the homeless and cats at the museum."

The mayor nodded. "I'm listening."

The reference was to the *Bee*'s series on homelessness and feral cats in Merryville after Fiona Castlebaum's infamous performance piece at the local museum. After that, Mayor Reed's office had picketers in front of Merryville City Hall for weeks. For all the trouble he caused, however, Phillip Pen was not to be ignored. He held a tape recorder in one hand and a notepad in the other. "May I quote you, saying it was your idea to do the new community garden project out by the hospital? The site of the old tire factory?"

Reed exhaled. This was a softball question. "Absolutely. When Ring Tires decided to relocate to Arizona, our beautification committee earmarked the area for nonprofit community use. The Merryville Horticultural Society took up the challenge and have already started transforming the eyesore into a place we can all be proud of." The elevator dinged and the doors opened.

The mayor stepped in the elevator with Phillip on his heels.

"But mayor," Phillip said, "isn't it true that one of your biggest political contributors was the tire factory that got a pass on cleaning up their toxic mess? A recent investigation by the Merida University Science Department has shown this garden project is only a big, beautiful band-aid on compounds leaching into the aquifer that provides our water. Do you have a comment on that?"

"Phillip," Mayor Reed said in a patronizing tone, "I haven't seen that study. But it sounds like it was ginned up just in time for the election. We have an environmental committee that ordered an environmental impact report to study this issue. They did their job and certified that Ring Tires had acted responsibly in their cleanup. That dirt is clean as a whistle and is now going to provide fresh fruits and vegetables to low-income folks in the area."

"Oh, the same pet committee led by Douglas Harker, the one that hasn't had a new member outside your golf group for the entire term of your office?"

This is why he hated Phillip. Once he had the whiff of a story, he was like a dog with a bone. "Where's this coming from?" Tom asked. "Can't you accept that sometimes good things happen in our community?"

The elevator stopped at the ground level, and the two stepped off. Three bohemian types held up protest signs. One sign read "No coverup for Ring Tires." The second sign read "You can't cover poison with Flowers." Tom sighed.

"Oh, you got your information from Francisco Gonzalez's campaign, didn't you? Was he involved in the study as a professor at the university?"

Phillip seemed unfazed. "I'm asking the questions. What do you have to say to them? And what about the makeup of the all-white, all-male environmental survey committee? Any quotes?"

One person in the small group chanted, "Clean air, clean water, clean air, clean water," while another sign-holder shouted, "Shame on you, Mayor Reed." A photographer appeared from out of nowhere and took photos of the mayor, the three protestors with their signs, and Phillip.

Tom was ready. "Well, Phillip, I hope you'll do your homework better next time. He pointed to the man's small notebook. "Write this down. I *have* appointed a woman from the LGBTQ community, who is actually part of the garden cleanup."

Phillip, for once, appeared blindsided. "Who?"

"Mitzi Fowler. Now, if you'll excuse me, I have city business to attend to. But before I go, let me say this." He addressed the small group with signs. "I share your desire for clean air and clean water and would add, a commitment to diversity. If Ring Tire has done anything wrong, they will be held accountable. Now I really must go."

As the mayor turned to walk down the hall to his meeting, he almost laughed out loud at the stunned look on Phillip's face upon learning Mitzi Fowler would be a part of his committee. He nearly stumbled when he heard someone yell, "What about the land? Isn't that owned by Windingle Developers? What about them?"

He acted as if he hadn't heard. Windingle Developers were possibly the biggest philanthropists in town. He needed to meet with his team right away for damage control. He also hoped Hortense Miller had already told Mitzi Fowler of her appointment to the environmental committee and that she accepted before the media got to her.

***

With the unseasonably cold weather, Mitzi and I were cuddled up on the couch by the fire in the late afternoon with our kitties, enjoying the mindlessness of the boob tube and being with each other. Mitzi got up to start dinner. I yelled from the living room, "How long do you think I'll have to keep this rag on here?"

"You rest, Panda Bear, and I'll come check it in a minute. Elsa should be up soon."

"You sound like Puddle. She calls me that."

"Hey, the name's catchy, and you are my little bear."

A couple of minutes later she called, "Panda."

"What is it?" I called from my throne on the couch, suddenly on alert.

Mitzi replied. "Twyla's here."

This made no sense. Twyla was in Peru. "What?" I used tongs to pick up a corner of the poisonous rag on my ankle and put it back in the pan before hobbling toward the kitchen. Mitzi stood at the open Dutch door face-to-face with Twyla, the fuck-up fairy. Mitzi had asked me not to call her that, but this was my first thought. I maneuvered into a chair at the table and said with my outside voice, "Twyla. It is you. What a surprise."

Talk about the unexpected. We hadn't seen her since we all returned from Peru about a month before. Well, she did appear once to me, disguised as a squirrel, when I was in federal prison, but that was a magically facilitated, brief appearance. Twyla always wanted to be helpful, but calamity usually followed her. According to my sister, she recently failed as guardian fairy for my brother, Brooke. Something that happened in New York. I didn't hold that against her since my older sibling could be a pain.

Still tiny and red-headed, Twyla stood in front of us. She wore a backpack over green overalls with a white T-shirt underneath it. "Hi. Aren't you going to invite me in?"

Mitzi unfroze and picked her up to hug her. "Sorry. Of course. I'm surprised to see you. That's all. What are you doing here, Miss Twyla?"

I waved from my chair. "Hey. I want to talk to you about a certain squirrel from when I was in jail. Good to see you. Come sit down and catch us up. Hungry?"

"I'm always hungry. What squirrel thing?" She didn't wait for an answer. As was typical for her, she changed the topic of conversation. "Hey, you changed your kitchen. I feel like I'm back in Germany at my Oma's house." She giggled.

Mitzi turned, one hand on the pan handle, and grimaced. The remodel was a sore spot. Ever the good hostess, she asked, "You're a vegetarian, right? I'll make a separate pan of spaghetti squash for you."

Mitzi turned back to the stove, and I gave Twyla a thorough assessment. The little fairy didn't look a minute older from the day we met. I was dying to know what happened in New York while she was guarding my brother.

"You're staring at me."

"I was thinking about how I met you in this very kitchen. Apparently, this is the place for magical people to show up. Do we have a portal in here?" I pretended to search, only half-kidding.

Twyla answered seriously, "I don't think so."

I patted the vinyl dinette chair next to me. "So fill us in. How was it living with Brooke in Manhattan?"

Mitzi went to the fridge to retrieve a jar of chopped garlic. Like me, she kept glancing at Twyla who, like all fairies, had a delicate air about her. Her red hair had grown a bit longer, and clear light blue eyes stared back at me.

"Well, as you know, I went to New York with Brooke after Peru. It was okay, but I'm not really cut out for cooking," she wrinkled her nose, "cleaning, and super urban cities. So many buildings. Not enough trees except for that big park, but that wasn't like the Hercynian Garden at all." She took a breath and sipped a glass of water my wife placed before her. "Anyway, Brooke really didn't know what to do with me, and, since his place was small, he sort of tried to make me the live-in maid." She scrunched up her button nose again. "It didn't work. This guy kept following me to the laundry room and asking me out. He wouldn't get the hint and I, ah, used some, uh, well magic, and he called the police. Uncle Ehren and Brooke decided it might be good if I left New York. It seems Brooke is so into his life as a stockbroker, or was," the way she jumped around on topics always drove me crazy, "that Wolfrum really didn't care about him much anyway. It was pretty clear you guys didn't know anything about Paititi or whatever that mythical city was in Peru either."

"So he's safe? Where is he?" I did my best to follow what she said.

"I think so. Safe I mean. As much as anybody is in this world." This made her giggle, which sounded more like the old Twyla. "Anyway, when he suddenly took a leave from work to go to that convent in Peru, I went with him. Ehrenhardt said it was okay since I was basically in between assignments."

"Except Peru is hot, and you didn't like it."

Twyla nodded. Mitzi seemed surprised I knew that, so I explained. "The phone call with Puddle before I called you today? She told me that."

"Exactly," Twyla said and stretched. She put two delicate hands on either side of her face. "This skin needs no sun. Do you see all my new freckles?" Twyla turned her face, showing each cheek. She did have a few freckles on otherwise porcelain clear skin. "I won't have that trouble here." She hugged herself. "I didn't know California got this cold."

"Are you on your way back to the Garden?" Mitzi asked. she was frying some zucchini, and both Twyla and I sniffed the air.

My stomach rumbled. "That smells so good."

Twyla said, "No."

"It doesn't smell good?" Her response was puzzling.

"No, I mean to Mitzi's question. I'm not going to the Garden now. I'm being posted in Merryville."

I grimaced. "Ah, we're kinda full up here. I guess we could—"

Twyla's laugh interrupted me. She sounded so merry. It was impossible not to laugh along with her. "You have your guardians already, silly. I'm assigned to the Goodens."

When no one immediately said something, she said, "Juniper and Valerie," as if we were wondering which Goodens.

Mitzi rubbed her chin. "Do they know it yet?" Mitzi was always so reasonable.

Twyla grinned sweetly. "Uh, no. Ehren said you two could break the news."

I rolled my eyes. "Your dad is so controlling," I said to Mitzi.

Twyla put her slender hand on her chest. "Panda. He is ruler of the Hercynian Garden, leader of all free creatures." Then she cracked up. "But yeah, pretty controlling."

Mitzi froze. "Why do our friends need protecting?"

"After all you four have been through? Even a nithling could figure that out."

I mulled over the word nithling in my mind before saying, "Maybe we should invite them for dinner."

***

THE GOODENS

Valerie was puttering around her indoor orchid garden when the house phone rang. She yelled over her shoulder, "Juniper, can you get that?" When two more rings went unanswered, she quickly pulled off her leather gloves and picked up the vintage handset. "Hello?"

"Hi, Val. It's Mitzi. Is this a good time?"

"Sure. I'm spritzing my babies."

"You sound like you're in a cave. Where's your cell?"

"Somewhere under one of Juniper's projects in the living room. I escaped to my happy place. What's up?"

"I wish I could come over and breathe in your orchid house, but I'm cooking dinner. Have you two eaten yet?"

Valerie laughed. "Actually, I'm starving. Juniper has taken over the whole house with this community garden planning, and I can't find the crockpot. I was going to get takeout. Why? You inviting us?"

"Yes. And, Valerie, we have a surprise guest."

"Really. Who?"

"If I told you, it wouldn't be a surprise."

"Hmmmm. Just a minute." Valerie placed the clunky receiver down and yelled out, "Juniper. Juniper. Put down the magic marker. We're going to the Fowlers."

Juniper responded in her usual dramatic voice, "I'm creating, Vava."

"You need a break." When that didn't work Valerie tried again. "Okay, then I need a break." That worked. She picked up the phone to tell Mitzi the good news. "We're in. Twenty minutes, okay?"

"Yes. Yay!"

CHAPTER SEVEN

Mitzi interrupted a deep conversation between me and Twyla to say Val and Juniper would be at our house shortly. "What are you two planning? When you two put your heads together, I get nervous." Mitzi turned away to give the sauce a stir.

I felt serious and punctuated my words with dramatic hand movements. "Twyla has seen an injury like my leg before. People have died from this back in the Hercynian Forest."

A grumpy Elsa entered through the back door. She had changed her clothes and acknowledged the new visitor with a frown. "Twyla, stop scaring the girls."

Mirroring her expression, like a wary cowboy in a Western movie, Twyla tipped her head. "Elsa." The relationship between them had cooled a bit when Twyla wasn't able to stop me from being kidnapped and taken to Peru. At the time, Twyla had heatedly pointed out that Elsa also wasn't able to stop Puddle from being kidnapped either. The difference was, Twyla, as a fairy, didn't hang on to things like that. Elsa, the elf, apparently did.

Elsa gave Mitzi a hug. "Smells good, honey, but it needs more garlic. Ekk will be down in a minute."

Mitzi visibly stiffened. I could tell Elsa's culinary suggestion irritated her.

Elsa seemed oblivious, and I stuck to the original subject. "Elsa, my leg hurts. I think it's getting worse."

Elsa gave Twyla the stink-eye and said, "We'll talk about it after dinner. I've been doing some more research and have some ideas. This is not a death sentence."

"I wasn't scaring Panda. I only said—" Twyla started to float, something fairies did when suffused with emotion. I put my hand on Twyla's arm to keep her in her chair, musing she was like a balloon slowly filling with helium.

"Elsa, I know you're still mad Panda got kidnapped on my watch, but—"

Trying to lighten the mood, I made a joke. "You had ONE job, Twyla."

Elsa was more serious than I'd ever seen her as she directed her anger at Twyla. "Yes, you did. And before you say it, yes, Puddle disappeared on my watch too. We both failed. We must do better." Suddenly, a lavender scent filled the room. The tenseness dissipated. "Okay, let me start over." She sat herself at the dinette. "I, I love these girls and the Goodens too. We cannot fail this time."

"Wow. That's the first time I've ever seen you use your flower magic on yourself," I said. "Twyla, you know I was kidding. I do feel safe, mostly. This morning I asked Elsa to teach me some magic for the times I don't." Everyone looked at me. "In case ya'll are not around, I'll be able to defend myself." I smiled but not one of the women smiled back.

Elsa sighed. "Panda, stop. We discussed this already."

Ekk appeared at the kitchen door holding Brutus, and he cleared his throat to get our attention. "Brutus got a ricochet blast that, if he weren't so tough, would have killed a cat his size. And you, Miss Panda, did a fine job of protecting yourself and him—without conjuring dangerous forces. Let's leave the magic to the pros." Blondie swirled at Ekk's feet. In a change of subject, Ekk addressed the latest arrival with a reserved voice. "Hello, Twyla. Your timing is uncanny. I heard from Ehren about your new job."

Mitzi dropped her spoon. "You heard from my dad? What did he say?" Mitzi had been missing him. "How come I didn't get to hear the message?"

Ekk placed Brutus on my lap and went to Mitzi. "He sent a very quick communication. Since I was temporarily in charge of the keep, he's been sharing more than he ever has with me. Mitzi, your dad loves you a lot, but this was strictly Garden business. Oh, he did say the ravens are chattering about danger to all of you and to your friends. Twyla was at loose ends, and the Goodens already know her. It makes sense that she is the one to protect them."

Twyla flexed a muscle and said, "I did save Valerie's orchids."

Elsa raised her eyebrows.

Ekk responded. "And that was temporary. They died soon after. Forget about all that. You must not be impulsive this time. Ehren's willing to give you another chance at being a guardian—even after…you know."

Twyla turned red. "What happened in Peru wasn't my fault."

Everyone else in the room knew accepting responsibility wasn't her strong suit. I studied Brutus' ear.

Twyla sagged. "My father, Frederick," she sniffed, and a tear went down her face, "never got to know Mitzi and Panda. Since we're related, it's my sacred duty to protect them and their best friends." She sat up straight. "I can do this. They're my family."

Apparently only Ekk and Twyla knew what her actual offense was in Peru, but it must have been a doozy. She certainly had created enough havoc in Merryville while Mitzi and I were out of the country, using magic to eradicate thistles at our house and other disobediences. Then a situation arose in New York with Brooke that apparently required Twyla to leave the country. Fairies in general were not good at following rules.

Mitzi went to Twyla and patted her silky red hair. "I'm so sorry I never got to meet Frederick." He was Ehren's partner, killed in combat with the Wolf Ravens before Mitzi and I were introduced to the parallel world. Twyla leaned in, accepting the affection.

The doorbell chime blared "Scotland the Brave." I'd thought about replacing it but, like every other quirky thing, the tune had become part of our lives. Getting up was painful, so I asked Ekk, "Would you mind?"

"Of course not." He hurried to the front door.

Elsa said, "Perfect timing, Let's all move to the dining room. We've got quite a crowd." She climbed up a step stool and counted out seven plates.

I watched from my vantage point at the kitchen table while Juniper and Valerie followed Ekk to the dining room and Twyla shyly joined them. After her dressing down by Elsa, she was a bit subdued. It didn't last long.

Valerie opened her arms wide. "Twyla, what a surprise. How are you?"

Juniper, always thrilled with the magical, grinned from ear to ear. "Are you just visiting? How long are you here?"

"I'm not sure yet how long I'm here, but it's nice to see you too."

Elsa glared at her in warning, and Twyla sat like a chastened child at the dinner table.

Mitzi entered the dining room carrying a large Pyrex full of spaghetti squash and placed it at the center of the table. "Dinner's ready."

I hobbled in as everyone took their seats and set a basket of garlic bread on the table. Valerie saw my difficulty walking and was instantly concerned. "Oh no! Do you think this is…?"

I didn't hold back. "It is. This is the same damn thing that almost killed me in the hospital."

Elsa tapped a spoon on her glass. "Okay, everybody, we all have lots to talk about with what's happening, but eating and resting at regular intervals is going to be very important considering what's ahead."

"What's ahead?" Juniper asked.

Elsa didn't respond directly to her question and simply said, "Ekk has things to tell us too—after dinner." She must have realized she was sounding cross and softened it a bit. "Besides, Mitzi has made us this lovely food, and I intend to enjoy it."

"Even though it could use more garlic," Mitzi whispered to me.

Ekk backed up his wife. "Thank you, Elsa, and thank you, Mitzi. Friends? Let's keep it light. *Bon appetit.*"

Everyone tucked into the food, and I observed a couple of furtive glances filled with curiosity traded between Juniper and Valerie. Ekk calmly ate as if this were a typical dinner.

Juniper sipped her drink. "Where did you arrive from, Twyla? Is Brooke here? Last I heard, you were guarding him in New York."

Twyla, still on her best behavior, gave an honest response. "Brooke Fowler no longer needs a guardian. He's going back and forth between New York and Peru to help those nuns raise money for the orphanage."

"That's good news, right?" Valerie said. "Things must be getting better. I mean, less dangerous."

"We aren't supposed to talk about it yet." Twyla gave Elsa side-eye and sipped her drink. Her hand was so delicate, the glass seemed huge by comparison.

"Twyla, is your dinner okay?" Mitzi asked, and giggled in spite of the tension.

Twyla had a small pile of spaghetti squash on her plate with garlic bread and said in an exaggeratedly polite manner, "This is delicious, Mitzi. Thank you for making me a vegetarian portion. Did you give up part of your dinner, Panda?"

I felt guilty. "I'm back on meat. I'd make a lousy fairy." I reached for a second portion that had meat sauce. "You're all vegetarians, right?"

Juniper seemed fascinated. "Wait, seriously? I never thought about this. What do magical creatures eat? Are you guys vegan?"

Twyla fairly twinkled. Her nature was light and sparkly. "Not all fairies are vegetarians, but we prefer it. We're highly evolved." Her blue eyes were clear, and not a trace of irony was attached to the comment.

Ekk jumped in. "Twyla's father, Frederick, was vegan, but that's not the norm. And fairies," he looked at Twyla, "are no more evolved than any other magical creatures. In fact—"

Elsa put her fork down forcefully. "All right, let's talk about the elephants in this room."

This was so abrupt, I stopped chewing and froze.

All eyes were on Elsa. "Ehrenhardt wants Twyla to move in with you two and guard you during this time. Something's happened."

This was news to Mitzi and me. We knew Twyla was going to Juniper and Valerie's, but not that something had happened. Conversation broke out all at once.

"What haven't you told us, Elsa?" Mitzi asked. "I've noticed you've been…um, on edge."

Juniper, in a colorful tunic, wilted a little. "Mitzi, is that why you had us come over?"

"No, I mean yes, but we always want to see you. Twyla showed up tonight, and Ehren suggested we should be the ones to tell you."

Juniper looked at Elsa and Twyla. "Why do Val and I need a guardian?"

Twyla took a deep breath as if to answer, but Elsa spoke instead. "All four of you have taken part in the two rituals to help balance the power between the magical world and this one." She looked right at me, answering the question I was forming in my mind. "The sharing of power between *Lupus Imperium* and the Hercynian Garden with the non-magical world brought you into this. Once that happened, I'm afraid you became, forever, a part of this fight."

Valerie, who had been quiet, asked, "What, specifically, has happened? I thought when Panda chased off that horrible Wolfrum, we were entering a nice, peaceful period. Not so?"

Ekk wiped his neat, well-drawn lips and put his cloth napkin down, keeping his hand on it. "Remember when Gary Smithers came here, to this house, and threatened to kill Elsa and me with a machete?"

I was nervous. "How could we forget? If not for Brutus coming to get me and Puddle and Mitzi at the museum," my voice got shaky, "you might not be here."

Ekk went on. "Well, that's the specific danger right now."

"Wait, isn't he in custody?" Mitzi seemed to have lost all interest in her food.

Ekk responded. "No. He's escaped the mental hospital where he was being held. It already hit the news. But that's not all. It's been confirmed he's part of *Lupus Imperium*, and…he isn't the only one. When Wolfrum came to Merryville, he was seeking people to turn."

My face paled. "Are you saying we may find more culties here in Merryville?"

Ekk nodded. "We think so. Thanks to Valerie and all of you, he left, but don't think for a minute he wasn't busy infecting people's hearts while he was on the ground here. That was his specialty."

I rubbed my aching leg. "Ow! Even talking about this is making my leg hurt more."

Valerie, a home healthcare nurse, couldn't stand it. "Panda, I want to see your leg."

Grumpy, Elsa barked at her, "I've got it under control."

The naked stare Valerie gave Elsa was one I'd never seen her do before. Resolute: a healer standoff. She stood up with fists on her hips. "Do you know Panda and Mitzi have been our friends for twenty years? Do you remember I'm a nurse with an actual degree? I have magic too, Elsa, called science. Let's not work against each other."

Elsa opened her mouth to continue in this vein, then crumpled and dabbed at her eyes. She exhaled heavily. "I'm sorry to be so upset, Valerie. Panda has a magical injury, and it needs Garden magic to fight it." She addressed the fairy with emotion. "Twyla, I'm worried about you having this level of responsibility. Everything is so serious." She pointed at the door. "That crazy ex-councilman could show up at the Goodens' house at any time. This is life and death! Or maybe even something worse than death." She dissolved into tears before stopping her outburst.

I took Mitzi's hand. "It'll be okay, Elsa," I said. "We've all felt disheartened at times over the past year." I inwardly resolved to stop complaining so much. It was clear the stress was affecting our guardians.

Twyla stood up and said, "My turn. Everyone is talking for me like I'm not here or like I'm a child. I can do this. Yes, last time I was here, the thistles in the yard backfired and Panda got kidnapped by Mitzi's yoga teacher…and then that thing in Peru"—a few at the table studied their silverware—"and New York. But, *but,* you are all here in one piece, right? Elsa, you seem to have a grudge against me, and well, please stop it. We all have to work together. My father thought a lot of you."

Elsa appeared stunned and wiped her eyes. "You're right, Twyla. I, I'm sorry. Frederick was a good man, and you are his seed." Twyla made a weird face, no doubt because she was of a different generation, one where no one would ever refer to being a daughter in that way. Elsa went on. "And, Valerie, you're right. We should work together, or at least coordinate."

Ekk beamed at Elsa. She could be a hard woman, and apologies like this were rare.

It was going well until she asked Valerie, "You know your herbs, right?"

Valerie opened her mouth like she was going to say something but exhaled instead. I believe her good heart refused to take issue with what had to feel like an insult. She simply said, "Yes, Elsa, I do."

This was nice, but I was hungry. "Well, somebody please check me out after dinner. Elsa said we need to eat. I'm eating now." I put a big spoonful of squash in my mouth. This broke the tension, and everyone settled in to eat. The mood was much better than when dinner started.

Once the plates were empty, Elsa and Ekk made eye contact, and Ekk nodded. Elsa's voice was more like her normal calm, collected self. Whatever anger had moved through her like a storm seemed to have passed. "Valerie, before we inspect Panda's leg, I want to take you to my, uh, workshop."

I grinned at Mitzi. She squeezed my hand under the table. It seemed the team was finally coming together.

CHAPTER EIGHT

PANDA AND BRUTUS' INJURIES

After dinner, Ekk helped me back to the elf hole and put me in a chair with my left leg on an ottoman he'd brought down from the house. Brutus lay heavy on my lap. Seeing two talented women I trusted working on our injuries made me feel hopeful. I was also still curious about the elf hole, which had a unique smell I couldn't quite identify. Valerie and Elsa stood side by side in front of rows of dried herbs, which were tied with red string and hanging off of hooks on a green, putty-like wall. Elsa gestured to various bunches, and Valerie pointed to something on the table. The acoustics of *grunzueg* were such that, although close, I couldn't tell what they said when they were faced away from me and conversed in low tones. Finally, Valerie pulled out a well-worn leather journal from her bag and laid it on the table next to Elsa's *Zauberbuch,* something which would have been unheard of before the truce. Elsa looked at her questioningly but stayed calm.

"My grandmother's," was all Valerie said, and Elsa nodded. In both Native American and elven traditions, wisdom of the elders was respected, and I knew what Brutus and I had must be serious to stump both of them.

Ekk took in the scene, knowing he couldn't do more than he already had. It was quite crowded. "You okay, Panda? I'm going to leave and give you guys some room."

"Of course. Thanks, Ekk."

Before leaving he stretched, pushing his hips forward, and surveyed the ceiling. "Is the ventilation better? I added a spout."

"Yes, Ekk," Elsa said, "it's *wunderbar.*"

I liked that. Even so engaged, she was mindful he needed kudos, too, sometimes.

"It's good," I said. "It does smell fresher in here."

He patted Elsa on the shoulder. "It's a work in progress. Let me know what you need. I'm going to help clean up everything." Elsa and Valerie were already deep in their respective books, and Elsa simply nodded. I turned my attention to Brutus, and Ekk took his leave.

The mysterious Blondie appeared from a dark corner and jumped on the ottoman, carefully stepping around my leg. The yellow and white cat had first shown up after Wolfrum's appearance in our kitchen, and she appeared to have come for the specific purpose of tending to Brutus, who seemed appreciative of having the cat around. Since Brutus was on my lap, I watched with amusement as Blondie picked her way around his wound and settled in with her body pressed close to him. Almost instantly I felt it. Blondie emitted some sort of low-level vibration that was cool rather than hot. It felt clean and comforting.

"Elsa, Valerie, I think I'm getting a cat healing."

Elsa turned. Her eyes were saggy, but some of her old cheeriness was present. After the confrontation at dinner with Valerie, she seemed to accept it was better for her to have another herbalist and healer on the team. Valerie seemed fixated on a page, her index finger carefully trailing down the page.

"Yes, Panda, all cats have it, but some are special healers like Blondie. Although a formal call out from the Hercynian Garden didn't occur, a feline collective conscious exists. All cats have jobs, and this one is doing what comes natural to her." She turned back to her *Zauberbuch*, leaving me with lots of questions about the animal kingdom.

"Kind of like when they show up at your house and turn out to be the perfect addition, even when you weren't looking for a pet. No such thing as a lost cat, only a cat with a new address." I laughed at my own commentary, but the others were too busy to respond. *What was Brutus' job*?

Valerie kept her finger on one particular entry and said loud enough for me to hear, "You know, Elsa, blue skullcap is effective for skin conditions, especially when fused with a ritual to call down wolf energy." Valerie was concentrating hard, trying to find a solution. The flickering light reflected off wire glasses she rarely wore. I was ashamed that after all these years, I didn't know she was an expert herbalist. She looked very much the scientist at that moment.

"Agreed. But we still need fresh wolfbane." Elsa took a deep breath. "You know, Valerie, I don't think I realized how much a part of the struggle between our worlds you played until the showdown at the Lutheran Church a month ago. I honor your ancient magic."

This was high praise indeed.

I piped up. "What about the Sun Dog ritual at the museum? I remember she morphed into one of her ancestors, or at least started to." They were ignoring me, although not in a mean way. They were busy.

Elsa held up a vial of something gold to the light and squinted. "I was too into my chanting spell to see much of the first ritual, but at the church, I saw it all." She put her hand on Valerie's. "I'm sorry for being cross earlier. We're all in this together."

"That's history now." Val's demeanor was calm, as always, but since Valerie's face-to-face with Wolfrum in the Lutheran Church, she did have the aura of ancient magic and a little more of an edge. "This magic, it takes many forms. We Utes call it ancestor wisdom." She spoke directly to me. "Anyone can access their own. It takes time to learn the ways. I believe everyone in your bloodline who has come before you has tossed something into the family knowledge reservoir."

I listened intently. "What if your ancestor is a notorious serial killer or a really bad person? Some reservoirs may have bad water."

Elsa turned to me and shook her head. "Stay focused. The evil we face now is very old. I don't even think we know the origin, but the Black Forest always has myths."

Valerie left her book and stood at the ottoman. She smiled at me while checking our wounds again. "Back to the reservoir metaphor— that's how family karma works, Panda—some good, some bad. The goal is, over the arc of time, a soul group has more wisdom than chaos, enough to absorb and teach the ones who have lost their way. Everything we do affects this reservoir. I wish more people realized that."

A light in my head switched on. "Maybe we need to pour something clean into *Lupus Imperium's* reservoir instead of fighting them all the time."

Valerie and Elsa shared a meaningful look.

"Maybe we do," Elsa said slowly. She turned back to her book, flipping pages quickly.

A stinging pain made me wince. "Like I know how to solve ancient riddles. How am I doing? My ankle is feeling very raw."

Valerie peeked under the bandage Elsa had applied with a healing poultice. Her smile dropped. "Elsa."

Elsa joined Valerie at the ottoman. She was very serious. "Get the skullcap. What sort of ritual do you have in mind for this?"

Valerie smoothed her silky hair and didn't answer right away.

I filled the void. "Ritual? Hey, you're talking about me. What do you mean, ritual?"

Valerie's eyes were sad. "The kind that will either cure you or kill you, I'm afraid." She closed her book with finality. "We need Twyla and Ekk to build a sweat lodge."

***

Mitzi burst into the elf hole, startling everyone. Elsa dropped her stir stick and frowned. The two cats on my lap barely stirred.

"Baby." I extended a free arm to my wife.

"Well, hello." Valerie said without turning, focused on mashing an herb in a mortar with a stone pestle. "Don't mind us."

Mitzi's eyes were bright. "Sorry to interrupt." She swallowed. "Glad to see you're fixing my darling." Mitzi went to me and took my hand. "How are you, sweetheart? I can see you're trapped."

"Yes, the kitties are determined to keep me here." I gave a pat to the intertwined pile made up of Blondie and Brutus. "What's up? You seem excited."

Without taking her eyes off the table, where she watched Valerie use a dropper to add something to a small bowl, Elsa said, "Do you two mind?" It was obvious that Elsa was getting grumpy again.

"Sorry." Mitzi lowered her voice and said, "I got a call from Hortense. Valerie, you need to hear this too. They want me on the city's environmental committee." When Valerie didn't immediately react, she added details. "You know, the one that oversees the community garden?"

Valerie turned away from the mixing table and frowned. "The mayor's committee? Well congratulations, but that's weird."

I was a bit stung. "Hey, be happy for her."

Elsa stomped to the corner, got earmuffs, put them on, and kept working.

It made us grin, as we exchanged looks behind her back.

Mitzi addressed Valerie. "Are you upset they didn't ask you? I mean, after all, you're on the board and know more about plants. I'm only a volunteer."

Valerie replied, "No, that's not it. The planning commission is a committee with five old, straight white guys on it. Always has been that way. I do keep up. The only person of color appointed to the committee didn't last long, and I know that appointment was political. So I worry about why they picked you. Although if it's real, that would be awesome."

Mitzi's jets cooled a bit. "I get it. I've wanted to find something to do other than travel, and it seemed, well, I'll tell them no."

"You'll do no such thing." I was serious. "I know you aren't challenged by helping me at the tax office and, let's face it, being gone as much as we have this year has hurt your tourism business." I pulled her close. "You love the environment. All the changes we've made around the house with solar and stuff were your idea. You can handle those old boys, and I think you should get on the Horticultural Society Board. They need you." I kissed the back of Mitzi's hand.

She relaxed a little. "I hope so." When Mitzi said this, she sounded sad.

Valerie wiped her hands on her apron and seemed to focus on a point beyond the clay walls. "Mitzi, not to be a killjoy, but I've been thinking about something, trying to sort it out. When I walked around the sand area earlier today, something didn't feel right."

Mitzi laughed. "Probably because it's been assigned to Hortense."

"No," Valerie said. "I've been wondering about how fast the whole thing got turned over to the club for this garden. I think we need to treat this like an opportunity to get more information."

Mitzi deflated a bit. "I was excited about something new and being more involved. Would you work with me on this?" She twisted one of her braids, thinking. "If they didn't do the environmental impact report correctly, I'll speak up."

Valerie nodded. "I'll put in your name for the board also." She turned back to her work.

I patted Mitzi's arm to get her attention. "They have no idea who they picked to be on this committee. Now, let's talk about me." I batted my eyelashes and pointed at my leg. "I need petting."

"That sounds good," Valerie said, "Pet her and keep her quiet." She looked over her shoulder at Mitzi. "Elsa and I are getting close to figuring out the best medicine for her and Brutus. Ute remedies and magical spells actually work surprisingly well together."

Mitzi laughed and hugged my head, as Valerie lifted one of Elsa's muffs and said, "Okay, grumpy, I'm all yours."

Mitzi and I petted the cats in companionable silence and watched Valerie and Elsa work.

***

The next morning I was feeling sorry for myself. Valerie and Elsa were finished with their examinations and left me on the couch in the house with my swollen ankle while they went in search of wolfsbane and other herbs. Ekk had gone to Taggart's Emporium with a list of supplies needed to build a teepee or whatever Valerie suggested. He had done some bookkeeping work at the hardware store for Ralph and that worried me. I hoped Ralph didn't steal him away from Fowler Tax Services. Babs, my one and only employee at the tax office, said things were fine. In fact, she had said with over exaggerated politeness, "Panda boss, you should stop calling if you want me to get all this stuff done."

Mitzi had left to find out more about the environmental commission she was invited to join. Twyla was at the Goodens' house, "guarding Juniper." This made me giggle a bit. I was alone and said to the cat, "It's you and me, buddy," but Brutus was snuggled up to Blondie, sleeping. "Or not."

I got up to retrieve my phone. Everyone was running around, being productive. I had a nagging feeling that danger was outside, and here I was, pretty much dead in the water with my injured leg and ankle.

Even though it was somewhat chilly, I wore shorts and a T-shirt. I was tired of rolling up my jeans to keep checking the wound, which was stinging again after all the poking and prodding. It wasn't getting better—that was clear. I tried to start a fire by saying, *Ignis*, like Ekk had done, but the logs in the fireplace stayed as they were, not even a spark. Left to my own thoughts, I noted that Valerie and Elsa had tried to look encouraging, but they couldn't completely hide their worry. In addition, the normally calm Elsa seemed frazzled and tired. At least she was listening to Valerie. Valerie, as a healer and the only one who had heretofore taken part in a sweat, said they needed to gather the right herbs at some botanica. That's where they were now.

I was scrolling through my cell phone when it rang. "Hello?"

"Whoa, were you sitting on that thing?"

"Puddle. Just bored. How are you?"

"I'm okay, how's our kitty boy? Any better?"

"He's hanging in there. I'm with him right now. He's cuddled up with his girlfriend."

"Girlfriend? Brutus has a girlfriend? Geez, Louise, what else have I missed?"

My sister always made me laugh. "I guess we have another cat named Blondie. It's another long story."

I stared at the tree through the window until Puddle asked, "Panda, what's up? What aren't you telling me?"

Rather than answering directly, I replied, "This call is so clear for once."

"It's a good thing I'm coming home."

"What? You're leaving Peru?"

"Left already. Dieter found some family, and I'm giving him time to get to know them."

I sat up straight. "Oh. Are you at the airport?"

Suddenly, the doorbell pealed out with "Scotland the Brave," and I shook my head.

"No. I'm on your front porch, weirdo. I thought it would be rude not to call."

I ignored the pain, got up, and dragged my leg to the front door. Puddle stood on the porch in her typical tie-dyed T-shirt and jeans, reeking of patchouli. She had let her big, frizzy hair fly, and new freckles adorned her tanned face. She gave me a big hug. "I could tell when we talked, something was really wrong."

I hobbled back to the couch. "I'd help you with your bags, but…" I motioned to my leg.

"Oh, wow." She frowned at my bum leg and asked, "Where should I put these?"

"Anywhere for now. We'll figure it out later."

Puddle, taller than me and somewhat skinny, hauled a backpack and two duffle bags into the house and stuck them in a corner.

"I can't believe you're actually here. We have a lot of catching up to do."

"You're telling me. Spill, little sister. Tell me everything that's happened since I left."

I opened my mouth to do so.

"But first I need the bathroom." Typical Puddle. I closed my mouth, but I felt my spirits rise.

Brutus lifted his head sleepily and blinked at Puddle, as she ran to him for a quick greeting. "Brutus boy. Is this your little girlfriend?" She petted his smooth, spotted fur. Blondie still had her paw on him protectively. She said to the new cat, "Okay, little mama, you got this. I can see that. Be right back." Her expressions were so comical, I realized how much I'd missed my unpredictable but loving sister.

When she returned from the bathroom with her hair tied back, I saw Puddle had aged. Maybe it was the tan. She plopped herself down near me, and I did my best to catch her up with all the recent crazy events.

I started my narration by saying, "You left at the end of July and, after everything we'd been through, I sort of had a spiritual meltdown."

"*Porque?*" Since going to Peru, my Spanish has gotten better. I knew *porque* meant because.

"Everybody in Southern California knows that, Puddle. It's like *bano* or *gracias*. Anyway, I'm talking about things we were introduced to this year. Elves? Fairies? They aren't exactly in the Bible."

"Yeah? You believe in air, and you can't see that. And how about gravity?"

"My crisis—don't sidetrack me. Father Bennington suggested a vacation and, you know Mitzi, she pulled a trip to Mexico together in a day." I snapped my fingers.

"Sounds like her," Puddle said. "It's lucky you married a travel agent."

"So we took a vacation and were on our way to Cozumel."

"I love Cozumel. The water's so warm and clear. How was it?"

"Listen. We didn't make it that time. Let me finish. Me and Mitzi and Elsa and Ekk were in my new Land Rover—"

"Saw that. You sure overcompensated for that tiny smart car."

It was impossible to change Puddle, so I went on. "With all our bags, heading down the street, and we got pulled over. I was arrested for aiding and abetting arsonists when some of the New Spirit Church tents in the park burned down."

Now Puddle sputtered. "Wait, what?" The two sisters stared at each other. Puddle was stunned. "You didn't think to call?"

"Now you sound like our aunt, God rest her soul. No, there's some stuff I still haven't even processed yet. I'm trying to do that now. And you're the one who doesn't trust telephones and such." I waggled my fingers on both hands mysteriously. "I mean, who knows if *Lupus Imperium* has a vast network of people listening in, you know, like NSA." I adjusted my leg on the pillow, as she crinkled her face.

"Loopy secta, whatsa what?"

"Oh, you haven't gotten the memo. Wolf Raven is no longer called Wolf Raven because the Ravens have broken their alliance with those guys. In fact, ravens have come to my rescue a few times."

We said together, "But that's another story," and laughed.

"I need a smoke." Puddle retrieved her backpack.

I went on. "Now they've rebranded as *Lupus*, which means wolf, *Imperium*, which is authority or rule."

"Sounds like a disease."

"Believe me, they act like one too. Anyway, I got arrested, and so did Ekk—"

"Little Ekk man got arrested? I need popcorn." Puddle jumped up and ran to the kitchen. I was used to my impulsive sister, who called out from the kitchen, "I'm still listening." The sound of the microwave indicated she was actually making popcorn.

I called out, "But it all turned out okay. I mean, the injury was caused by Wolfrum, but having an ankle bracelet—"

"Wait a sec." Soon Puddle was back with a bowl full of delicious-smelling popcorn and sat down. "That creep's back? You have an ankle bracelet? House arrest? Got any kombucha?" Puddle got up again.

"No, that stuff's dangerous and tastes like, well, I don't like it. When you left your little home brew in our shed, it blew up and made quite a mess."

Puddle held out the bowl to me. "Sorry."

I grabbed some popcorn. "Speaking of explosions. Someone served me an exploding casserole when I was in federal prison."

Puddle dropped back down and put a handful of popcorn in her mouth. "You're making this up."

I put my hand over my heart. "Swear it's the truth." I was still physically hurting, but I felt better, even with all the interruptions. "Mitzi and I decided not to tell you all of this while you were out of the country. It feels good to tell you now. We were worried you might have flown back and been right in the middle of it, maybe even gotten hurt. Then, after things died down, no one wanted to relive it in the telling. Now you're pretty much up to date except, what happened with you know who, my leg, and, oh, Twyla's here."

After fishing around in her backpack, Puddle declared, "This requires a smoke. Let's go outside, and I want to know about your leg and hear the details and the rest of the story. Can you walk? I want to hear it all, blow-by-blow."

"Yes, let's go in the backyard."

I was grateful for the company and the change of scenery. I brought a blanket from the couch. With Puddle's help, I hobbled out to the backyard and resettled, no longer feeling sorry for myself. I knew that once Puddle had a few puffs of pot, she'd be better at listening.

"Let's start at the beginning of this last adventure," I said. "Remember that tent church that came to town?"

CHAPTER NINE

THE COMMUNITY GARDEN

Janet poked her head in the Horticultural Society trailer. She had curly brown hair with silver streaks and her eyes showed excitement. "Sylvia, there's a Francisco Gonzalez to see you." In a whisper, she said, "He's that professor from the college who's running for mayor."

Sylvia was going over the plot assignments, and she looked up through her stylish red glasses. She was warming up to Janet and appreciated her support. "I know who he is. Thanks, Janet. Send him in." She gave her blouse a gentle tug to straighten any wrinkles from sitting and gave her smile full wattage. It had been a long time since she and Francisco were classmates together at Merida University.

Francisco, tall and on the thin side, entered after a token knock on the side of the trailer. He wore pressed jeans and a traditional Mexican Guayabera shirt, black hair pulled back in a man bun. He was handsome with a wispy black mustache on his smooth, brown face. "Sylvia, *ha sido un tiempo* ." He flashed a toothy grin and approached to hug her. She gave him a warm hug back, smelling his expensive cologne, and held him at arm's length.

"Frankie, sit down. Want some coffee?" She motioned to a folding chair across from the table. "It has been a long time."

He sauntered over to the coffee pot and poured himself a cup before returning to the seat.

"Uh, not Frankie anymore, Francisco. I'm head of Chicana and Chicano Studies now. Can you imagine? Professor Gonzalez. You and I have come a long way since the protests to include this area's accurate history into the curriculum."

"Congratulations. I did keep up with you. It's great you kept the program going and turned it into a department. Now you're running for mayor? Wow."

After taking a sip and carefully putting down his coffee cup on a folded napkin, he pressed his lips together while seeming to collect his thoughts. He spoke with resolve. "I finally realized that to change the white man's world, you need access to power. I'm tired of crumbs from the political table and token tolerance that's meaningless lip service. Change must come from the inside, but you know this. You left us and went to Silicon Valley to become a role model for our young Merida girls. You figured out this power thing before me. I especially like that you showed the good old boys that Mexican Americans, men and women, can play in their world and win." He reached across the table for her hand. "We could be a real powerhouse together, Sylvia."

She was surprised. "Well, thank you, Frank—Francisco. But you know I'm retired from all that. This community garden is my thing now."

He retracted his hand. "Yes, you retired young and rich. I can't believe this garden thing isn't a springboard for something else."

"I'm not interested in running for office, if that's what you mean." She reached for her Louis Vuitton purse. This visit had to be about fundraising. "Tell me about your platform. The Horticultural Society can't endorse since we're a nonprofit, but I'm happy to write you a personal check."

Now he frowned and put up his hand in a stop motion. "It's not about that. Well, a check is welcome, but I'm here for something deeper, and I'm hoping a little of the old Sylvia Arviso will be interested."

She rested her hands on the table. "I'm listening."

"It's about this place we are sitting in the middle of." He spread his arms out, indicating the five acres.

She took a breath and said, "Does this have anything to do with the defaced sign and water tower?"

He shook his head. "You call it defacing, but maybe it's correcting. I personally had nothing to do with it. But there's a generation of young people who can't wait for institutions to do the right thing." He paused. "Merryville." He made a grimace as he said the name of the town. "It was *Merida* before the whites stripped us of our history."

Intelligent eyes nailed him like a prosecutor. "So it was your students? You're confusing me. You say you want to be part of the institutional power, but at the same time you fire up your students to wreck my project?"

He fixed his intense brown eyes on her, using silence like a weapon.

"Because somebody," she used air quotes, "used spray paint to cross out Merryville on our sign out front and wrote in Merida."

She noted Francisco wore a mask of innocence.

He spoke. "Many people are outraged that our town, which goes back to a Spanish land grant, was renamed after a wealthy white woman, wiping out all our history."

Sylvia sat, holding her own cup with both hands, elbows on the table. "And? Why are you here? If it isn't money, what exactly is it you hope to accomplish?"

"We want you to change the name of the nonprofit. Show those Windingles and Harkers and Millers that they are participating in a new genocide by denying this area's culture and all the brave men and women who died defending it from the white man. It's the least you can do." His words were challenging.

She laughed and shook her head. "Is this your platform? Cuz if it is, you're going to lose this election."

His face flushed, a sign the tension was ramping up. "That's not all. You asked what I want? I'm here to do you and this community a favor." His index finger punctuated his point, pressing down so hard on the table the tip was white.

Sylvia had a short fuse herself. "I'm sorry you oppose what I'm doing, but why you chose this effort to grow fruits and vegetables to focus on is mind-boggling, Francisco. The project is going to help underserved communities. It's a food desert in this part of town."

His face clouded with anger. "So. The rumors are true. You've completely sold out. I guess you're a white girl now."

"Francisco. You're better than that. *A white girl?* If I'm a girl, are you a boy? You don't know me. I haven't seen you in what, fifteen years? You walk in here and demand we change the name of Merryville Horticultural Society to Merida? Virginia Merry literally founded this club in 1897 and donated her house to us. She has a legacy too. I was hoping we could donate food to your nonprofit, but I guess you don't care about that." She threw up her hands, also showing anger.

He dialed it down a notch. "Sylvia. You know this was a tire factory, right? Your community garden is full of poison. Your little project is just a convenient place for the mayor to get rid of poison property with a false clean report from his fake environmental task force. Dr. Sliwa—"

"You actually believe this." She was stiff, and the room had definitely lost its former friendliness.

"Well your friend, the mayor, made a sweetheart deal with Windingle Developers and Ring Tire that if they donated this land, he wouldn't make them pay for the cleanup. Now all those vegetables you're planting for our people? They're going to spring up full of polychlorinated biphenyls." He leaned across the table on his forearms and softened his tone. "How can you be a part of this?"

Sylvia met his gaze. "So this is why we need to use our scant resources to paint over a skull and crossbones on the water tower? You're wrong about the science, Francisco. She pulled out a slim notebook and pushed it across the table. We got the Environmental Impact Report. I read it, and I'm not an idiot. The property was cleaned up. Under the conclusion on the last page, you can see—"

Again the stop motion with his hand. "Then you might want to see the parts they left out." He reached down into his drab, olive-colored satchel and brought out a thick stack of papers which he placed in front of Sylvia. "Dr. Sliwa from Merida had her agricultural group do their own testing. This is the whole report. Call me after you've digested it. Thanks for the coffee. And you're right. I shouldn't have called you girl." He pointed at her. "But mark my words, you don't want your name on this project."

She stared at the eight and a half by eleven-inch papers, bound by a two-pronged fastener. It was so much thicker than the environmental report she had. Sylvia sat, stunned.

Before leaving he turned. "And tell Mitzi Fowler she's being used."

"Where did you get this, and what does Mitzi Fowler have to do w—?" but he was already out the door.

***

Mitzi parked her Miata on the curb outside of Douglas Harker's home in one of Merryville's better neighborhoods. She was dressed in what she believed to be classic business attire, wearing a navy skirt and jacket with a tailored white blouse. She hoped it struck the right chord. It surprised her how much she wanted to get involved with the environment at this level, and she wondered if she wasn't trying to be someone she wasn't by wearing the suit.

A man in his sixties with thinning blond hair, wearing pressed jeans and a cashmere knit sweater, opened the front door. He was handsome and fit, and his pale blue eyes matched his sweater. He reached out his hand and said with a cultured voice, "You must be Ms. Mitzi Fowler. I'm Doug Harker, board chair. Come on in."

"Nice to meet you, Mr. Harker."

"Doug, please." As he closed the door behind them, she glanced down a hall that resembled a fancy hotel lobby. The shiny wood floor was covered by a green runner, leading past a wall of oil paintings reflecting English hunting scenes. An entryway table made of Carrara marble held a full bouquet of fresh flowers that smelled marvelous. It was clear the Harkers weren't hurting for cash. She followed him toward laughter that came from behind double doors down the hall.

As they entered the room through an impressive archway, Doug said, "Everybody, this is Mitzi Fowler, our newest commissioner."

After some claps, someone said, "Come on in."

Doug turned back to her. "Should you accept of course."

Mitzi saw a scene that seemed right out of a movie about privilege and class. Four white men reclined, smoking cigars and having drinks. The largest animal skin she'd ever seen covered much of the floor, and various elk heads were displayed around the room. Each man had a thick-cut crystal glass with amber liquid sitting by them. Doug finished the introductions by pointing to each man in turn. "This is Ben, Mark, David, and Monte."

She waved and said weakly, "Hi."

Monte put his cigar in an ashtray near him and nodded, while the rest gave her a little wave. The scent of expensive tobacco filled the room and was surprisingly pleasant. She wondered if they would offer her one.

"Your timing is perfect," Douglas said. "We met for a drink and were about to get down to business. We're ready to move into the dining hall. Drink?" His tanned hand waggled a cut-glass container with a silver label around it, secured with a tiny chain.

"Nothing too strong. Maybe some water?" Mitzi replied.

"Sure." He bypassed a decanter on the counter, probably used to make Scotch and water, and poured her a glass. "Ice?"

"No, I'm good," she said. "Hey, I was at the community garden project earlier today. I'm looking forward to learning more about what the commission does."

The men were all between late fifties to early seventies and cut from the same cloth—expensive cloth. Ben was rotund, Mark sported a scowl on his face, David wore an unfortunate toupee, and Monte had the whitest hair and teeth she'd ever seen. "Nice to meet you," came the chorus, except from Mark, who turned his back and left the room first to go to the dining hall.

Mitzi had led the occasional tour with guys like these and their entitled wives. She didn't take offense. "I started volunteering on Hortense Miller's committee. She extended the invitation from the mayor. I guess they're tight." She was babbling. "I'm really excited to be here. Can you catch me up on your side of what we're doing? I haven't seen the EIR."

Eyebrows lifted, and she wondered whether she was being too direct.

"We'll get to that," Ben responded with a smile, but it didn't match his eyes, which were fairly beady.

It dawned on her then that she'd been invited to the meeting but not to the "meeting before the meeting" for drinks in the library. She wondered what that meant. Still, everyone seemed nice enough, so she chalked it up to the same-day invitation and her nerves. Next time she would have more notice. She clutched her water and followed Douglas into the opulent dining hall.

***

Juniper walked downstairs while securing an earring, dressed for what she considered "butch" shopping.

Twyla was already by the door, waiting in cute overalls. "Valerie took the car."

Juniper was unperturbed. "You look cute," she said, while her hand floated over the key rack, finally alighting on a set of keys. She dangled them from her fingers. "Val took the Citroen, but she left us the truck."

"We have a truck?" Twyla had only recently moved in to be the Goodens' guardian, and she brightened at that. "Goody. I've got the list of what we need. Do you have a store where we can get some," she viewed her list, "wood, tarps, blankets, sage, cedar, eucalyptus, and rocks?"

Juniper headed toward the garage at the back of the house. "Not sure about the rocks, sage, or eucalyptus, and I know of only one place in town for the rest. Come on."

Once they were on the road, Twyla's brow furrowed. "I've never made a sweat lodge before, but it shouldn't be too hard. I've seen pictures. I made a yurt for some dwarves once."

Juniper took her eyes off the traffic to glance at Twyla. "I thought you knew how to do this."

"Don't worry. I saw one in Colorado and can tell you if it's legit. It's like an art installation, right? Plus, Valerie will oversee the construction as soon as she and Elsa return. In fact, they'll be at Panda and Mitzi's house soon with the herbs. Let's call them and see how they're doing."

Twyla called Valerie as they pulled up to Taggart's Hardware Emporium that was about to close. "It went to voicemail," she said, as she craned her neck to see where they were headed.

Juniper was worried about this whole project even though she kept it hidden well. The stakes were high, and it seemed to her nobody from Ehrenhardt to Elsa to Ekk really had a handle on what exactly they needed to do to save her friend. She adjusted her mirror and said under her breath, "I understand this good against evil thing is timeless. With all due respect, how has the Hercynian Garden lasted as long as it has?"

Twyla looked at her with wide clear eyes and answered brightly and confidently, "Because we're good."

***

Elsa read the address to Valerie as she drove her Citroen slowly down the street. It was hard to see the numbers in the dusky light. Elsa folded the shopping list of herbs they were seeking and tucked it in her pocket. She rolled down her window to get a better look at the tired strip mall. "Have you ever been here before? I haven't." Merryville didn't have many seedy areas, but this one qualified for sure. Some storefronts were boarded up, and trash littered the street. Apparently, gentrification had not made it to this part of Merryville.

"I've only been here once or twice," Valerie said. "Most things I grow myself or get online." Valerie didn't give up her secrets easily. She slowed down and pointed. "That's it."

Elsa took in the sketchy neighborhood and wondered how they would find fresh herbs in this place. Absently she commented, "I'll know if it's a real herbalist store or not."

Valerie parked and glanced at Elsa. "And I wouldn't know?"

Elsa shook her head. "Sorry. I'm on edge and frankly, a little worried. If we do this sweat with wolfsbane, it should counteract the poison in Panda and Brutus, but if it's the wrong type, it could kill them."

Valerie kept quiet and let Elsa finish her thought.

A tear went down Elsa's cheek, and she wiped it with the bottom of her apron. "I'm supposed to be Panda's guardian and should never have left her alone. This ritual must be perfect."

"I share your worry," Valerie said calmly and without offense, "but stop blaming yourself. That's not helping our friend. Let's get moving." She looked right and left. "Two women sitting in a car in this neighborhood isn't smart." She indicated with a subtle nod of her head the denizens in the shadows of the parking lot not far away. A scraggly group appeared to be sizing Val and Elsa up already.

Elsa said, "That I can fix." She closed her eyes for the briefest of moments and the scent of cinnamon wafted around them.

"You're making me want a cinnamon roll, Elsa," Valerie said. When the men started walking away, she said, "And apparently them too."

At Valerie's tilted head, Elsa said, "I noticed a donut shop down the block."

Valerie grinned, as they watched the men lurching like zombies toward the big W donut shop. The well-lit, enormous, cement donut sign was the brightest thing on the street.

Safe for the moment, they got out of the car and walked across the parking lot to The Eye of Horus, a botanica with an Egyptian eye painted on the glass. Wedged in between a laundromat and a cannabis store with flickering neon signs, it appeared the rest of the strip mall was closed.

"This is definitely it," Val said, as they approached the front door. A cold breeze gave them the shivers while they read a small sign with the hours of operation.

"It's closed," Elsa said unnecessarily before pressing her face against the glass with hands on either side to prevent any glare. "I don't see any light beyond the purple curtain at the back of the window display."

Through the window, they saw various dusty artifacts on pedestals, surrounded by purple silk folded artfully. Icons of Catholic saints presided over plates with faux fruit and religious candles. A black cat slept among the dusty items. She turned to Valerie. "What now?"

Valerie pulled out her phone. "Wait a sec. I'll call."

Elsa rubbed at the goose bumps on her upper arms while Valerie punched in a number and said, "We're here." Soon, a dark-skinned man, who appeared as if he could be Egyptian, unlocked the door, releasing the smell of nag champa from the store. He had large brown eyes and said with a deep voice, "I was about to give up on you. Come in." He squinted in the dim light at Elsa and said, "Hell-ooo."

He appraised Elsa, and she knew he was really seeing all three and a half feet of her. Then it hit her.

"Hello, Ali. It's been a unicorn's age."

Valerie started. "You two know each other?"

Elsa's mood brightened considerably. "Actually, yes. Ali spent several seasons as the herbalist in residence at the Hercynian Garden. I wondered what happened to you." He picked her up and gave her a squeeze, putting her down gently again.

Valerie was momentarily struck dumb. She offered lamely, "He helps me with herbs for hospice. How did…? Never mind."

Elsa handed Ali their piece of paper with the list of various herbs required. He locked the front door behind them.

"Please don't be offended," he said to Valerie. "I didn't know you were connected to the cause, although I sensed you have healing in you. My work depends upon secrecy."

"Did you come to Merryville because of the portal under the Lutheran Church?"

"No, I just heard about that actually," he answered. "Ehren said to make myself useful in his daughter's neighborhood." He gestured to the store. "So I did, spreading protection spells around town. Come to the back, and let's see what's on your shopping list."

After rattling the front doorknob to make sure it was secure, he walked through his fragrant store, crowded with rows of jars on wooden shelves. The blend of scents was wonderful.

"Nice neighborhood, Ali," Elsa commented jokingly.

He called through a curtain of beads, "It's perfect. Most folks think this is a run-down botanica for older Catholic ladies, and as we all know, it's better our work stays out of the limelight. Selket keeps watch." The sleek black cat brushed past them, following Ali. Valerie and Elsa walked through the hanging beads into a well-lit laboratory with no dust at all. He motioned to the pristine table with burner, vials, and charts. "This is where the magic happens." He laughed at the saying that was actually true in his case, his deep bass tone rumbling through the small shop.

Elsa's eyes immediately lit up, and a light citrus smell wafted through the air. "This is perfect. Now, we need a very pure strain of wolfsbane."

Valerie nodded. "Fresh."

"No problem," Ali said and reached toward the top row of herbs. Selket gave a bored meow and went back to the front room.

Elsa turned to her friend. "Sorry I doubted you, Valerie," she said. "So many stores claim to have these herbs but sell ordinary plants. I had no idea it was Ali."

Valerie was not ego-driven and didn't appear to take offense. "Let's get to it. We have patients to tend to."

Ali pulled up a metal stool and sat. He perused the rest of the list, tilting his glasses to better read the handwriting. "Yeah, I've got all of this, I—"

Hissing from Selket in the outer room drew Ali's attention from the conversation. "Wait here."

Valerie and Elsa exchanged glances. They heard Ali say clearly, "How did you get in?"

Elsa started opening jars and placing herbs in her pockets. She was glad to see that Valerie did too.

A low voice responded, but from their position, it was impossible to decipher what was being said. Elsa saw Valerie freeze in place, the hair on her arms standing on end.

They heard Ali's deep voice again. "Nobody's here but me, so why don't you go back to whatever hole you crawled out of?"

Not wanting to waste any more time, Elsa searched for the top-shelf wolfsbane, but the jars were coded in a language she didn't know. She closed her eyes to feel the magical signatures and upon opening them, pointed to one particular jar near Valerie, who nodded and placed some of the herb in a pocket by itself. Elsa reached out a hand for Valerie to take. She led Valerie to the tiny bathroom behind the laboratory and whispered for her to stay put.

"Stop! Stop! The treaty!" Ali shouted. Suddenly, Elsa heard a series of pops that sounded like firecrackers, and the unmistakable sound of broken glass. Selket screeched and hissed.

Elsa whispered to Valerie, "Don't make a sound, and don't come out, whatever happens." She ran into the other room and shouted, "Let him go."

A male said with a creepy voice, "Ooooh, an elf. This is a prize. Where's the other one? We distinctly saw two enter this store."

"Just me. You saw Ali and me."

"*Kuondoka*," Ali said with a forceful voice. It was Swahili, meaning leave.

"Your voodoo won't work on me," the creature spoke in a strange tone, as if someone other than he was using his voice box.

"Who are you?" Elsa asked.

Not taking his eyes off the man, Ali said to Elsa, "It doesn't matter. He's only a vehicle for *Lupus Imperium*."

Elsa angrily brought up the rules they should all know. "This can't happen. There will be serious consequences in the human world. The treaty says—"

The intruder mocked Elsa in a falsetto voice. "The treaty says, the treaty says. Please, you sound like a parrot. Of course, the Eye of Horus has been on our radar for some time." He focused on Ali., "Talk about breaking a treaty. You've been helping the Hercynian Garden all along. Tsk, tsk."

"Only as a Guardian," Ali replied. "That means the Ravens have been watching, too, and they are no longer with you."

The creepy man cackled. "You really have no idea what's going on, do you?"

"The Ravens defeated Wolfrum," Elsa stated.

The man snapped his head in an unnatural way toward Elsa, enunciating through a snarl that allowed his yellow, rotting teeth to show. "We have a new leader now. And the Ravens only listen to that foolish human, Panda Fowler, not that she has any idea how to control them. No, I'm afraid by the time your loved ones read about this in the paper, you will be part of the ashes of this annoying place." With that, he took his hand out of his pocket and threw a small box at the dusty shelves.

This action seemed to release Ali, who lunged for him. The box must have contained something magical, since Ali's eyes rolled back into his head, and he went down hard at the same time the glass jars in the room started popping again. This time flames appeared.

Elsa tried to conjure a calming vibe, but the magic against her was too strong, and she felt depleted. She focused on calling Panda telepathically instead.

Valerie, after hearing all of this, burst into the room with a glass vase to throw, but she was no match for the evil in the front room. She was soon tied up on the floor next to Ali and Elsa, the heat in the room increasing as the herbs caught fire. The perpetrator left, locking the front door behind him.

CHAPTER TEN

SISTERS CATCHING UP

"I'm so sorry I couldn't be here for Ekk and Elsa's wedding. We were river rafting when you called, literally on the water. Couldn't they have, like, picked a date and sent out invitations?"

"Says you who arrived without notice," I responded deadpan. "We have a video. Things came up pretty fast. When I was in the hospital, it made us all realize how things can change in the blink of an eye." My stomach contracted hard. "Speaking of which…" The sensation was on the level of the one I'd experienced right before Wolfrum appeared in our kitchen. It was also like the one I'd had when in prison, although I hadn't understood what it meant at the time. This new sensation could not be ignored.

Puddle reacted. "Sis, what's wrong?"

Right in front of me, Elsa, in a hologram form, appeared and yelled with my voice, "Eye of Horus. We're in trouble."

"Eye of Horus, who's in trouble?" Puddle responded. "Am I supposed to say something that rhymes with that?"

I reached toward her and said sharply, "Puddle."

She stared at me with glassy eyes. "Eye of Ra, I'm seeing double." She started giggling.

I snapped my fingers in front of her face. "Puddle, listen to me."

She put down her joint. "What, sis? I know you don't approve. I have cut down."

"No, it isn't that. I need you to drive me someplace. It's hard to explain, but our family has sensing magic, and I got a message from Elsa, uh, loud and clear, with a hologram or something."

"I know about the sensing thing. That's why I came home, sort of. I was feeling I needed to be here."

I shook her. "Well, this is a freaking magical 911. Come on. Let's find Elsa. She'll know what to do."

"I drive better stoned," Puddle said. "Don't worry. Where are they?"

"Someplace called the Eye of Horus."

She pointed to Panda's leg. "Are you sure you're up to it?"

My gut was going crazy. "Yes, hurry."

Puddle helped me into the Range Rover and drove carefully down the street.

I had a panic attack. "Hurry! Drive faster!"

Puddle increased the speed. "Won't do to be pulled over right now."

I exhaled and rubbed my face. What was happening? I hoped that the poison or whatever it was in my leg wasn't making me crazy. Visions. I had seen Heloisa at the prison. In fact, that saved me from my exploding casserole, but nothing like that had happened since. I was frustrated for not being able to drive myself and called Mitzi. After three rings, it went to voicemail. "Mitzi, call me. I'm having that feeling again. Me and Puddle are going to find Elsa and Valerie. We're going to Eye of Horus." I called Elsa next, and it went to message. I clicked off as Puddle slowed the vehicle. "Are we lost?" I asked.

"No. I know exactly where it is."

Thankfully, the streetlights had come on. She put on her turn signal, and I wished she would respond more quickly. When stoned, Puddle's reactions were delayed.

"It's right next to a, ah, store I go to when I'm here." Puddle turned the Rover into the strip mall parking lot and said, "Oh wow. That's it but what the hell?"

A flickering reddish glow emanated from within The Eye of Horus, as if from a fire. No one was around. I pointed and shouted, "That's Juniper and Valerie's car."

With the vehicle barely stopped, I was out of the car, dragging my leg. I heard Puddle call my name, but I didn't slow down.

The front door to the store was locked, so I pounded on the glass, which was hot. "Elsa. Valerie. Are you in there?" I yelled.

I heard small explosions from inside and looked around for anything to use to break the glass. Puddle caught up with me as I took a piece of broken brick from a planter border and used both hands to slam it right in the middle of the door.

"Careful, sis. I'm calling the fire department." Puddle's eyes were wide, as she pulled out her cell phone to call 911, chanting, "Shit, shit, shit!"

The door glass shattered, and dangerous shards fell to the concrete. I reached in and unlocked the door.

Puddle waved her hand frantically. "Sis, don't."

With no time to lose, I covered my nose with a sleeve and charged into what was obviously a room on fire. Through the smoke I saw figures on the floor in the reddish light, the heat almost intolerable. Smoke was everywhere and full of strange scents. Once inside, I saw Valerie, Elsa, and a large man tied up and lying on the floor, unconscious. I coughed and yanked at the rope, but they were collectively too heavy to move. I went to the door. "Puddle, I need your help," I yelled. I heard sirens in the distance.

Puddle's eyes were wide with emotion, but we both took deep breaths and then dove through the smoke to where the three were lying on the floor. Puddle grabbed Valerie, and I grabbed Elsa. Adrenaline helped us drag the women out the front door. By this time, fire personnel arrived. Two firefighters reached out to take Valerie and Elsa, and another yelled over the now raging flames and firetruck noise, "Anybody else inside?"

Gasping for breath, Puddle said, "Yes," and pointed vigorously. The fumes from the herbs were overwhelming. We were pushed aside as firefighters with proper gear entered the store. In seconds, they brought out the man, and an oxygen mask was immediately clapped onto his face. He looked like he got the worst of the heat and smoke.

I coughed so hard it racked my rib cage. Puddle put her arms around me. "You okay, Panda bear?"

"No." Immediately, my leg collapsed under me, and I experienced pain like I've never known. Puddle helped me hobble to the front seat of the Rover. It was noisy, and water was everywhere in the parking lot. I watched Puddle return to see about Val and Elsa. Water streamed out of the front door of the botanica, but it appeared the flames were out. Elsa was untied and sitting up on the wet asphalt, going through Valerie's pockets.

"Elsa, are you okay? Why are you picking her pockets?" I heard Puddle ask, as she knelt next to her.

"Later. Thank you for saving us." Elsa coughed. "Where's Panda?" Puddle pointed at me, seated in the Rover with the door open. We nodded at each other, still breathless.

"Get her home," Elsa said, still gasping for air.

"I will," Puddle said solemnly.

Paramedics moved Puddle out of the way as they approached with a stretcher on wheels and loaded up the man, the most injured, first. The paramedic said to Elsa, "Smoke inhalation. You should come too." She shook her head no. Valerie was placed on a stretcher. She lifted her oxygen mask and croaked out weakly to Elsa, "Let Juniper know."

"Of course."

"Ma'am, we've got another ambulance coming for you," a paramedic said to Elsa. Elsa refused the offer to go to the hospital, and walked over to the Land Rover. "This is very bad." She coughed deeply.

"I need to get back to my workroom. In fact, you need to come with me, Panda."

A couple of police black and whites arrived, lights revolving on top. Radios crackled as an officer approached Puddle.

"I need everybody's names and," he pointed at me, "she needs to go to the hospital." Apparently, he'd seen me struggling to walk.

I was so tired, but I focused on getting home. "My name's Panda Fowler, number nine Thistle Drive. This is my sister Puddle Fowler and our friend Elsa Schmidt. They all live with me. We're going home."

"You need to be seen in the emergency room."

"Oh, this?" I gestured to my wounded leg. "It's a trick knee. I'm okay."

The policeman didn't seem completely convinced, but he wrote down our information and went back to the center of activity. Thankfully, he hadn't smelled the cannabis on Puddle over all the other smells of burning herbs.

Still afraid my sister would be arrested for driving under the influence, I watched as the young officer who took our information talked to someone before he returned to us to ask, "Can you tell me what happened? Why were you tied up?"

Elsa answered. "I came with Valerie Gooden, the woman in the paramedic van. We were shopping for herbs when someone came into the store. It must have been a robbery. We were in the backroom and didn't see him. The owner, Ali, went to speak with him and the next thing we knew, we were on the floor, tied up with fire all around." He eyed her with suspicion, sure she was hiding something. "Wasn't it closed at this hour?"

Elsa told a white lie. "No, it was open."

"Was it open?" he asked me.

I shrugged. Pointing to my leg again, the officer said, "Ma'am, you really should go to the hospital and let 'em check you out."

I shook my head. "I want to go home. I had this," I gestured to my leg, "before the fire."

"Well, you all were lucky. They're not sure the man they brought out will make it. We'll have more questions later. Next time, let the fire department do their job."

I tried to be reassuring. "We'll cooperate and give statements tomorrow. My friends and I need to rest."

He handed me a card. "Call us tomorrow."

After the officer walked away, Elsa said, "Someone should go with Ali. Juniper will meet Val at the hospital, I'm sure."

Surprisingly, it was Puddle who spoke up. "I'll go. You go home. Someone needs to be there when he wakes up." After a beat she said, "If he does wake up."

"Ali means champion," Elsa said fiercely. "He's strong and magical. And thank you, Puddle. I remember he has an adult daughter locally. His last name is Badawi. I'm trying to remember her name. Becca? See if you can find her."

The paramedics were about to close the door of his ambulance when Puddle sprinted over and tried to jump in the back.

"Are you his wife?"

"No."

"Then you can't ride in the back. We're going to Valley General."

"But—"

As the paramedic climbed in, he said, "No exceptions," and closed the door behind him.

After the two ambulances pulled out, sirens blaring, Puddle returned to us at the Land Rover.

"Who's gonna call Juniper? She's going to go nuts."

"I'll do it," I said and fished my phone out.

The fire crew was packing up, as someone in uniform took pictures of the burned-out store.

Elsa suddenly stood up straighter. "Do you hear that?" She turned toward the store. Following Elsa's line of sight, we saw a burned-up black kitty wobbling toward them.

"Selket," Elsa shouted. "We have another patient. Get the blanket out of the back." Elsa went to the kitty, who was still smoldering.

She talked to it quietly while Puddle ran over with a soft blanket. The two wrapped her up and carried her to the car. Elsa studied Puddle and said sternly, "You are not driving." It wasn't a question.

Puddle was so concerned about the cat, she asked with a weak voice, "Can you drive the Citroen? I've never seen you drive."

Elsa appeared frustrated. "Let me try something." She put her hands on either side of Puddle's head and mumbled a bit. "You're going to have a headache for a while, but at least I won't worry you'll get into an accident while stoned. Really, Puddle, you may think what you do doesn't affect anyone else, but it does."

Puddle shook her head. "Don't judge me. Who knew I'd be driving a car? I was at the house telling stories with Panda Bear."

Elsa got very serious. "I'll say this only once. During these times, we don't know when danger will happen. You need to be alert. It's not judging. I didn't say you were selfish, but it isn't smart. We need you in your right mind."

I tried to lighten the conversation a bit. "Are you sure she has one?"

Puddle's eyes got large. "Message received." She shook her head like a wet dog trying to dry itself. "Man, you did something. My head does hurt, but I'm straight. Meet you at the house later." She held out her hand for the keys.

Elsa nodded and jumped on the running board of the Rover. She opened the door and maneuvered herself onto the seat, and then pulled out the leg contraptions that made it possible for her and Ekk to drive and snapped them in place.

I was surprised, as I had never seen Elsa be so commanding or drive a car. I suspected Elsa let Ekk do a lot that she was probably also capable of doing. Puddle drove the Citroen away carefully. After that, I was in so much pain, I was glad it wasn't me who had to drive. I called Juniper and Mitzi, holding the cellphone between my face and shoulder while I cradled Ali's cat gently.

***

"Listen," Monte said. "We set the ribbon-cutting for the community garden right before the election."

Doug replied, "Do you want to tell Hortense? The flower show is always in March. You know that. She'll flip her lid."

Monte was firm. "And I told you, it has to be now. Mitzi, can you help with this?"

"Actually, Sylvia Arviso is the current president. I can talk to her." Mitzi's phone rang. With all that had been happening with Panda, she didn't dare let it go to voicemail. It alarmed her when she saw she had already missed a call.

"Excuse me." She walked out of the dining room and put the cell to her ear while the men inside continued to argue.

She returned to the group only to say, "I'm sorry, but my wife has an emergency. I've got to go." The men seemed relieved, although they made noises like they cared. Back in her Miata, her head spun while thinking about Elsa and Valerie in a fire. She felt guilty about leaving them for this stupid meeting in the first place, and now she felt bad about leaving the meeting before it really even got started.

***

The bell tinkled as Juniper and Twyla entered the store. Juniper pulled out her cell and called Valerie again, this time leaving a message on voicemail. "Honey, don't forget the sage and eucalyptus, and please have the truck tires aligned. I don't know how you drive this thing. We'll meet you at Panda and Mitzi's." She waved at Ralph, who was already searching for items on the list Twyla handed him.

"How big a tarp do you need?" Juniper heard him say, as he and Twyla walked to the back of the store. Juniper had to admit, it was nice to have Twyla around, even if she had the attention span of a gnat. She was strong and cheerful, and she didn't seem to ever get tired. Even better, Twyla said she would be happy to take over dog-walking duties and wanted to make something of their garden.

Juniper's phone rang, and she brought it to her ear right away, thinking it was Valerie. It was a call from someone at the museum with a problem, and she talked them through it while the only other two in the store shopped.

Ralph and Twyla returned to the front with Twyla pulling a hand-truck laden with the wood pieces, a tarp, and other supplies. "I hope we've got everything," she said. "Juniper, can you prop open the door?"

"I'll do it." Ralph wedged a doorstop against the door and turned the open sign to closed. "If you tell me what you're making, I could tell you if you got everything." His eyes were filled with curiosity. He turned to Juniper. "She won't tell me what she's building, but I would love to see it."

Twyla made the zipping-her-lips hand motion.

Juniper said somewhat absently, "My wife is Ute Indian. We're building a teepee in our friend's backyard." Twyla nodded vigorously.

Ralph moved behind the counter and said in his drawl, "A teepee. Now if that ain't interesting. Yes, I'd love to see that. I had a Lakota friend who took me to one of them sweat lodges," he said, as he rang up the items. "If that's what you're doing, you're gonna need some willow branches."

Juniper and Twyla turned their heads toward each other, eyes wide. Willow branches. No one had put that on the list. As she handed him a credit card, Juniper said, "Not saying we are, but if we were, where might we find some of those willow branches?" She gave her best enchanting smile. Twyla giggled and secured the pile on the hand-truck.

"Right behind my wife's memory care unit. I can give you the address."

Juniper's phone rang while she waited for Ralph to write it down. She noticed she had missed several calls. She put a manicured nail up to halt the conversation with Ralph, then said into the phone, "Hello?"

"I'm in the hospital. There was a fire. Panda and Puddle came and, oh, hold on a minute." Valerie's voice sounded hoarse.

"Valerie? What?" Juniper's face paled. She heard voices in the background, but couldn't understand what they were saying. "Who are you talking to? Where's Panda? I—"

"Listen, just come to Merryville General," Valerie said. "I have to go."

"Oh my god. I'm on my way." She scribbled her name on the credit card receipt, said a quick, "Thank you," to Ralph and dashed out the door. Twyla started to push the cart outside to the curb.

Juniper practically screeched at her. "Twyla, leave it. There's no time. We need to go to the hospital. The botanica caught fire." Juniper's voice caught. "Valerie was taken by ambulance."

Twyla looked at the tarps, boards, and other supplies.

Ralph jumped in. "I'll deliver it for you. Address?"

"Number nine Thistle Drive. The Fowlers' house."

"You girls do what you need to do. I'll drop it."

Juniper wasn't listening. Her entire focus was on getting to her wife at the hospital.

When Twyla was in the truck's cab, she asked Juniper, "What happened?"

"Valerie took Elsa to a botanica to buy herbs for the sweat, and somehow it caught on fire. Panda and Puddle showed up in the nick of time and called the fire department."

"Puddle? She's in Peru." Twyla scratched her head. "Was in Peru, I mean. I was but now I'm not, so I guess she could be here." Shaking off this train of thought, she said, "Are they okay?" Twyla started to levitate but her seatbelt held her down. Fairies couldn't help their emotional reactions sometimes.

"I don't know." Juniper shook her head. "I don't know anything right now." She pulled the truck into traffic and headed to Merryville General Hospital.

✳✳✳

After Juniper and Twyla drove away, Ralph started his closing ritual for Taggart's Emporium a few minutes early. It was probably good to vary his routine anyway. Predictability could be deadly. He thought about his brush with the former city councilman and knew if he never saw Gary Smithers again, it would be too soon. He took the cash drawer back and was relieved to see the back door to the alley was still secure and that Ratter was sleeping on the work desk in a circle of light from a lamp. He was pleased to see that Ekk had tidied the receipts, and he allowed himself a little spark of hope that the business might be saved as he patted the cat. "I'll be back tomorrow, little fella. You watch the store while I get some willow branches and make a delivery."

He took a moment to put some cat food in a bowl and fill Ratter's water dish and noticed that Ekk had started to organize the boxes in the backroom. Aurora loved bringing in items from Europe, and unopened deliveries had piled up from when she started forgetting to put them in inventory. Some of these dusty boxes he hadn't seen for years, and it made him long for the old days when he and Aurora worked side by side. Those were the good days.

Ratter meowed, bringing him back to the present and the delivery he needed to make. Ralph rubbed his hands together and spun the combination he knew by heart on the old safe. He swung open the heavy door and put the till inside, noting the meager stacks of cash in reserve. His little spark of hope for the business died. "Who am I kidding?" Ratter meowed again, as if he knew how his owner felt. Not being able to understand the language of cats, Ralph locked the safe and turned out the overhead lights, leaving the one desk lamp on for the cat. It was colder than usual, and Ratter probably enjoyed the warmth from the bulb. He grabbed the handle of the handcart loaded with the sweat supplies and wheeled it to the front of the store where he saw Ekk standing outside. Ralph twisted the lock to open the door. The bell tinkled. "Ekk, what are you doing here?"

Ekk was still dressed as he was earlier in the day when he worked at the store for a couple of hours, but he'd donned a heavy jacket. "I'm here to help you with our delivery. Juniper called me on her way to the hospital."

"I heard her wife got hurt," Ralph said. "She's at the hospital." He asked, "You know where to take it?"

"I hope so. That's my address too."

"Oh. I told them I'd bring it."

"Maybe if we both do it, the job will be easier," Ekk said,

"Let me pull my truck around. You can follow me," Ralph said. Ralph pulled his 1950s Ford truck to the corner and double-parked. The two men quickly got the supplies loaded. "I appreciate the help. Where's your car?"

"I don't own one. I took an Uber," Ekk said.

"Now that's an act of faith, son. I mighta already left." He laughed his deep bass laugh.

"But you didn't." Ekk moved to the passenger side of the cab. "It's number nine Thistle Drive."

Ralph's door closed with a creak and a heavy metal thunk. "Yep, but we've got one stop first. Merry Hearts Memory Care."

"Uh, we need to hurry."

"I know."

Ekk started to say something, but Ralph emphasized, "I already know." He surveyed his new friend with deep brown eyes under thick eyebrows. "You got a sweat lodge to build. In the dark. I threw in a couple of lanterns for us too. Now get in. If you're gonna' do a sweat right, ya'll need willow branches. I know where to find them."

"Willow branches," Ekk said, "how did you know...?" He didn't finish his sentence. As they headed to Merry Hearts Memory Care Ekk asked, "This is where Aurora lives?"

"Yup. My bride. She don't even know where she is most times." Merry Hearts Memory Care was on the outskirts of town in front of a man-made lake. Sure enough, willow trees dotted the landscape around picnic tables. "My wife loved these trees. We used to have 'em down South. I had some put in here for her."

They had to walk through the facility to get to the lake where the willows were, but Ralph stopped at a door and said, "You go on and get us some switches. I'll only be a minute."

"I'd like to meet her," Ekk said.

"Sure, Ekk, come on."

Ralph knocked on the door and a frail voice said, "Come in, Ralph."

Ralph's eyes got big. "She used to always do that, before." His voice caught in his throat, and he rushed in. "Aurora?"

Her watery eyes fixed on Ekk. She grinned and pointed. "Friend."

Ralph gently took her hand. "Yes, baby, this is my friend. He's helping me down at the store."

Ekk stopped and his mouth dropped open. "Hi, Aurora, it's been a long time."

CHAPTER ELEVEN

MERRYVILLE GENERAL HOSPITAL

Valerie was doing better after being administered oxygen, but she was still in an ER bed, arguing with an orderly. She lifted her mask. "I need to leave. Where did you put my clothes?"

"Whoa," the orderly said. "Smoke inhalation can be serious." He frowned. "The doctor hasn't seen you yet. Please rest. She'll be here soon."

Still woozy but starting to feel alarmed, Val responded, "No, I need to get discharged right away."

The nurse came in, a cheerful smile on her face. "Now what could be so important?"

"I must go. It's a matter of life and death."

The orderly and nurse exchanged dubious glances. "I'll get the doctor," the orderly said, and rushed off.

Thankfully, Juniper's demanding voice could be clearly heard through the curtain around her bed, "Where. Is. Valerie Gooden? Who's in charge here?"

Relief flooded through Valerie's body. "In here," she shouted as loud as she could, which triggered a coughing fit.

"Valerie?" Juniper's voice again.

"In here."

The curtain opened dramatically, and Valerie saw the worry in Juniper's eyes.

"There you are." Juniper exhaled heavily. "Are you okay?"

Valerie coughed and said, "I'm fine, but I need some water."

"Twyla, water," Juniper said.

"On it."

After they were alone, Juniper asked, more quietly, "What happened, Val? You smell like smoke…"

Valerie's face was serious. "Elsa and I went for the herbs we needed." She grabbed her wife's arm like a lifeline. "Juni, there are more *Lupus Imperium* forces still in our town. One of them set the botanica on fire and tried to kill us. Get me out of here. Panda and Puddle found us and," her voice broke, "if they hadn't come, we'd be dead."

"Oh my God!"

"Panda's doing worse than me with her leg. I have smoke inhalation but will be fine. We need to get her into the sweat immediately."

"I'll get you discharged."

Valerie started to get up and Juniper moved to help her.

With a wave of her arms and another cough Valerie said, "Go. Twyla can help me." Twyla had returned with the water and held Valerie's shoes while hunting for other clothing.

Soon, Juniper returned with a woman who wore a hospital lanyard around her neck. The woman clutched a clipboard with forms Valerie needed to sign. After Valerie signed the release forms and promised to follow up with her primary care doctor, she was cleared to leave. The woman then pulled over a wheelchair so she could transport Valerie out of the hospital. Juniper and Twyla walked beside the chair until they reached the truck.

"Good luck," the woman said to Valerie when she got out of the chair.

"Thanks," Valerie said, and Juniper helped her into the truck.

"Poor Ali and Elsa," Valerie said, "it all happened so fast."

Juniper kept one hand on the wheel and another on Valerie's thigh. "You don't leave my side for a second until we know what's going on."

Twyla popped her head through the truck window from the bed. "Don't worry. I'm your guardian and will not leave either of you, no matter what."

Valerie pulled a dubious expression but said nothing, and soon they were parked in front of the Fowlers' house.

"Whose truck is that in the driveway?" Valerie asked. She referred to the 1950s Ford truck.

Twyla was already out of the back to open Valerie's door.

"Probably the Taggart's delivery," she said. "Let's get you inside."

***

BUILDING THE SWEAT LODGE

After helping Valerie out of the cab, Twyla ran to the back of the Fowlers' house and found a beehive of activity. Lanterns on the table and hanging from the oak tree lit the area. The skeleton of the lodge in the green space made the area feel like a campground. Ekk and the man from the store she and Juniper went to earlier were building the frame of the sweat lodge with willow branches.

"It's about time," Ekk said to Twyla. "Ralph's been here an hour."

"We had to get Valerie from the hospital. Let me help." She ran to where the boards were stacked against the fence and tripped over a hose. She went sprawling.

Ralph helped her up, and Ekk said, irritated, "Why don't you get the tarp?"

"Right. Yes, absolutely." Twyla ripped open the plastic package and pulled out the large blue tarp, as Mitzi emerged from the elf hole beneath the tree.

Valerie and Juniper entered the backyard, and a chorus of "Valerie. Are you okay?" greeted them.

She was pale but moving okay as she walked to the lodge. "Looks good, but where's the animal skin?"

Ralph and Ekk paused and looked at each other. "Didn't have one. We got a tarp."

Valerie shook her head no. "Plastic won't do. At least find a natural substance, something of the earth." She appeared exhausted. "I need to go help Elsa."

Ekk said, "She's downstairs with Panda and the cats. I'll take you."

Valerie nodded and followed Ekk to the secret entrance. Juniper followed and said, in spite of the circumstances, "I can't wait to see it."

Ekk moved in front of her. "Sorry, Juniper. It's pretty crowded under the tree, and Elsa is stressed." His tone was apologetic. "Let Valerie and Elsa do their work, and I promise to show you later."

"Of course." She gave Valerie a quick kiss and watched her disappear in the magic thistle bush. Juniper embraced all creative things and was also a good organizer, having organized many installations at the museum. "Okay, people, where can we get enough animal skin, or at least leather, to finish this lodge?"

Mitzi wrinkled her nose. "I saw a large zebra skin rug today at Doug Harker's house in his downstairs parlor, but that's obviously off limits. Do you think the Windingles would have anything like that in their mansion?"

Juniper laughed. "No. Charlotte is a vegetarian, at least this week. She purged the house of all her father's hunting trophies years ago. What else can we use?"

Twyla pulled Juniper aside. "I'll be back in a few minutes. You'll be okay if you stay here with Ekk. Can I have the keys to your truck?"

"I guess. I'm certainly not going anywhere." Juniper was puzzled. "Where do you need to go?"

Her face was solemn. "Fairy business. Top secret."

Juniper handed the truck keys to Twyla before asking Ekk, "Did you get the willows?"

The brainstorming went on, as Twyla slipped away.

"I want to thank you, but you don't need to stay," Mitzi said to Ralph. He and Ekk shared a look. He dusted his hands on his apron slowly.

"I'm happy to help. I—"

Ekk cut to the chase. "Mitzi, Ralph is married to Aurora. She's magical. He knows."

Ralph scratched his balding head. "Well, I know enough, but certainly not everything."

Mitzi said tiredly, "Okay, so he's magic adjacent. I can't keep up. Is that in the rules?"

In spite of the tense situation with Panda and the cats, Juniper laughed. She was never far from laughter because she saw the world through her creative lens. "That sounds like something Panda would say. I'm magic adjacent if you want to put it that way."

Mitzi let out a breath. "I guess it's every hand on deck then. Thanks, Ralph. Is Aurora coming too?"

He responded, "She's in memory care, Mitzi. I wish she could."

"Oh, I'm sorry," Mitzi said. "Well, welcome to the team."

***

Valerie and Elsa stood at either side of the table where Panda lay with eyes closed. Elsa said urgently, "You better get Mitzi."

Before leaving, Valerie suggested, "Maybe we should take her to the hospital?"

"They couldn't help her last time, but my salve worked," Elsa responded. "What is worrisome is that I put the same gel on her leg, and no response. We need the sweat to activate it. Hurry and see how they're coming above ground. Panda may not have much time."

Valerie went upstairs, sweaty and tired, face solemn. Since their ministrations of herbs, Panda had, they thought at first, fallen asleep. Now it seemed she was comatose. This was bad. When she emerged, she saw Ralph seated at the patio table, shivering. Ekk was nowhere to be seen.

The lodge was pretty much complete. In place of the plastic tarp, Ekk and Ralph had used cotton blankets.

Mitzi ran to Valerie. "It's bad, isn't it?"

"It's time," Val said. "Go to her, Mitzi. I'll do what I can here to help."

Mitzi, without comment or delay, dove into the illusion of thistle that hid the door to the underground lab where Panda lay.

Juniper approached Valerie. "We found cotton blankets. Mitzi had some with no dyes or anything she brought back from Egypt. It's as close as we could come to what we need."

Valerie exhaled. "It's not ideal, but we need to do something now." It was clear that things weren't going well.

Ekk emerged from the open flap in the lodge. "Val, please check it out and let us know what else we need."

Valerie and Juniper went to the opening and saw a pallet for Panda next to a bucket of water with a dipper, a circle of stones in the center, and pillows against the lodge wall. Embers were already reddish and covered by ash. She frowned at the cotton walls of the healing tent, sighed, and picked up a handful of sweetgrass. She threw it on the embers, where it immediately flamed.

Ralph moved closer as Ekk, sweating and dirty from the work, watched with intense concentration on his normally merry features.

"Shall we bring Panda in?"

"Yes, now. There's not a moment to lose."

***

From the corner of the Harker's street, Twyla saw a light shining through a window on the third floor of his home. After parking, she turned off the headlights on the truck and studied the situation. The front yard was well lit, with a hedge-lined driveway, revealing a black Tahoe parked in front of the broad porch. The stakes were so high.

She knew that Panda's life could literally depend upon this sweat going right, and they needed an animal skin. Ekk would be so proud of her if she brought back the animal skin rug they needed for the lodge, but it wouldn't be easy. The light in the upstairs window told her at least one person was still up, so she'd wait until it went out. From what Mitzi said, the rug would be on the ground floor. Isn't that where parlors were? She slipped out of the truck cab, wincing at the squeal of the metal door. She walked silently and willed herself to blend in with the scenery. Being one with the scenery was much easier to do in the Hercynian Forest than Doug Harker's front yard. What a spread. It was about fifty feet from the curb to the three-story manse. An ornate fountain and low, well-lit beds of flowers and shrubs formed an intricate pattern fit for such a stately residence. Thankfully, trees also lined the long driveway, which circled around the landscaping and led back to the street. Twyla grinned. Trees were home to fairies, and she would use them like her own personal highway to avoid being seen.

After successfully hopping from tree to tree, she was almost to the house and started descending to the ground when a loud dog howl from below made her freeze. She had calculated that since there was no fence, the dog or dogs must be in the backyard. She was wrong. As soon as she dropped to the ground, a Doberman Pincher with bared teeth came flying around the corner toward her—fast. She scrabbled back up the tree in the wink of an eye, wondering how this was so. A guard dog. Surely, they wouldn't leave that lethal animal to roam the neighborhood freely. She used low faerie tree magic to keep him quiet, but she couldn't do much more than that without violating the rules she had taken an oath to abide by in this world. She focused on a metal sign affixed to a pole, announcing the invisible, electronic fence. Doh.

The dog growled low in its throat and sat staring up at her. It was a standoff. She needed that rug, but now she felt trapped and regretted not telling anyone where she'd gone.

***

GARY SMITHERS

"Where do you live?"

"I'm still at the Salvation Army," Bud blurted as he drove. Bud had briefly worked for Wolfrum and was now on the radar of every other bad actor that worked for *Lupus Imperium*.

Gary paused to give his accomplice a withering look. "Bud, I can't stay there." He shook his head. "Don't you have anyplace I can hole up other than this reeking van?"

Bud's face was blank. "I gotta get it back before six. What about one of your old friends?"

"Gee, that's a great idea. Oh, wait. Apparently being charged with attempted murder and declared insane is hard on friendships. Who knew?" Gary's tone was dripping with sarcasm. Even though he considered Bud an idiot, he did have that one secret friend…

"Buddy, drive me to Lincoln Road and drop me." He said this as he pulled a T-shirt over his head that he'd stolen from a collection center in the Shoprite parking lot.

"Okay, but what are you going to do?"

"Nothing you need to know. Keep that burner phone I gave you and await instructions."

"You bet. You know, I just got out of jail myself." He laughed so hard he snorted. "With all that magical gobbledygook going on, they didn't think they could get a conviction. I'm very grateful, Gary, for all the help that Loopy, uh, *Imperius* organization gave me by hiring a defense attorney."

"Nice for you. They dropped me like a rock."

Bud appeared terrified. "Don't say that. You-know-who would be mad."

Gary went to the front of the van and held a knife to Bud's neck. "You need to worry about me."

"Uh, sorry."

"Sir. Say I'm sorry, sir."

"I'm sorry, sir." The van swerved a little.

Gary put away the knife. "I may need you again."

"You got my number. I mean, you called me. My phone is always on. Do you want me to wait for you?" He was babbling.

Gary snapped at him, "Keep your mouth shut. Once you drop me, leave the area immediately. If anyone asks, you don't know a thing. Got it?"

Bud nodded and followed his instructions, driving into the nicest part of town. This neighborhood was called "The Presidents" by locals, because all the streets were named after them. Merryville Hospital was only about a mile and a half from Lincoln Street, so it didn't take long. He slowed, pulling to the curb, and Gary ejected himself from the back of the van before it even stopped rolling. Gary ran down the street, sticking to the shadows.

***

Twyla was stuck in the Harker's tree, pondering a magical float to a window on the second floor, when she saw a man come loping down the long driveway. Although he tried to stay in the shadows, her tree-fairy eyes picked him out quite easily. The dog must have sensed him too and immediately left for the greater threat. This was her chance to shimmy down the tree and make her way to the French doors at the side patio.

What luck. It was unlocked. With the dog and security cameras, the house owner probably felt safe to leave it open. She could hear the guard dog barking in the distance, then silence. What did that mean? She had no time to muse. She was on a mission. The French doors led into the parlor. More good luck. It was dark, but she clearly saw not one, but two animal hide rugs on the shiny wooden floor. Just when she thought it was time to grab them and run, the front doorbell rang. Twyla hid behind the first thing she could find, a thick, velvet curtain. Even despite the circumstances, it almost made her giggle because it was so cliché. She had tried improving her relationship with Ekk by watching his silly old movies, and she had seen this trope many times. Soon, she heard a man's voice say, "What are you doing here? Get in before someone sees you."

"This is like old times, Dougie. Is the wife home?"

"Oh god, no. Gary, you shouldn't be here."

Twyla's eyes widened, and she had to fight to keep from levitating. *Wait, Gary? The political guy who tried to kill Elsa and Ekk? That Gary?*

"I thought you'd be glad to see me."

The parlor light went on, and Twyla stood still as a statue behind the heavy drape.

"How did you get past Cesar?"

"If I told you, it would spoil the mood."

"What mood? There is no mood. If you hurt my dog…you need to leave." This voice, she assumed, must belong to Doug Harker. He sounded both angry and afraid.

The intruder's voice sounded entitled. "You owe me after all I did for your little development projects."

Doug sighed heavily. "Sit down. I'll pour us a drink."

"That's more like it."

She wished she could see, but she didn't dare chance it. The sound of ice cubes in a glass was all Twyla heard for a while.

"You were faking the crazy, right?" Doug asked. "I mean, I never did understand what happened."

"And you never looked me up to ask. That hurt."

"Gary…"

"When is Laura coming home?"

Doug cleared his throat. "Not until this weekend."

"Then I guess I found a place to stay. I'll need clothing. These clothes won't do."

"You need a shave too," Doug said, which surprised Twyla.

She was puzzled. It sounded like they were friends and had some sort of relationship going on while Gary Smithers was a councilman. Twyla felt like she'd been hit over the head and realized Gary Smithers was infected by Wolfrum.

She heard rustling. One of the men softly said, "It's been a long time."

"It has."

The two men left the parlor and turned out the light. She chanced a quick peek and saw them walking hand in hand up the stairs. She whispered under her breath, "*Ach du meine gute.*" It was German for "Oh my goodness." Twyla, despite this turn of events, needed to finish her task. Carefully rolling up the two rugs, one inside of the other, she crept out the French door, hoping Cesar was otherwise engaged. She walked down the long driveway and found him lying on his side, with an empty syringe lying in the grass nearby. She didn't want to delay, but being a huge animal lover, made sure he was breathing before leaving with her prize. She hoped she got back to Thistle Drive in time.

CHAPTER TWELVE

SWEAT LODGE

It took Ekk, Valerie, and Mitzi to maneuver Panda up the stairs and out of the elf hole. With Ralph's help they got her across the yard to the sweat lodge. Juniper held open the lodge flap so they could lay her on the pallet. Brutus and Selket soon followed, although Blondie strangely drew back to a place on the fence where she could monitor the situation, seemingly watching the humans at their tasks.

"Who needs to be in here?" Ekk asked.

Panda moaned and thrashed her head from side to side as if dreaming.

"Elsa and me," Valerie responded, "and maybe Mitzi."

"Hell yes, Mitzi." Mitzi was already half in the lodge.

The three women were soon in place. Mitzi sat next to Panda's head, cooing to her, as Elsa applied more salve on her ankle and leg. Valerie chanted softly. Ekk dropped the makeshift canvas to keep the heat inside and sat outside, ready to stoke the eucalyptus fire if needed or put water on the rocks. Ralph sat with Juniper at the patio table, silently watching smoke escape through the hole in the lodge.

Ralph asked Juniper, "Where's your little friend?"

"What? Uh, she had to do something. I don't know." She seemed to wake from a daze. "Tell me about your wife, Ralph. How long have you known she is part of…" she moved a hand around in a circle, gesturing toward the lodge, the tree, and the general surroundings, "this."

He rubbed his chin. "Funny, I just found out about ya'll in particular, but I guess I knew about Aurora all along. Looking back, she was always at the center of every good, impossible thing in our lives." He stared at the tent. "Uh, oh."

Uh, oh indeed. The thin walls were turning brown from overheating.

He jumped up. "Ekk, water."

Ekk came around from the other side of the lodge with a hose. "The sheets are too thin," he said, as he used a muted stream of water to dampen the fabric and keep it cool. Silence reigned. Everyone outside the tent could hear Mitzi crying.

Elsa came out through the flap, dark circles under her blue eyes. "I feel like we're missing something. Ekk, call the Garden."

***

It was hot inside the tent, and dark and cold outside in the backyard. The lanterns in the trees swayed with the wind. Ravens started arriving and perched on limbs of the old oak tree, cawing softly. Juniper and Ralph sat outside to be near the lodge, and when Juniper noticed Ralph shivering, she asked. "Can I get you a blanket?"

He blew on his hands. "I won't say no."

Juniper went inside for her own coat and a blanket and called Puddle at the hospital across town.

She quickly answered. "I was about to call you guys. What's that noise?"

"I'm making coffee. We're freezing to death. How's the man from the botanica?"

"Ali? He's coming around. The hospital contacted his daughter, and I'll leave when she gets here. He woke up and said, 'Who are you?' I told him in that voice Ekk uses sometimes that he was in the Land of Oz. He laughed so hard he started choking. He'll be fine. He's already asking about you guys. How's Val?"

Juniper paused. "Val's pretty shaken up but physically okay. As soon as Ali's daughter arrives, you come home. We've started the sweat."

A note of anxiety entered Puddle's voice. "Without me? Shit. How's it going?"

Valerie's voice sang out strong. "It's going."

"I'll be to the house in ten minutes."

"Good, your sister needs you now."

Juniper put on her coat, went outside, and wrapped a heavy blanket which she had taken from the back of the couch around Ralph's shoulders.

"Thanks."

"I put on coffee too."

They sat together and watched smoke spiral out of the top of the homemade lodge. Ekk kept a close eye on it and sprayed water on the lodge walls when they got too hot.

Thrump, pa pa, thrump, pa pa, thrump, pa pa.

Juniper asked her new friend, "Ralph, did you bring drums from Taggart's?"

He shook his head. "No, but I hear 'em too."

Over the span of twenty minutes, Ekk ran out of the lodge and into the kitchen several times for more water, and Juniper could tell he was irritated.

"What can I do, Ekk?" she asked.

"Nothing. Twyla should be here helping. Where is she?"

"I don't know. She said she had 'fairy business' or something."

Ekk did a frustrated, palms up appeal to the sky. "Ugh, I knew this would happen. As soon as things get tough—"

Juniper interrupted him. "How's it inside?"

He shook his head negatively. "We need something thicker for the walls, and an element is missing. Both Elsa and Valerie feel it. I tried calling the Garden, but this healing ritual is indigenous to America. They're working on it, but Valerie is our expert." He looked away for a moment, his eyes watery. "We're running out of time."

A crash made the three turn their heads toward the side of the house. It sounded like a herd of elephants was coming.

Ralph stood. "What's tha—"

Twyla flew into the backyard and fell on her backside.

Ekk was furious. "Where have you been, Twyla?"

"Here are the keys to the truck, Juniper," she said defensively, as she held up the car keys.

Juniper took them and asked, "Where did you go?"

"To get the animal skin." She noticed the lodge with its smoking walls and being a fairy felt the tenseness. "Sorry, got here as soon as I could."

Ekk's eyes lit up. "You got a skin?"

"Right around the corner, I dropped it. That's why I fell."

Ekk disappeared around the side of the house and came back into the yard, tugging a rolled-up animal skin toward the open area. As if choreographed, everyone grabbed a side and helped. Ralph and Juniper, who were the tallest, removed the thin cotton and carefully wrapped the Zebra skin around the lodge. Valerie came out, face shining with sweat, and nodded her approval. "This is exactly what we need, but one animal skin doesn't completely cover the area."

Twyla, still breathless from exertion, pointed toward the street. "In the bed of the truck is another one." Ekk darted down the side of the house with Juniper and Ralph following. Sure enough, another animal skin rug was in the bed of the truck. As they carried it into the backyard, Juniper commented, "This one's muddy."

Twyla looked sheepish. "I had to drag it."

Elsa appeared and marveled at this development.

"Where did you get this?" she asked, as they finished wrapping the teepee shaped contraption.

"Doug Harker's house."

"Oh my goodness, you didn't," Juniper said, scandalized.

Twyla continued to speak. "Wait, there's more, he—"Ekk cut her off.

"Later. No time for talk now but," Ekk squeezed Twyla's hand, "you did good." Elsa impulsively kissed the young fairy's head before going back into the lodge. This turn of events gave them all renewed energy.

***

Inside, Panda was indeed sweating, eyes closed, her face lit by flickering firelight. Herbs brewed in a pot on the hot rocks, and Valerie kept checking to make sure Elsa had put in the proper proportion of ingredients. Brutus was stirring, but Selket was still. Elsa had worried that this heat so soon after the fire might scare him, but he sat like an Egyptian statue. Valerie was singing her heart out. Elsa could tell something was happening and the wolfsbane was helping, but it wasn't enough to overcome the evil that had gotten into Panda's leg. Elsa stuck her head out of the flap and said, "We missed something. We need ideas."

Juniper started Googling on her cell phone furiously. Ralph had his eyes closed, bowing his head as if to pray.

In the midst of this angst, a weary Puddle walked into the backyard. "Hey guys, what—"

Ralph's head jerked up. "I know what we're missing. I've been trying to remember from when we did this in Alabama. It's tobacco. Do any of you have tobacco?"

Puddle reached in her pocket. "Will pot do?"

Ralph shrugged. "Maybe." He extended his hand, and once Puddle placed the pot in it, he made a hole in the dirt beneath the lodge and buried the stash.

"Puddle, this is Ralph from Taggart's," Juniper said.

"Nice to meet you. That was some prime stash." Puddle looked longingly at where it was buried. "It was my last bit from Peru."

"You carried that on the plane?" Juniper gave her a "what were you thinking" stare.

Puddle shrugged.

"You're lucky you're not in jail."

"I have to tell you guys what happened when I went to Doug Harker's house." Twyla was interrupted by a voice from inside the lodge.

"Whatever you did, that's not it." Valerie sounded frantic.

Puddle became thoughtful. "I think that's a sign."

"What, that when a once in a lifetime magical event to save your sister happens, your pot doesn't work?"

"I love Panda so much. I'm gonna' quit for her."

"Good for you, but that's not going to help right now."

Juniper got up and ran into the house, returning with a pack of cigarettes.

Twyla sat next to Puddle and asked, "Are you feeling guilty?"

She cried a little bit and didn't answer. Instead, she addressed Juniper. "Who smokes American Spirit? Where did you get those? Can I have one?"

Slightly guilty, Juniper said, "Okay, busted. I'm giving you one, but let's get some regular tobacco in too."

"Come on, girl," Ralph said to Puddle. "Let's save your sister."

Each took a cigarette from the pack, removed the paper, and went to various portions of the lodge, tucking the tobacco inside holes. Val paused in her singing to say, "Better." Her throat was hoarse.

Ralph dug out Puddle's pot and gave it back to her.

Puddle appeared to be making a decision. With the pot in her hand, she walked to the composter and put it in, saying only, "It's organic." This raised a few eyebrows, but Panda in the lodge was the main event.

Twyla sat at the outdoor table, uncharacteristically quiet. She appeared crumpled and spent. "This has got to work. It's got to."

Ralph patted her hand, and they all in their own ways prayed for a good outcome.

"What was your name again?" Ralph was staring at Puddle, who lit a cigarette.

"Puddle."

"Like a pool of rainwater?"

"Yeah. It's a long story. My brother's name is Brooke. Panda's my sister."

"Oh. Thanks for the help. That Valerie gal said it's working."

Puddle got up and brought the outdoor heater from the storage shed to the patio table. "I don't remember Merryville being this cold in September."

The heat and some coffee made everyone a little more comfortable. At least an hour went by while they listened to Valerie sing, watched smoke pour from the top of the lodge, and listened to the soft drumming coming from somewhere in the distance. Puddle thought she could hear the nuns from Sister Lucia's convent in Peru as ravens circled overhead. It was hypnotic, and in spite of the caffeine, Ralph nodded off. After another hour of this, the ravens thinned. Twyla pointed this fact out at the same time Blondie sauntered calmly into the makeshift lodge and a few minutes later, out again. She jumped up on the fence and disappeared into the night. It was a sign that the sweat was coming to a close.

"That's the healing cat," Juniper exclaimed, waking Ralph. "Why did she leave?" All eyes were on Twyla.

"Because she's finished," Twyla commented somewhat blankly.

"Is that good or bad?" Puddle asked her.

Mitzi staggered from the lodge, sweaty and disheveled, as smoke stopped pouring from the top of the structure. "It's done." She came over to the table and drank a glass of water.

Ekk came out and said, "All we can do now is wait."

"But how is she?" Juniper asked.

Mitzi walked back to the lodge. "I don't know."

It was then they noticed Valerie had stopped singing. A hush blanketed the backyard, and no one spoke, wanting to know but afraid to ask whether the sweat was successful. Twyla and Puddle moved to the tent behind Mitzi to see for themselves.

Mitzi returned to the place on the ground where she'd sat during the whole ceremony, cradling Panda's unresponsive head.

Puddle cried, "No!" because Panda wasn't moving. "Why is she like that? What's happening?"

Mitzi held a finger to her lips. "Shhhhhh."

Juniper, Puddle, and Twyla wormed their way in the now overly crowded space, garnering a frown from Elsa, who said, "We need space." Panda lay still on the pallet with Selket and Brutus nearby. Elsa stared up to where the last of the smoke had escaped. It had to be over one hundred degrees in the tent. Valerie sat and stared at her friend and said, "It's in Spirit's hands."

Ralph, sensing the private nature of the event, went to Ekk. "Is there anything I can do?"

"No. Thanks for what you did. At least we know we had the right elements. Go home. It's cold." He patted Ralph on the back and walked him toward his truck in the driveway.

The old man nodded. "Call me?"

"Of course." The two men had reached the old Ford when Valerie's voice rang out clear and loud from the tent. "Great Goddess in the Sky."

Ekk and Ralph ran back to the lodge and peeked through the flap. What they saw was amazing.

Selket and Brutus were up and, although a bit wobbly, very much alive. It was hard to see Panda's face with Mitzi covering it with kisses. Elsa lifted the blanket and showed off Panda's leg. "Ladies and gentlemen, the evil has literally gone up in smoke." They all cheered.

This was short-lived because Valerie, completely spent, fainted.

***

Mayor Tom Reed spit out his coffee after opening the morning paper. *The Merryville Bee* was spread out on his polished burlwood desk. The headline blared up at him:

COMMUNITY GIFT OR GRAFT?

Below the headline were two color pictures from the kickoff of the community garden a year ago. In the first one, left to right was an image of himself, smiling widely, next to Charlotte Windingle, Sylvia Arviso, and Douglas Harker, who were posed with shovels. The next photo was taken at city hall as he exited the elevator with Phillip Pen. He now knew he'd been set up. The caption on that photo said, "Mayor Reed on the hot seat over possible cover-up of the environmental impact report."

The most eye-catching, however, was the color picture of the water tower on the back of the community garden property with a black skull and crossbones painted on it.

"Margaret!" Tom yelled to his secretary. "Get me Doug Harker's number—now!"

"On my way," she called through his open door.

Tom put on his "cheaters" and held up *The Merryville Bee*. His eyes tracked down the page to the article, titled "Tainted Produce?" printed in the lower right corner and continued on page three.

> *Constance Sliwa, head of Merida University Agricultural Department, issued a press release about tainted dirt left behind by the new community garden's former lessee, Ring Tire Company. In July the Bee reported Ring Tire ended its thirty-year lease, citing what the CEO called, "ridiculous and restrictive new California regulations." That article focused on the loss of good-paying jobs, but now it seems the toxic chemicals used at the site may have harmed the local community in other ways. So far, Douglas Harker, chairman of the Merryville Planning Commission that issued the permits, has not responded to our requests for comments.*

> *Residents hailed Tom Reed as a hero after he negotiated with the Windingle Development Company to donate the land to the city for a community garden. That may not be such a good outcome if the fruits and vegetables grown harm residents. Did the Windingle company donate the land to avoid a costly cleanup? Did our city leadership do a proper environmental impact study? The Bee will continue to dig for answers. Calls to the mayor's office for a comment were not immediately returned before publication.*

Margaret placed a post-it note with Doug Harker's phone number on the desk in front of him.

He remembered that she had given him that number to him many times before and said by way of apology, "It's in my cell phone, but I left it in the car."

She smiled, her default expression, and returned to the safety of her desk.

His friend answered on the second ring.

"Doug, it's Tom."

"You don't think I'd recognize our mayor's voice?"

"Have you seen the paper this morning?"

"No, I was, uh, sleeping in." His voice sounded uncharacteristically nervous. "What's up?"

"Find a paper and call me back. No, better yet, I'm coming over."

"But—"

"See you in fifteen." Click.

GARY

After showering, shaving, and dressing in better clothes, Gary could pass for normal, except for his strange eyes. His hair needed to be cut, but it was washed and combed. He slipped his feet into Doug's Cole Hahn loafers and wiggled his toes. "We used to be the same size. Funny how eating slop not fit for pigs will make you go off your feed and lose weight."

Doug watched nervously in Dockers and a polo shirt. "I'm sorry for everything that's happened to you, Gary, but I had nothing to do with that. Look, I can give you some money…some clothes, but you can't stay here." His cell phone rang, and he picked it up from the dresser. When he saw who it was, he grinned and put a finger in the air to indicate Gary should be quiet.

"Laura, so how is the conference?"

Gary hummed in front of the mirror, talking to himself as Doug continued the call. He heard Gary muttering to himself, "I almost feel human." Doug should have known Gary wouldn't remain quiet.

"That's nobody darling, the radio's on." While Laura spoke, he covered the receiver with his hand and put his other index finger in front of his lips in the universal "shush" sign. Then, "Oh, I would pick you up from the airport, but we have a press conference about all this weather. Yes, it is strange. Okay, doll. See you."

Doug clicked off the call and stuffed the cell in his pocket.

"Gary, not only is our mayor on his way here right now, Laura's coming home early. And by the way, what happened to my expensive rugs? Laura will have a fit."

"I don't have a mayor, Doug. I'm an outcast, a man without a country. And Laura never liked those old dead things anyway."

Doug bit his lower lip and said with his most persuasive voice, "You can't be here."

Gary sauntered over to him and ran his finger slowly down Doug's face. "You keep saying that, Dougie, but I think I can stay wherever I feel like." He tilted his head and wrinkled his nose. "How do I look?"

Doug was unwilling to play the host any longer and stayed serious. "He'll be here in five minutes."

"Then you better pour the drinks." Gary appeared unperturbed. "And I'll be in your safe room. You still have that, don't you? We spent some good times monitoring, didn't we? And, oh, I know how to turn on all those computer monitors, so watch what you say. And"—the maniacal gleam in his eye was scary—"lest you think your problems would be resolved by having the authorities come get me," his expression turned menacing, "you're wrong, so very wrong." Gary pasted a smile on his face and said, "Now, what's for breakfast?"

***

THE MAYOR

Doug sat on one of the white wicker chairs on his broad porch to wait for Tom. He waived when he saw Tom's Mercedes pull into the driveway. He parked, tromped his leather-clad feet to the porch, and lowered his big self onto the empty porch chair next to Doug. Two bloody Marys sat on a table in between them. Tom picked one up and took a gulp.

Doug's light blue eyes were curious as he said, "Morning, Tom."

"Laura home?" Tom asked.

"No, Junior League conference. Drink okay?"

"It needs a couple drops of Tabasco."

Doug tapped a couple drops into Tom's drink. "What's up? You're scowling."

Tom opened the *Merryville Bee* and held it with one hand while smacking it with his other one. "You see the news this morning?"

Doug shook his head. "I meant to, but I got distracted." He thought about the "distraction" now in his safe room, probably watching them this very minute. He took a sip of his Bloody Mary and read the title of the article. "That son of a bitch!"

Tom forced a laugh. "Which one?"

"That Francisco Gonzalez, who else?"

Tom responded with disdain. "That peepie-squeakie professor from the college? Please."

Doug opened a mini-humidifier and handed Tom a thick Cuban cigar. "Light?"

On a roll, Tom waved him off. "Dammit, Doug, things were looking good for the election until that nobody started bashing my new community garden project with all that politically correct horseshit. Don't people know this is a good thing? Vegetables, for eff's sake. I swear, Doug, it's damned if you do and damned if you don't in politics."

Doug puffed on a cigar, thinking, before he rested it in an ashtray. He was sweating a little as he tented his fingers.

"It'll blow over." He wanted Tom to leave.

"The EIR is solid, right?"

"Of course it is. Boris contracted it to professionals."

Tom leaned forward. "Gimme one of those things." He selected a cigar and took some deep draws to get it lit before speaking. "I thought so, too, until this landed on my desk."

"Let me see." Doug picked up the paper and scanned the article again. "At least they got in that Mitzi Fowler is on our committee, even though she's only been to one meeting, and she left early."

"How come?"

"She said her wife had an emergency."

Tom took a long sip of his drink and stared out at the fountain. "Wife, gimme a break."

After Tom left, Doug stood for a moment, watching as the Mercedes receded down his long driveway. As soon as his friend was out of sight, he raced inside his home to insist that Gary leave. His marriage, position in society, and livelihood were all at stake, and he felt panicked. Meeting with the mayor woke Doug up. Fearing the loss of his comfy life more than Gary, Doug yelled directly at the camera, "I can't take this. You've got to go." He was ready to have a showdown. Upon reaching the safe room, he found it unlocked, and he took a deep breath before opening the door. He exhaled upon realizing the room was empty, but he sagged after seeing a note. "Don't get lonely. I'll be back. Keep your doggy tied up."

CHAPTER THIRTEEN

THE FOWLERS' HOME

After my ordeal, I was resting upstairs. I'd taken a hot shower, and my skin was pink. I said to Mitzi, "The cats want some cinnamon rolls. Could you?"

"The cats, not you?" She quipped.

Brutus lifted his head and gave Mitzi a curious kitty appraisal.

"It's for my healing. Sugar helps, and I'm hungry."

"I'm shocked."

I was propped up on the bed with Selket on one side and Brutus on the other. The two cats were becoming good friends. "Well, it's not like I can get up and go to the kitchen myself. You know the cat rule."

Mitzi's phone interrupted our banter. "Hello? Hi, Hortense."

I petted Selket and eavesdropped, only hearing one side of the conversation.

"This Friday? You know, I've only been to one meeting, and I had to leave early when my wife, ah, took ill."

Mitzi flicked her beaded hair over her shoulder and studied me, wallowing in my post sweat lodge sympathy. She rolled her eyes and said, "She's fine now."

Mitzi listened for a moment and said, "No, I haven't read the story. Sounds like I need to read the environmental report, too, and talk to Doug."

Mitzi was quiet for another moment. "I understand. Sylvia emailed it to me, but…" During the pause before she answered, Mitzi's face showed concern. "I want to read it before I say yes."

I could now hear Hortense's' distinctive voice.

"It won't take long, Hortense, I'll call you in a bit. Bye."

Mitzi lifted her eyes to the ceiling and shook her head. "That woman." She sat on the bed and stroked Selket, our temporary charge until we heard from Ali regarding what he wanted to do about his cat.

"How's Horse Face?"

"Panda."

"Well, she doesn't call very often. What's up?"

Mitzi gave a big sigh. "She said the mayor is calling a press conference about the community garden at noon Friday. Something about an article in the *Bee.* They want me on the stage with him."

"But you just got on the committee. I don't like this. They're using you."

"Gimme the paper."

I always read the paper, but today's edition was on the bedside table with the rubber band still around it.

She reached for it over Selket, who hissed. Mitzi said, "I'm ready for this cat to go home."

"Elsa said he doesn't like being petted. He takes his job as Ali's familiar very seriously."

She unfolded the paper and found the story. "Holy shit." Mitzi moved Brutus and scooted next to me so we could read it together.

I was alarmed. "And with you on the environmental committee, this is bad. At least they didn't mention your name." I squinted. "Oh wait, they did. Ms. Mitzi Fowler, I stand corrected." I gave her a sympathetic gaze, not knowing what to say.

Mitzi said, "I need to do something, like, now."

I nodded. "Go."

"You sure you can wait for your cinnamon rolls?"

"I'll make them myself. Call Sylvia."

"I will, but first I'm reading every word of the EIR. Valerie said something didn't feel right when she was walking on the land. I need to know what's going on before I agree to tell the public, while onstage, that all is well. I'll call Charlotte too."

This made me smile. "Oh, look at you with all the notables on your Rolodex. By the way, how is Valerie doing? She's been through a lot."

"I know—the fire at the botanica, then she fainted after pouring her heart and soul into the sweat." Mitzi became serious. "We owe her. When this is done, I'm sending her and Juniper on a cruise."

I comically addressed the cats. "Okay, kids, convalescent time is over. Let's see what's in the kitchen for you."

Selket leaped over me gracefully and waited at the door. Brutus followed, unwilling to be far from his new friend. Both cats reacted as if they fully understood what I had said.

Mitzi commented, "First ravens, now cats?"

"You may refer to me now as Dr. Doolittle." We each went to our tasks.

***

Elsa was already in the kitchen when I entered, baking her little heart out. It was one of the things I loved about having Elsa and Ekk in our home. They always seemed hungry and didn't mind cooking for everyone.

"How are you doing, Elsa?" I moved to the stove and gave her a hug. "Thank you, thank you, thank you."

"For what?"

"I'm alive. Whatever you're baking, it smells wonderful."

Elsa grinned at me and the cats. "You sound like the old Panda. This time, I think we totally got it."

"Meow, Meow." A chorus rang out from below.

She said, "And you, too, my little furry friends."

Brutus was so big, and Selket so skinny, they made a funny pair. Both now had energy and bright eyes. Ekk entered through the back door and sat at the dinette. "Morning, Panda. How are you feeling?"

"Excellent. It's Elsa and Valerie I worry about."

"I'm fine," Elsa said, feeding the kitties some treats. "All this worry. I'm only a bit tired."

I sat in my chair next to Brutus' pet bed. "Wow. It all started here a little over a week ago. Hard to believe so much has happened since then."

Brutus stepped into his bed and made room for Selket, who curled up in a little black ball. I recalled how desperately ill my kitty boy had been two days before and marveled at all our recoveries. "Brutus seems to like company. Where did Blondie go?"

Ekk responded, "Blondie was a special breed of cat. In fact, I'm not sure she was really a cat at all. When needed, the Hercynian Garden healers can inhabit small, simple creatures. It's one way we've done work here without triggering an imbalance in the magical forces and starting another world war."

I thought about this. "Cats working below the radar—that makes so much sense."

Elsa said, "Yes. When the healing was truly finished, she moved on."

I thought of what Elsa had been through and asked, "Is that like what happened to the zombies you told us about at the botanica the night of the fire?"

Elsa nodded. "Those unhoused people were under the influence of magic, except it wasn't healing energy in them, obviously. Dark energy can also inhabit simple creatures, even people if they're drug addicts and have no mental defense. That part of town is full of vulnerable people."

I accepted a plate of cinnamon rolls with a pat of butter sliding down the side. "Thanks, Elsa. Was it always this way? Has this evil always been in my hometown right under my nose? I don't remember anything like this growing up."

"The longer we're here, the more we learn about how far *Lupus Imperium* has penetrated Merryville," Ekk answered. "Remember, before you met Elsa and me, you didn't know about the Hercynian Garden either. We still don't know why Wolfrum, or whoever is in charge now, is focused on this town since the portal under the Lutheran Church is closed forever. I think when Wolfrum was here last, he worked hard to infect people, places, and things, perhaps out of pure meanness. I don't know. We'll have to monitor it."

"So it could be raw, random evil. Why would that be?" I really wanted to know.

He sighed. "Evil beings hate to see happy people go about living their lives. The light in their souls bothers them."

"Well, it feels very personal," I said around my roll, "and thank you again, both of you. I don't know what we would have done without you. Elsa, please sit down and eat. These rolls are amazing."

Elsa pulled out a chair. "I think I will. Oh, by the way, Ali's out of the hospital. Puddle went to pick him up."

"In what?"

From the living room, Mitzi called, "My Miata. She had to put the top down for him."

I said loudly, "Nothing wrong with your hearing." This made her laugh. "How could that big guy even fit in your car? Is this a new boyfriend? I suppose she's going to want to go to Egypt now."

Not wanting to keep talking, Mitzi said, "I'm reading now." I knew she was reading the Environmental Impact Report about the Merryville Community Garden.

"I've known Ali for a unicorn's age, and that actually wouldn't be a bad match, Puddle and Ali," Elsa said.

I thought of the crowded conditions on Thistle Drive and commented, "Well, I hope she doesn't ask him to move in here. What about his cat?"

"Since he's staying with his daughter, who is allergic to cats, he's asked us to keep Selket until he figures out what to do next," Elsa said. "He'd been living in the back of the botanica."

"Well, that's no longer an option." My mood darkened, thinking about the destruction and near fatality of my friends due to the fire. After we ate rolls silently for a bit, Elsa called to Mitzi in the other room. "I saved some cinnamon rolls for you."

"Good thing," Mitzi said. She entered the kitchen with a sheaf of papers in one hand. "I finished reading the EIR. Some professor at the university says we have a problem with the community garden. I don't see it." She put two rolls on a plate and took the fourth seat at the yellow dinette. This was what I liked best. Cinnamon in the air, the kitchen warm from the stove, and everybody in a pile.

I asked, "Did you make your calls to the other ladies?"

"Yes," Mitzi answered. "I'm going to pick up Valerie and meet Sylvia and Charlotte at the project. I'll need the Land Rover."

I changed the subject by asking Ekk, "What's going to happen to your, uh, little hidey hole under the tree now?" After getting over being miffed at not being told about it, I'd become fascinated with the secret space.

"I only built it for Elsa to have a place to work," Ekk said. "Now that we have it, let's keep it."

I thought of all the trips Ekk made to Taggart's Emporium. "Yeah, you put a lot of work into that space."

"Not just that but," he winced, "if an emergency happens and we're not around, it's where you girls need to go."

Mitzi's face drained of color. "What kind of emergency? Haven't we been through enough?"

Elsa gently took her hand. "You're not completely out of danger. I don't have any idea what's coming down the road, but it's good to be prepared. I mean, Panda found me, Valerie, and Ali tied up on the floor of a burning botanica not that long ago."

"Oh yeah," I said.

Ekk rolled his eyes. "How quickly they forget."

Mitzi shook her head. "So sorry to think only about myself. I was hoping things might finally get back to normal."

Elsa patted her arm. Ekk said, "We'll be fine. We do need to stick together."

I picked up the morning paper and turned the newspaper around so they saw the article about the Merryville Community Garden. "Check this out." I turned the page so they could see a picture of Gary Smithers above another article. Elsa shivered. "Until that guy is caught, this is our normal. We need to be on guard."

"This is the guy who almost chopped your heads off," I said, a perfect example of how my mouth worked before my brain sometimes.

Ekk did a thousand-yard stare out the kitchen window and swallowed. "Yes, we know." Elsa stopped chewing and folded her arms.

The memory of Gary towering over them with a sharp machete had to be terrifying.

"That was a bit blunt, Panda." Mitzi pushed her plate away. "But I see your point. I guess I've been in denial about a lot of things. Anyway, I need to meet Sylvia and the board for an emergency meeting about our dirt in a few."

I licked my fingers and replied, "You're not going anywhere without me, now that I'm in good shape." I patted my leg. "I'm tired of being home all the time, and I want to see Val."

Mitzi's eyebrows raised. "FOMO?"

Elsa asked, "What's FOMO?"

"Fear of missing out," Mitzi said. "Panda's got a bad case of that." They all laughed, knowing it was true. Mitzi put her hand on my arm. "Please don't take this the wrong way, Panda, but this is my thing. I'm the one on the commission."

I wilted comically. "Okay."

"Panda, look." Elsa distracted me by pointing to Brutus, who lay with his furry cat arm around his new friend, Selket, who snuggled into him. "Don't miss out on that."

"Yeah, the cats and I all bonded in that sweat lodge experience." I reached down and with one finger gave the jet-black cat a little scratch on the head. Selket answered with a hiss. "Or not."

My sister appeared at the door. "Get your beauty sleep?" I asked.

"I smell cinnamon. Speaking of Selket." Puddle entered, yawning, and pulled up a chair, "Selket's daddy, Ali, wants him back. But he's got to go to Cairo first. When Ali gets back to Merryville, he's renting a space and starting over."

Mitzi asked, "For his botanica?" at the same time I asked, "He's coming back?"

Puddle answered Mitzi. "Yes, but bigger. He's talking about getting a place on Main Street."

"So much for dusty strip malls on the wrong side of town," I commented. "Good for him. I guess I'm surprised, being from Egypt, that he likes our little American city."

"He really does. When things settle down, I want to have him over for dinner," Puddle said.

Mitzi stared at Puddle and asked, "I take it you and Ali hit it off?"

Puddle blushed. "Actually, yes. You know how I said I kind of like it here too? Ali and I are talking about going into business together. He's gonna' go back to Egypt first, though, to see family."

"Oooh," I said. "A new boyfriend." My eyebrows did the hubba, hubba dance. "What would you be doing in this new business?"

"I dunno. Yoga class? He could teach me to do the herbs."

Ekk asked, "What about Mitzi? Can she get in on this too?"

"Ekk—" Mitzi started.

He continued, effectively ignoring her. "No, seriously. You and I spoke about your travel business. You've outgrown the space here. You could put your office in with the botanica."

"That would be rad." Puddle was all in. "A yoga travel botanica."

"What about Dieter?" Elsa asked.

Puddle took a cinnamon roll. "It's fine. I think we knew we were done when I left Peru."

I shook my head. She changed boyfriends like some people changed brands of soda.

Mitzi stood to put her plate in the sink and said, "Travel, yoga, herbs. I'll give that some thought."

***

Valerie and Mitzi bumped down the unpaved road toward the trailer, the golf cart's tires kicking up dust behind them. Overhead, clouds were gathering. They entered the temporary clubhouse and saw Sylvia sitting at the folding table with a slender bespeckled woman in her thirties, who wore a thin sweater over a white blouse and a warm scarf around her neck. Her hands were very white, and she hugged herself as if cold. Sylvia and the woman had coffee in front of them, and Mitzi wondered if she and Valerie were late, and where the rest of the group was.

"Where's Charlotte? Denise?" Mitzi asked.

"Charlotte has a migraine, and Denise is at a Junior League conference." Sylvia looked grim. "I left messages for the rest of the board."

The woman Mitzi didn't recognize cleared her throat audibly and said, "I appreciate this invitation, but time is short. Ladies, it appears you have a big problem. This meeting is your last chance to do the right thing."

The aggressive start caught Mitzi by surprise. Sylvia asserted her role as president of the club. "Valerie, Mitzi, let me introduce you to Dr. Constance Sliwa from the agricultural department at the university."

The visitor practically bristled. "Actually, I head the department." Lightning flashed, followed by thunder. It was like a Disney effect introducing the villain.

Valerie said a soft, "Wow." It wasn't clear whether this was a comment on the weather or Dr. Sliwa.

Sylvia managed a tiny laugh. She lifted her hands in surrender. "Sorry. Let's start over." It was clear she didn't want to begin on the wrong foot, but Dr. Sliwa was making it hard. To Mitzi and Valerie, she said, rather unnecessarily, "Dr. Sliwa is here at my invitation because of the article in the *Merryville Bee* about the soil on our five acres."

"It's the sandpit, isn't it?" Valerie quietly asked. Rain pelted the roof, sounding loud on the metal and giving the already tense meeting a further feeling of urgency.

Dr. Sliwa stood and shook hands with Mitzi and Valerie, formal and rather frosty. She intently studied them up and down. To Mitzi she said, unsmiling, "You're wearing beads in your hair. Are you indigenous?"

"Uh, no, German and American mutt. Pleased to meet you," Mitzi said after receiving a limp handshake.

"I see." The woman gave her a rude appraisal. "Well, you won't be pleased in a minute."

Mitzi squinted her eyes. "Why do you say that?"

Dr. Sliwa leaned her weight on her two hands on the table and did this weird side scrunching thing with her mouth while appearing to think. After the pause she said acidly, "Aside from your obvious appropriation of indigenous culture, aren't you the Mitzi Fowler who is part of the mayor's planning committee? The one with Monte Hunt, Douglas Harker, Ben Dunning, and David Smith?"

"Yes. They added me as the environmental liaison to this club."

"Did you even know who I was before today?"

"Not before the article in the *Bee*," Mitzi said.

Dr. Sliwa shook her head. "Well, we know who you are."

"Excuse me?"

"We refer to you at the Uni as the toxic five."

"What?" Mitzi was shocked.

Valerie stepped in. "Hold on, Dr. Sliwa. First, not everyone who wears beads in their hair is appropriating my culture."

"Oh? Your culture?"

"Yes. My maiden name is Chipeta, or, as you white people translate it, White Singing Bird. I'm Ute. My friend Mitzi likes beads. So what?" Valerie rarely got irritated, but this was one of those times.

Mitzi was about to speak again, when Sylvia intervened.

"Dr. Sliwa, I asked you here in good faith. The Horticultural Society—"

Their visitor cut her off. "Is a bunch of white women who play in the dirt and like to see their names in the paper. Meanwhile, we at the university are actually working on ameliorating the effects of climate change and promoting sustainability. So forgive me if I'm not here on a social call."

"That's a lot of hostility. What did we ever do to you?" Mitzi asked. She was genuinely interested. She and Panda were not part of the history of the club and had only recently joined.

After a big sigh, Dr. Sliwa said, "This site for the community garden, that we weren't asked to assess by the way, is a disaster. We didn't care when you all were just socialites playing gardener, but *this*," she gestured with both arms at the land beyond the walls of the trailer they were standing in, "this can hurt people."

"What do you have to tell us about *this*," Valerie calmly asked.

Dr. Sliwa pressed her lips in a straight line. "Let me be clear. It's bad."

She moved to the front of the table and switched on the overhead projector. "To be honest, I was surprised when Ms. Arviso called me." She lifted her pretty brows.

"Well, you're here. What do we need to know?" Mitzi flatly asked.

Dr. Sliwa gathered herself and dialed it down a notch. "Some say your club is a part of Mayor Reed's effort to whitewash the problems with what should be a superfund property. Has it occurred to you, Ms. Fowler, that you're being used by the mayor's political agenda for optics?"

Mitzi was taken aback. "I was asked to be on the planning commission. They picked me because I, ah, care about the environment."

"Oh, sweetie. They picked you because you're queer and not a man. I heard you were a travel agent before this. Now, I can't stay long, so let's talk about what you asked me to come and talk about."

Mitzi was mad and deeply hurt, but sat quietly.

Dr. Sliwa placed a transparency on the lighted projector, showing the tire-making process. "I'll break it down for you non-scientific types." This woman would never win any personality contests. "The problem is chemicals leeching into the soil over a long period of time. Ring Tire didn't bother to capture their manufacturing runoff. For three decades they turned raw materials into rubber. That's a lot of pollution that's seeped not only into the soil, but probably into the aquifer."

Valerie asked, "What's in the soil?"

Dr. Sliwa continued. "They used polychlorinated biphenyls and other compounds. Here's the bottom line." She put a new slide up showing shortened lives of humans who had even small amounts of the toxin in their system. She pinned each woman present with her piercing, milk chocolate-colored eyes. "Clearly, all the tainted soil must be removed before any food use or anything can be grown on the property."

A stunned silence followed, broken by Mitzi.

"Are you sure about this? I mean, an EIR was done." She clutched her copy of the one she printed out from Sylvia's email and smoothed it out in front of her on the table.

Dr. Sliwa sighed. "The version relied upon to get this project through the city has been manipulated. We're contemplating a lawsuit, but our resources are limited. You'll find the scientists who did the testing are on the payroll of a large oil company affiliated with Ring Tire. It appears at least two members of your commission are former shareholders."

Sylvia held up a thicker stack of papers than the one sitting in front of Mitzi. "Dr. Sliwa brought me the uncut version that is nothing like the one we were given."

"How can we trust this?" Mitzi asked as she picked up and leafed through the document. "How did this happen? And how do we know this is real?"

The woman was irritated by her comment. "Ms. Fowler? I'm an expert in this field and verified the unofficial tests done by some of my students. Trust me, the cleanup wasn't done." She snapped off the overhead. "I'm sorry to be the bearer of bad news, but now you know." She crossed her arms.

Valerie asked Sylvia, "Are we going to pull the project?"

"We need to have a full meeting, and with all due respect," she turned to Dr. Sliwa, "we need some time to digest this information and perhaps get a second opinion."

"I've got to go. You have the information. What you do with it is up to you, but, honestly," Dr. Sliwa shook her head and pressed her lips together, "I'll do everything in my power to stop you if you decide to go forward."

After Dr. Sliwa left, the executive board sat in silence for a beat. Steaming, Mitzi said, "What a bitch."

"She's passionate in her beliefs. To her, we're the bad guys," Sylvia said.

Mitzi flipped her beads back, her tell when she was angry. "What did we do wrong? We're going to bring fruits and vegetables to an underserved community."

Sylvia countered her. "Not if what she says is true."

The heater clicked on, and the dejected women looked at each other. At least the rain appeared to be slacking off.

"When I walked the space, it felt okay, except maybe for the sandpit." Valerie appeared to be remembering, head tilted sideways. "I was raised with a great respect for the earth and its gifts. But even so, with all these bad feelings in the community, I'm not sure we want this gift anymore."

"Did you hear her? Toxic Five?" Mitzi was still fuming. "Doesn't it seem a little cozy? I mean, that Francisco Gonzalez running for mayor is a professor at the same college as Dr. Sliwa."

"Don't take it personally," Val said.

Mitzi snorted, arms folded.

"If you're going to be in the public eye, Mitzi, you need a thicker skin," Sylvia responded. "I know Francisco. We go way back. The science doesn't lie, and he's a true believer. Here's a lesson for you in politics. It doesn't matter why Francisco's using this issue or how pissed off we get at his messenger, Dr. Sliwa. We still have to deal with the fact that the community garden has issues."

"What's it going to take to fix it?" Valerie asked. "I mean moneywise."

"That is the ultimate question, isn't it?" Sylvia appeared depressed. "It's going to take a complete removal of the topsoil going down about fifteen feet. Also, testing of the water below that. Proper disposal of what is removed after that, and I don't know what they do if the aquifer is poisoned. Plenty of companies do this, but it's expensive. I asked Charlotte to have her people make a few calls. It's millions of dollars."

Mitzi played absently with one of her braids and commented, "I can see why Charlotte has a migraine."

"Yes, because that puts Windingle Development, who donated the land, on the hook too," Sylvia said.

Mitzi asked as she got up, "Did you know the mayor wants to do a presser here on Friday to reassure the public about this project? I'm supposed to be on the stage."

Sylvia said, "Don't quit the commission yet. I have an idea. I hate to say this, but we need Hortense Miller. She has some pull."

Mitzi glared at Sylvia. "Oh, I'm not quitting the commission." She walked out, leaving the new, thicker report on the table.

CHAPTER FOURTEEN

THE GOODENS' HOME / DOUG'S SECRET

Twyla was eager to be where the action was, and Juniper was about to leave. "Now that Panda's healed, I'm ready to help with whatever you need, Juniper. Can I go with you to the museum?"

Juniper paused her going out the door ritual. "Sorry, love, but I've got a luncheon at the yacht club and meetings after that. It's going to be a late night."

Twyla wilted. "But isn't your job art? I thought you would be dealing with paintings and statues and interesting installations."

Juniper sighed. "Don't I wish. Sometimes it's like that. We're in between major exhibitions right now and into fundraising mode. I'm meeting with several patrons of the arts, although they've been less generous than in past years. Everyone is blaming the pandemic."

Twyla bounced up and down on her heels, always at odds with containing her energy. "But that was years ago. What should I be doing while you meet?"

The Goodens lived in an old Craftsman with a generously sized garden in the backyard. "My dear," Juniper said, "you've already transformed the garden, our eaves are repaired, and I can't think of a thing. Don't little fairies ever rest? Read a book for heaven's sake. Valerie will be home later. Maybe you and she can figure out something for you to do. She's been through a lot, and she probably wants a nap. You can protect her." She picked keys off the hook by the front door. "Wish me luck with the Harkers. That family—"

"Oooh. Doug Harker?" Twyla had her hands on either side of her face, like the painting, *The Scream*. "I knew there was something I was supposed to tell you."

Juniper jingled her keys. "Give me the short version, please."

"Doug had an affair with that city councilman who tried to kill Ekk and Elsa, um, Gary—that's his name."

The two females stood, facing one another. Whatever Juniper had expected to hear, it wasn't that.

"Excuse me? Wait, what?" Her hand that had been poised to open the front door, dropped to her side.

"I got the animal skins from that Harker guy's house. It must be the same family, right?" Juniper froze, her blue eyes fixed on Twyla's animated face. "And?"

"Well, I had to hide—I mean I was trespassing—behind a curtain actually. It was so like in the movies. You know, where the bad guys are coming and—"

Juniper snapped her fingers. "Twyla, focus. This is very important. You do realize Gary Smithers is the one you're protecting Valerie and me from? Oh my god." Juniper picked up her cell and punched in some numbers. "Maribel, I'm going to be a few minutes late."

Twyla heard a woman talking on the other end, but not the words.

"I know, I know. Trust me, this is important. I'll be twenty minutes."

She led Twyla back into the living room and perched on the couch. Next, she dialed Valerie, who answered right away.

"Are you still with Mitzi?"

Valerie laughed. "No, I'm on the porch. Open the door."

Juniper walked to the door and let her in.

Upon seeing her expression, Valerie asked, "I leave for one hour and obviously something's happened. Now what?"

Juniper took her hand and led her to the living room. "You have no idea."

***

Mitzi was in a down mood when she got home after her meeting. She filled Panda in on what had happened at the trailer.

"That cow. First, she accused me of appropriating indigenous culture," she lifted one of her beaded braids, "and then attacked us about the garden."

I was livid. "What a bitch."

Mitzi's cell phone rang. "It's Juniper." She punched the green connect button.

"Hi, Juniper. I'm glad you called. Did Valerie tell you what happened?"

"She did. But we have some news for you guys."

"What? Let me put it on speaker so Panda can hear."

Juniper repeated what Twyla told her.

"Wow," Mitzi said, "Doug and Gary. What a hypocrite that guy is."

"A murderous hypocrite, even worse," I said.

"This is explosive news," Juniper said cautiously. "You'd better make sure this is true before you do anything with this information."

"I'm not a liar," Twyla said.

I heard Valerie in the background. "I agree. I can't imagine she would make this up."

"Would have been nice if Twyla told us the night of the sweat," I said.

"I tried to," Twyla said. "Everyone was too busy to listen."

"We need to tell Ekk," Mitzi said.

Juniper said, "If it's true, that reporter, Phillip something, needs to know."

"I know what I saw," Twyla said. "Why is this such a big deal?"

Mitzi responded. "Closeted people do hook up sometimes. It's not easy to be yourself when you're gay in this world. He's hiding behind his marriage and doesn't have the courage to take the heat. We need to think about why we're doing this before we tell anybody."

"Um, because he tried to kill Elsa and Ekk and maybe us?" I suggested.

Valerie, always wise, said, "If this goes public, it invites people to hate him, but for the wrong reasons. Yes, he's a hypocrite and an adulterer, but then he's no longer crazy or a homicidal maniac. He becomes a gay homicidal maniac."

We were all silent for a couple of beats.

"And I bet his wife probably doesn't know," I blurted out.

Juniper finished up the call. "Well, I needed to tell you. This is as far as it goes. Right? I gotta do some fundraising. I was actually going to the Harkers' house next, but Maribel called and told me their secretary canceled it. Boy, I'd love to be a fly on that wall. Ta-ta for now."

We said our goodbyes, and Juniper ended the call.

Brutus said, "Meow," as Ekk walked in. "What's he talking about?"

"You better get Elsa." I was still shaking my head.

***

Ralph entered his wife's nursing home and stopped to sign the visitor book. He put a brown paper bag on the counter while he did so. The hallway smelled vaguely of Fabuloso cleaner. The area was free of the usual wheelchair traffic, as it was near dinnertime. He fished in his pocket for a sweet.

A young woman in colorful scrubs with "Merry Hearts" stitched under her name looked up. "Good evening, Mr. Brown."

She was fairly new, but they all knew him from his regular visits. Ralph placed a hard candy on the chart in front of her and answered, "Good evening, Brittany. I'm paying my toll."

She snatched it up and, after expertly disposing of the wrapper, popped it in her mouth. "Thanks." It made them both grin. This was his routine with all the girls.

Relph returned the pen to its holster next to the visitor's book and carefully made his way across the shiny floor to his wife's shared room. A man pushing a cart full of dinner trays passed Ralph. "Hey, Mr. B," he said.

Ralph nodded. "Hi, Buddy." He shook his head. They all seemed so impossibly young to be running a memory care unit. When he reached Aurora's door, he gave a little knock and asked, as was his routine, "Is my bride in here?"

Aurora's roommate's bed was empty. He was glad they would be alone. His wife was in a wheelchair, staring out the window at the willow trees in an unfocused way. She turned at his voice and, for a second, he allowed himself to believe she recognized him. Her hair was wild.

"Hi, baby. I brought you something." He opened his bag slowly, stopping to massage one hand with the other. She sat, unresponsive. Ralph pulled out a hairbrush and showed it to her. "Let's do your hair." Even though she had receded to a place he couldn't go, her smell was the same, Ivory soap.

It was one of the things that made him fall in love with her, her scent. When she first came to his little country store in Hartselle, Alabama, she was trying to find her favorite brands, and he had personally escorted her to the appropriate aisle. A young man then, he couldn't help but notice the woman with the print dress, who was so serious about facial soap and Persil laundry detergent. When he was about two feet away he leaned over to help her read a label and inhaled the chemistry of soap on skin. A country girl, she did her best to "gussie up" when she went to town, and he remembered she smelled so clean. He stood transfixed for so long that his boss had yelled, "Ralph," reminding him of his duties. She must have felt a little electricity, too, since she didn't seem to mind him being so close and wasn't in a hurry to get that soap and leave.

"Ralph." Her cracked voice brought him back into the room.

He was startled. "Aurora?"

She said with difficulty, "Soap." Tears rushed to his eyes. Even with her disease, she must have picked up his reverie. He started brushing her hair. She always seemed to know what he was thinking.

"That's right, baby. We got that soap, didn't we?"

Over the next hour, Aurora didn't show any other indications of realizing her man was with her, holding her hand and telling her stories from their past.

When he finally left, Ralph stopped at the front desk and asked for the charge nurse.

"She's gone home. Is everything all right?" Brittany had a schoolbook in front of her. It was quiet on the night shift, and he supposed he couldn't blame her for getting in a little studying.

He didn't want to scare her but decided to warn her anyway. "Brittany, that man who used to be a city councilman, ah, Gary Smithers, escaped the prison mental hospital. Did you hear?"

"We do have a TV in the breakroom. I heard something about it. Why?"

He carefully chose his words. "This man has a vendetta against me, and I want to make sure Ms. Aurora is safe."

Brittany's mouth fell open, and her hand went to her necklace. "Do you think he'll come here?"

"I don't know. He might. Do you have security?"

Shaking it off, she said, "Yes, hold on." She picked up a microphone and held down the switch. "Security to the front desk." To Ralph, she said, "She'll be here in a minute. She started her shift," Brittany looked at the clock on the wall, "five minutes ago. Have a seat, Mr. B."

Ralph rested his old bones in a molded, plastic chair in the hallway. He closed his eyes, and wondered how Gary got loose. He worried what this would mean for them.

The sound of squeaking leather made him open his eyes. A woman in a Merryville police uniform approached the front desk. He stood and walked over to join them.

"Mr. B, this is Officer Tuigamala."

The officer, a woman of size with dimples, stuck out a hand. "I'm Officer Tuigamala. Call me Lulu. Here to protect and serve."

"I-I expected security, not an on-duty police person." He turned to Brittany. "I'm sorry, Miss. I didn't mean for you to call 911."

Lulu gave a belly laugh. "This is my night gig. My day job is at Merryville PD. I haven't had a chance to change out of uniform."

A man in a hospital gown made a beeline for the security guard. Ignoring everyone else, he said, "Lulu."

Lulu addressed him. "Hello, Jerry."

Jerry, eyes shining, implored Lulu, "Come play chess with me." He abruptly turned without greeting anyone else and wheeled himself down the hall. Over his bony shoulder he yelled, "Come on."

"Cool your jets, Jer. I've got some po-lice business to handle." Her face broke out in a broad grin, and Ralph could see this was more her natural state than the stern cop.

She put her thumbs on her leather belt. "So, what do we got here?"

He said it straight out. "Gary Smithers, the old city councilman?"

Her smile waned, and she got serious again. "Yeah. What about him?"

"He may come here. My wife's here, Officer…I'm sorry, what's your name again?"

"Call me Lulu. It's easier. What's your wife's name?"

"Aurora Brown, and I'm Ralph."

"Well, Mr. Brown, don't you worry. This is a big city and, frankly, I see no reason for this escapee to target a patient here."

Ralph couldn't tell her about Gary's threats to him at the store. "Anything you can do would be appreciated, officer." He fished out a card for Taggart's and handed it to Lulu. "My cell phone's on it if you ever need to call me."

Lulu furrowed her brow and tucked it in her pocket. Turning to Brittany, she said, "We're going code *puipui* tonight."

"Got it," Brittany said, and picked up her handset.

Ralph was puzzled. "Pui-pui?" His Southern accent made it sound like pooey-pooey.

"That's Samoan for protection. I protect." She gave her shiny gold badge a pat. "Don't you worry."

He scratched his head. "Well, okay." Lulu walked Ralph to the exit leading to the parking lot. He hesitated and said, "Maybe I should stay. This man, he's very dangerous."

She grinned, "So am I. Now, with all due respect, sir, you look dead on your feet." Lulu shifted her weight. "Go home and get some rest."

He nodded. As he hauled himself into the driver's seat of his truck, Lulu called out from the front door of Merry Hearts, "And lock your doors."

***

An hour later, when Lulu knocked on Aurora's door, she saw her staring blankly out the window.

"Mrs. B?" Aurora gave no response, but truthfully, Lulu hadn't expected one.

"Your husband asked me—Jesus, Mary, and Joseph, it's snowing!"

At that, Aurora turned to her. When she spoke, it might as well have been to the walls. Her watery eyes were not in focus. "It's happening. I need to find it."

"What's happening, Miss Aurora? The snow? Yes, that's a surprise. I'm checking in on you to make sure you're safe. That's all. I'll come around again in a bit. You just stay put, okay?"

Aurora swiveled her head toward the window again and said nothing. Lulu left, thinking how terrible it was to lose your ability to think.

She walked down the hallway toward the nurses' station. She popped a piece of gum in her mouth and sought out Jennifer, who was at the front desk tonight. She found her studying a textbook. Jennifer was in her early twenties, juggling work and school like Brittany. "Hey, Jen."

The young woman barely registered her presence and said absently, "Hey, Lulu. I made a new pot of coffee." She pointed toward the reception's little breakroom and kept reading.

"Thanks. I can smell it. Uh, Jen?" She wrinkled up her face. "I've been in Southern California for five years and never seen weather like this. It's snowing. Is that normal?"

Now Jen raised her head. "It doesn't snow here. It's probably misting."

Lulu squinted at the white stuff falling from the sky. "I may be from the Pacific Islands, but we get Currier and Ives Christmas cards, Jennifer. I think I know snow when I see it." Jen got up and both women walked to the glassed-in front doors.

The young woman's mouth dropped open, but she was not as alarmed as Lulu. "Weird. I'll go crank up the heat."

Lulu's big brown eyes fixed on her. "That's all you got to say? It's weird?"

Jennifer wasn't the friendliest. "And that I'll crank up the heat. I'm tired, and I have a final tomorrow."

Lulu watched as a few residents in wheelchairs started down the hall to check out the spectacle. It must be boring to see the same thing every day. This was an event.

Jen shrugged and offered her opinion. "It has been a cold fall."

Lulu instinctively knew something was very off. "Please, be on alert."

"For what?"

Mildly irritated at the stubborn attitude she said, "For anything else out of the ordinary. I'm going to do my rounds."

The front desk phone rang. Lulu heard Jennifer promise to send a blanket to a room. Lulu came back and inquired, "What is Aurora's husband's name?"

The young student put a pencil to her lips, thinking. "I'm not sure. Do they own that hardware store in town, Taggart's Emporium? I always call him Mr. B."

Lulu tucked her thumb in her belt and nodded. "B. That's right. It's Brown," she said, remembering the card he gave her. She walked the hall again.

***

"So it's clear to me that this Gary Smithers is possessed by *Lupus Imperium*, and he's using this other guy, this Doug Harker? To do what?" Elsa processed aloud.

"He probably needs a place to hide," Mitzi responded. "His assets were seized when the depth of his criminality and all the bribes he took were revealed. The paper said he'd been putting the squeeze on small business owners and amassed a fortune. But the hypocrisy after his public comments about the LGBTQ community makes me furious."

I poked at the fire. "Remember his ridiculous family values picnic? They had a big sign out front that said "Make Merryville Great Again with Traditional Marriage."

"That was before we arrived," Elsa said. "This new information really doesn't change things. Stay focused. If Wolfrum turned Gary Smithers to their cause, and he's still after you, that's what we need to deal with. We need a plan. Whether it's that or if he's simply murderously insane on his own, same thing. I don't think any of us should go anywhere alone."

Mitzi nodded. "What if we call the police with an anonymous tip?"

I'd been staring through the front window and sat up straight. "You guys." I pointed out the living room picture window. "Snow!"

Normally, the large square window would reveal a rather plain front yard with one tree, some flowers, and thistles bordering the grass. At this moment, the thistles were dappled white under a flurry of snowflakes.

All three of us stood in front of the window for a minute. Mitzi said, "Okay, time for the rest of it. Elsa, do you think this weird weather is connected to *Lupus Imperium*?"

"Yes." Elsa remained calm but serious as we all sat down. "Cold as a weapon has been used in the Black Forest in Germany."

"This sounds like the start of one of those fairy tales," I remarked.

"Fairies are in this story," Elsa said. "Just because something is a fairy tale doesn't make it untrue."

Mitzi hushed me with a stern gaze. "Go on."

Elsa leaned forward, her face lit by firelight. Ekk sat back quietly and let her have the floor. "The Hercynian Forest, home of Schwartzwald Castle, is very cold naturally. In fact, the Black Forest got its name because the canopy is so thick, day seems like night in the forest."

"We've been in that spooky place, thank you very much," I said.

"But not in the dead of winter."

This made me shiver, and I put my arm around Mitzi.

She went on. "And this is worse than a cold winter, if it's what I suspect. We all know that cold can be deadly if you're not prepared for it. The snow is pretty now and a novelty."

"The yard does look good," I said.

Elsa went on with her story. "Imagine it gets so cold that everything is covered in thick sheets of ice, and even your heaters aren't enough, or they break. In Southern California some people don't even have heaters."

Mitzi covered her mouth. "And the unhoused folks, oh my god."

Elsa nodded. "Over the centuries, it's rumored, *Lupus Imperium* has dedicated a special cell of monks to meditate and focus the cold like a laser, and they've made some devices to enhance the effect. They've used it effectively on individuals, but as far as I know only in Europe."

"We're thousands of miles away. Couldn't this be climate change? Everything can't be about us." I could tell Mitzi was trying to be rational, as her arm swept toward the window.

"Mitz, snow in September?" I raised my hands in an isn't it obvious pose. "It's about us."

Mitzi jumped up and began to pace. "Right. But okay, say we accept this snow is part of the whole *let's kill the Fowlers* program. Why? And why hurt everybody else in Merryville to get us?"

Elsa hesitated. "*Lupus Imperium* cares nothing for collateral damage. Hurting you, Mitzi, is really the only way they can get to Ehrenhardt and the free creatures. He's well-protected at the keep in the Garden. That's why he'll want you safe with him. Remember, that's the whole reason Ekk and I were sent here in the first place. You're precious to him. When you humiliated Wolfrum at the Lutheran Church, Ekk and I worried about the backlash. But I must say, we didn't see this coming." She traced a pattern on the floor with her Mary Janes.

"What?" I stared at her, now able to tell when Elsa was avoiding a subject.

Elsa took a deep breath. "At the botanica, right before the fire, when I mentioned Wolfrum, the man who started the fire said, 'We have a new leader now.'"

Mitzi responded calmly, "And you're just telling us this now?"

"I talked to Ekk about it. We didn't want to unnecessarily make things more frightening than they already are. It could have been a bluff. We had to report it to the Garden." She bit her lip. "They want us all to go to the Garden keep to be safe until this new threat is sorted."

I put my hands on my hips. "Well, I'm not surprised. I'm almost glad the shoe finally dropped. I knew it wasn't over." I turned to Mitzi. "My gut's been in an uproar for a while now. Tax season's starting up soon for people who got extensions, and I don't think we should go. We can handle this, Mitzi."

Mitzi wasn't impressed by my confidence. She burst out laughing. "I can't believe you said we should stay because it's tax season. I guess somebody has come into her own."

This wasn't like the old me, to be sure. "I have ravens," I said, "if I can figure out how to call them. And you're a half-griffin. Doesn't that count for something?"

Elsa quietly watched us, her expression hard to read.

"It's been so long since I flew," Mitzi said. "I haven't thought about it. This weather could keep me on the ground, you know. Like ice on a plane."

Elsa nodded. "Exactly. Which may be why this form of attack was chosen."

"Didn't we just have a talk about not keeping secrets? No more holding back. We aren't helpless, you know." As I made my point a particularly loud gust of wind sent a stick into the glass and made me jump.

Ekk picked up the remote and turned on the TV. "How big is this storm anyway?" Sure enough, the "Breaking News" ticker scrolled on the bottom below a picture of town square, blanketed in white. Our usual talking head, Jessica Walters, was dressed in a parka suitable for Alaska, —a little over the top for the current light dusting of snow. She stood on Main Street in front of children trying to make a snowman, and the vibe was playful. She had a microphone in one hand and the other up by her ear, as if listening. She nodded and looked back at the camera "Thanks for that weather report, Fritz. So this is mysterious. Christmas in September. Strangely, the unusual weather event is focused on Merryville only, and neighboring towns appear to be unaffected. Scientists say—"

"Panda, let's batten down the hatches," Mitzi said. "I'm going to put up the convertible top on the Miata."

"I'll dig out some jackets. We need to get Puddle here."

Elsa said, "I'll call her."

The doorbell rang. I ran to it and saw Juniper, uncharacteristically serious. "Hey, Juniper, come in." Mitzi walked up behind me.

"Can't." She hugged us. "I'm taking Valerie to Colorado. We're driving."

"This is sudden," I said.

Twyla let their dog Layla out of the car, and she made use of the grass. Brutus joined us on the porch and hissed at the dog. Selket was a bad influence.

Valerie stayed seated in Juniper's Citroen. Twyla waved, smiled wanly, and put the dog back in the car.

"What's going on?" Mitzi said. "Trouble on the res?" She was concerned and walked toward the car.

Juniper caught her arm and said, "No, it isn't that. I wish we could stay, Mitzi, but we got, well, Twyla got a call from the Hercynian Garden asking us to leave Merryville for a few days. And I've been worried about Valerie, anyway, since she fainted. I know everyone's been through a lot, with that sweat and the fire—it's too much. She needs to rest, be with her people."

"But we're her people," I said, selfishly.

Mitzi reached for Juniper's hands. "We would never talk you out of leaving. In fact, I think it's a good idea. When this is over, though, please come back."

"Of course," Juniper said. "It's only until this crazy weather stops."

"We'll miss you so much," Mitzi said, "but we want what's best for you both."

I nodded vigorously and pointed to Mitzi. "What she said. In fact, leave now before this crazy weather gets any worse."

I walked to Valerie's side of the car and observed her through the window. She was on the thin side, anyway, but she appeared especially frail. When she noticed me, she opened the window to talk.

"Hi, Panda. We wanted you to know right away. I guess we need some rest. Are you and Mitzi going to leave too?" This was so typical of her, to worry about others.

I reached through the open window and said with more confidence than I felt, "Nope. We're going to hold the fort here."

Twyla popped up from the back seat, arms around Layla. "Ehren's gonna' be pissed."

"You do your job, and I'll do mine," I said to her.

"Panda, I promise I'll keep them safe. We got a call from the Garden saying this is what we should do. You'll be getting one too."

"Thanks for your input." Fairies sometimes invited drama, and I wasn't biting.

Mitzi leaned in, tucked up Valerie's blanket around her, and gave her a kiss on the cheek. "We're going to be fine. Call us when you arrive."

Juniper got behind the wheel and revved the motor.

"I will," Valerie said. "Let us know what happens with the community garden."

After waving goodbye, we stood in the cold at the end of our driveway, waving, until the heavily loaded Citroen was out of sight.

***

Francisco Gonzalez stood in his small campaign office among signs announcing FRANCISCO FOR MAYOR, TIME FOR A CHANGE. Young and passionate campaign workers argued, wanting to stay despite the freezing weather. Francisco was adamant. "Folks, your safety is first with me." This safety thing was becoming a brand, and he made a mental note to work it into his speeches. He waved at his enthusiastic young students as they reluctantly left, some picked up by parents.

He decided to see for himself what this snow was all about and walked through the strip mall, observing Merryville citizens acting like this was a good thing, a holiday. Families were outside in jackets, taking selfies. Did they not understand this was a sign of severe climate change? He hoped Sylvia had taken his words to heart about the poison in the community garden. It hurt being on the outs with her. Francisco entered the crosswalk as the walk countdown turned to a solid red hand. Busy with his own thoughts, he barely missed being run over by a "Handy Van" driving fast on the slippery streets.

***

Bud was behind the wheel of the work van, sweating despite the cold. Having just received a call from Gary Smithers, he was on his way to pick him up, which would make him late for his next official pick up. He really didn't like that guy.

Bud came within a hair's breadth of nailing some Mexican guy crossing the street in front of him. He didn't worry about the pedestrian, only seeing the near miss as proof the world was against him. Meeting Pastor Wolfrum had, at first, seemed a great stroke of luck. He got Bud this very job and filled him with talk of helping the new order that was coming. He was also helped by Reverend Morry and his tent church community. With them, he felt large and in charge, and it seemed his life would finally straighten itself out. Then, he saw Wolfrum carried away by thousands of ravens through a round window in that Lutheran Church like something out of a horror movie. After that, Reverend Morry packed up his tent and left town.

Bud skidded to a stop at a red light and cursed. Gary Smithers had called him out of the blue, saying Pastor Wolfrum had given him the number and to drop everything and pick him up. He didn't realize that getting out of jail with help from whatever church Wolfrum belonged to would commit him to serving them for life. He honked at a family crossing the street when a child fell and made him wait. Traffic was terrible. What idiots.

When he heard Gary's voice on the phone, it made his hair prick up on the base of his neck and put him on edge. He wanted to keep driving out of Merryville and maybe go back to living on the streets, but "Yes, sir," is what he said. Tired of thinking, he cranked up Slayer to an ear-splitting level and drove toward Lincoln Avenue, near where he'd left him the night before. He saw Gary slouched on a bus bench and pulled over to let him in for whatever fresh hell was next.

***

Inside Merry Hearts, Lulu was making her last rounds before taking a nap. Jerry was finally sleeping, their chess game over, and the snow had lost its novelty. She had spoken with colleagues at the police station, who informed her a bulletin was going out soon, asking folks to stay off the streets. She thought about the things she'd seen months ago at Fowler Tax Services when she was a security guard at the strip mall. She suspected something otherworldly was afoot. She didn't dwell on the past, but she had a feeling her brush with strangeness wasn't over.

She stretched and poked her head into each patient's room to do a head count. When she reached Aurora's room at the end of the hall, the door was closed. She almost kept walking but thought it better to have a thorough count. She quietly turned the doorknob and saw that the bed nearest the door was still empty. A curtain between that bed and Miss Aurora's bed, which was next to the window, was pulled for privacy. She peeked around the curtain and saw that her bed was empty, too, as was the wheelchair parked in its usual spot by the window. She checked the bathroom and headed to the nurses' station to see if they knew Aurora's whereabouts.

***

Meanwhile, Ekk was at Taggart's, talking to Ralph about the heating, when the wall phone rang. Ralph picked it up and squinted, like that would make him hear better. "Who? Oh, yes, Miss Lulu. What?"

Ekk listened as Ralph hung up and relayed the news that Aurora was missing. "I'm going to find her. You comin'?"

"I am." They locked up the store and piled into the truck. Traffic was heavy with a line of cars headed out of town. They turned down Main Street and saw snow piled up at the base of buildings and traffic lights. This was more than the earlier flurries. The news channel was on, and an announcer said, "By order of the mayor, all citizens are to return to their homes and keep the streets clear for emergency vehicles. Until it is known what is causing this climate anomaly, we ask all residents to voluntarily comply. This is a public service announcement."

Ekk saw red lights up ahead. An officer was directing traffic and knew they would be deterred from their mission. "Ralph, trust me on this. We're not going to find her this way. Take me back to the store. Go down this side alley and turn around."

Ralph was fierce. "No! This is my wife, Ekk. She's probably out in the snow. I'll walk if I have to in order to find her." He reached for the door release.

Ekk put his right hand on Ralph's sleeve and said, "Ralph, buddy, you're both in your eighties. It won't help Aurora if you end up in the hospital or dead with the cold. Trust me. She's magical, and we can track her down with a little help. I need a quiet place to contact the Garden."

Ralph seemed to understand the wisdom in this plan. "Then let's go back to the store. I got boots I can wear in the snow." Ekk nodded, grateful.

When they pulled the old truck to the front of the store, the door was encased in a thin sheet of ice. "This is a bad business," Ralph said. He got a tool out of the back of the truck to crack the icy shell and dug in his pocket for the key. "Seems like the store is getting the brunt of this storm."

Ekk was thoughtful and didn't respond except to say, "That's curious."

CHAPTER FIFTEEN

The Goodens and Twyla had left for Colorado, and Puddle was now home tinkering in the shed. After an hour or so of decompressing on the couch, I said to Mitzi, "When's Ekk coming back? He's been gone for a while." Elsa came rushing in through the sliding glass door from the backyard. She'd changed her Mary Janes for bright blue boots. She wore stretch pants and a sweatshirt that said, "Let it Snow." Her hair was only half braided, and I'd have laughed, except Elsa's expression was serious.

"Do you need help with your hair?" Mitzi asked, and suppressed a smile.

Elsa frowned. "Girls, we received a message from the Garden. Things are happening now. Where's Puddle?"

Mitzi got serious immediately. "Out in the shed. What things? And where's Ekk?"

Elsa sputtered. "He-he's with Ralph. Aurora's missing."

I tried to make sense of it. "Ralph's wife? But she's in a facility."

Elsa held up Ekk's dagger and waggled it. "She walked out twenty minutes ago. Let's get our message." Elsa placed the dagger on the floor near the dining room table. When she moved a ruby, the dagger started to spin. This was the method Ehrenhardt chose to deliver news, something about it being part of an old treaty that, if used in moderation, wouldn't trigger a violation of the no magic rule in the human world.

Mitzi, now a pro, asked, "Is this a live message or a recorded one?"

"I think it's recorded," Elsa said. "Now hush."

A tiny three-dimensional image of Mitzi's father in his chambers appeared. "Greetings to my daughter and guardians."

"Don't mind me," I whispered. "Am I chopped liver?"

"You're a guardian too." Elsa said this quickly, and I was stunned to consider that.

"Oh."

Puddle entered from the backyard. "Hey, guys," was immediately followed by, "Oh wow, what's that?"

"Communication from the Hercynian Garden," I replied.

My sister was riveted. "Cool."

Now all three of us shushed her, as Puddle joined us around the hologram.

Ehren stated, "When I returned from your world, we had much cause for celebration. Although Wolfrum also returned to Germany, he was diminished. We heard his own monks have put him in the dungeon at Schwartzwald Castle. We don't know yet who ordered that. Apparently, they have a new leader who is outside of Germany."

"So he's not dead," I said with wonder.

Mitzi shivered and took my hand. "Been in that dungeon. It's not nice."

I squeezed her hand. I knew that Mitzi being kidnapped and kept in that evil place was no picnic.

"A new leader has emerged," Ehren said. "Things are shifting. All we know is they are taking over. It's not a singular person."

Puddle asked, "They?"

"He can't hear you, Puddle," I said.

Mitzi and Elsa shushed us both again.

"I want you all here with me. It's become too dangerous for you in Merryville. We have heard of the cold, and it's only a taste of what is to come. This new leader or leaders may be in Europe, but the origins are a fog. Oh, and one of ours has awakened in Merryville. Bring Aurora to the Garden."

As the vision faded, I asked, "Ralph's wife? From the store?"

"That's the only Aurora I've ever heard of," Mitzi said. "Elsa can you make anything of this?"

"Only what you heard. At least Wolfrum is no longer a threat to us."

"But they? Them? Sounds like a bad fifties movie," I said.

Elsa cocked her head at me.

"You know, science gone wrong?" I shrugged, Ekk would have gotten the reference.

"I'm not hiding in the Hercynian Forest," Mitzi said. "My father and I talked about this. My life is here."

"I don't think we have a choice, or at least Ekk and I don't," Elsa said. "Ehrenhardt's our leader and we must obey." She wore a sad face. "We swore an oath. I'm going to call Ekk now." She left to get her phone.

"Man, I remember when this place used to be boring," Puddle said. "Ali's daughter took him back to Egypt. I think Ehren had something to do with that too. No one's supposed to know about it."

"Good thing you can keep a secret," I said, irony dripping off my words. "Are we the only magic people in town?" I was starting to doubt my decision to stay.

Mitzi put her beaded hair behind her ears, and commented, "Think about it, Puddle. Now me, Panda, Elsa, and the cat know too. I wonder who else does." Brutus lifted his head from his warm spot on the hearth and gave a meow, probably saying he knew too.

"Shouldn't we be leaving as well?" Puddle asked. "Maybe it's a good idea to go to Germany, you know, the Garden. I'd love to actually see it, get the full tour."

Mitzi's lips were pressed in a resolute fashion. She glared at us.

I sort of agreed. "And, I mean, how can we human people fight this evil?"

Mitzi put her hands on each of my shoulders. "I'm not just people. I'm half-griffin."

Elsa stood up straighter and said, "And I have my *Zauberbuch*."

"And maybe I have ravens?" I said uncertainly. "Haven't seen one in a while, so I'm not sure."

Elsa said, "I'll talk to Ekk, but maybe we should push back a little."

Puddle ran her hand through her hair and said, "Hoo. This was a bad time to get sober."

***

It had been surprisingly easy to leave the facility. She was quiet and walked toward a side door that was usually armed. She lightly touched the bar with both hands. It had been a long time since she used her gentle magic. The door swung open silently, and she knew the universe worked with her because she was on an urgent mission. She walked in a daze, knowing nothing except where she must go. Not dressed for the weather, wearing a nightgown and simple robe, her slippers quickly became wet from fallen snow. She didn't feel the cold as she was drawn toward the place where she'd spent the most wonderful years of her life with Ralph.

Ralph—she wanted to tell Ralph but didn't know how to find him. She would do the work that must be done herself. Taggart's Emporium was six blocks away from Merry Hearts Memory Care, and, although she occasionally slipped, she kept moving determinedly forward.

***

About three blocks away from the facility, Bill slowed down his silver Volvo and pulled to the curb six feet in front of Aurora. Hortense rolled down her window and yelled, "Bill, hurry and get her in the car. That's Aurora Brown."

Bill stepped out of the car to guide Aurora toward the back seat, but she resisted.

"No, I must go to our store."

"Mrs. Brown, Aurora, it's freezing and the store's closed. Get in the car, and I'll take you wherever you want to go. We need to get you out of the snow. You're not dressed for it."

She hesitated, and Hortense got out of the car. "Aurora, darling, it's been a long time. Where are you going?"

"To find that box."

"Where's Ralph, honey?"

"The store."

"I really think—"

Aurora's eyes were fierce and focused as she stared into Hortense's eyes. "TAKE ME TO THE STORE!"

Bill and Hortense locked eyes. Sometimes married spouses didn't need words. Hortense was sure Bill agreed that they weren't taking this addled senior to the store.

"Okay. Get in the car, and we'll take you to Taggart's," Hortense lied.

With that, the old woman allowed herself to be guided into the back seat. Hortense said to Bill, "I'll sit back here with her."

Bill turned up the heat in the car and headed toward Merry Hearts Memory Care facility.

In the back seat, Aurora started singing:

"It's time for the change
I can feel in my bones
The world must rearrange
In the Circle of Stones."

"That's lovely, Aurora. Did you learn that as a child?"

Aurora didn't answer. She turned to the window and watched a rivulet of moisture drip down the glass.

***

Gary Smithers reached for the van's passenger door before Bud had even stopped the vehicle. He clutched a long bundle in his right hand and jumped in. "What took you so long? Go, go, go!"

"I got here as soon as I could. Traffic is terrible."

"Take me to that memory care place."

"You mean Merry Hearts?"

"Yes. Are you deaf or something?" With that, Gary went into the back of the van, sat on a box, and unwrapped his bundle. Bud saw it was a long gun of some sort.

Gary opened it and barked, "Keep your eyes on the road."

He did and heard the thing being loaded. At a red light he turned around and saw that Gary, in his haste, had dropped several shells. They rolled around on the metal floor as the light turned green. "Wha-what are you going to do at the old folks home?"

In his most sinister voice, Gary said, "Here's what you need to know. Just pull around back, and then go about your business. You didn't see me. You know nothing."

Bud pulled up near the willow trees in the back of Merry Hearts, and Gary snatched up his bullets and gun. "Bud, I know where you are and what you're doing at all times. You should remember that."

With those words, he went out the back of the van. As soon as the sliding side door slammed shut, Bud pealed out.

***

Lulu was fit to be tied. She had let Aurora slip through her fingers after promising to protect her. After talking to her police colleagues, who searched without success, and watching the weather get worse, it was with great relief that she saw a silver Volvo pull up in front of the center with Aurora in the back seat. "Thank God." She picked up her phone and hit redial. "Ralph. Aurora's back. Hang on, um, stand by."

She was out the glass doors in a hot second and helped bring Aurora in, still holding the cell phone. "Where did you find her?"

Hortense answered with an appalled voice. "My husband and I were on Main Street and saw her freezing in this flimsy gown. How can this happen? Are any other residents missing? I—"

Lulu cut in. "Thank you very much, Mrs.?"

"Miller. And I think Bill and I will wait right here for an administrator. I don't know her well but—"

Jennifer, a nurse, came rushing up and said, "Aurora, let's get you in some warm clothing." She said to the Millers, "Let's all go inside."

Lulu said into the phone, "Mr. Brown, a Mr. and Mrs. Miller found your wife and brought her back. Yes, yes, I'll sit outside her door until you show up."

They had barely cleared the entrance doors when a bullet destroyed the glass, and Bill Miller grabbed his ear. Blood ran through his fingers.

Although trained for active shooter situations, Lulu didn't carry a gun on her rounds at Merry Hearts.. She yelled, "Active shooter, everyone in their rooms!" Lulu grabbed Hortense and Bill and shoved them together into the first room that happened to be empty. At the same time, Jennifer crouched on the floor of the hall with her patient and covered Aurora, who appeared to be frozen in place. The bland music Merry Hearts played that normally could barely be heard above the daily noises, echoed cheerfully in the empty hallway. Lulu poked out her head and stage-whispered to Jennifer, "Go into the nurses' lounge." She pointed twice for effect and Jennifer nodded. Lulu's cell phone was still connected to Ralph, so she said quietly, "Shot fired. Don't come. Aurora's okay for now. Call the precinct and tell them Officer Tuigamala needs back up. That's Tui-, no Tuiga—Just say Lulu. I'll call you as soon as I can."

She clicked off and edged out into the hallway when another shot rang out, driving her back into the room with the Millers. Her phone rang, but she silenced it. Brittany, at reception, was under the desk, but at least Jennifer was able to get Aurora into the nurses' lounge. Brittany must have hit an emergency button because a pre-recorded voice said, "Stay calm and return to your room. This is not a drill. Stay calm and stay in your room until further notice."

Gary walked through the shattered front door and shouted, "Aurora, I've come to get you."

***

Ralph had been jiggling cold metal keys into the lock at Taggart's when the call from Lulu came in. At first, he and Ekk were relieved. Aurora was found. Ralph had rushed into the store to grab boots for the snow and to throw a hunter's cap on. Ready to leave, he broke out in a grin. "Hallelujah."

That changed seconds later when Lulu whispered, "Shot fired. Don't come." Without waiting for Ekk he ran out into the snowy streets, only to slip and fall hard.

Ekk helped Ralph and left him leaning on the brick wall outside the store. "I'll get the truck."

Ralph grabbed his hip and said through gritted teeth, "But the traffic."

Ekk responded, "We'll get to Aurora faster and safer even with the traffic. It's dying down anyway. People are getting off the street. You okay?"

"Not really. Just get the truck."

By the time they reached the memory care center, the façade was bathed in red and white pulsating lights. Police surrounded the perimeter. Ralph opened the truck door before they were even stopped but found he couldn't get out unaided. "Ekk, I did something to my hip."

Ekk, so much shorter, helped the six-foot former footballer as best he could, and Ralph hobbled toward the police line. He shouted, "My wife's in there."

An officer approached him. "Sorry, sir, but you have to stay back. Let us do our jobs."

Ralph tried to push past the crowd but grabbed his hip again and cried out in pain. He really had hurt himself when he fell. Ralph cried in frustration. "Aurora." Ekk grabbed his arm and dragged him toward a bench. "Sit here. We need help."

Ralph said "Who?"

Ekk pointed at the Land Rover. "Those people right there."

***

Mitzi parked the Land Rover, and she, Puddle, Elsa, and Panda poured out to surround Ralph, who was clearly in pain.

"Puddle, you stay here with Ralph," Ekk said.

Ralph said, "No, I'm coming." When he moved, he groaned.

Puddle said, "You're in no shape to do that. You and I need to stay put, okay? Let them do their thing."

Ralph asked, "How are you going to get past the police?"

"No time to explain," Ekk replied, "but you stick with Puddle."

Puddle waited with Ralph on the bench when a man in his thirties, with PRESS on a lanyard around his neck, approached them. "Hi, I'm with the *Merryville Bee*. Aren't you a friend of the Fowlers?"

"I'm Panda Fowler's sister. Why?"

"I need to speak to her wife, Mitzi, and would love to talk to her, too, actually."

Ralph let out a groan. He tried to get up again, unsuccessfully.

Puddle said, "Excuse us, his wife is in Merry Hearts." She indicated with a head movement toward the building.

Instantly, the reporter sat down next to Ralph. "I'm Phillip Pen, a reporter. I'm so sorry, sir. What's your name?" He pulled out a pad.

"I'm Ralph Brown. My wife's name is Aurora. Maybe you can get me closer." He broke down crying as they heard another blast.

"Sorry, sir, they won't let me in either." Phillip handed his card to Puddle. "I know this isn't a good time, but we want the truth about everything going on in our town. I'll find out what I can, okay?"

Ralph nodded.

To Puddle he said, "Please ask your sister to call me."

Puddle tucked the card in her back pocket and put her arm around Ralph.

***

Ekk Turned to the rest of us and said, "Panda, you and Mitzi come with us." He and Elsa led us to a corpse of trees where thick bushes blocked us from view.

Elves were able to do simple magic to carry out their duties as guardians. One of the most practical pieces of magic was the creation of an elf hole connecting one place to another underground. Elsa also had the additional power to calm a situation temporarily. She concentrated while Ekk did calibrations for the elf hole. To Mitzi and me he said, "Okay ladies, once we're in, we need to move quickly."

I was scared but nodded.

Mitzi said, "Quickly, and get Aurora."

We heard more shotgun blasts. Mitzi flinched at each one.

Elsa turned and said, "It's done." She stepped aside to reveal a roughly hewn hole in the ground that was completely dark. "Go now. This won't last long."

I was worried. "What do you mean? Will it close up? Is the hole all the way through to inside?"

"It's fine, no time for a long discussion. Yes, it goes through to the hospital place. Who do you think I am, Twyla?" Elsa was irritated, but I knew it was because she was under so much stress.

I edged toward the hole in spite of my fears, but Ekk said, "Wait, I should go first. I'll text you when it's safe to come."

"My shoulders are tingling," Mitzi said with surprise. This was a sign her wings might deploy. Her eyes were wide with alarm.

He gently laid his hand on her shoulder and gave it a shake. "Trust us." Ekk quickly checked to ensure his cell phone was securely zipped in a pocket. "Now, let's go save these people."

Elsa put her arm around Mitzi. "It'll be okay. Physics exist even in magic, so your wings won't spring out in a tight place."

With that, we all watched Ekk dive headfirst into the dark hole.

Mitzi pointed to Elsa, and we saw her stand in the snow, eyes closed, lips moving.

"I think she's inside the center calming things down," I said. "At least, I hope so."

We kept checking our cell phones, not sure which number Ekk would use. Two minutes later we both got the text. "Temporarily calm. Come now."

Without hesitation Mitzi jumped in, and I jumped in right behind her. What if we ended up under the tree in our backyard? What if the tunnel collapsed? I really needed to ask more questions if we made it through this. The tunnel smelled of dirt, but I was kept in the center of it as if gravity kept me from hitting the walls. The sensation only lasted a minute before I came spinning out of the hole onto a shiny floor in the cafeteria of Merry Hearts. Mitzi quickly followed, which was puzzling. "How did I get ahead of you? You went in first."

Ekk stood at the door of the cafeteria. "Shhh. Later. This door leads to a hallway," he whispered.

"I'm dizzy," Mitzi said and shook her head. "What's the plan?"

CHAPTER SIXTEEN

Sound from outside Merry Hearts hospital drifted in, and I heard someone speaking into a microphone. "Gary Smithers! The hospital is surrounded. Come out now and nobody has to get hurt." There was silence, as if the person who made the announcement waited for a response. Meanwhile, Ekk, Mitzi, and I worked our way toward the hallway. I whispered to Ekk, "We don't have a weapon."

"Yes, we do," Ekk said. "Well, a shield anyway."

Elsa slid onto the floor and said, "I'm okay. I can hold him for about a minute." She stayed where she landed and closed her eyes. "Go."

I opened the cafeteria door, and Ekk and I ran into a man in a wheelchair who demanded to know, "What's going on?"

Ekk said quietly. "Go in the kitchen with my wife and stay quiet."

"Where's Lulu?"

I stepped forward and grabbed the handles on his wheelchair to guide him in. "Here we go. What's your name?"

"Jerry. Where's Lulu?" He was being belligerent, but I saw he was scared.

"Lulu?"

"Yeah. The security guard. She and I play chess." Mitzi motioned for Ekk and me to go while she kept Jerry quiet as Elsa concentrated. I knew we needed to move fast so as not to lose the brief respite Elsa was providing.

Ekk led as we walked down the shiny hallway. I was hoping the security guard was my old friend from the strip mall. I also hoped ravens would somehow show up, as we really had no plan. I could hear soft music playing from the overhead speakers, punctuated by sobbing from various rooms. Another blast from the shotgun made us both jump. I pointed and Ekk nodded, as we now knew which hallway to go to.

The voice from outside, which I assumed came from a police negotiator, rang out again. "Gary. You're surrounded with nowhere to go. Let's end this. You'll be safe if you come out now."

I heard Gary sing through the now open front door, "Whatever it takes, I will do what I gotta do."

I looked at Ekk and said, "He's singing Gabriella Cilmi songs." We moved stealthily down the hall toward Gary's voice.

***

Lulu heard who she assumed to be Gary Smithers shout out, "I'm on fire. I'm on a mission." Then another shotgun blast echoed through the building. She scanned the room for a place to hide Bill and Hortense. The tiny closet in the corner would only hold one of them, so this room wasn't an option.

"This is crazy," Hortense said and rushed toward the door. "We've got to get out of here." Lulu pulled her to a stop and put a finger to her lips to quiet her when Hortense began to whimper.

She motioned for Bill to follow them and pulled Hortense through the Jack and Jill bathroom into the next room. She heard what sounded like Gary kicking doors open, and she knew it wouldn't be long until he reached where they were.

She pulled soiled bedding out of an industrial sized hamper and put a chair beside it to allow Hortense and Bill to climb in. Once they were in, she covered them with bedding. "Be quiet and don't move," she whispered.

Lulu barely contained her girth in the closet, when she heard the door to the room they'd just evacuated kicked in. She quickly turned off her radio and held her breath. She wished mightily that she had her police weapon. For this security job, it hadn't been deemed necessary to carry one. The thought was an armed guard might disturb some of the occupants. She did have a billy club, and her hand went to it.

She heard crying down the hall and was itching to smash the shooter over the head with her truncheon. She prayed he wouldn't shoot one of the patients or staff. She listened carefully to what was going on and waited silently for Gary to walk past the room where she hid. She wanted to step out behind him with a surprise attack.

"One of you needs to say where Aurora Brown is. You send her out and we can all go home." He laughed maniacally. "Oh, that's right, you are home." Another blast rang out. "Aurora, come out, and no one else needs to get hurt." He giggled at that. "You and I both know why I'm here."

"Okay," he shouted, "this is fun, but I'm done playing, Aurora. If you don't come out now, I'll start picking off residents one by one. I'm going to count to three. One, two—"

***

Inside the nurses' lounge Jen tried to hold Aurora back, but she was surprisingly strong. She shook off the nurse and walked into the hallway. She had grey hair with streaks of auburn and pale, watery eyes that fixed on Gary. Her robe hadn't been replaced, and she left wet spots on the ground wherever her soaked slippers stepped.

"You found me, you bastard."

Gary said something to Aurora that Lulu couldn't make out. Unexpectedly, some characters she never thought she would see again turned the corner and stood behind her. Everyone in the hallway paused a millisecond in recognition.

***

Gary said, "Well, well, well. Ekk Schmidt. Thank you for bringing your little friend Panda and making my job so easy. Now I don't even have to come hunting for you."

I wondered anew why I was going to be "hunted" by Gary. I prayed Elsa was still doing her thing and wondered why Gary didn't hesitate as he pointed the shotgun toward us. Where were my ravens? It was true, I hadn't even tried to call them and didn't know how. This was all so new. Even so, time had run out.

Thank goodness Ekk shouted, "Gary, you're going to kill us for sure, so one more minute won't make a difference. Why do you want to kill Aurora? She's done nothing to you."

"Nothing. Not yet. And now, she won't." He giggled.

Aurora looked blankly at Ekk and Panda. She turned around. "Ralph?"

I said, "Ralph's outside, waiting for you."

"I must help him at Taggart's."

Gary said, "How heartwarming. If this were a Hallmark movie, we'd all start hugging. But alas." He reloaded and snapped the gun shut with a metallic sound. "It's not." He lifted the shotgun, ready to shoot.

Mitzy rounded the corner and said, "Gary. We know you and Doug Harker had an affair. I know your image was built on a lie." She was beautiful. At some point after coming out the elf hole, her white wings had deployed, but instead of making her fly, they trailed behind her, like a cape. She was regal, like an angel, or the true daughter of a king.

He frowned and pointed the shotgun at her, as she put a wing in front of her face. The gun jammed. Lulu, a strong Samoan woman, rushed Gary from behind and head-butted Gary's shotgun arm up. The rifle unstuck, and it went off, destroying a ceiling light fixture. Hortense came running and beaned the shooter hard on the head with a bedpan. He staggered but wasn't completely down. He lifted his hands and yelled, "*Animatus.*"

Suddenly, seniors began shuffling from their rooms like zombies, adding confusion to the scene. Mitzi calmly walked toward Gary and said, "*Mora.*"

"Mitzi?" I asked.

She turned to me. "It means delay. Oh, watch out!"

The man who had earlier identified himself as Jerry was in a motorized wheelchair aimed directly at me. I turned around and got painfully nicked by his foot support as he sped by. He then aimed at Ekk.

While Ekk and I dealt with this threat, Lulu gamely wrestled with Gary on the linoleum floor. Hortense stood over them with the bedpan and tried to hit him, but Lulu kept getting in the way. Elsa finally entered the scene from around the corner. She was limping, probably another victim of Jerry's wheelchair. She closed her eyes and was able to chill things out for a brief moment before slumping to the floor.

Ekk ran to her. The spell had been broken, and patients came back to themselves, meandering, stunned, and confused.

Lulu wrenched the shotgun from Gary's hands and leapt to her feet, turning it around on him. The man actually growled at her, and Hortense gave him another mighty whack with the metal bedpan. She seemed willing to keep hitting him, but Mitzi stopped her. "That's enough, Hortense. Thank you." Bill finally poked his head out of the room where he'd been hiding, blood on the left side of his head.

Hortense drew up to her full height and stared at Mitzi. "You're wearing a costume?"

My wife turned halfway so she could get a better look at her wings. "Nope, they're real."

Hortense reached out and lightly stroked one of her wings gingerly as they began to recede. Lulu kept her eyes on Gary as she got on her radio. "All clear. Subject has been subdued."

A mighty cheer rose up outside, as officers flooded in. Jennifer and Brittany began herding the elders back to their rooms.

Hortense, after checking that Bill was stable, walked to where Mitzi and I stood, sharing a hug. Any evidence Mitzi had sported wings mere moments ago was gone. "Mitzi, I…" The woman was at a loss for words. Of all the things Hortense could have said, she only managed, "You know Latin. You said *mora*."

Mitzi laughed. She'd been through a few of these magical showdowns and was not as discombobulated as Hortense. "Thanks for saying my name right."

Hortense pointed to where Mitzi's wings had been. "Are you an angel?"

Ekk cleared his throat, a warning to Mitzi not to say too much.

Mitzi simply said to Hortense, who had treated her like a dummy, "There are more things in heaven and earth, Hortense, than are dreamt of by your philosophy."

Hortense tilted her head with respect. "Shakespeare, well done. Hortense instead of Horatio." She smiled. "Clever." She looked back at Bill, who was pitifully holding his bloody ear with a shaky hand. "I need to take care of Bill, but I'd like to talk later."

Mitzi said, "Yes, we need that."

It was me, as usual, who broke up the seriousness of the moment. "By the way, Hortense, way to go with that bedpan." I lifted my hand to high five and got a half-hearted tap back. Ekk, Elsa, and Mitzi laughed at that, and we watched a handcuffed Gary being perp-walked down the hallway to a waiting police car.

Lulu came over to us and gave me and Mitzi a big hug. "I'm so glad you're okay."

Mitzi grabbed her shoulder. "Thank you, Lulu. Hey, I thought you were a cop?"

Lulu adjusted her leather belt and replied, "I am. This is usually my easy side job."

"Why work so hard?" I asked.

"I'm saving up for a house." She pointed toward Ekk. "This guy." Lulu made hand gestures at Mitzi in the shape of her now retracted wings. "And you, Mitzi. I want to know more. We never did get to talk about it after last time at the tax office."

I put my hand on Lulu's arm. "Awwww. You need closure. I'm so sorry. That's my bad. This year has been so crazy busy that—"

"It's okay, um," she pulled out a card from her wallet and handed it to me. "Call me and let's have lunch or something, okay?"

Ekk said to Lulu, "Please tell no one about, you know. And by the way, you appear to make quite a guardian."

"It's my job." She laughed from her belly. "I'm a natural." At his quizzical facial expression, Lulu continued. "Guardian. That's what I do. I protect." She impulsively mussed Ekk's hair, which he awkwardly received. "Thanks, little buddy. Glad that motorized chair didn't take you and Panda out." She took them all in with her merry eyes and said, "Now, I gotta go debrief with my team."

Mitzi, in high spirits, did a salute and said, "Thanks, officer.

Ekk smoothed his hair and said, "Little buddy?" He chuckled.

***

Doug Harker and Monte Hunt sat across from the mayor at his desk when a call came in from the police chief. Tom Reed gave his friends a thumbs up as he said into the phone, "Thanks for the call. You just make sure that son of a bitch never sees the light of day."

Monte sighed. "They got him? That's great."

No one in the room appeared more relieved than Doug who said, "Hallelujah. Make sure they throw away the key this time."

Tom got up. They'd been discussing whether or not to go forward with the press briefing the next day. "Now let's get back to the plan for tomorrow. It's time to talk about our fabulous Merryville police. Find me that officer who was inside the memory care." He clapped his hands. "That sure takes the wind out of Francisco Gonzalez' sails. Ha."

Doug exhaled. "I can already feel the Ring Tire problem receding."

"What a relief," Monte said. "It'll be nice to have the press conference without having public safety thrown in our faces by that Francisco. Talk about timing."

"I'll call my committee members. I'll see you at city hall at noon tomorrow." Doug stood and put on his jacket.

Tom said, "Hey, wait. This calls for a drink." He reached into a deep drawer. "Stay, Doug. I've got some special cognac here. Let's have a toast." He pulled out a cut-glass bottle and three shot glasses.

Doug jingled the keys in his pocket. "Sorry, guys, but my wife's been out of town. She'll be getting ready for dinner when I get home. I'm taking her somewhere special."

"You two are like honeymooners," Monte said.

"Okay, if you have to leave the party, tell me quickly about the committee first. We need to know Mitzi Fowler is one hundred percent on board. I don't need any more surprises."

"She's intimidated." Doug said. "She knows she's not at the same level as the rest of us. She'll be fine." He imitated her with a mincing voice. "I'm just so pleased to be asked."

The men laughed.

"That's good," Tom said. "Now go on. Get out of here, you lovebird. We'll see you tomorrow."

Doug left and dropped the smile as soon as he was out of sight. As the door closed, he saw them pour shots to celebrate Gary Smither's capture.

Margaret, long suffering secretary to the mayor, must have caught the expression on his face.

"Everything okay, Mr. Harker?"

He quickly pasted on his smile again. "Sorry, Margaret, I'm thinking about those poor people who were held hostage at the memory care center."

She nodded with solidarity. "I know. Thank goodness they caught him." She was probably impressed about his care for others.

Doug walked out of the office, silently praying any connection he'd had with Gary Smithers would never be discovered. He would be on the straight and narrow from now on, no matter what it took. He needed badly to go home and take his wife out to dinner, maybe that fancy place she'd been bugging him about.

***

Laura Harker was glad to be home from Atlanta. She had many files with her from her Junior League conference and lots of ideas for the local crew. It had been a productive time, but she was tired. Her loving husband had sent a driver to pick her up from the airport, and all she could think about was a bath in her jacuzzi tub. A snippet from "Hello" by Adele sounded from one of her bags. She located her iPhone and put it to an ear after seeing Denise McGreggor was the caller. "Denise. On my way home from the *aeropuerto*. How are you?"

She listened, and her face crumpled a bit. "Surely that can't be correct. I'll talk to Doug, but I'm sure whoever you talked to has their facts wrong. Thanks for the call. I'll get back to you."

The call disturbed her, but what she found at home later disturbed her much more. Cesar greeted Laura at the door and loped behind her as she made a beeline for the bedroom. She and Doug each had their own bed and bath. Hers was all French and pink while his was decorated with more masculine colors of tan and brown. The maid had prepared her a bath as ordered, and it smelled scrumptious, almost wiping the call from her old friend Denise out of her mind. In fact,

Denise must be out of her mind. After Denise came back from Europe to Merryville married to a woman, Laura had distanced herself a bit. Now Denise was claiming her husband's planning committee had done something wrong with that garden for the poor. The woman was turning into a very left-wing wacko in her opinion. Tired, she shucked her clothing and walked through her picture-perfect designer bedroom into the bath. She stepped into the bubbles, slid down until the hot water reached the bottom of her chin, and closed her eyes. Heaven. Her pedigree Doberman, Cesar, was happy to see her but somewhat agitated.

The dog kept coming into the bathroom and whining. She opened one eye and said, "What is it, boy?" He came up to the edge of the bath and dropped what appeared to be a rubber ball in it. She laughed and said, "Oh, baby boy, we can throw the ball when daddy gets home." She fished around for it in the suds. The ball wasn't a ball. It was a butt plug. She only knew about those from the very brief time during their marriage when her husband was trying to spice up their sex life. While raised to defer to men, Laura had drawn a line, banning such things. They never spoke of it again.

She asked him, "Where did you get this, Cesar?" He lay on the bathroom rug, staring at her. She closed her eyes again, thinking Doug had better have a good reason for not throwing away the sex toy years ago.

CHAPTER SEVENTEEN

THE AFTERMATH

Puddle told an officer posted near the smashed front door of Merry Hearts that Aurora's husband was outside on the bench and needed to see her. She waved over his shoulder at Ekk, Hortense, Mitzi, and Panda. Mitzi waved back. They appeared to all be in one piece, and she was relieved at that.

While those involved in the active shooter situation answered questions, Nurse Jennifer, after putting her patient in warm clothing, took Aurora Brown out to see her husband.

As they approached him and a frizzy haired girl on a bench, Jennifer called out, "Hello, Mr. B."

He tried to stand but grimaced. "Hello, Miss Jennifer. Aurora. Come here, baby." Ralph held out his arms. It was cold, but at least it had stopped snowing. Aurora let herself be hugged, then stepped back and said, "Ralph, we need to go to the store. We've got work to do."

He patted her back. "Honey, you're retired, remember?" A paramedic came over and said, "We need to take you to emergency now, sir. You may have a broken hip."

Aurora got that stubborn, clear, fixated stare she had worn inside Merry Hearts. "I must go to Taggart's. Then I'll come see you. I have work to do." She glanced at Jennifer. "Take me to Taggart's."

"Ralph, I'm sorry, but I had to tell them you got hurt," Ekk said.

Puddle said, "I did too. He's in a lot of pain."

A young paramedic rolled a gurney up. "We're taking Mr. Brown to Merryville General to check him out. Come on, sir."

Ralph was agitated. "Do I get a say in this? Gah!" He was clearly in pain.

After the paramedics got Ralph on the gurney, he grabbed Ekk's shirt sleeve. "Do me a favor? Here are my keys to the store. Take Aurora and bring her to me at the hospital if I'm still there. And check on Ratter. *Please.*"

Ekk fixed his blue eyes on Ralph and said, "Sure, we'll see you soon." He put the keys in his pocket.

"Aurora's not going anywhere," Jennifer said. "I need to get her inside." She put her arms around Aurora protectively to gently guide her back.

Ekk pulled himself up and said firmly, "Nurse, I think this man and his wife deserve whatever they want right now. She wants to see where she used to work."

As they wheeled Ralph toward the ambulance, he called out to Jennifer, "It won't hurt nothing. These are good friends. Let 'em take her."

"Mrs. Brown has been involved in a traumatic experience," Jennifer said.

Luckily, Elsa walked up, and the scent of lavender surrounded all of them. Jennifer's expression turned relaxed and trusting. "Okay. But you be sure she's back for dinner. We eat at five p.m." She turned and went back into the building to make her statement to the police.

"Well done, Elsa," I said. "What's happened to Ralph?"

"He couldn't walk," Puddle said. "This feels like *déjà vu*. After the fire at the Eye of Horus. Ali, Valerie, and now Ralph have all had to take ambulances. At least those first two are on the mend."

"Ralph's no spring chicken." My two cents.

"I saw it happen," Ekk said. "Ralph fell pretty hard on the ice in front of the store."

"Ice?" Mitzi was incredulous. "Not snow?"

His brow furrowed. "The cold is worse at Taggart's. I think we all need to go investigate. Elsa?"

Elsa moved to Aurora and put her arm around her. At her touch, Aurora's eyes lit up. "Take me to work."

I quipped, "You heard what the lady said. Something's going on at Taggart's." Mitzi, Aurora, and Elsa went with me in the Land Rover. Puddle and Ekk followed us in Ralph's truck. None of us knew what to expect when we arrived at the store.

***

Sylvia drove to Francisco Gonzalez's campaign headquarters hoping to catch him, but it was closed. The snow was falling gently and, although alarming and strange, was actually pretty, covering cracked sidewalks and dirty streets. Downtown Merryville streets were fairly empty now, as people had either left town or gone home. On the radio, one story after another covered the big news in Merryville. If it wasn't about Gary Smither's capture, then it was all about the snow. She'd been shocked to hear Hortense Miller and her husband Bill were at the care center when the hostage situation occurred and wondered how she was.

She'd spent so much time thinking of Hortense as the enemy that wondering about her well-being was a new thought. When interviewed on the radio, Hortense uncharacteristically had few words to say. "But for the courageous actions of a few, this terrible incident would have ended in tragedy. Thankfully, my dear husband, Bill was only grazed by shotgun pellets. That's all."

Curiosity made her drive by Merry Hearts since it was on her way home. The crowd was dwindling in front of an area marked by yellow police tape. Her mouth dropped open when she spotted Bill and Hortense getting into their car. Bill sported a large white bandage on his left ear. Sylvia pulled her Mercedes to the curb behind them, got out, and called, "Hortense."

***

Sylvia sat in a vinyl-covered booth near the window lost in thought and watched people scurry like ants in the strange weather. She didn't notice the woman she was waiting for until she heard, "Well, I'm here." Hortense towered over the table, wearing a parka and gloves. She scooted in the booth and removed the gloves from her fingers, one by one.

"I'm glad you agreed to meet. It's high time we really talked." Sylvia stirred her Waffle House coffee. For the last half an hour, she'd sat in the booth, thinking of what to say.

Hortense adjusted herself and her bag on the vinyl seat, which made a crackling sound. "Thanks for waiting for me. Bill really needed to get home."

She sipped coffee. "I know, poor man. Poor you. Can you tell me what happened?"

"In time. But is that why we're here?" Hortense smiled her predatory smile at the server, who placed a thick cup in front of her.

The woman wore a hoodie over her uniform, a nod to the cold. Although it wasn't snowing on the outskirts of town, it was still chilly.

"We didn't have Earl Grey tea. I hope this'll do."

At first Sylvia thought Hortense might send it back. She radiated disapproval.

"Did you put the milk in first like I asked?"

"Yes, ma'am."

"Good girl." The server, who was easily over forty, made a pained face and walked back behind the counter.

"Sorry, this was the only place open what with, you know." Sylvia's eyes indicated the snow outside.

Hortense sipped her tea. "Lipton's. It could be worse."

As current president of the Merryville Horticultural Society, Sylvia felt it was her duty to extend an olive branch. "Hortense, I hope we can do a reset."

"Why now?"

"We've all been through a lot this past year, and the club has suffered. Now I'm afraid we have even more bad news about our community garden project."

"Oh? I don't think much could surprise me anymore."

"First, can we bury the hatchet? I know we have differences of opinion."

Hortense snorted. "I'll say."

"But there must be some middle ground for the good of the club." A couple of construction worker types passed the table and turned their heads at Sylvia, who was dressed as if she were going skiing in Aspen.

"The important meeting I missed because you called it at the last minute?"

"I tried calling you earlier. It was the only time Dr. Sliwa had. The professor at Merida University?"

"As you now know, I was busy being held hostage, but go on. Before you do, though, anything that woman has to say is suspect because she's friends with that Francisco Gonzalez." She made a face, and Sylvia was unsure whether it was due to having to say Francisco's name or due to the taste of the tea she had just sipped.

"That's the same thing Mitzi Fowler said."

At the mention of Mitzi's name, Hortense uncharacteristically said, "Well ,her instincts are good."

This surprised Sylvia. "Dr. Sliwa is a respected scientist in topsoil. Hortense, the project is tainted." She reached into her bag and pulled out the complete report. "As in, *completely polluted* by Ring Tire Company. The city is being accused of covering that up for some monetary reason."

"Really? I'm not so sure." Hortense put her rather large hand on the thick report and pulled it to her side of the table. "I'll read it, and tell you what I think. But. Remember an EIR has already been done on the property. Isn't Charlotte Windingle one of your friends? I'm sure her lawyers would have gone over the donation of Windingle property with a fine-tooth comb."

Sylvia pushed her saucer away. "Hortense, I'm not going to lie to you. I adore Charlotte, and her heart is always in the right place." For a moment the only sound was the clatter from the kitchen. "She's also impulsive and leaves the 'boring' parts to others. She's sick about this whole situation too."

Hortense lifted her eyebrows. "Well, when I was in charge of the club—"

Sylvia hit the table with the heel of her hand, making the crockery jump. "Dammit, Hortense. This is bigger than old grudges. I'm the president now, so get over it."

Hortense stiffened. "Is that why you called me here?" She started scooting herself out of the booth. "To curse at me?"

"Wait. I'm sorry." Sylvia took a deep breath and forced herself to say the next words. "Hortense, we need you."

Comically putting a hand to her ear, Hortense said, "I didn't hear you. What?"

Sylvia put her resentments aside. "We need you. And I'm sorry. I didn't ask you to this meeting at what must be an awful time to fight with you. I called all the board members. We need to halt this project now and get back to basics. This project is finished."

Hortense scooted back into the booth. "If you've already made a decision as president, then why do you need me?"

They stared at each other while a person bussed the table noisily at the next table. Sylvia heard sirens through the window.

"We both know you have juice in this town. The Merryville Horticultural Society needs to speak with one voice."

Hortense, always calculating, appeared interested. "And what will this one voice say?"

"That both the city of Merryville and the club will be suing Ring Tire for the cleanup. They created the pollution. They need to pay for it. All the donations that people have made we'll need to return, and that will become part of the damages. We'll be plaintiffs too."

"What about Charlotte?"

"Unfortunately, we'll probably need to name Windingle Development as a defendant. Her company has already tendered this to insurance. She's willing to do whatever it takes to make sure the Windingle name is on the right side of this fight."

"What does Mitzi Fowler say about this? She's on the commission. Shouldn't she be here?"

Sylvia wore a pained expression. "She's trying to walk a fine line. Honestly, I'm not sure what side she's on."

"Let's call Mitzi, and don't be so sure about the whole project being trashed."

Sylvia was confused.

Hortense laughed. "You really do need me." She tapped an index finger on her thick mug as if trying to decide. She waved at the server walking by. "Miss, I think I'll need another cup of tea."

***

Aurora said nothing on the way to Taggart's, and I started to wonder if this journey would be a bust. I turned the corner to where we could see the front of the store encased in ice, and that changed. Ekk rolled down his window and with frosted breath called out to me, "I'm going around the back to see if that's any better." I parked and waited, the heater on full blast to keep my car warm. Aurora scrambled to get her door open. When the scent of lavender filled the car, she settled down again. Pretty soon, Puddle and Ekk returned on foot, and I got out, saying to Mitzi, "This is gonna' take a minute. You two wait here with Aurora." I knew Mitzi and Elsa wanted in on whatever this action was, but Mitzi reluctantly agreed to wait and even climbed in the back.

"I'll stay and help keep Aurora in the car," Mitzi said. With Mitzi on one side of Aurora and Elsa on the other, she wasn't going anywhere until we got through the ice and into the store.

Puddle, Ekk, and I stood before the front door to Taggart's, and studied the solid ice. "What does this mean, Ekk?" Puddle asked, and pulled her coat tightly around her body.

He rubbed his chin and shivered. "It means we need to get inside and see what's going on."

I knocked on the block of ice. "Pretty solid. Looks like somebody forgot to defrost the freezer."

Puddle asked, "Do we need an ice pick?"

"Nope." Ekk raised his hand and said, "*Ignis.*"

Nothing happened where we were standing, but when I turned toward the cars, I saw Aurora becoming quite agitated. She flailed her arms as she said something I couldn't hear. A moment later Aurora, Mitzi, and Elsa exited the car.

Soon Aurora stood next to Ekk in front of the door. He tried to melt the ice again by saying, "*Ignis. Ignis.*" It reminded me of someone using a Bic lighter to melt a glacier.

"*Kowlleski,*" Aurora said with a strong voice, and water rushed down and covered our feet as the ice disintegrated under the instant magical heat.

"Well, okay," Puddle said. We all saw Aurora in a new light.

"You have some powerful magic," Elsa said, her voice filled with admiration.

"*Kowalski?* Some Polish last name?" I was curious. How come everyone else got these cool magic skills but me?

Elsa answered. "No, Panda. *kowlleski* is Cornish, from the southern part of the United Kingdom."

"Oh, Cornish. Huh. Now what?"

Ekk said to Aurora, "Let's do this one more time. Then I can open the door. Do you know what work you need to do?"

She didn't answer but lifted her arms and said, "*Kowlleski*" again. Any remaining ice melted, and even some ice on the other side of the door melted on the floor, some escaping under the bottom of the entryway.

Ekk said, "This is some pretty strong magic, girls. You better wait for us in the car."

"Girls?" Mitzi asked, scoffing. "Please. Get the door open."

He was surrounded by women on a mission and did as he was told. Upon opening the glass front door, lots more water rushed out. I charged in first, looked around, and pointed to the backroom. "It's coming from the storeroom." The cold was biting and seemed much more intense than it was outside the store.

Mitzi ran to the clothing section, slipping and sliding to stop in front of a rack of down hunting jackets. She handed them out. "Won't do to freeze to death while we're figuring this out."

The plastic flaps separating the back supply room and office from the retail part of the store were stiff with ice. They cracked when Ekk tried to move them. He said, "*Ignis,*" and nothing happened. Frustrated, he stepped back and let Aurora do her work. After another round of rushing water, this time from the storeroom, we all entered. It was dark. I flipped the light switch, but nothing happened.

"Be careful, Panda. With all this water, I don't want you electrocuted," Mitzi said. She had a point.

I said, "The electricity was probably knocked out by whatever this is." My arm sweep took in the area. It was clear we'd reached the eye of the storm.

Ekk ran back into the main part of the store and brought back lanterns. It took a minute, but soon the room of ice was lit, albeit with some shadows. An empty cat bed sat atop the antique safe.

"Oh my god, the cat. Didn't he have a cat?" Mitzi became frantic. The entire store was frozen solid, and that didn't bode well for a kitty.

Puddle said, "His name is Ratter, and Ralph loves him."

"He's a tough cat, and cats are smart," I said. "Mitzi, I bet he left when it started to freeze." I hoped against hope this was true and that we wouldn't find a frozen kitty body in this watery, icy mess.

With the lights revealing the storeroom, the view wasn't encouraging. Puddle asked, "Now what?" She studied the piles of boxes that stretched into the darkened corners of the room. Most of them wet and some still encased in ice. My feet were soaked.

"I've only worked here a few weeks," Ekk said guiltily. "We had a plan to work on it."

Mitzi stood surveying the many stacks with her hands on her hips, overwhelmed.

Aurora walked toward a pile stacked haphazardly and pointed. "Here."

"Okay, we have a place to start." Ekk asked her, "What do you think it is, Aurora?" Aurora was somewhat more aware than she had been and addressed Ekk, ignoring the others. It was as if they were the only two in the room. She simply said, "*Gorfen.*"

"*Gorfen*?" I asked Elsa. "What does that mean? Is that Cornish too?"

Elsa said, "Yes, it is. My Cornish is rusty, but I think it means *time.*"

I quipped, "Cornish. From Cornland?" Everyone ignored me.

Mitzi said, "She's saying we're running out of time. Open the boxes!"

Mitzi, Puddle, and I started toward the pile Aurora pointed to and simultaneously started ripping boxes apart. Ekk was still staring at Aurora, encouraging her to say more.

"Careful," Elsa yelled at us. "We don't know what's really in any of these containers."

The wet boxes opened easily and contained pet food, now ruined, screws and nails, and all the things one would expect at a store such as Taggart's. Once we inspected all the boxes in that pile, I started to doubt Aurora.

Her expression was vague again, as she pointed to another pile. "There."

Again, we attacked the pile with vigor, but we found no answers.

Tired and cold, Puddle said, "With all due respect, this is crazy. I'm freezing, and I'm not nearly as old as this lady." She hooked a thumb in Aurora's direction. "We should probably take her by the hospital and get her back to the, uh, you know."

"Memory care," I said.

But as vague as she appeared, she'd heard what Puddle said. "No. Work to do." So, freezing, wet, and somewhat discouraged, we tackled another new pile she indicated. Soon, I lifted a box triumphantly as if it were the cub in *Lion King*. "This one has German writing on it."

"Set it down gently," Ekk and Elsa said together.

Aurora looked tired. "That's the one." Some moisture dripped on her, and she shivered. Her eyes became vague again, and whatever energy had driven her to get to Taggart's had clearly left her body.

"Ekk, I'm worried about her," Elsa said. She's cold. I'll put her in the car with the heater."

He responded, "Good idea."

Mitzi went to Aurora and gave her a hug. "Thank you, Aurora. You did your work." This got a wan smile out of her.

"Mitzi, Puddle," I said to get their attention, "you should go too." I pointed at the mystery box. "You know, just in case." I tossed the car keys to Elsa. Aurora let Elsa lead her outside to the promised warmth of the car.

Mitzi shook her head. "If you stay, I stay." We stayed.

Puddle shivered but was resolute. "Nope."

"Ready?" Ekk sloshed closer to the box that was about a two-foot cube, as Mitzi moved a lantern closer. He said, "It's from Europe. It could be anything, but I'd bet my last ruby whatever is inside this box has caused all this." As he said this, he waved his short arms around, keeping his eyes on the mystery.

I nervously moved closer. "Could it be a bomb?" I was dying to know what this thing was but a little afraid to know at the same time. "Seriously, Mitzi? Maybe you should go outside with Elsa. You, too, Puddle."

Puddle was giving the box her rapt attention. "Uh-uh. Not a chance, Panda bear."

She moved some nearby boxes away so we could see what the German box said.

"I don't sense danger, but this is clearly magical," Ekk said.

This prompted me to say, "You know? I don't either. Let's open it."

Ekk was the one who went to the box and held his hand out like a surgeon. "Scissors?"

Mitzi placed scissors from Ekk's bookkeeping desk into his hand. "Here we go."

***

Outside, Elsa helped Aurora into the front seat that was only possible because she was compliant. She climbed into the driver's seat and immediately turned on the engine and cranked up the heat. It took a minute for the engine to warm, and she feared Aurora would get pneumonia with her wet feet. She turned the windshield wipers on to remove some of the snow from it so they could see, and they waited. Downtown Merryville was blanketed in white with literally no one on the street. The "Not Your Mother's Coffeehouse" and the old movie theater appeared to be out of a winter scene. She said to Aurora, "This snow has made downtown charming, although nothing can hold a candle to Germany when it comes to quaint villages." Aurora said nothing.

Elsa turned on the radio that announced a citywide curfew would be in effect through at least Monday by order of the mayor. Climatologists were brought in to study what has been dubbed the "miracle snow," and the phenomenon was garnering national attention. When the news changed to Gary Smithers, Elsa snapped it off. She knew what happened with him and didn't want to relive it.

While they waited to hear something from those inside, Elsa decided to try a little low-level treatment on Aurora with her magical scents. One scent she rarely used was poppy. It was known as the forgetfulness flower, and her elder friend certainly didn't need that. What many didn't know was that reversing the scent could be done quite easily and perhaps even reverse memory loss. She wondered…it could be a cure if Aurora's dementia was caused by magic. Ordinary mental difficulties could be overcome with magic but, like all magic in this world, would only be temporary. That was simply the physics between their worlds. Finally heat started pumping out through the vents in the dashboard. Now where was her *Zauberbuch* when she needed it?

Puddle tapped on the window. "I'll take her to see Ralph, Elsa. There appears to be a magic problem inside and you would be more help than me."

"Thank you, Puddle. That's a good idea. Your lips are blue." She patted Aurora's hand. "You and I are going to spend some time together soon." Aurora didn't respond, so she went back into the store to face whatever awaited.

CHAPTER EIGHTEEN

THE BOX

The cold near the box was biting, and a low hum was felt by us all. This was definitely the source of something. Ekk opened the top of the box with two gloved fingers and peeked inside. He said nothing, his facial features bathed in a light blue glow that emanated from inside the box.

Mitzi and I moved closer. Mitzi asked, "What is it?"

Ekk stared at the thing in wonder. "A Winter Stone. Oh boy. I suspected it might be but have never actually experienced one."

My wife hugged herself. "A rock? Is it dangerous?"

Ekk nodded. "It can be if left like this. Something, or someone, has switched it on."

I gestured toward the thing with my hands. "Well, switch it off."

"Panda, relax," Mitzi said and hugged me. "Ekk's got this."

He looked sheepish. "Actually, we need Elsa."

"I'm here." Elsa sloshed through the wet floor in the outer store.

"What's a Winter Stone?" Mitzi asked.

Ekk stroked his chin. "I've heard of stones like this that control the weather. Like good and evil, all are a matter of balance. They're supposed to be in a protected circle with guardians and should never be left singular like this—you see what has happened."

Elsa peeked in the box. "It's actually only a piece of a Winter Stone," she said. "We got lucky."

"Of course, you're right. The big ones are about the size of the ones at Stonehenge," Ekk said. "If the whole thing was here, all of California would be under ice and snow right now."

I shivered. "You said balance. Is this a good or evil stone? What did you mean?"

Ekk went into his lecturer mode. "It's neither good nor evil, Panda. The balance is about how it's used." He gestured with his hands to mimic a scale. "You'll never be able to eradicate either good or evil, so in our lives we must build as much good around ourselves as we can and give a wide berth to evil. Avoid it. Most of what happens to us occurs in the dynamic tension between the two. Cold and heat are like that in a way. We balance it out."

Mitzi's teeth chattered. "Speaking of cold."

"A weather stone should never be used like this. Its presence here is clearly intentional and meant to harm," Elsa said. "We must return it to its place in the circle."

Ekk walked around the box marveling at the stone, which was about a foot in length and six inches high, unremarkable, except for the blue light around it and the vibration it gave off.

Mitzi asked Elsa, "How's Puddle? We made her leave when her lips turned blue."

Without taking her eyes off the stone, Elsa replied, "Puddle's taking Aurora to the hospital to see Ralph. She's turning into quite the caregiver."

This wasn't sitting well with me. "Hey, people. How can you be so relaxed? This…this thing has made our town into the North Pole."

Elsa laughed. "I'll show you why." With that, Elsa said to Ekk, "Ready?" He nodded and took her hand. "Stand back."

"Dons meyn, dons meyn, we'll say it again
Cessya or the earth shall moan
Birth, aging, death brings payn
Omberthi the circle of stones."

"Nothing happened," Mitzi said, stating the obvious.

"Oh," Elsa said. "You two need to hold hands with us. Make a circle around the box."

So we did. Bathed in blue light, we stood in melted ice water in the back storeroom of Taggart's Emporium. Good thing the box wasn't any bigger, as elven arms weren't very long.

Elsa said, "Repeat after us. *"Dons meyn, dons meyn, we'll say it again."*

We did our best to follow by saying the words together. After Elsa said a line, we repeated it. Even though it wasn't exactly correct, it was enough. The energy in the room changed, and the pale blue light switched off with an anticlimactic click.

"That's it?" Mitzi was incredulous. "And who's this *Don Main*?"

"Pretty much," Ekk said. He was still staring at the stone. Elsa broke the circle. "*Don Main* isn't a person. It's Cornish for "Dance of Stones." It's an old nursery rhyme elves are taught as children."

I tried to reach into the box, but Ekk and Elsa said in unison, "No!"

I froze. "You said it's harmless now. What?"

Ekk physically pulled me back by my parka. "No, not dangerous now, but there are some protocols associated with handling numinous objects."

Mitzi and I stood observing what appeared to be a very ordinary rock. I asked, "What's a numinous?"

"Numinous means sacred." Ekk said. "This stone being here is so wrong, so out of balance. It shouldn't be here."

"I'll say." Was I the only one still freaked out?

Mitzi smiled at me but addressed her question to Ekk and Elsa. "Now what?"

Ekk examined the box, tilting his glasses to read it better. "Now, we need to return it to the circle, once we figure out which one. Something or someone switched it on. We can't risk that happening again. You saw how we got winter in September."

I sensed another trip coming. This wasn't welcome news, as we were only recently adjusting to being home. "Return it where? I don't see a return address."

"It shipped from Germany, but that doesn't mean it originated there," Ekk offered, rubbing his brow.

"Cornwall?" Mitzi guessed.

"It might be, but rumor has it once the big stones were destroyed, these smaller pieces were scattered all over the world. The earliest magical folx placed them where they would do no harm."

Elsa closed the lid on the box, took a few steps back, and stood with hands on hips. She broke their fixation on the rock by exclaiming, "Look at this place. What a mess."

They surveyed the storeroom that was filled with water-soaked boxes. Mitzi said, "The water ruined so much of Ralph's inventory."

Elsa went to the back door and opened it, allowing some water to escape. "We need to clean this up before it starts to mold."

"Cleaning is her coping mechanism," I said to Mitzi.

"Clearly," Ekk agreed. "And Ralph can't do it by himself, but now isn't the time."

Mitzi asked, "What do we do with the stone? We can't just leave it here."

"True," Ekk said. "Panda, help me get it in the truck. We'll take it to the, uh, special place at home."

***

Ralph sat up in his hospital bed, grinning, when our crew entered. Aurora was in a chair next to him, and they held hands. Puddle met us at the door.

Puddle said, "Wait 'til you see this. Elsa, take my chair."

Mitzi, Ekk, Puddle, and I fanned out to find a spot to perch, as Aurora and Elsa were using the only visitors' chairs.

"See what?" I asked.

Puddle pointed at Aurora.

Aurora spoke slowly. "Hello, friends. Thank you for helping us." Her blue eyes sought each one out in turn. "Ralph needs hip surgery." She turned back to him. It was short, but coherent, and she was present.

Elsa explained to the group. "As you know, Aurora is one of us. Although she has a little ordinary dementia, someone used a spell to make it worse. That's the part I was able to help."

Ralph's face darkened. "And I know who."

Ekk went to Ralph and Aurora and said, "Hi, Aurora. Remember seeing me at Merry Hearts?"

She grinned. "Friend."

Ekk nodded. "From the Garden."

Her face went dark. "And that horrible, horrible Gary too. He stole my life with Ralph from me." She put her other hand on Ralph's, holding his one with both of hers.

Mitzi said, "Wait a minute, you knew Gary before this, uh, hostage thing happened?"

Ralph sighed. "Let's get you some more chairs. I think this is a good time to tell you about me and Gary from when he was our councilman."

***

Ekk and Elsa took the Winter Stone into the elf hole below their treehouse for safekeeping and to study it. After the shooting, the snow, and the discovery of the Winter Stone, I was spent. The adrenaline rush left all of us tired, and we went to our respective corners.

Puddle went upstairs and finally, Mitzi and I were alone. We shared a wordless hug, as Brutus rubbed against our legs. "I'm beat," I said and took her hand. "What say we go upstairs and get a little sleep?" She nodded and followed me to our waiting bed.

After only a few hours' sleep, Mitzi's phone rang.

"Aargh," I said. "Throw that thing away."

"Oh, that's adult." Mitzi lifted it to her ear and brightened. "Mayor Reed. I haven't forgotten. Are you sure you need me? We've had—uh-huh. Okay I—." Her shoulders straightened. "See you soon."

We were both still in pajamas. "Come on, Mitz. We just got home."

"New day." Mitzi's eyes were bright. "Duty calls. I'm on the Merryville Planning Commission, and that was the mayor. He wants me at the press conference."

"But—"

"I've got to call Sylvia." She went to change and make her call.

I lay back down with the cat and closed my eyes. It seemed like Mitzi was really energized by being an insider of city hall.

About fifteen minutes later, the doorbell rang out "Scotland the Brave." Puddle was closest to it, having descended the staircase, and she opened the door. I got to the door moments after she did and saw a man weighed down with a camera and other bags.

She laughed and said to him, "You moving in?"

"Uh no, I need this for the presser. Hey, remember we met at the hospital yesterday? I'm—"

She snapped her fingers in recognition. "You're that newspaper dude." She called over her shoulder, "Pandaaaaaa!"

My head hurt. "I'm right here."

"Oh, sorry. Company's here."

The reporter came in as Mitzi entered the room. She said a puzzled, "Hello."

He wasted no time. "Phillip Pen with the *Merryville Bee*. Do you have a minute for a couple of questions?"

Mitzi had changed and was ready for prime time. Although still wearing beads in her hair, she presented herself a tad more conservative than usual. "Actually, no. I'm on my way out." She picked up her purse as if to punctuate the point. "What's this about?"

Phillip gave her a cheesy smile, set his heavy bag down, and spread his hands in supplication. "I only need two minutes, please. Where to begin? I'm covering the story about Ring Tire and the new community garden. Dr. Sliwa at Merida University says your garden club is going forward despite problems with the soil. Can you give me a comment about that?"

At the mention of Dr. Sliwa, Mitzi stiffened.

Having heard all about that meeting from Mitzi, I knew she was still sore at Dr. Sliwa. I said politely, "Listen, ah, Phillip, we're all pretty busy. Can you do this another time?" I frowned at Puddle for letting him in. Puddle shrugged and went back upstairs.

Mitzi in a clipped voice said, "I need to be at a press conference at city hall in," she checked her watch, "forty-five minutes."

Phillip was relentless. "That's the point. What I write has to be published right after that. You can have your say, or you can read what I write based on other interviews and research. Your choice." He sat himself down.

Mitzi gave him a frosty glare.

I commented, "That was pretty aggressive." Brutus even glared.

Phillip was nonplussed. "It's all First Amendment stuff."

I'd had enough. "What about the right to privacy?"

He turned his attention to me. "I have questions for you, too, Panda Fowler. I was on this very lawn the day that the press conference was here earlier this year. They were looking at you for making her," he pointed at Mitzi, "disappear. Then you were arrested for burning down the New Spirit tents, although the *Bee* was sure to print you were innocent. I mean, what's going on here? Now, with this new controversy…"

My face went red. "Then you should write it was the idiots who—"

"Panda." Mitzi took a step closer in warning.

He wouldn't stop. "Then, the two of you were somehow inside Merry Hearts Memory Care when Gary Smithers showed up with a *shotgun.*" Phillip took out a recording device. "Listen, you don't know me, but my job is to let the people of our town know what's going on and, for whatever reason, you and your little family are usually right in the middle. This is important."

"So, if we don't talk to you, are you going to camp out in that chair?" I was getting loud.

Mitzi inhaled a deep breath and appeared to be calming herself. She said in an even voice, "Mr. Pen, I can't speak for either the Merryville Horticultural Society or the planning commission. So if you want answers, you're going to have to come to the press conference."

He reluctantly stood, reminding me of a cat after you told it to get off the table. They don't do it until you are physically close enough to scoot them off. "Then can I get a comment from either of you about what happened at the Memory Care facility? I mean, how did you even get into the place?"

"I think it's time you left," Mitzi said firmly.

"But—"

I was more direct. "Can you not take a hint? Out." I walked to the door and opened it.

Phillip turned to go, realizing he would get nothing. We all turned as two very excited short people burst through the backyard sliding door shouting excitedly, "Panda. Mitzi. We found out where the Winter Stone came from."

CHAPTER NINETEEN

PRESS CONFERENCE

Mitzi drove, and I worried a little about the lack of conversation in our car. Since Phillip had left our home, Mitzi remained quiet. Usually, we talked about everything. She hadn't wanted me at the meeting about Dr. Sliwa's allegations, and it was unlike her to keep her cards so close to her vest. We had lots of other stuff to talk about, but I supposed she needed to focus herself for the big meeting. It was hard to be kept in suspense. The city hall parking lot was already filled when we arrived. "Wow, the whole town's here," I said.

Mitzi rolled down her window when an officer tried to direct us to the overflow parking lot. "I'm part of the program. Where do we park?"

"Yes, ma'am, pull around to the back." He waived our car through.

I pondered this new, privileged Mitzi. In the past we'd be driving to wherever directed and would probably sit in the cheap seats. Was being on the commission going to her head? Her normally free-spirited self was sounding like she embraced the perks of power. As we were guided to premier parking behind the building, she finally spoke. "Don't take it personally, Panda. I'm meeting with the mayor, and that would make anyone nervous."

"You'll be great, babe. What are you going to say?"

"It's more complicated than people think. You'll know soon."

Did that mean she was siding with the planning commission? What *was* their position?

To keep her talking, I asked, "It feels funny to be on this side of a public event. Is Sylvia coming?"

"Oh yes, the whole Horticultural Society will be here, except for Charlotte Windingle."

"Poor Charlotte. She's such an exuberant, childlike person."

"Remind you of anybody?" Mitzi asked and finally smiled. "I think she'll be okay."

"What does that mean, when you say that it's more complicated than people think?" I asked.

"Exactly that." Mitzi reached for her purse behind the seat.

I changed the subject. "Do you think the reporter heard Ekk and Elsa when they came in talking about the Winter Stone?"

Mitzi picked a spot and pulled the car in. "You've asked me that already. I have no idea what he thinks and don't care. It really pisses me off that he came into our living room and was so pushy."

"Uh, Mitz, news people are nosy. That's the job. And before, I asked you if he heard, not if he knew."

Mitzi was on edge and slammed the car into park rather harder than was required. "Don't defend him. I hate being put on the spot." She opened the driver's side door of the Miata and was met by a flash photographer. A member of the mayor's staff hustled us into the building.

My eyebrows were raised at the paparazzi. "You were saying about being put on the spot?"

Once inside, we were given badges. I guess I was given privileges too. A man said, "Ms. Fowler? Come with me to the green room." When I tried to follow, he put up a hand. "Sorry, only those who are part of the press conference are allowed."

"Okay. Good luck, Mitzi."

"Thanks. If you see Sylvia, send her back." And with that, Mitzi was led to a side room where the politicos were presumably gathered. I strolled out to the lobby area and watched the circus unfold. I felt alone.

***

Mitzi straightened her skirt and stood in the circle around Tom Reed. He was ramping up his energy and was very dramatic. "Thank you, all. I guess you know how important this press conference is. We've got various groups under this very roof today who want to tear down the city. The city we love. Do you all know your content?"

Monte Hunt said, "I'm not even sure why I'm here. Doug usually handles this stuff."

Tom sighed and put his hand on Monte's shoulder. "Doug walked into a door, Monte. Did you not see his sunglasses?"

Doug lifted them and showed Monte the shiner. Mitzi was sympathetic, but Monte laughed. "Wow, what does the other guy look like?"

Doug appeared to be in a foul mood. "A door."

Tom turned to Mitzi. "So after Dr. Smith speaks, I'll talk about Gary Smithers' capture. Then I want you to come up to the podium and reassure these citizens that the Merryville Community Garden has your stamp of approval." He turned back to the men.

"How do you know what I think?" Mitzi asked. "You haven't asked me yet. Sylvia's not even here."

The men shuffled a bit. Monte said, "We don't have room for her on the dais."

Tom raised his eyebrows. "Well, Mitzi, what do you think?"

"Our group met with Dr. Sliwa, and she showed us the chemicals in the ground. Apparently, at least two different EIRs are floating around. How do we know which one is right? It sounds like not enough due diligence has been done." She folded her arms, resolute. "I really think Sylvia Arviso should be here. She's the president of the club."

Brad Butler poked his head in and said, "Two minutes."

"Too late to make changes," Tom said. "The committee did its work."

Monte said, "Mitzi, Sliwa is biased. She's full of liberal horseshit. People who can't do, teach. We do business in this town and wouldn't risk our reputations on bad science." He snarled at the mayor. "I told you it was a bad idea to put a travel agent with no credentials on this commission. She shouldn't talk to the people until we sort this out."

"Excuse me?" Mitzi said.

"Her name's in the program," was all Doug said.

Mitzi flipped back her braids and poked Monte in his chest. "What are your credentials, Monte? I've been doing my homework. Best I can tell, your father made your family's money in oil, and your claim to fame is being on commissions and playing golf with the mayor."

Monte looked at Tom like an angry child who was challenged on the playground. "Now see here, young woman…"

Doug said nastily, "You don't know what you're playing at."

Mitzi whipped around to face him. "Seriously, Doug? I can imagine how you got that black eye once your wife got home."

His mouth dropped open. She said, "Oh yeah, shall I fill in your buddies?"

Tom said, "This was a mistake. Ms. Fowler, you're off the commission."

Mitzi turned to Doug again. "Do you want me off the commission, Doug? I bet Phillip Pen has an empty seat next to him." She made as if to go out the door.

"Wait." Doug addressed his friends. "Hear her out." He added hastily, "about the community garden."

The men stood, all eyes on Mitzi, as she stood next to the refreshment table with bottled water and crudites. She picked up a carrot and snapped it in two. "Monte, how would you feel if you saw your grandchildren eating a carrot that might make them sick? You, Mayor? How about you, Doug?"

Jeremy Dap stood at the door. "Is everything okay? It's time."

Tom growled. "Close the door, Dap. Let me know when Rowan Smith gets here."

Jeremy held up his Google watch but, seeing four sets of eyes on him, he said, "I'll do a long intro, but please hurry."

Mitzi said, "Here's what I think we should do."

As she finished her thoughts, a door opened, and a man rushed in. "I'm sorry, with the roads all icy."

Mayor Reed stomped to the door. "Dr. Smith. Glad you're here. It's showtime."

***

The program started. A local scout group carrying flags tromped onto the stage and stood off to the side. All eyes were glued to the stage as the same man who asked everyone to take their seats marched out, leading the mayor, Mitzi, Doug Harker, and a man I didn't recognize. They took their seats. Doug was wearing sunglasses. I thought that was weird since we were inside.

"Thank you all for coming, I'm Jeremy Dap, the Merryville Public Information Officer. First, Local Troop 450 will lead us in the Pledge of Allegiance. All stood and most put their hand over their hearts. The kids were dressed in green uniforms and were very disciplined. After the words died out, Jeremy said into the mic, "Thank you, future leaders."

He took a breath and then dramatically began. "Today we've called this press conference to share, in a transparent way, the challenges Merryville has recently faced—is facing. Originally, this press conference was only to give you an update on the community garden. This is still on the agenda, but first we will address the unprecedented weather. You'll hear from Dr. Rowan Smith from Sacramento. We will also address the recent hostage situation at Merry Hearts. First, the freezing weather. Dr. Smith is the chief climatologist for our state. Dr. Smith?"

The man next to Mitzi stood up and shuffled to the podium. He was in his mid-fifties and wore a gray suit and white shirt. "Good afternoon. Sorry for the late start. I ran into a bit of weather outside." Surprisingly, the crowd laughed a little. "Although I think Snowmageddon is a little over the top." They laughed more.

He pushed his heavy black glasses up his nose. This buttoned-down dude had a sense of humor and was a good choice. "The first thing I need to say is that this phenomenon is passing. I flew here from Sacramento as soon as reports of snow flurries came in and have been working with our top climatologists. Historically, Southern California has never had this type of cold weather as long as such records have been taken, and that, of course, includes Merryville. So in the interest of transparency…" He leaned into the mic. "At this time, I don't have an explanation." People burst out with comments to each other in surprise. "We're going to be studying this for a long time. Questions?"

Lots of hands went up, and Bradley Butler patiently walked from citizen to citizen, holding a microphone. Dr. Smith handled questions volleyed at him for about fifteen minutes, answering them honestly and with humor. He promised to keep a handful of scientists on the ground and to make sure the city got regular reports. I couldn't help but wonder how they could study our freak weather since it was only a local issue. It would be interesting to see what they came up with for this magical event. I glanced over at Mitzi, and she didn't seem as nervous as I'd expected.

Mayor Reed was already standing, as Dr. Smith left the podium and took his seat in the front row. Reed, an imposing man, seemed to know how and when to look serious. Jeremy looked ready to do the next introduction, but the mayor grabbed the mic and said, "Good afternoon, Merryvillians." The lights shone on his forehead, and his expression exuded the right amount of concern. "And thank you, Dr. Smith. We're lucky to live in the Golden State where science leads the way. We take climate change seriously. Merida University has already cleared space for your field office, and my office will get you anything you need. Thank you again, sir." People around me clapped and I joined in.

"Public safety," Mayor Reed said. "Let's jump right in." No one could say he was a shrinking violet. "You've all heard that since this press conference was scheduled a couple of days ago, our outstanding police force captured Gary Smithers."

The crowd clapped again, and I heard a verbal ripple of reaction from the crowd. A heckler yelled out, "Yeah. The guy *you* supported for city council."

I grinned at that and wondered how the mayor would respond.

The mayor shaded his eyes and called out, "Who's doing lights? Can we shine a light on that fella? Give him a microphone?"

That wasn't the response I expected from him and couldn't wait to see the showdown. A spotlight sought out the loudmouth, and I saw it was a youngish man sitting with the Gonzalez camp. Bradley Butler moved down the aisle with a microphone and handed it to him. The heckler didn't seem prepared for this and shrunk a bit.

From the podium, the mayor put him on the spot. "Son, let's hear what you have to say. It's one thing to yell out and interrupt a speech. What's important enough that we all need to hear you instead of me?"

"You, mayor," the young man said into the mic, "you appointed Gary Smithers, a homicidal maniac. He went to the memory care yesterday and could have killed elders. Now you take credit for his capture? Give us a break." He sat back down.

Mayor Reed responded in political speak. "Young man, I hear your anger. First, let's be glad Gary is now in the mental health unit facing additional charges. He's being dealt with according to the law. Mental health is a serious problem. I see you're sitting with my opponent. Well, it's good to see our youth engaging in politics, no matter which side." Bradley took the microphone back from the young man, who apparently had more to say and grabbed for it unsuccessfully.

"But I'd like to focus on the *positive*." The spotlight turned off. "Thanks to our excellent police force, and the hero of the day, who happens to be right here, what could have been a tragedy is now setting the stage for change."

Phillip Pen, the annoying reporter from this morning, grabbed the microphone from Bradley and said loudly, "Excuse me, Mr. Mayor. I have a question for Douglas Harker about this. There are allegations—"

Brad snatched back the microphone and nodded to security. Security grabbed the reporter within seconds, and he fought back. Things escalated fast, and I heard the tussle over the loudspeaker.

"You can't stop the power of the press," Phillip shouted as two beefy officers regained control and escorted him to the back of the room toward the door. "The truth will come out." Doug turned paper-white.

Mayor Reed took control. "Now where was I? Before I talk about this new mental health program, and it appears to be sorely needed,"— Panda heard titters from the audience—"would Officer," he glanced down at his card, "Lulu Tuigamala come up to the stage, please?"

I was stunned because it seemed the reporter who was in our living room hours ago knew of the Gary-Doug connection. This thought was pushed aside, however, because I was thrilled to see Lulu, in full dress uniform and white gloves, make her way to the stage as people stood and clapped. Lulu stood, all five feet nine inches of her, like a deer in headlights next to the mayor.

"Officer," he looked down at the card again, "Tuigamala, your sergeant is here with something for you." A male officer in dress uniform walked on the stage.

The whole thing felt like a gameshow, but people were transfixed. Her superior officer saluted her and said, "Officer Tuigamala, you showed bravery last evening. That reflects well on your uniform. You ran toward danger when others might have run the other way, and not one life was lost. We salute you." He gave her another crisp salute.

She saluted back, as a teardrop slid down her cheek. Her buttons almost burst as she whipped her white gloved hand to a place right above her eyebrows. The crowd roared with approval.

I tried to catch Mitzi's eyes, to see her reaction. She was hard to read, and again I wondered what she was thinking and feeling about this press conference and her role in it. But dang, even though calculated, it was sure nice to see Lulu get the praise she deserved. Whoever put this together was pretty smart. After the news that scientists had the climate issue in hand, and the emotional honoring of Lulu, much of the earlier tension had left the room.

Jeremy again took the mic. "Now for the community garden issue. These, as you can tell from the outbursts here today, are turbulent times. You have read in the news that the property donated by the Windingle Foundation has been vandalized, and rumors state the former lessor didn't properly clean up their byproducts. This is what we will now address. It was the original reason we called this press conference."

"Tell the truth. You're only having the press conference because of Francisco Gonzalez," another heckler from his group called out in a loud voice.

Jeremy continued. "If you wish to have a candidate's rally, go outside. This is not the time or place. I'm happy to introduce the newest member of the Merryville Planning Commission to speak for the commission. Ms. Fowler is the first female to serve on the commission and is the liaison for environmental issues. Mitzi Fowler has taken tours all over the world and has first-hand experience with how different countries and cultures relate to their food sources. She brings all her experience to us today. Ms. Fowler?"

Of course, I knew it was coming but was still shocked to see my wife get up and walk to the mic. She was poised and appropriate. "Hi, I'm Mitzi Fowler. I think it's time for a reintroduction. I'm the newest member of the Merryville Planning Commission but to be honest, this isn't my first time in the news."

A voice yelled out, "You got murdered." A few around the person laughed. It was a reference to the press conference which occurred when she and I returned from Europe at the same time local officials were announcing progress in the investigation of her "murder."

I searched to find the source of the loud comment but was drawn back to the stage. This was my wife in the limelight. Jeremy got up to address the interruption, but Mitzi motioned him away. "Any reports of my being murdered were, well," she leaned into the microphone, "inaccurate." People burst out laughing. She had the audience in her hand at this point and any laughs were at the expense of the city.

She nailed the press in the front row with her eyes. "So remember, not everything you hear in the newspaper or in the gossip chain is true. This is why I'm on the planning commission. We need ordinary citizens to get involved and, yes, government needs more transparency."

Another loudmouth yelled out, "The community garden is full of poison." I looked around and found the heckler. It was another from Francisco Gonzalez's group.

Mitzi maintained her poise, and asked, "Are you sure, though? Let me address that. Ring Tire leased the land from the Windingle Company and says they remediated their industrial waste on the land. Dr. Sliwa, the *head* of Merida University Agriculture Department, says it's polluted and a community garden would be harmful to the neighbors we're trying to help. They can't both be right."

Mayor Reed seemed to be looking for someone in the audience and I followed his gaze to Hortense Miller. She stared back at him and smiled, all innocence. That was interesting, but my wife was on stage, and she was my priority.

Mitzi's hands firmly grasped both sides of the podium, and her beads glittered in the spotlight. "Now, some of you think we at the Merryville Horticultural Society are a bunch of white ladies who only care about roses and seeing ourselves in the press." She looked directly at Dr. Sliwa when she said that. "That we are a bunch of women easily manipulated by others. In fact, the society has worked in this neighborhood for years, cleaning up yards, providing tools, training, and seeds, and we only want what's good for our community. Before we continue, I'd like all the members who are here today to stand up where you are so we can recognize you." I saw beads of sweat sparkle on the mayor's brow, and Monte whispered something to him.

"House lights, please." At least thirty women and two men stood up. "We are your neighbors, and we care about the truth. I hope you all do, too, instead of wasting time shouting out provocative things or believing everything you hear without evidence. The mayor and our planning commission want you to know we listened to all of you and made a decision."

Her eyes glittered with tears. "So it's with great sadness that I must say we're pausing the project while we bring in more experts to study the site." The audience started murmuring. Mitzi waited for the reaction to settle down, then cleared her throat and continued.

"If what Dr. Sliwa and others say is true, a remediation will have to be done, period. If that means a lawsuit against Ring," both Monte and Doug visibly winced, "we'll leave that to the legal types. I don't know at this point. I'm here to reassure you my interest in this project is from my heart, and this city and the Merryville Horticultural Society will work hand in hand with *anyone* who wants to help. We will provide fruits and vegetables to this underserved community eventually, whether at this space or another. That's how we move forward. Thank you."

She sat down and, after a stunned silence, people clapped vigorously. Doug sat stone-faced and Monte was a bit green in color. Mayor Reed stood and clapped, appearing to be as happy as a clam. He wasn't called the "Teflon Mayor" for nothing. I shook my head. What a con artist.

But then Francisco Gonzalez stood and so did his group. They noisily left the building. Public Information Officer Jeremy Dapp acted as if it was simply time for the crowd to leave since the press conference was essentially over. "Thank you all for coming," he said. "The mayor will make sure you're informed as events unfold. For now, Gary Smithers is in custody, the snow appears to be over, and it seems," he turned to include Mitzi in his gaze, "we have the right people working on the right things. Stay safe."

They cut the spotlight and the mayor, Mitzi, Monte Hunt, and Doug Harker marched off the stage single file through a throng of reporters shouting questions. The mayor posed for a quick photo with Dr.

Rowland Smith, who then made his exit. Doug Harker never stopped and headed out the back door, head down. The group continued single file toward the green room, and I fell in line behind them. There was no way I was going to be left out again.

When we got to the room, Monte noticed me and ushered the others inside before slamming the door in my face. I saw Mitzi frown as the door shut. I heard shouting and leaned my ear against the door so I could hear better.

Monte exploded at someone I assumed was the mayor. "What was that, Tom?" I smiled when my guess was confirmed, as he continued. "I heard from Mitzi, for the very first time, that we're going to sue Ring Tire? Did you suddenly forget we entered into a deal in which the city signed off on cleanup?"

"What?" Mitzi asked sharply. "Is that true, Tom?"

The door suddenly opened, and the mayor rushed through. Luckly I'd jumped back before the door rearranged my face. The mayor said over his shoulder, "Monte, let it go for a couple days. Doug had a big fight with Laurie. The community is riled up. Let's meet and talk about this as a group."

Mitzi wasn't done. "But—" The mayor stopped and glanced at her. "Right now, I've got another meeting and, er, Mitzi, at least you staved off a riot. Thank you." He patted Mitzi on the arm.

Mitzi said, "I publicly promised the community we would study the situation. You need to tell me that's going to happen, that I didn't just go out there to buy you all time to cover your asses."

Monte shook his head and left without saying another word, clearly angry.

I waited patiently for them to leave. Mitzi was the last to come out, and I ran up to her. "Baby, you did great. I mean, the whole auditorium…" Seeing my wife's tears, I enveloped her in a hug.

"Take me home," was all she said.

CHAPTER TWENTY

THE WINTER STONE

The Winter Stone was now on a stool between Ekk and Elsa. The stone was silent, no more buzzing or a blue light now that it had been deactivated. Its box sat on the floor. Else couldn't help but wonder who sent it here, and when. "How long do you think this has been here?" she asked.

Ekk picked up the shipping box and tilted his glasses to magnify the faded stamp. "The postage is from 1986, so thirty-something years?"

"It's high time that storage gets cleaned out," Elsa said. "No telling what else might be from someone magical. We need to talk to Ralph."

"He sure has been a good friend. I don't know what's going to happen to the store now. Eighty-year-olds don't fare so well with a broken hip."

"You know, Ekk, we haven't talked about *Lupus Imperium's* influence on Gary Smithers. He may be locked up, but he's going to keep trying to carry out their plans."

"I don't think he set the Winter Stone off purposefully. I remember from elf school that if you give off magical vibes merely being around a solitary stone can do it. For all I know, it was me working in the backroom that set it off."

Elsa was energized. "Let's you and I go to Taggart's now and see what we can do. We have to find out if there's another stone in that big mess. We also need to stop damage from mold now that the ice has melted."

"I agree. I still have the key. Get your wellies, honey. After we do a safety check, maybe we'll go see Ralph. The Stone will be okay here until we figure out what to do with it."

Elsa and Ekk found Puddle lying on her back with her feet up on the couch armrest when they came back into the house. Elsa was puzzled to see her there. "I thought you'd go to the press conference," she said.

"They left without me. I think Panda's mad because I let that reporter in, and he heard you guys. And that's not my thing anyway.

Ekk scratched the back of his head. "Oh, that's right," he said. "We were talking about the Winter Stone. That was my fault."

Elsa put a hand on his arm. "If he did hear, he wouldn't know what that meant anyway. Don't worry about it, honey." She grinned at

Puddle. "We're going to Taggart's to clean up the mess. Would you like to come?"

"Yeah, I'm bored anyway."

"You and your sister," Elsa said. "She gets bored too."

Ekk went to the key hook and grabbed Panda's keys.

Elsa asked Puddle, "Do you have wellies?"

Puddle's brow wrinkled. "Wellies? I haven't a clue what you're talking about."

"Rubber boots," Elsa said. "You do remember how wet it was?"

"Oh yeah, that's so British, but no," Puddle replied.

"Well, they'll have some at the store," Elsa said, and noticed Ekk was writing something. " Now what are you doing?" she asked him.

"Leaving a note for the girls." He put the pen down and went to pull Puddle from the couch.

Puddle yawned and stretched. "What's the plan?" she asked.

"Today we're going to check on things and sweep out all the water we can. I think I saw a warehouse size squeegee in there." Elsa was on a mission. When it looked like Puddle might meander off, she said, "Get in the car."

"Maybe it's not as bad as you think," Puddle said as they drove downtown.

Ekk parked the car in front of the store. "We'll see."

Taggart's looked normal from the outside, but water ran over their shoes as soon as Ekk opened the front door.

"I guess more ice melted," Puddle said and reached for the light switch on the wall.

Ekk yelled and reached out his short arm. "Don't. It's not safe yet."

"But it's dark in here."

"Wait here," he said and went down an aisle and returned with a pair of boots and some lanterns."

Puddle put on the boots. "They're a little big." An irritated glance from Elsa quieted her.

"Let's get some of these lanterns spread around," Ekk said.

Puddle, wearing boots up to her knees, grimaced. "Wow, what a mess."

"Upstairs won't be as bad," Elsa said. "Why don't you check that out for leaks." She handed Puddle a battery-operated lantern. "Don't turn on anything electric. I don't want you electrocuted."

Puddle said, "No problemo. I'd hate that. Hey, Ekk, l guess you and I are unemployed, eh?"

"Don't be so sure," he responded mysteriously, sloshing down the aisle. Puddle started up the stairs while Elsa placed lanterns in strategic places. "It looks like everything from the second to the bottom shelf are toast. Above that will be okay."

Ekk called upstairs, "Puddle, if you find any dry wood, bring it downstairs for the stove."

"Whoa. I found something better than that."

Ekk and Elsa looked up and saw Puddle standing at the top of the stairs holding Ralph's beloved cat, Ratter, in a brown blanket. "He was curled up inside a pile of Taggart's fleece souvenir blankets."

Ratter said, "Meow," and then something like "wowowowo."

"Hey, he's talking."

Elsa put down a lamp and said, "He certainly is."

"We need to take him to the hospital to see his daddy." Ekk took out his cell phone and took a picture. "I'll send him this for now."

***

Mitzi graduated from tears to anger. "Those two-faced bastards!"

Sylvia, Hortense, and the others from the Horticultural Society were waiting for Mitzi outside the auditorium. "Well, I must say you should wear skirts more often," Hortense said, and Mitzi simply lifted her eyebrows.

The comment was so silly I started laughing hysterically. Mitzi usually wore long pants, and it struck me as hilarious that in this moment, that's what the woman would say.

A smile tugged around Sylvia's lips. "You did handle yourself well up there."

"Thanks," Mitzi said and gave Hortense a dubious look, "I guess."

Done with my laughing fit, I said, "Yes. Yes, she did. She's a natural." I patted my wife on the back and surveyed the group.

We were a diverse group indeed. Me in jeans, Denise perfectly matched to the winter weather in a pastel-colored ski outfit, and Hortense, Lidia, and Florence dressed for the 1950s in pearl button sweaters over dirndl dresses. Janet joined the group breathlessly, saying by way of explanation, "What did I miss? Bonnie had a thing."

Mitzi exhaled and said, "I'm so angry."

"What's the matter, dear? I thought you did rather well, considering." Hortense was being uncharacteristically nice, or was she?

"Considering what?" Mitzi asked. I could tell the adrenaline of being on stage had ebbed.

"I'm talking about our hospital ordeal." Hortense gave Mitzi a meaningful look, no doubt to remind her that Hortense now knew her secret, having seen her wings and all.

Denise, Lidia, and others nodded and murmured support for Hortense, Mitzi, and me, and Sylvia added, "Mitzi, we've all been through a lot, but I can't imagine the situation at the hospital. No one would have blamed you for not even showing up today. You did the club proud with that speech. It's sad we have to pause the project, but we have to until the science proves one way or the other what's going on with our community garden."

Hortense drew herself up to full height, towering over the rest of the group. "Well, I tend to think it will all be fine, with the exception of my sandpit." She narrowed her eyes at Sylvia. Even though they had a truce of sorts, the animosity ran deep.

Sylvia responded, "Don't reflexively say that Hortense. You're automatically siding with the mayor—"

Hortense cut her off. "I'll have you know—"

"Guys, please," Mitzi interjected as she wiped her eyes.

"You mean ladies," Hortense said to correct her. She was smiling, which was infuriating, and I could tell she was enjoying this. Hortense seemed to love getting under people's skin.

Mitzi's hands made little chopping motions in the air, emphatic. "Whatever, *ladies*. Listen, you don't understand. Tom Reed, Monte Hunt, Douglas Harker, and the rest of them have no intention of stopping this project or suing anybody. Those men are going to keep ramming this thing through. I was standing right there when Monte asked Mayor Reed if he forgot they'd made a deal with Ring Tire."

"What?" Lidia asked.

"Tom wouldn't do such a thing," Lidia said. "I've known the Reeds for decades. They wouldn't allow poisoned ground to happen on their watch."

"I don't trust them." And I wanted to punch somebody. "They made Mitzi cry. She doesn't cry easily."

"Excuse me, uh Panda, is it? Are you part of the Horticultural Society?" Florence Dinwitter asked.

I swiveled toward her, and she flinched. "Yes, I am. I'm your free accountant, so be nice to me."

Denise, always a cool head, said, "I can ask my lawyer to do a little digging around whatever deal was or wasn't entered into."

Sally Johnson spoke up. "Jack can help too. He knew these guys when we started the roofing company and still goes to the same golf club."

"Okay, anyone else?" Sylvia asked. She was back to her professional self. "We need neutral science."

"I think you'll find that difficult in this town right now," Denise said. "I mean, you've basically got the university scientists, who are with Francisco Gonzalez, and you've got the political and business guys with their oil industry scientists saying it's all fine. Where else can we get an expert?"

Sylvia said, "I've still got contacts in Silicon Valley. CTI does this. It's run by all women."

"Seriously?" Florence, from the old board asked. "You're picking this moment to advance some feminist, politically correct agenda of yours?"

"No. They're simply the best at what they do," Sylvia retorted. "We had a situation similar to this on the Techlife campus, where I used to work. CTI is their name. Not sure what that stands for. Check out their credentials for yourself. They brought drills, went down about thirty feet, and then sent samples off somewhere. If you all agree, I think we should bring them in."

"Who's going to pay for this?" Janet asked.

"We will." The group of ladies turned to see Charlotte Windingle had quietly joined them. Denise McGreggor nodded. As the two most well-heeled women in the Merryville Horticultural Society, they were a financially formidable twosome.

Sylvia cried, "Charlotte. I didn't see you here." The group opened to let her in.

She chuckled. "Of course not, I'm wearing sunglasses. Just like Doug Harker. Did you see that?" She went on. "My family has the most to lose, and I want someone we can trust doing the testing."

"Why are you doing this, Denise?" Janet asked. "It can cost millions for the Windingles and maybe even the club if the ground needs to be cleaned properly."

Denise, fresh off her Junior League conference, was still dressed as if she'd skied off a black diamond run. On her feet were fluffy white *apres* ski boots. "Our family of companies has a philanthropic arm. Since coming back to Merryville, I've realized how important this place and all of you are to me and Bridgette. In for a penny…"

"In for a pound. Yes." Hortense cleared her throat. "Before we have a group hug, some of us need to discuss other matters as well. I feel myself, Lidia, and Florence have been kept at arm's length. Sandpit indeed. That needs to stop."

Lulu sidled up to the group, and they all turned to her. "Sorry, ladies. We're closing the venue. I'm going to have to break this up." She softened the statement with a grin.

Hortense brightened. "Officer Tuigamala. I'm so glad to get a chance to thank you."

"Yes, triple that," I said.

"You were pretty good with that bedpan," Lulu said and told the story.

After hugs and congratulations, the group disbursed, with the future of the community garden still very much up in the air.

***

Ekk, Puddle, and Elsa worked their fingers to the bone. After three hours of squeegeeing out water, tossing out waterlogged boxes, and taking stock of what still needed to be done, they sat around the metal stove in the entry area and rested. "This coffee is amazing, Elsa." Puddle blew the hot liquid before sipping again.

"I put a little cinnamon in it. You know, Ekk, this place could be made more successful with some organization. Did you see the faucets are next to the pool noodles that are next to the porch flags?"

Puddle chuckled. "I think it's part of this place's charm. It reminds me of the stores in India. They were colorful and chaotic, the smell of *nag champa* in the air." She twinkled her fingers for effect.

"Not everybody loves chaos, Puddle, or incense. Do you see how I keep my kitchen?" Elsa referred to her tiny kitchen in the tree house. It was compact and cozy but shone with cleanliness.

"You Germans," was all Puddle said. "Shall we go see Ralph now?"

Ekk had been leaning back with eyes closed. He sat up. "The accounting's the same way, pretty messed up. Since Aurora retired, Ralph's done his best, but he apparently isn't a numbers guy."

"He's also eighty something," Puddle said, offering another reason. "It's time for him to retire."

Elsa turned off the coffee pot and used a poker to make sure the fire was down to a few embers behind the iron grate. "Think it's safe to leave it like this?"

"Ekk flicked a hand toward the potbelly stove, and it went cold. "Now it is."

"Ekkhard Schmidt."

"Come on Elsa, I'm tired. Let's go."

CHAPTER TWENTY-ONE

MERRYVILLE HOSPITAL

Ralph was alone when they arrived, resting with his eyes closed. "Knock, knock," Elsa said as she rapped her knuckles on the door frame. Ralph had to be tired, but he put on a smile for them.

"If it ain't my wife's heroes. Come on in. Some gal took one of the chairs, but we can get it back. Thanks for coming." He had a cast covering his hip to a few inches below his knee and must be in pain.

"Your Southern hospitality is showing," Ekk said.

Puddle hovered near the door. "I'll get a chair. Do you need anything?"

"Yeah, my cat." He squeezed the bridge of his nose and shut his eyes for a moment, as if avoiding tears. Apparently, he hadn't checked his texts. "Sorry." Ralph lifted his eyebrows. "Actually, can you go to the cafeteria and see if they have any pudding?"

Puddle gave Elsa a secret smile before pointing at Ralph and saying, "On it." She disappeared out the door into the hospital hallway.

"We came straight here from Taggart's." Ekk held up the keys and jingled them.

"I'm afraid to ask. How is it?" Ralph grimaced with anticipation.

Elsa put on her glasses, pulled out a list and a pencil, and gave her report. "We got the water on the floor out, but it damaged the walls and floor. It's going to need new drywalls. The storage unit took the biggest hit. We had to throw out a number of boxes that were soaked." She added quickly, "Don't worry, I took pictures for insurance." Ralph appeared surprised at her efficiency. Elsa felt like everyone was staring at her. "What?" she asked.

"I guess I didn't know you were such a good business lady is all." Ralph scratched his head. "About that insurance…" He grimaced again. "It lapsed a couple years ago. Things haven't been so great at the store." His hands fiddled with the top of his blanket. "Aurora's care is expensive."

Elsa put a hand over her mouth. "Oh, Ralph."

He wiped his face with a big hand. "I know, I know. It's probably time to close up shop anyway. I just hate—"

"No." Ekk was resolute.

"No, what?"

"You've had that store since the 1960s. We'll help, Elsa and I." He motioned unnecessarily between the two of them. "We can run the store."

"You don't have to. I appreciate the help and all, but I'm old. Now that Aurora's doing a little better, I can rest up at her memory care. Kinda' looking forward to that."

"What about the Windingle paint?" Ekk brought up the special purple that Aurora Brown invented years before. "Who's going to mix that up?"

"Not much of that left. That's another thing I can't do."

"But I can." Elsa made a note on her pad.

"Huh?" Ralph asked, a puzzled look on his face.

Ekk smiled. "It's easy for her. She has a, ah, recipe book."

"Come here, you two." He held out his arms and Ekk and Elsa each accepted his hug.

Ralph's eyes were merry. "Thanks. You wanna buy it? I'll make you a great deal."

Ekk was about to answer, not sure if his friend was joking or not.

Puddle entered. "Sorry, no pudding, but I brought something better."

"That's all right. What you got going on, girl?"

Puddle grinned from ear to ear and scanned the hallway for nurses before she closed the door. She then pulled out a bedraggled Ratter, who was none too pleased at having been crammed under her sweatshirt.

"Meow."

"Put him on the bed," Elsa told her.

She did, and the cat ran up Ralph's cast like it was furniture and collapsed in a lump on Ralph's chest. He stoked Ratter's fur and cried freely. "Thank you. Oh Lord, thank you."

***

"This pot roast is excellent." I blamed Elsa for my failed vegetarian experience. She could walk into our kitchen, pull out any form of protein from the deep freezer —chicken, beef, or pork—and turn it into something delicious.

"Thank you, Panda. It's a simple dish. Something I threw together."

I mimicked her, flipping my imaginary long hair. "Just something I threw together." She swatted at me.

"You know," Mitzi said, "before all this latest stuff happened, Ekk said you'd like to see the United States. Like a tourist."

"I would," she said, "but that's got to wait. We still need to respond to Ehren. He expects us all back in the Hercynian Garden soon—with Aurora."

"Until this 'latest stuff' gets figured out?" Mitzi said. "How long will that take?" Mitzi was still of the opinion that we weren't going. "We have lives here." She looked at me for support.

I wasn't sure where I landed on that issue. Being home was great, but the possibility of losing Mitzi, Ekk and Elsa, or our friends to this evil because we stayed made me sick with worry. "What do you think we should do?" I asked Ekk.

"It could be a very long time until we know what we're facing," he said. "Now that Wolfrum's been defeated, a new leader has filled the void. Ehren wants you two in the keep under his protection."

"Tell me something we don't know." I was exasperated that both our guardian elves always folded when it came to Ehren. "I want to know what you think."

He bit his lip. "You can close your office for a season, Panda." He turned to Mitzi. "Your travel business is pretty much on hiatus too."

"We're under your protection. So, no, we're not going. I'm on the planning commission and can't run away because of what might happen." Mitzi was calm, and I suspected her mind was made up. "May I have some of that squash, please?"

I handed her the squash. "Ekk, can't we harden this target?"

"Sounds like you've been watching CNN again," Elsa said. "Isn't that what they say when somebody shoots up a school?" She buttered a roll and passed the breadbasket.

"Speaking of active shooting situations," Mitzi said. "Did you all see my wings deploy at Merry Hearts? That was new. Instead of flying, they hung like a cape. It was weird."

I remembered the incident and said, "And Hortense saw it. Thank god Lulu was there."

Elsa giggled. "And how about Hortense with that bedpan?"

We all ate in silence for a few minutes. Ekk finally said, "To be honest, I'm really not in a hurry to go back to Germany either. Merryville is drawing all these energies, and it's only partly because Mitzi is here. I'm going to talk to your father, Mitzi, with your blessing of course. Maybe he can send someone for Aurora."

I lifted my glass of ginger ale. "Hear, hear." Elsa smiled in such a way that I knew she had been a part of this decision.

This was shocking in a good way. Both elves were loyal to a fault to the Hercynian Garden. Ekk had even led it for a time while Ehren was in Merryville. Ehren trusted him so completely that a conversation might be fruitful with getting him to agree to keep things as they were, at least for now. Mitzi got up and walked over to Ekk. She hugged his blond head, making his wire-framed glasses crooked. "Thank you."

He patted her arm and straightened his spectacles. "Now for Panda's favorite part of the meal."

I squinted at him. "In case you haven't noticed, I've lost a few pounds since the showdown at St. Olaf's."

"I have. I have. But you still have a sweet tooth."

Mitzi said, "Yes, she does."

I shrugged.

Mitzi stacked the dirty plates and said, "I'll get dessert."

Elsa got up and she and Mitzi took the plates to the kitchen.

I said to Ekk, who was picking his teeth, "After the press conference, I felt we needed to go walk the land. Valerie said she felt something, and so did I. This," I openhandedly circled my gut area. "Something magical drew us to the sandpit.

Ekk leaned back. "This is what I mean. We're not done here. Something new is going on, or maybe something old that we were unaware of. I wish Ali was here. In any event, maybe I can use that to convince your father-in-law."

***

It was Saturday, and I slept in. Mitzi had been up for at least an hour and brought me a latte. She told me Puddle was with Elsa, cleaning up Taggart's, and Ekk had gone to Merry Hearts to check on Aurora for Ralph. He also needed to call Mitzi's father, who wanted up-to-date information.

Mitzi said she was going to go through the two different Environmental Impact Reports page by page to compare any differences. I heard her on and off the phone all morning, only calling upstairs to tell me Denise McGreggor was going to stop by if she had any information to report.

I got dressed, finished my drink, then called Juniper in Colorado. "Hi, Juniper."

"Panda. How are you, darling?"

"Fine. It's a beautiful, sunny day."

"Oh yeah," Juniper said. "I heard. The mystery snow phenomenon and its passing is all over the news."

"How's Val?"

"Valerie's doing much better. She's been spending time with her mom, Etsy, and that's good medicine. Everyone's glad to see her. I've been taking some time to sketch the desert scenery. It's been nice, but I'm ready to come home. Now that things have died down, we should be heading back in a couple of days. They need me at the museum."

"Has Twyla gotten any more messages from the Garden?" I asked and Juniper laughed.

"Well, if she hadn't left her receiver, or whatever it's called at home, we would know, now wouldn't we?"

"She didn't. Oh, Twyla."

"Don't tell Ekk," Juniper said. "She's really worried about that."

"I won't. What does she think of the reservation?"

"She's fascinated with the horses here. Right now, she's out riding with one of Valerie's cousins."

"Isn't she supposed to be protecting you?"

"Please. My dog, Layla, offers more protection than that fairy." Then Juniper said to someone else, probably Layla, "Good girl." She said to me, "We do like Twyla, but sometimes I wonder who's protecting whom."

"How could you not?" I replied. "She's adorable. And she did come through with the animal skin for the sweat."

"True."

I asked, "Do you want me to go by the house and look for the receiver?"

"Oh, that's a good idea. Twyla told me it's a tiny dagger she tucked under her pillow. The keys—"

"Are under the pot by the back door. I know."

"Well, if you get a chance. How's Mitzi? We saw part of the press conference on CNN. She was impressive."

"This whole year has changed us both a lot. Mitzi's coming into her own. To be honest, the travel stuff is fun for her, but she's capable of so much more. Right now she's in the dining room making phone calls and doing her due diligence to find out how bad the soil actually is at the community garden project."

I heard Juniper sigh. "That whole poison thing is such a shame. Those people around the old tire factory will get the shaft over and over."

This got me thinking. "I know. Everybody's fighting and using the project like a football in the election. Maybe even corruption's involved. Ugh."

"Well, I'm so glad you called," she said. "You beat me to it. If you do get the receiver thing, put it someplace safe."

"For sure. Talk to you soon." We ended the call. Now I had a mission.

I ambled into the dining room. Mitzi had her serious glasses on as she scribbled notes.

"You're up."

"Hi, babe. What have you found?"

"It's really insidious. The report Sylvia got is legit, but the methods used and areas tested are different from the one that Francisco brought to her. Five acres is expensive to test. I'm also starting to wonder if the university simply picked the worst place to test. It's like they tested a completely different place than the city study."

I pulled out a dining room chair and sat. "Let me see." I was good with money, but no scientist.

Mitzi laughed. "This is not your forte."

"No, it's not. When you get ready to follow the money, let me know." I kissed her and made to leave.

"Where are you going?"

"Juniper said Twyla left her receiver dagger thingy at their house. It's kind of important to find, don't you think?"

Mitzi nodded. "Uh, yeah. Are you going to get it?"

"Yes, after I stop by Taggart's. Please don't tell Ekk."

"Of course. Be careful, honey. You remember what happened to Potts." Her phone rang, and I heard her say, "Charlotte. Okay, tell me more…" as I got my car keys and left.

***

I parked down the street from the store and noticed every shop on Main Street was cleaning up after the storm. The proprietor of Not Your Mother's Coffeehouse was sweeping the sidewalk, and someone from the flower shop was dumping ruined plants and flowers on the back of a truck for hauling away. Merryville merchants were busy. The door to Taggart's was open to let in air, but a slender chain draped across the doorway held a sign that said, "Temporarily Closed." I ducked under and called out, "Hello."

Wow. Elsa and Puddle had been busy. The interior shelves were empty and at least four large fans were on, drying out the store. "Hello," I called louder.

"We're back here," Puddle yelled. The storeroom door leading to the alley was propped open to allow the sunlight to flood in, making it easier to survey the damage. Elsa was directing a couple of young men to move boxes, and a big pile of rejects were stacked on the side. She pulled off a leather glove and approached. "Are you ready to get your hands dirty?" I suddenly felt guilty after sleeping in.

"Sure, I'll help. I wasn't aware you were taking on this whole project."

"I need a break," Puddle said. "Let's get some coffee."

We walked to the front, near the potbelly stove. It was one of the few undisturbed places. I grabbed a mug off the wall, poured a cup of coffee, and sat down. Puddle poured her coffee and joined me.

"So what's happening, Puddle? You're really motivated to help Ralph."

She leaned back in her chair and stretched her legs. "And myself. We're talking about buying the store from him and Aurora, or maybe being partners."

"Seriously? You're going to run a hardware store?"

She put her Taggart's mug down. "No. We're going to run a hardware store and travel agency botanica."

"Um, that's unique." This seemed like another wild idea of my kooky sister. "What does Elsa think?"

"She thinks Ralph and Aurora need to retire all the way, so that they can make up the lost time from what Gary Smithers did to her. That guy was so bad. He was ripping Ralph off for years and afraid Aurora would put a stop to it. When she started having memory problems, he used magic to make it worse. She's really coming around."

"Wow."

"And Ekk already works here. He'll probably get you involved, too, since you're such a whiz with taxes and bookkeeping."

"Again, wow."

Elsa walked up with Ratter following and sat with us. "I'm pooped," she said, but she was smiling. "Did Puddle tell you what we're thinking?" The cat jumped on her lap.

"You brought Ratter back?"

"He lives here," Puddle said. "He's got his bed on top of the giant safe in the back."

"This feels right," I said, "although a hardware store, travel agency, and botanica sounds a little eclectic."

"We need to involve Ali in that," Elsa said to Puddle. "Nothing's decided yet."

"Have you heard from him?" I was curious to see if this was a new boyfriend thing.

Puddle's face fell. "He's been busy, I guess."

Elsa petted Ratter. "He's a guardian like me, Puddle. He could get reassigned somewhere else. We don't know if he's coming back yet."

She responded, "So we're going to do something here. It has so much potential."

"Mitzi will have some input, too, I'm sure. I'll start doing some research on what the cost to run this place will be."

Puddle got up. "That's the boring part. I'm going back to work. You coming?"

"I'll come back. I'm on my way to the Goodens. Twyla—" I remembered she didn't want Ekk to know she'd left her dagger at home. If I let it slip, Elsa would have to tell him. "Juniper wants me to check on things. You know, make sure all is secure."

Elsa eyed me suspiciously. "Did something happen while they were away?" My eyes were big, all innocence. "No, just giving them some peace of mind."

CHAPTER TWENTY-TWO

THE GOODENS

I arrived at Val and Juniper's house about eleven a.m. I picked up a few newspapers lying on the front porch and walked around to the back. The gate was unlocked, and I reflected that this was the very place where Hortense Miller's husband, Bill, had brained detective Charlie Potts months ago. I closed the gate behind me and entered the backyard, thinking about how so much had changed. Now Hortense was an ally, and we hadn't heard from Charlie or Alexandra, Charlie's defense attorney wife, for a while.

The garden looked much better than the last time I saw it. Juniper had mentioned how Twyla could work miracles with growing things, and she wasn't kidding. It appeared she was even partway through building an orchid house for Valerie, which would free up the back bathroom in the house.

It was so pleasant, I sat at a patio table and rested before going inside the house. I didn't want to ponder anything in particular, but simply enjoy the beauty of the tulips, one of the few flowers that could have survived the biting cold that had passed. Things were okay but still uncertain. That was my feeling. Mitzi was as engaged as I'd ever seen her, but we still faced a danger we didn't ask for or truly understand. Even so, I was happy.

I went to the back door and retrieved the key from under the pot. Inside, I saw signs of a hasty departure. Juniper's latest project was strewn around the living room, and the kitchen still had some cups in the sink. I missed them already. The snow was upon us two days ago, but now it seemed like a false memory. I found Twyla's dagger under her pillow, as she said, and it was buzzing. I called Mitzi first, but she didn't pick up. Then Twyla.

"You got it." She sounded relieved.

"Yes, and it's buzzing."

"Oh no. That means messages have come in."

"What should I do?" I stared at it, buzzing on her bed in the guestroom.

"Press the green, no the red, button. It's actually a jewel."

I did. A hologram of an angry Heloisa appeared, telling Twyla to stay in Colorado with the Goodens and to report to the Hercynian Garden immediately."

"Uh-oh. Can you get the dagger to me?"

"I guess. Give me the address where you are."

***

"You what?" I'd never seen Ekk so upset.

"I went to the Goodens, got the dagger thing, and sent it overnight to Twyla at the reservation in Colorado."

Mitzi was agitated too. "Honey, why didn't you call first?"

"I did. You didn't answer."

She collapsed into the chair and picked up her phone. "Dead. I'll plug it in."

Ekk was like a dog with a bone. "Okay, Heloisa said to call the Garden? Tell me again exactly what she said."

"She seemed really mad and said for Twyla to keep Juniper and Valerie in Colorado and to report to the Hercynian Garden."

"Oh no. Something else must have happened. I've got to call Ehren."

Mitzi piped up. "I thought you did already. Weren't you going to talk him out of us going to Germany?"

He reddened. "I was going to do it after checking on Aurora. But she's no longer at Merry Hearts."

Mitzi and I both exclaimed, "What?" at the same time.

He sighed. "Twyla's not the only one dropping the ball." He took another deep breath and said, "Panda, call Elsa and Puddle and get them back from Taggart's. We need everyone here. I'm going to call the Garden." He walked toward the back door to go to his treehouse.

"He's my father," Mitzi said. "I'm coming too."

Instead of arguing with her, he nodded, very distracted, and led the way.

I called Elsa and instead of a hello, she said, "Panda, are you coming back to help?"

"Not right now."

"Honestly, you can be so lazy." It was good natured, but I felt the sting of a little truth.

"No, Elsa, well yes I can be, but something's happened. I'd rather not say on the phone. Please lock up Taggart's and bring Puddle home."

"We'll leave immediately."

***

Mitzi wasn't used to seeing Ekk on the defensive. He was their little old man in a way, full of wisdom. This time he'd sided with them and was willing to push back a little at Ehrenhardt. Unfortunately, some of the very things Ehren feared had happened, and Ekk was certain to face his leader's wrath. Ekk placed his dagger on the floor of his and Elsa's tiny front room. It was a happy little thing—bejeweled, sharp, and shining. As usual, it spun, and spun, and spun.

Instead of the almost instant connection, nothing happened. Surprised, Ekk tried again. The communication device spun quickly at first, then slowed and stopped. "Uh-oh." He looked at Mitzi. "Let's try it in the house."

She looked worried too. "Has this ever happened before?"

He said a quick, "No," picked up his dagger, and headed for the door. Mitzi and Ekk quickly descended the ladder leading from the treehouse to the backyard. He looked up and saw a couple of ravens. Mitzi had never heard him attempt to speak with birds, but this time he did. "Raven. What do you see?"

Before the dark birds flew away, they croaked, "Too late. Too late."

This sent a chill down Mitzi's spine. In all the local drama about the community garden and her role with the mayor's commission, she'd let herself forget they were still players in a war they didn't choose. "Let's get in the house."

***

"What does this mean?" I asked Ekk again. We were in the living room, waiting for Elsa and Puddle to return.

"It means we should have gone when Ehren asked us."

"I'm not so sure," Mitzi said. "We have a mortgage to pay, obligations…"

"Which won't mean a thing if we're all dead," he snapped uncharacteristically.

The front door opened, and Puddle rushed in followed by Elsa. "What's going on?"

"We have some news," Mitzi said.

"You know," Puddle said, I have a hunch about something. Give me your cell phones."

After a short argument, Puddle had Elsa's, Ekk's, mine, and Mitzi's cell phones and took them to the shed. Upon returning she said, "I bought a Faraday cage when I was here last time. It was too big to take to Peru. Humor me about this. It seems like this invisible other side is always one step ahead of us lately."

"Faraday?" Elsa said.

"Cage," Puddle finished. "It's practically the only way to block electro-magnetic influences."

"My darling sister has always been paranoid about people listening in," I said. "The box is like a fancy galvanized trash can, but it blocks eavesdroppers."

"Science magic is good, too, I guess," Elsa said, "but as long as we're at it, didn't you tell me you had a smart TV?"

"Yes," I said. "Anything else you can think of, Mitzi?"

"I don't know. I can't think right now. Let's not go crazy. We can move to the treehouse, no TV."

We all tromped into the backyard and climbed into the elves' home. To say it was a tight fit was an understatement. It was, however, secure. Ekk put his dagger on the floor and tried to contact the garden again. We all focused our attention on the little device and waited. It spun, then stopped like before. I had a sinking feeling in my stomach.

"What could this mean?" I looked at Ekk and Elsa, who were pale with fear. This scared me more than anything.

Instead of answering directly, Ekk asked, "When does Twyla's device get to her?"

"Tomorrow morning."

"Folks. I think we should all pack one bag each and wrap up whatever you got going on here. We need to get to the Hercynian Garden."

Mitzi finally spoke. "Don't you have another way to contact them? What if we get there and find, I don't know, they've moved?"

"The Garden has been continuously protected back to the mists of time," Elsa said. They can't pick up and move." She looked guilty and sad at the same time. "They can't."

I sensed she was holding back. "What aren't you telling us?"

"It's the last outpost."

Now it was Mitzi's turn to look pale. "What do you mean? We used to have other outposts and we lost them?"

Ekk took a minute to answer. "Yes. I guess now is as good a time as any to tell you. You may have noticed Elsa and I have been nervous.

The activity you've seen here, first Wolfrum, then Gary Smithers, these are minor skirmishes. If the Garden falls, you'll see complete chaos in the world like no one has ever seen."

I commented, "I have noticed people are edgy—"

"Hello," a man's voice hollered from outside the treehouse. "Anybody home? Don't make me climb that ladder. It'll break."

Puddle perked up. "That's Ali." She climbed over me and Mitzi to get to the door. "Up here."

I'd never seen her act that way, even with her last serious boyfriend. Ekk said, "Well, come on. Let's go."

Soon we were all standing in the yard, sharing hugs. Elsa said, "I'm so glad you're okay."

"I came right from the airport. Wasn't sure they were going to send me again after what happened last time." We understood this was a reference to the fire at the botanica.

"Did you call us first?"

"No, and you all need to ditch your phones for a while." His eyes got large to emphasize what he was saying.

"Already on it," Puddle said. "They're in the shed in a Faraday cage."

Now his expression turned to admiration. "Good thinking, Puddle. I didn't call and that's why. This new attack uses all modern technology."

"But that's in complete violation of the treaty."

He looked sad and said to Elsa, "The treaty is no more."

We all took a second to let that sink in and started talking over one another.

Everyone had questions for Ali, but Ekk put his hands up in a stop motion. "Everybody, quiet. Let the man talk. What's going on in the Garden? We can't get through."

Our jolliness at seeing Ali diminished a little as we waited to hear his answer. It couldn't be good. "That's why I'm here. I got a message in Cairo telling me to high tail it here as soon as I could. I'm supposed to hold the fort while you all," he pointed at Mitzi and me and our elven guardians with his big hand, "go see Ehren. There's a blackout on communication until he gets a handle on this new threat. All messages are through direct contact or ravens."

"Exactly like we're doing." Puddle seemed pleased with herself.

"Except the ravens aren't very reliable," I said.

"Keep working on it, Panda." Ekk turned to Mitzi and said, "You see why we need to go to the Garden now."

I looked at my wife, half expecting her to object, but she seemed resolved, saying, "I need to make a few calls. Then I'll be ready."

"What about me?" Puddle said spontaneously. I knew she felt abandoned. Ironically, my sister was okay, as long as she was the one leaving, but she hated to be left.

Ali went to her and put his big arm around her. "You and I are going to hold down the fort." He laughed uproariously as he hugged her tight. This guy was really growing on me. We were facing an existential threat and had to leave all we were used to on a moment's notice, but I felt his genuine warmth. He was also good at staying in the moment.

He addressed Puddle. "I brought bales of herbs from Egypt. I need a helper to set up shop again. You game?"

Puddle looked suddenly shy. "Sure."

"We need to find a space."

Her face lit up. "No, we don't. I think we've got one."

"Great. Let's talk about that in a minute."

He addressed me next. "I know you've got a tax office. Can you keep it going from abroad?"

"I'll call Babs. She's my office manager. We hired temporary accountants who are at the end of their agreement, but maybe they'll stay on."

"That should work, Panda," Ekk said.

"Ladies, don't overpack," Elsa said. "We need to travel light." I heard relief in her voice when she said, "Thanks, Ali. You've no idea how timely this is."

I poked Mitzi. "Hear that, wifey? Don't overpack." I laughed and got a dirty look.

Ali's return seemed to have relieved Ekk, and he said to him, "Come with me. I want to show you how my dagger is acting." It reminded me of guys at a party growing up, hood raised on some car in the driveway while a barbeque progressed in the backyard. They excused themselves and walked over to the glass table where he placed his dagger/receiver.

Puddle was happy with a mission. "I want you to call me every day, Panda."

"I'll sure try," I said, "but phones."

"Oh. Then Instagram pictures."

"This isn't a vacation, Puddle," Elsa said, She looked glum. "And someone needs to call Ralph. We still don't know where Aurora is."

At that, the good feeling we had when Ali arrived evaporated.

***

Ali and Ekk went to see Ralph, while we all packed and made phone calls to take care of our obligations in Merryville.

Mitzi got online and made reservations to Baden-Baden, the closest city to the Black Forest.

"I got us economy plus," she said. "Hey, Elsa, whoever is tracking us can see that, right?"

"I suppose so, Mitzi, but there's no other way."

"What about an elf hole?"

She laughed without humor. "Elf holes are emergency devices and only for relatively short distances. The longest one Ekk ever made was to Stockton to see your mother and get the Octopus Pendant."

As she said this, I smacked my head. The Octopus Pendant was an ancient amulet of protection. "How could we forget something so important?" I said and ran upstairs to get it.

"One of you girls should be wearing it every day anyway. *Ach du lieber.*" This last could be translated as "Oh heavens."

Puddle retrieved Ali's things from his rental car, as he was going to stay in the house with her while we were gone. With everyone set to their tasks, I had a little time. Given the danger only being hinted at, I hoped we would be returning, but I wrote out a quick will just in case.

***

Ekk knocked gently on the hospital door.

"Come in, Ekk," Ralph said and squinted. "Who's that with you?"

Ali approached his bed and offered his hand. "Ali Badawi, sir. I used to run a botanica here in town."

"Nice to meet you." He turned to Ekk. "Is this the fella you told me about?"

"Yes. It was his store my wife and Valerie went to for herbs for the sweat lodge. Unfortunately, it burned down."

Ralph said, "I'm glad everyone survived. What aren't you saying? Do I want to hear it?"

"You are perceptive," Ali said. He settled his big frame in a chair. "In fact, Ekk and I have some news that will be upsetting."

"It's hard to hear bad news when you can't jump up and fix it." Ralph braced himself. "Tell me quick. Is it about Aurora?"

"I'm afraid it is," Ekk said. "I went to Merry Hearts, and the security guard said they've moved her. Wouldn't tell me where." Ekk kept his eyes fixed on Ralph's face, ready for an angry reaction.

Surprisingly, Ralph laughed. "Good. I had 'em do that. She wasn't safe there."

Ekk looked hurt but relieved. "You didn't tell me."

"I was going to. I'm still waiting for the lady to bring me my phone."

"What lady?" Ali and Ekk said almost in unison.

"Jennifer from Merry Hearts."

Ekk furrowed his brow and said, "She doesn't work here, Ralph."

Ralph swatted the air. "I know that."

Ali was direct. "Where is Aurora?"

When Ralph hesitated, Ekk prompted him. "We know a place that's incredibly safe. It's called the Hercynian Garden. We must get her there to protect her."

"I don't think so," Ralph replied. "I need her here where I can keep an eye on her."

"But Ralph," Ekk said, "how are you going to protect her with your hip in a cast?"

"That's my business. You give me your story first." He was a smart old guy, playing his cards close to the vest. "And with all due respect," he motioned to Ali, "I only met him a minute ago."

Ali acknowledged the point with a nod. "I am trustworthy, but you are right with not taking anything at face value. Do you want me to leave?" He started to stand.

"No," Ekk said, "you stay. Time is short." He concentrated on Ralph. "I'm asking you to take a leap of faith. All our lives may depend on it."

Ralph nodded and moved his hand in a "proceed" motion.

Ali looked around and casually asked, "Are there any cell phones in the room?"

Ralph, eyes still on the big man, answered, "No, they say it interferes with their equipment on this floor. Why?"

"That's all part of the story," Ekk said, as he got up and closed the door for privacy.

CHAPTER TWENTY-THREE

COLORADO

Federal Express arrived at a town near the res, and Juniper drove Twyla to get her package. "Thank you for driving me," Twyla said. " I hope we haven't missed anything too urgent." Twyla was nervous—that was clear.

Juniper smiled and parked the car. "We'll know soon enough." When Twyla started to get out, she said, "Why don't you wait here."

"No, I want to see how this Federal Express thing works."

"Suit yourself."

The ladies went inside, Juniper tall and colorful, and Twyla much shorter and dressed in jeans, a pullover, and sandals. "If anyone asks," Juniper said, "you're my teenage daughter." Twyla smiled at that. While Juniper produced her identification, Twyla studied the interior of the business center. She hadn't been in California long enough to get her ID yet. This had been a subject of conversation in the car.

"But you drove my truck," Juniper said.

"Just because I don't have a license doesn't mean I don't know how to drive a car," Twyla said.

"Well, your privileges in that regard are withdrawn until you get legal. This is a rental."

Juniper shook her head, and thought the teenager analogy was apt.

Twyla tried to look suitably contrite, but fairies were like cats, immune to guilt.

Juniper received the small box from the attendant. "Thank you."

As she walked out, Twyla tried to grab it from her, and she deftly moved it to the other side. "Patience."

Once in the rental car, Twyla again grabbed for it and with a sigh, Juniper let her have the package.

"Please, please, please, be okay," she said as she ripped open the box and pulled out her undamaged dagger. She hugged it to her chest.

Juniper felt like her mother. "I can't believe you left it at our house."

***

"Should I get a ticket for Aurora too?" Mitzi called from the dining room table. She'd made this area her temporary office since the community garden issues started to blow up. She sat amidst the computer, reports, yellow pads, and other paperwork spread out all over.

"How can you?" I asked. "Wouldn't you need her birthdate and passport number? Does she even have a passport? Besides, last I heard, Ralph's not giving up where she is."

Mitzi looked tired and put her hand on her head. "That's right. Elsa, how are we going to get Aurora to Germany?"

Elsa sat on the dining room chair next to Mitzi and stared at the screen. "Oh, dear. We always count on the Garden for things like that. They provided Ekk and me with the passports we needed to travel. We'll get that when we go."

"They're not answering their phone." I put a fine point on it.

"I'm not sure what we're going to do." Elsa headed out the back door.

I asked, "Where are you going?"

"To find something to pack the Winter Stone in. We need to bring it with us."

Mitzi completed our reservations and said, "Tomorrow morning we'll be going to Germany again. I'm not sure how I feel about this."

I hugged her. "Me neither. Sure hope your dad's okay."

She hugged me back. "And Jay. Think about it. This guy follows my dad back to some magical place he's never heard of and what, turns into a superhero? He's not. He makes coffee for a living."

"He was smitten by your father." I smiled and shook my head. "That's one of the only things that makes sense right now, love. This is why I'm not letting you out of my sight." I kissed her head.

Mitzi's phone rang. She picked it up, and I moved away to do my own tasks. It sounded like another last-minute leaving notification. She said, "Thank you for understanding, I'll call you as soon as we get back."

Although I put on a brave front, I wasn't at all sure we could fulfill any promises we made to return.

***

The next morning, Mitzi, Ali, Elsa, Puddle, and I said our goodbyes.

"Ekk told me there was no way Ralph was going to crack and tell us where Aurora was." I was nervous about that.

"Your sister will keep working on him," Ali said and looked at Puddle.

Puddle hugged me hard. "Please be okay, sis."

"I'm planning on it. But just in case, our estate plan is in my drawer upstairs."

"That makes me sad."

"I'm being practical. You get the house." We both hugged again and cried a bit. "We'll get a message to you somehow. Get me on the prayer list at St. John's."

Mitzi's eyes were red. No one had slept well. "I decided not to tell my mom." She wore the Octopus Pendant around her neck and was ready to go. "I hate to say it, but I can't trust her after all that went down when she was here."

I thought about how Mitzi's mom had betrayed her several times and said, "News flash, no one else trusts Susan either." I didn't want to be mean, but I felt it needed to be said.

Elsa squeezed Mitzi's hand, and a light scent of lavender surrounded us.

A honk out front drew my attention. "That's us. Somebody get Ekk."

"I'm here." Ekk staggered in, carrying a bowling bag.

"In case we get bored in Germany?" Mitzi quipped.

"Do they even bowl there?" I asked.

Elsa said, "We Germans are the most enthusiastic bowlers in Europe."

I giggled. "Wow, bowling and accordions too. Whoo-hoo."

"Haha, let's go," Ekk said, We all knew he was carrying the Winter Stone.

My phone rang while we were waiting at the Lufthansa gate. Elsa said, "That should be in the bag."

"I've been waiting for this call." I turned my back to her. "Hello?"

"It's me," Twyla announced. The package arrived. Thank you."

"And?" I was trying to be cryptic. We were still wary of using our phones. Elsa moved close to my ear to listen. Mitzi was at the gate desk helping Ekk with trying to convince a flight attendant that the *bowling ball* was actually a carry-on and didn't need to be checked.

"It's working here in Colorado, I guess. Things are just weird in Merryville."

"Uh-huh. And?"

"Willow said—"

"Who's Willow?"

"It's code for tree," Twyla said.

I heard Juniper say, "Give me that," and she came on the line. "We're okay here. Heloisa told us reinforcements are coming, and other things I'd rather not say on the phone." Elsa glared. "That I'm about to put away."

"Gotcha. So Heloisa got you the message?"

"Sort of, complicated. Panda…be safe."

I unexpectedly teared up. "You too. I'll be in touch."

The line disconnected as our group was called for boarding. Mitzi wore a triumphant expression, and I noticed Ekk still had his bowling ball.

"Shall we?" Mitzi loved to travel, and, even in these circumstances, that didn't change. On board, she and I were seated behind the wing. Ekk and Elsa were somewhere near the front. Our reservations were made too late to have the four of us seated together. It didn't really matter. We'd all get there at the same time. My wife and I held hands when the plane took off, which was our custom. There was nothing to say, and many hours in the air ahead. I fell asleep.

***

GERMANY

We arrived at Stuttgart Airport fourteen hours later and took a train to Baden-Baden. I felt guilty, having slept most of the way on the plane. Mitzi was a wreck. I think much of that could be explained by her worry for her father. She'd only met him in March of this year, discovering at the same time he was a griffin and leader of the magical community. Now, she'd seen him in Merryville as a man, experienced being half-griffin herself, and together we had faced down Wolfrum. The train joggled us back and forth, carrying us into only heaven knew what. Mitzi was clearly uncomfortable, trying this way and that to reposition herself. I handed her my neck pillow. She tucked it around her neck and closed her eyes. It was lame, but sometimes little things like that were the only way to say I love you.

Wide awake, I listened as Ekk and Elsa chatted in German, something they did less and less at home, and I said randomly, "I need to learn to speak German."

"Oh, sorry," Ekk said, and pushed his wire-framed glasses up his nose. "It comes with the territory, I guess." He gestured to the window.

"This is where I spent many winters working." The temperature on the train was chilly by California standards. Mitzi opened her rolling bag and found a fleece, saying, "I think we've had enough winter."

I had my own jacket on and thought I should find some gloves. I replied, "At least this is a normal winter."

"Oh, honey," Elsa said, "this is only fall. Winters are something else. One December, it was so cold, all our windows were sealed in ice."

Mitzi closed her eyes and leaned on my shoulder, putting the fleece over her like a blanket. I looked out the window, but there wasn't much to see in between lit stations since it was nearly midnight.

"Next stop Baden-Baden," the conductor announced in both English and German. Ekk leaned in and tapped Mitzi. "Okay. Here's what's next. We're going to rent a car and go straight into the forest."

My wife gave up trying to sleep. "No Little Prince? I'm disappointed. Juniper told me how enchanting it was." Poor baby, it would have been nice to regroup before heading into the Black Forest.

"Sorry, Mitzi," Elsa said, "but time is of the essence. *Der Kleine Prinz* may be crawling with the enemy. We don't know what we're going into. Can't trust anyone here."

"So how smart is that? Couldn't we be driving right into a trap?" I asked.

Ekk and Elsa were quiet as the train slowed and we entered the station. Ekk finally said, "Panda." His red eyes betrayed how tired he was. "Let's see what happens when we get there. I hope all in the Garden is reasonably well and this is a voluntary communication blackout. Until we know, don't let your thoughts go dark. Let's find out if Heloisa, Ehren, and many others we care about are okay. Then we can relax."

Mitzi frowned. "Sorry, Ekk. I forgot you led the Garden while my dad was in Merryville. This has to be hard for you."

He looked out the window into the darkness, and his reflection in the glass was of a sad elf. "It is," he said.

Upon arrival at the Baden-Baden station, Ekk quickly got us a Kia Sorento from the sleepy attendant.

"Thank goodness you speak the language," Mitzi said.

Elsa shrugged. "Most Germans speak English. You would have been okay without us."

"Let's hope we never have to find out," I said, as I helped Ekk load our four bags in the truck, along with our bowling ball. Heater blasting, tucked in, we were off.

***

THE BLACK FOREST

Ekk couldn't reach the peddles without his adapters, so I drove. As we headed into the forest, my gut was singing, a sign that some sort of magical event or creature was near. "Remember when we first met?" I asked Elsa, who sat shotgun. "Yes. I can't believe it was only this year. That time you were in the back seat."

Ekk and Mitzi sat in the back now, buckled in. There were no streetlights, so I drove with the brights on. The trees were dense, and it was rough-going once we left the paved roads. I hit a pothole and Mitzi said, "Slow down."

"Sorry." The trees made every twist and turn similar. "Okay guardians, I need directions. This is one place GPS has no clue."

"Mitzi's right," Elsa said. "Go slow. We're getting close."

"I can feel it," I said and squinted to try to see better in the dark. "Or at least I feel something. Do we need to walk and find that rock like last time?"

Elsa was practically on the dashboard, peering into the night forest. "No. We're driving in."

From the back Ekk said, "I had them add this option when I was in charge. Hopefully we—"

"There." Elsa pointed to a particularly uninviting area in the dark. It was a collection of rocks and trees. "Drive right up and it should open."

"Like platform nine and three quarters? What if we crash? No offense, but how do you know?"

Elsa gave me the stink-eye.

"Maybe she's right, Ekk said. "We don't know what we're going into. Let me try to walk it first."

Ekk opened his door, and I felt a cold blast of air rush in. Mitzi got out, too, so I had to get out. Elsa rolled down her window. "Walk forward like normal, and you should be able to enter. We need to hurry."

I followed Ekk with Mitzi right behind. We walked to the rocks, and I bumped my shin. "Ow!"

Ekk moved a couple of feet to the left and similarly couldn't enter. "It's solid, Elsa."

She shined a light on a map in her lap. Meanwhile, my gut was on fire. "It's to the right," I said and pointed to an area about twenty feet ahead. Unfortunately, there was a crevice in the ground between us and where I thought we should go that would be dangerous to traverse.

"Panda, dear, I know you have, uh, some sensing ability, but that doesn't line up with the coordinates we received before the blackout." Elsa appeared panicked and this wasn't something I wanted to see.

"Humor me, Mitzi?" I held out my hand and she and I carefully made our way to the crevice. It would surely twist any axel on a car and destroy the tires. She hung onto a thick branch and held one of my arms as I stretched my body into it. Sure enough, my foot and ankle entered a warm space, a hallmark of the Hercynian Garden.

"This is it."

Ekk and Elsa were quiet as we piled back in the car to drive into an illusion that seemed certain to destroy us all. Even though I'd assured them, Mitzi squeezed her eyes shut and even Elsa winced as we entered. Thankfully, the front tires of the Kia straightened out on a smooth road, and the atmosphere lightened once we were fully in. It was night in the Garden, with stars and a bright moon overhead instead of thick trees. It almost seemed bright compared to the Black Forest. At least we could see.

"Who goes there?" A voice called out in German. Like when we were in the Garden before, understanding other languages was no problem. The Hercynian Garden must have some sort of magical universal translator woven into the space.

Ekk rolled down his window and called out, "Ekkehardt Schmidt."

"Ekk?" It was Shrumm who, sword in hand, revealed himself. "Ekk!"

"Shrumm, what are you doing on guard duty?" The two men hugged through the window. "We're all on guard," Shrumm said. "Lots going on. Let's get to the keep."

"Climb in. It'll be quicker."

Shrumm squeezed into the back seat.

My relief that this place was still here, coupled with the warm air and having a magical creature in our car, bolstered my hope for a good outcome.

"How did you find the opening?" Shrumm asked. "We've had to move it several times."

"Our driver, Panda Fowler, has some pretty impressive sensing magic," Elsa admitted.

I looked at her in the rearview mirror and grinned.

We were tired, but here we were, driving a Kia from the human world on paved roads toward the keep. Mitzi was now wide awake, and the smile she gave me spoke volumes. The sky was dark blue, and the fields were guarded. Dwarves mostly stared back at us as we drove slowly by.

"Report, Shrumm," Ekk said, then laughed. Apparently, that was part of his leadership style when he was in charge of the Garden for a period of time.

"Actually," Shrumm said. "I will. Ladies, I saw you when you were here so long ago after your rescue of Mitzi,"—time worked differently in the parallel world—"but we were never introduced. I, Popkin Shrumm, am the first person." Ekk and Elsa gasped.

"But Harold has been first person forever," Elsa said.

"What happened to the old first person?" Mitzi asked.

"We have an ideal community here," Shrumm answered, "but even free creatures still die. He died in honor, protecting your father, Mitzi."

Our frivolity died. There was a war going on.

"Here is our state of affairs. Communication is an issue."

"We heard about the phone situation," Ekk said. "Ours are in a Faraday pouch in my suitcase."

Shrumm was thin, and tall for an elf. He used his hands expressively. "That's no longer a problem here. All of your cellular phones were completely blocked once you entered. We're working on a fix for when you eventually leave, and also for our regular dagger communication devices."

Mitzi asked, "Tell us what's happened, Popkin."

Shrumm, Ekk, and Elsa gasped. Ekk said, "You didn't know, Mitzi, but we only call him Shrumm. If someone says the first name of the first person, it's a signal that something's wrong."

We still had so much to learn. Mitzi apologized.

I thought, *Well, he did tell us his first name.* I kept my mouth shut and drove.

Shrumm still seemed embarrassed. "Anyway, Ehrenhardt will tell you what we know now, but we were hit hard by our new enemy right here at the keep. Thus, the blackout."

"No," Elsa said. "That's unprecedented. They actually breached the keep?" It was interesting listening to Ekk and her talk to Shrumm. This reminded me they had other close relationships and a different life and were part of this world before coming to Merryville.

"There were injuries, and I think the shock brought on Harold's death. I'm now first person to your father, Mitzi. He has had me walking the perimeter for weeks now, expecting your arrival."

This made me feel guilty, and I'd bet the farm my wife did too. We'd been resistant to Ehren's call to come back here for protection. At this moment it seemed selfish to only think about our work and the community garden in Merryville. This was the Garden we should have prioritized.

"I'm sorry for the delay, Shrumm," was all Mitzi said.

We pulled the car into the keep. "You've made some changes," I commented.

"That was under my leadership," Ekk said proudly.

"Yes, you really were innovative. Ehrenhardt was impressed." Shrumm patted Ekk's shoulder.

"What about Jay?" Mitzi asked. "What's he doing here?"

Shrumm pointed as we pulled closer to the buildings. "This is new. Coffee *Wirtschaft*. It opens in the morning. The apple fritters are truly delicious."

I cracked up. "The keep has a coffeehouse."

"Park here," Shrumm said, and we pulled into an empty stable and got out of the car.

"Is my dad okay?" Mitzi asked him.

"He's fine, but he's very busy. You get your bags, and I'll announce your arrival." Shrumm went to Ekk, who was already at the open trunk of the Kia. "Do you have it?"

Ekk nodded, "I do." Ekk handed him the bag with the Winter Stone.

"Nice bag." Shrumm rushed inside and Ekk continued to unload our scant luggage. Mitzi took her bag, and I gave her a hug. "You okay?" She nodded.

A young female elf in green ran out of the keep's main hall. "Greetings, Ekkehard and Elsa Schmidt." She bowed to us. "Welcome Mitzi and Panda Fowler. I'm Sasha. Follow me. Do you need help?" She talked fast, with the energy of youth.

Each of us had a bag in hand and said variations of "No, we're fine." Lights were coming on in the immediate vicinity, and several of the keep's denizens sleepily came out to observe our arrival.

"Our arrival is a big deal," Mitzi whispered to me. "Now I really do feel guilty for delaying it." I did, too, and walked behind Sasha into the entrance, which appeared different than before. I recalled it used to be ornate. This one was simple and really nice.

Inside, the large chamber looked the same, but a bit smaller than I remembered. When we were first here many months ago, everything was new and overwhelming. Now I was getting used to the walls made of *grunzueg,* and my sensing magic told me we were in a safe place. That felt good.

Sasha took Mitzi and me to our room, which was cozy and sweet. The *grunzueg* used to build here was a great insulator. It kept the room from being too cold during the winter or too hot during the summer. The bed was covered with a puffy quilt bearing the image of a griffin in royal blue. I longed to jump into the soft bed after all our travel, but a late evening meeting with Mitzi's father and maybe a snack were in order.

I risked a quick lay down while my wife brushed her hair and refreshed her face. She asked, "Where did Sasha take Ekk and Elsa?"

"I think Ekk already had quarters from before," I answered. "You know he lived here for quite some time."

"Oh yes, the time thing," she said. "Speaking of which, don't get too comfortable. How do I look?"

"Beautiful."

"Your eyes are closed."

I made myself get up because surely I would fall asleep if I remained lying down.

"Uh, Panda."

"Yes?" I was ready to go, still wearing my travel clothes.

"Change your blouse and brush your hair."

Here we were almost six thousand miles away from home in a magic keep, and her comment struck my overtired mind as silly. "Just like home." I wiped tears of laughter from my eyes and did as I was told, donning my least wrinkled blouse. We walked outside our room to look for the dining room and were startled when little Sasha popped up from a chair and led us cheerfully down the hall. I was glad for her quiet company, as she led us to the informal dining room. I thought things must not be so bad if she could be so happy.

The smell of stew was in the air, even before we entered the rustic kitchen dining room. I loved it. The place was adjacent to the kitchen and was intimate. The fireplace was huge, and a giant copper pot hung over the flames. Fragrant woodsmoke scent hung in the air, and I wondered if Elsa had conjured yet another magical fragrance. She met my eyes and commented, "It's natural, not me." She and Ekk were seated at the heavy wooden table in the center of the room, which was laden with delicious-smelling food. Ehren waited for us, dressed in his informal purple outfit. He stood next to Jay, who looked great in a flowing white shirt and tight jeans. The handsome men enveloped us in hugs. The fact that time passed more quickly here than at home hit me again. Ehren and Jay vibed like a long-time couple, but they'd only met six or so weeks ago in our world.

Ekk and Elsa were tired, too, and somewhat subdued. After hugs, Ehren held Mitzi at arm's length and said, "Finally. Why didn't you come sooner?"

I knew Mitzi would be grumpy at that, but before she could answer, Jay said, "Ehren, let the poor girl eat, then talk." I was impressed. Ehren could be overbearing, and I was interested in how he would react.

Surprisingly, he said, "Jay's right. Eat. You all must be tired. We won't keep you up too long. Is your room okay?"

Jay was really rocking the host role in this relationship. I thought about Twyla, and wondered how she would feel about that as her late father used to be Ehren's partner. I answered, "It's cozy and wonderful. Thank you."

"I love it," Mitzi said. "I wish I could write about it on Trip Advisor."

"What's Trip Advisor?" Ehren asked.

Mitzi answered, "It's a thing at home. Online reviews for travel."

"Oh." The culture gap between them was palpable. "Well, you know you can't do that."

She smiled. "I know." They awkwardly made small talk, but I wasn't listening because my attention turned to the food. I recognized dishes Elsa made for us at home and some new purple vegetables that tasted like potato. Elsa commented, "It's been so long since I had *Rinderroulade*, delicious."

Since we were enveloped in the Hercynian Garden, I understood what that was. *Beef roll.* We could do this at home."

"Yes, we could," Ekk said and grinned.

Jay's eyes were merry. "Panda, are you the cook back in Merryville?"

"Uh, no." I said as Mitzi and Elsa laughed.

"But she is our main eater," Mitzi said.

I changed the subject. "There was one funny thing at home, Jay. You should have seen your old friends at Not Your Mother's Coffeehouse. In about two minutes they had a snow scene in the window and served new hot drinks called things like 'Snowball' and 'Winter in September.'"

He laughed, and I wondered if he missed his friends. "The owner is very creative, but wait until you see my coffeehouse."

"Your *Wirtschaft*?" I loved this dual language thing.

Jay brightened. "Yes, we serve food too. Come by tomorrow and I'll give you some baked goods. As it turns out, some of the locals were dying to have a place to showcase their baking, and I was thrilled for them to do that. It's they who are making it the place to be."

Ehren turned to Jay. "You're too modest."

Wow, Ehren was truly smitten.

I pushed away my plate. "I'll be there." I hadn't intended to eat so much, but the food was so good.

Kitchen staff cleared plates, and tiny shot glasses of something alcoholic were brought. I declined, but the amber liquid reflecting the fire in the grate was pretty.

"Ekk," Ehren said, " how was your flight? Did anyone follow?" His manner had become serious again. I noticed Ehren asked the male, none of us females.

"I don't think so, but we don't know what we're dealing with yet." Ekk picked his teeth. "I see your new first person is here."

Shrumm had joined us near the end of our eating. To Ehren he said, "I put the Winter Stone in the vault. Do we want to do the briefing now or in the morning?"

Ehren stood and stretched. "It's late. Let's meet here for breakfast." He gave us the once over and said, "They should have at least one night of undisturbed sleep."

After sleepy goodnights, we shuffled down the hall to our room. Mitzi and I both piled into bed, assuming our normal spooning positions. I couldn't help but wonder what was so terrible it would disturb our sleep.

***

I got up the next morning before Mitzi and decided to find my way to Jay's coffeehouse. The staff in the keep all knew their jobs, and I saw elves, fairies, dwarves and the occasional human busy with their various tasks. Everyone seemed to know who I was, and no one stopped me as I went out the front door. Coffee was a powerful draw for me. I was a woman on a mission.

Daylight showed a community on edge. With this new threat we were facing, this was no surprise. Even so, there were greetings of *Guten*

Morgan—good morning—and nods to meet me all the way to the *Wirtschaft.* The open sign was written in at least six different languages, and the smell of cinnamon wafted through the front door. A couple of dwarves sat at the outside tables, enjoying giant croissants. I went inside and ordered a latte and pastry.

Jay spotted me from the back and came out to say good morning. "I see you found the streusel. Good choice. Give me a sec and I'll join you."

I sat at a table near the window and sipped coffee while people-watching creatures in the surreal scene. Jay seated himself across from me at the French-inspired, decorative, wrought-iron table and chairs.

All I could say was, "So wow!"

His cup couldn't hide his smile and upon placing it down he said, "I know. Wow."

"This is incredible, Jay. How long has it been in your time?"

He scratched his head. "It's flown, I can tell you that. Probably a year or two? Every day is so amazing. It's hard to describe."

"Are you happy here? Miss home?"

"Very, and maybe a little, but this is home now. Is Mitzi sleeping in?"

"Yes, she was so tired. It was a long trip." I tucked into my streusel. "This is amazing."

He jerked his head toward the kitchen. "I'm telling you, it's the bakers from the keep. I just provide a place to sell their stuff." He checked his watch. "We're having breakfast in about forty-five minutes, so don't eat too many."

"You sound like Ehren." We shared a smile. "He looks happy."

With a telling sigh, Jay responded, "As happy as he gets. He has a big load to carry here, and I'm glad to support that. He'll tell you more after breakfast."

"By the way, I suspect you had a hand in redecorating the keep," I said. " Love the new entrance."

This made him smile. "We call it the main house now. And yes, the first time I saw that over-the-top green design…" He clucked. "It was so Emerald City that I couldn't stop thinking about the *Wizard of Oz.*" We both laughed. "The rustic opening fits better with the surrounding garden and forest theme."

Some cinnamon dropped on my white tunic, and I dipped my napkin in water to sponge it off. "I think so too." We chatted amiably a bit more before I went back to the room with a packaged streusel and coffee for Mitzi. Part of me felt like I was on vacation, but my gut told me the information we were about to receive would change all that.

CHAPTER TWENTY-FOUR

It was a rare sight at the community garden. At six on a Saturday morning, almost the whole board was present. Sylvia Arviso, Hortense Miller, Florence Dinwitter, Janet Bruce-Pippin, Denise McGreggor, Sally Johnson, and Charlotte Windingle all stood side by side and watched the CTI environmental engineers do their work. Janet bit her nails, Sally hummed, and Charlotte mostly sweated, having walked from being dropped off at the end of the street. "Did we have to do this so early?"

"CTI does their work better without a crowd," Sylvia explained. "We were afraid if we did this later, all the opposition groups might try to interfere. This town loves a good protest."

Charlotte grunted. "I sure hope we get a good result." This was the day they would, hopefully, begin to find out who was telling the truth about the quality of the soil.

The owner of the all-female company, Rhonda Flowers, directed another woman who was drilling in the second of five sections plotted out for testing. They had an impressive amount of machinery standing by and boxes full of tubes to collect samples. "You gals don't need to wait," she said. "It's going to be a while. We're testing every acre." Her bright smile was reassuring.

"That's okay," Denise McGreggor said. "We can't help it. Our club has a lot riding on what you find, but I wouldn't mind a latte." Sally giggled.

"We have coffee in the trailer. It's not a latte, but it's hot," Sylvia said. "We can wait inside and not stare at these women while they do their work."

Denise and Florence turned around to leave and saw a group marching down the dirt road toward where they stood.

"Oh no," Florence said. "Who invited them?" She pointed toward the six or seven new arrivals and then pulled down her sun hat over her ears, as if it would protect her identity. The rest of the club ladies turned to see Phillip Pen and a photographer walking with another group of young people. Francisco Gonzalez led them with Dr. Sliwa at his side. Hortense frowned.

"It's okay," Sylvia said. "We're playing with an open hand." She started walking to the group.

Not able to resist making a quasi-legal comment, Florence said, "It's not private property so I guess we can't stop them." With that, she walked toward the trailer. "I'll be inside."

Charlotte, who probably had the most financially riding on this outcome said, "I'll join you." She didn't want to be interviewed by the *Merryville Bee.*

As Hortense and Janet followed Denise, Hortense asked her, "Did you find anything out about what Mitzi Fowler said? Did the city let Ring off the hook illegally?"

Denise put a finger over her lips. "Inside."

***

When the group was within twenty feet or so, Sylvia waved in a friendly manner, as if she were leading a tour and had been expecting them. "Good morning. For those of you who don't know, I'm Sylvia Arviso, president of the Merryville Horticultural Society." She motioned to where CTI was digging. "We've got some testing going on, so I ask that you don't come closer for insurance reasons." She smiled her Silicon Valley smile.

"At six in the morning?" a young man in Francisco's group yelled. "What are you trying to hide from us?" Francisco put up a hand to shush him and walked to the front.

"Good morning to you, Ms. President." He sounded vaguely mocking. "What's going on so bright and early?"

"I don't answer to you, Francisco, but I will tell you and Dr. Sliwa." She nodded a greeting to the woman who, as before, wore a facial expression appropriate if someone had put dirt in her Wheaties that morning.

"You were at the press conference," Sylvia said to the group.

"The propaganda conference," a young woman in their group said as her friends snickered.

With the hoopla, no one noticed Hortense leave the trailer and hand her niece the club's camcorder.

Sylvia went on as if uninterrupted. "Mitzi Fowler said it best. We have paused the project until science gives us the truth. The Horticultural Society will proceed accordingly once we have results."

Dr. Sliwa said derisively, arms crossed tightly, "Science has given you the truth. We gave you the results already."

Rhonda Flowers seemed to be drawn in by the spectacle and walked toward Dr. Sliwa. She pulled off her leather gloves and said, "Hello, everyone. What's this all about?"

"We want to know who you are and who hired you." Francisco said.

"I'm CEO of CTI, an environmental consulting firm. Whoever pays my bills is none of your business unless they choose to tell you. And you are?"

"I'm Francisco Gonzalez, professor at Merida University."

"And candidate for mayor," Sally Johnson added sweetly. Rhonda wore an amused expression.

"Are you a scientist?" Rhonda asked.

Dr. Sliwa answered for him. "He's not, but I am. Dr. Sliwa. I'm head of the agricultural department at Merida. It was our students who first recognized the potential for disaster in turning this tire factory into a farm."

Rhonda, a professional, simply said, "I see. Nice to meet you. I'd love to have you explain to me what areas you tested and the testing methods used. I can show you how we're proceeding. Are you interested?"

Rhonda was fit and exuded health and good cheer. It would have been hard for anyone to turn down her offer. The crowd watched as Dr. Sliwa seemed to struggle with how to respond.

She looked at the reporter. "Of course, but I'm bringing the photographer."

"Some ground rules," Sylvia said. "We, the society, are paying for this testing. This isn't your project. I'll allow one or two photos, but these folks have an important job to do and have a right to do their work without interruption."

Phillip Pen said with snark, "You mean without witnesses."

Ms. Flowers took offense. "Excuse me, young man. Who are you to say that about my company?"

The crowd parted a bit, and although anyone else would have regretted that smartass comment, he doubled down. "Phillip Pen. I'm a reporter. The stench of backroom deals with the tire company is all over," he waved his microphone around, "and this attempt to appear benevolent to the underserved community is going to be embarrassing once the truth comes out. This project has been shoved down the public's throat—"

Rhonda pulled back and said in surprise, "Whoa. Agenda alert. We're here to deal with facts, not pre-drawn conclusions."

"Phillip, are you serious?" Sylvia sputtered. "Corruption? Shoving the idea of healthy vegetables down the public throat? You sound like Dr. Sliwa's crowd."

Dr. Sliwa said, "See here, Sylvia—"

"No, no, let them come," Rhonda said to Sylvia. Then to the hostile crowd, she said, "I only ask you to pick some representatives who will stand ten feet back."

She got a glare from Sliwa, who crossed her arms. It appeared this woman wasn't going to budge.

"You can take all the notes you want," Rhonda said, "but this crowd needs to go home. I have my people to think about too." She wasn't backing down either and spoke with authority.

Dr. Sliwa finally pulled Francisco aside and spoke to him. When he came back he said to his group, "Okay, you all go back to the campaign office and make your calls. I'm going to stay with Dr. Sliwa. We'll get to the bottom of this." His entourage didn't seem to like being dismissed but did as they were told.

Phillip Pen followed Rhonda back to where her crew was boring into the soil and said, "I've won awards and don't have an agenda. This will be a truthful article."

"Looking forward to it," Janet called out, video camera to her eye as she filmed.

"Who's this?" Francisco asked. With his crowd around he hadn't noticed the large woman filming.

"This is Janet, our club archivist," Hortense said. "No offense, but I think we need our own record of events." She smiled and went back to the trailer.

Janet Bruce Pippin, power point operator for the club and all things technical said to Phillip, "Okay, Mr. Merryville Bee, I caught all of that confrontation, so you better get this right when you print it."

Francisco took a few steps away from Phillip.

Sylvia was never so glad to have both Hortense and her niece Janet on board. She brightened considerably and said, "Let's do this."

***

MERRYVILLE HOSPITAL

Puddle and Ali went to pick up Ralph and take him to Taggart's. Puddle was surprised to see Aurora in the room with him. She was glad to see that Aurora appeared happy and fairly focused. She wore street clothes, and her hair was combed. Ralph was dressed in overalls and sat on the bed, ready to go.

"Hi, Ralph, so glad to see you both." Puddle put emphasis on the both. Ralph had only recently agreed to travel to the Hercynian Garden with his wife. "Aurora. Remember me? From Merry Hearts?"

Aurora looked at her husband. "Ralph, do we know her?"

"Yes, darling. This is Puddle. She's going to take us to Taggart's." It was probably smart not to bring up Gary Smithers and the shooting.

Her countenance brightened. She said to Puddle, "I'm Aurora Brown."

Puddle pointed to the tie dye T-shirt she wore and said, "Puddle Fowler." She picked up Ralph's small bag as Ali's large frame filled the door, pushing a wheelchair. "Your ride is ready, sir."

Aurora stared at him.

"Hi, madam. I'm Ali Badawi."

"From Egypt." She said, surprisingly.

"Yes, I am."

Aurora lifted her hand and pointed a crooked index finger at him. She said, "You knew someone I knew."

He smiled knowingly. "Yes. We know the same people."

Puddle understood this was a magical person connecting with another magical person. It was cool.

Ralph picked up on it too and asked Puddle, "Is he?"

She nodded. "The botanica was here so he could help keep an eye on Merryville, my sister, and her wife."

Ralph said, "For me as a mere mortal…well, it's a lot."

Ali said, "I know, sir. I know." He motioned to the door. "Shall we?"

Puddle was eager to see how Ralph, and now Aurora, would take to the alterations they'd made to Taggart's. She changed the subject, as magic seemed to make Ralph a little uncomfortable. "Are you ready to see the store?"

At that, Ralph brightened. "Let's go. But I need someone to bring me my new horse to put in the car."

Puddle frowned, confused. "Horse?" She wondered if he was not getting dementia too.

Aurora laughed. "He calls that walker in the closet his horse."

Ali loaded Ralph into the wheelchair, and pushed him toward the lobby. Puddle retrieved his walker and pushed the "horse" beside them. Aurora walked slowly next to her husband, using a cane. Ralph asked Puddle, "Have you heard from Ekk?"

"Not yet. Hopefully soon."

As they reached the lobby, he said, "I'm afraid to ask. How bad is the store?"

"Not bad at all," Ali said. "We got all the damaged goods out. Elsa made a good list of what we had to discard. That freed up some shelving. I, ah, filled those shelves up with some botanica type items."

Puddle looked at Ali but said to Ralph. "It's a good mix. New customers are already stopping in."

Reception signed Ralph out and, as they waited for the car, Aurora asked, "What items?"

Ali said, "I'm an expert with herbs, but I made sure it was framed in a Taggart's style. You need to see it because I want your approval." He was quite a salesman.

Ralph patted Aurora's hand and asked Ali, "Don't get me wrong, I'm grateful you two were able to keep the store open at all, but a botanica?"

"Yes. I used to sell herbs, candles, and incense, all designed around the mysteries of Egypt and the pyramids. I used to own a store called The Eye of Horus.

Ralph winced. "I hope we're not going to smell incense and see beads over the door." Ali laughed.

Puddle pulled up with the car, and it took the two of them to put Ralph in the front. With the seat pushed back, Ralph had enough leg room to accommodate his hip cast.

"Are you sure you don't want to go home and see this later?" Ali teased.

"Nope," Ralph said. Any observer could tell Ralph was anxious. Taggart's represented not only his livelihood but also his history with Aurora.

***

Mitzi and I were at the breakfast table first, eager to find out why we were summoned and what new enemy we faced. Ekk came in shortly after us and pulled out one of the heavy wooden chairs.

"Where's Elsa?" I asked around the roll I was eating.

"Elsa," he said, "is visiting her grandmother."

I looked at Mitzi, and she gave me a puzzled look back. "She's still alive?"

He seemed mildly insulted. "In the Garden, elves can live to about a hundred and twenty-five. She's unwell, which is another reason we needed to come."

"Oh my gosh, Ekk, I feel so bad. We delayed Elsa seeing her grandma." I put my roll down.

"But she was willing to stay with us…" Mitzi said.

"You are our mission. That comes first," was all he said. When he could tell we were going to keep talking about it, he said, "It's okay."

I felt selfish not knowing more about the Schmidts, and it humbled me. Ehren and Jay entered, like the royalty they were, and took seats at the ceremonial table. This table, unlike the kitchen dining room, was shiny and had a colorful runner from end to end. Shortly thereafter, Shrumm and two attendants I didn't know took seats. A neatly dressed dwarf of indeterminate age turned out to be Alaric. He had a comical pencil-thin mustache. It looked drawn on, but his expression was serious. The other person was a large woman in flowing purple with wavy reddish-brown hair in a thick braid. She wore glasses framing intense eyes that kept studying us. Ehren greeted her. "Woda, come meet my daughter."

While we made introductions, kitchen staff brought potato omelets, apple pancakes, and sausages. Jay and I made eye contact. He said, "See what I mean? These are the best cooks and bakers in the world."

Ehren waited until we were almost done eating, then began. "I think you have all been introduced. In addition to Shrumm, Woda and Alaric have been invaluable with fighting this new face on an old enemy."

"I'm surprised Heloisa isn't here," Mitzi said.

Shrumm explained. "Heloisa is our chief guardian. She is visiting each of the nine provinces in the Garden to make sure we're secure."

"That does make me feel secure," Mitzi said. I agreed with her.

Ehren cleared his throat.

"Father, you wanted us here," Mitzi said, "and I'm glad we came. It's so good to see you. We're very curious to hear why we were summoned."

"Thank you, daughter. I'm glad to see you too. We have some answers." Ehren stood and nodded at Alaric, who pulled a small device from his pocket. He pressed a button and a screen descended from the ceiling. "Alaric is our new head of technology."

I had to ask. "Excuse me, didn't you tell us before about a treaty that prevented your use of modern technology?"

"That was then, and only for weapons," Ehren said. "It's been years since you were here. The treaty has been broken so many times in that regard, we stopped trying to honor it. No more swords and bows and arrows."

He paced like a general or someone crushing a Ted talk. "You know about the communication blackout. We discovered that the enemy knew our every move and traced it to our cell phones and our own dagger communication devices. Alaric?"

Alaric was small for a dwarf, and he wore the purple robes of Hercynian Garden leadership. He stood on a stool and gave us a fairly comprehensive lesson on radio waves. He ended his presentation with, "It's astonishing how something so old and simple could penetrate all our safeguards."

Woda spoke up for the first time. "That's because we were still following the treaty."

Ehren explained. "Woda is the equivalent of your state department. She believes in diplomacy and has guided us well. Unfortunately, things have changed, but she will guide us in this new area."

"I still haven't given up on making a truce." Woda was clearly a force to be reckoned with.

"The stone changes everything," Shrumm said. "Until we secure the other stones, there will be no peace."

A kitchen worker came in quietly to pick up plates. Ehren said, "Leave us and finish later." She closed the door on the way out.

Ekk had remained quiet, but now he spoke up. "Elsa and I heard about the stones from childhood, but they were more myth than anything."

Ehren waved at the screen, and a picture of the Peruvian jungle appeared.

"We were there a couple of months ago," Mitzi said, unnecessarily.

Ehren showed patience. He had a soft spot for his daughter. "Yes." He looked so fit since becoming human, his tawny hair curled around his collar. "This was the fabled home of the Summer Stone. We now know that the alliance the old Wolf Raven made with the Amazons was all about finding the Summer Stone in Paititi."

"But we never found it," Mitzi said. "We couldn't even enter Paititi. In the portal I saw magical illusions beyond my reach, but that's as close as we got before the portal closed."

"We know," Ehren said. "Every time you and your friends and guardians are involved in a portal opening, or an event with the organized evil *Lupus Imperium*, we do an analysis. Woda and Shrumm led the scholars and found indications the stone they sought was never even in Peru."

Shrumm spoke up, excited. "At least now we know they were after a magical stone. We had no idea at first what it was."

"As I was saying…"

"Sorry," Shrumm said. He was clearly intensely involved in all of what Ehren was saying, but a pecking order existed.

Right now, Ehren had the floor. "This is why I'm more relaxed about you two going back to Merryville. Now that the Winter Stone is safely in our vault, it takes away their reason for attack."

"Is that the only reason they came?" I asked.

"Initially, they probably believed kidnapping Mitzi, or worse, would be a way to get at me, but I think they know by now you two aren't the easy targets they thought you would be." Ekk patted Mitzi on the back.

"In fact, you're actually being considered for a mission—"

Elsa knocked and entered. "Sorry I'm late." She took the last empty chair next to me.

Mitzi and I were both super curious. "Please tell us more," Mitzi said.

"Ekk, take over." Ekk stood and took Ehren's place at the front of the table. I was impressed he had such a big role in this, but he did run the place for a while when Ehren was in California.

Ekk cleared his throat. "Woda, Alaric, so glad you're on the council. Ehrenhardt, thank you for your leadership as always." He looked at Elsa, then at all of us. "Friends." I noticed he included Shrumm with friends, and I realized they must be quite close. "Some of you know most of what I'm about to say, although for some it will be new."

Alaric asked, "Do you want me to do the pictures?"

Ekk cracked his knuckles. "It's been a while, but I can do this." He waved at the screen and the image of Stonehenge appeared. "You've all seen this iconic image. Ancient peoples aligned these huge stones with the sun, moon, and stars. It's a sacred place, and at different times has served as a burial site." He switched the picture. "Our historians have studied Stonehenge and all the other stone circles in the United Kingdom. There are stone circles in Avebury and Wiltshire." He changed the image. "Here's a circle in Stanton Drew and at Cove, Somerset. We don't have all the answers, but we have learned that, even if broken down, certain smaller stones have magical properties. Over time a few have been switched on, for lack of a better term, and affected the weather. This Winter Stone, we believe is from St. Cleer in Cornwall, England. Unfortunately, these stones existed before written history, and we don't know much beyond what I told you."

Woda spoke. "There's some controversy on that. Some of our researchers say their qualities weren't written down because it was too dangerous. Better to leave it in oral history." I was curious to hear more from her.

Shrumm said, "Let's keep it simple."

A picture of our stone filled the screen. "That's the one sent to Taggart's Emporium," I said, earning me glances from everyone in the room.

"Yes," Ekk said, like a tired teacher.

"Ekk and I were able to deactivate it by repeating an old nursery rhyme called "*Dons meyn,*" Elsa said.

Jay had been silent through all of this Garden business, but now asked, "How did you know to use it?"

All the magical people in the room looked at him. "We all share knowledge of the ancient wisdom in fables and rhymes," Elsa answered. "It's an open secret, so if you're in this room, keep it to yourself. *Meyn* is stone in Cornish and many rhymes we take for granted are actually common magic passed down through the innocents. This child's rhyme popped into my head as soon as we saw the stone."

"Yes," Ekk said, "we all learned it growing up."

"Could it have been any poem?" Jay asked.

Woda, Ehren, Ekk, and Alaric shared a worried glance. "That's one of the things we don't know." Ehren said.

"I said the Cornish poem because I lived with my Oma for a while in Cornwall," Elsa said. "We had stone circles everywhere, and that image popped into my mind. When I saw the stone, it reminded me of the poems we learned there."

"That was pretty lucky," Mitzi commented.

"Not luck," Ehren said. "Every guardian is carefully selected for their task, Mitzi. I chose Elsa for you because her intuition and knowledge of inanimate magic potential is solid. She and Ekkehard are a good team." He gave them a rare smile. "In more ways than one."

I wondered what his words "knowledge of inanimate magic" meant.

"As long as it's kept away from a magic person who might use it for ill, it's harmless. Even at its worst, it can only create wintery conditions. The problem is—"

Woda couldn't hold back. "The problem is there are four cardinal stones. And we don't know what would happen if they were all brought together in a circle."

Alaric said, "Woda—"

She turned on him. "They were separated from each other for a reason." She spoke this in a serious manner, and I started calling her *gloomy grandma* in my head. Some of the lightness left the room. This woman had gravitas. To make sure we were sufficiently depressed she said, "You only have a piece of the one."

My hope that we were close to being done with this Winter Stone thing died. "Aren't they all in Cornwall?" It seemed logical.

Elsa said, "Not all of them. I was able to learn a bit from my Oma. She repeated a fable about the stones that ended with them being broken and flung to the four corners of the earth."

"Well then, I guess since the bad guys know it's not in Merryville, does this mean we can go home now?" I asked hopefully.

"Soon," Ehren said, "but there is still more for you to know. Alaric." A world map appeared on the screen. "The Winter Stone was in California, and we don't know who sent it to Aurora or why. By the way, where is Aurora?"

"Err, her husband has secreted her away," Ekk said.

Woda was direct. "Ekk, we need her. There's a reason the stone was sent to her. It's only a miracle it wasn't activated sooner."

"I'll get her here," Ekk said. "We need a little more time."

Ehren said to Ekk, "I'll grant it but, frankly, I need you here too."

My stomach dropped. Did he mean for a minute? Years? Elsa and Ekk were now a part of our family.

Mitzi got back to the most important thing he'd said. "What's this mission you mentioned?"

"Since you appear to be human and you do tours," Ehren said, "no one will become suspicious of you traveling to Africa. Besides, you won't be alone. When we have better intelligence, I'll put together a special tour group."

My mouth went dry. "Africa?"

Mitzi sat up straight, her eyes lit with interest. "How long until we leave?" Now I wanted to kick her.

"That's up to Panda," Ehren said. "We have some time. She must mature into her gift with her ravens."

"My ravens? As far as I can tell, they don't even like me."

Ehren stopped to stare me down. Woda, Alaric, Shrumm, and even Ekk and Elsa were very quiet.

He went on as if I hadn't interrupted. "What kind of world do you want to live in?"

"Ehren, that's not fair," I said. "I'm a tax preparer, not a superhero." Ekk looked sad when I said this.

Elsa jumped in. "That's not true, Panda. You were the one who could get through the barrier at St. Olaf's to complete the compass. You survived Wolfrum and somehow called the ravens when he attacked you in our kitchen." Elsa's words touched my heart. I loved that she felt enough a part of our family to say "our kitchen."

Ehren made his strongest pitch. "Panda, if we can remove these stones from the wrong hands, there will be fewer powerless humans and other free creatures dying at the hands of *Lupus Imperium*." He lowered his voice and put his knuckled fist on the table in front of me and leaned in. "You need to tell me if you're up for this task." Jay put his hand on Ehren's shoulder, and he moved back a bit.

"When do we go?" I asked shakily. Mitzi beamed at me.

Ehren turned off the images and sat. "Maybe never. We don't yet know exactly where they are, but we're making progress."

I felt small inside. All eyes were on me. This was one time that our worlds squarely crashed into one another as the mission ball was passed to my wife and me.

Mitzi put her arm around me, a show of solidarity. "She can do this."

"I'll do my best, sir," was all I could manage to say.

Smiles erupted around the table. Shrumm got up and rang a bell. Soon the kitchen staff returned to clear the table. Everyone got up like normal. My head was still spinning because Mitzi and I were going across the world when, and if, I could master my magic.

"You all leave tomorrow for Merryville," Ehren said. "Ekk, you and Elsa need to come back and bring Aurora and her husband here."

The weight of our possible future mission was heavy. It would depend upon me mastering my magic. I wouldn't be a coward but had no clue how to start. As the others talked about Elsa's grandmother and Jay promised to make us a care package of baked goods, I worried. *What if I'm the one holding up progress in this good against evil because my magic isn't strong enough? What if the ravens changed their birdbrains again?* Sheesh. No pressure.

CHAPTER TWENTY-FIVE

TAGGART'S

Puddle parked at the green curb in front of Taggart's and Ralph said, "I can't believe the city finally painted the curb. People been leaving their cars in front of the store and walking down the street for a two-hour lunch. It's not good for business." He paused. "Uh, was this magic?"

"Politics," Puddle responded. "Mitzi talked to her new buddy, Mayor Reed. Ekk told her you've been trying to get the city to put twenty-minute parking here for ages."

"Get this door open," Ralph said. "I want to see the inside."

Puddle and Ali helped him and Aurora out of the Land Rover. Puddle was nervous but opened the door while Ali got Ralph's walker out of the back. They both got out of the way as Ralph used his walker to enter Taggart's. He stopped cold in the lobby area, his gaze sweeping left to right, taking it all in.

Aurora stood behind him and Ali. Puddle brought up the rear. A faint woodsmoke scent wafted in the air, and a pile of fragrant pine was neatly stacked by the potbelly stove. A fresh coat of Windingle purple paint on the walls and a neon sign in script up near the ceiling that said "Taggart's, Est. 1955" in glowing green greeted them. It was beautiful. The shelving was organized so that gifts were separate from camping gear, which was separate from the tools. The floor was clean and the counter uncluttered. A non-magical person could never have accomplished all this in so short a time. Ratter strutted through the plastic flaps, which separated the storeroom from the main store, and greeted them.

Ralph seemed angry. "I can't afford this—"

Ali said, "It's paid for. I hope it's okay, but Ekk arranged for the Garden to pay for the cleanup in return for you letting me have a few shelves." Ali and Puddle waited for Ralph to absorb that.

"You mean Ekk is…?" He shook his head. Ratter rubbed his walker.

In his booming voice, Ali said, "Yes, you know he is. For whatever reason, you're surrounded by magical people."

Puddle said, "You and I, Ralph, are what we call magic adjacent. Let me show you Ali's botanica."

Ralph looked a little worried but hobbled with his walker back to the shelves now redesigned as "Taggart's Apothecary." Ralph laughed and scratched his head. "Much better than I thought. You made it look all, um, 1800s."

Ali beamed with pride. "Exactly. Like in a Western town."

Puddle took Aurora's hand and showed her a special section with Ivory soap products next to Persil detergent. "Does this look familiar?" She grinned at both Aurora and Ralph.

Ralph turned to his wife and asked, "Honey? What do you think?"

They waited. With a tear on her cheek, Aurora picked up some soap and put it in her pocket. She smiled. "It's good." Apropos of nothing, she said, "I need to make coffee."

Aurora toddled to the potbelly stove with Puddle right behind her. At least for the moment, everything was going to be all right.

***

THE COMMUNITY GARDEN

It had been a week since CTI Environmental finished their work. The executive board called a meeting at the trailer to receive the final results. Sylvia sat in her usual seat, going over the agenda, when Denise arrived. They all knew Charlotte wasn't an early riser.

"Denise, I'm breathless with anticipation. Any news?"

"Good morning, Sylvia. I wanted to give you what I know before the others get here."

After sitting across the folding table, Denise leaned forward with her hands clasped. "None of what I'm about to tell you leaves this room."

"Okay."

"When Ring Tire put in their termination of lease notification with Windingle Development, it was a year before they physically planned to move. That was according to the terms of the lease I got from Charlotte."

"That should have been plenty of time to assess the damage," Sylvia responded.

Denise put on her cheaters and pulled a stapled sheath of papers from her bag on the floor. "The notification was sent in February. I've got a copy of that too. Apparently, Boris Hunt, chief negotiator at Windingle, dropped the ball big time. Charlotte says it's because he thought Ring moving out of state was simply a negotiating tactic for the lease option. It wasn't."

"So, they didn't test the soil during this period?"

"No, they didn't. A good nine months went by while this idiot, Boris, played golf with the CEO at Ring, thinking they had it covered. When it became apparent Ring was dead serious about moving the plant, and all those jobs, Boris called his brother Monte on the planning commission in a panic and asked for help."

"How did Charlotte find that out?" Sylvia asked, then it hit her. "Wait. *That* Monte Hunt? Oh, now we're getting close to the mayor."

"She has sources. That's not all. When Monte got the call, who did he turn to? More golf buddies. Get this, Gary Smithers and Douglas Harker."

"Oh dear god, they were all involved. This can't be all from Charlotte."

"It's not." Denise suddenly got up and poured herself some coffee, not meeting Sylvia's eyes. "Doug Harker's wife, Laura. We've known each other for years and served on the Junior League Board together. After she found out…some private things, she grilled Doug until he told her everything."

"Is that why he had a black eye at the press conference? Remind me never to get on Laura's bad side. Did she know if they ever tested the land?"

Denise sat back down, cup in hand. "Here's the kicker. No. This is where she wasn't sure what happened. Either Gary falsified the report— he was the city councilman for this area—or Douglas Harker paid someone shady to do it. The whole thing stinks to high heaven. She's filing for divorce."

"Wow." Sylvia's brow furrowed, a faraway look in her eyes. "But why would these guys want to give Ring Tire a pass? What was in it for them?"

Denise was blunt. "It's always about money."

"And what did Mayor Reed know?" Sylvia asked.

Denise shrugged her shoulders. "I haven't a clue. Your guess is as good as mine."

A few minutes later, Hortense, Lidia, Florence, Janet, and Sally joined Sylvia and Denise. Charlotte, Valerie, and Mitzi were the only board members missing. It was time to give out the results of CTI's report. The room was soon abuzz with caffeine, chatter, and speculation.

"Ladies," Sylvia said, "we all know why we're here. Let's get right to it."

There was no power point this time, so Janet asked, "Would you like me to read the results?" Sylvia had been about to do it but said, "Sure." She handed Janet the twenty-page neatly typed report.

The first part was all about timing and methods. Everyone leaned in when Janet began reading the section labeled "Results and Recommendations."

"Of the five acres that comprise the land formerly occupied by Ring Tire Company, four can be categorized as within EPA safety limits for growing food." The ladies broke out in a cheer.

"However," Janet went on, "the fifth and final acre that contains the sandy area is thoroughly contaminated with polychlorinated biphenyls and other chemicals. Although it comprises a small part of the acre, it is our recommendation that the entire acre be remediated. Fortunately, the contamination has not penetrated the aquifer. It is this engineer's opinion that this acre, even remediated, should not be used for food production."

Janet looked up. "This is good news?" She surveyed the faces.

Denise nodded. "It is. It could have been a lot worse."

"I told you about that sandpit," Hortense said.

"I admit it," Sylvia said. "You did. Now, going forward, you are all members of the board, and I expect you all to maintain complete secrecy about what you've heard until we have our next steps in place. I'm counting on you."

"The executive board will be meeting with the lawyers this afternoon," Denise said, "and we'll call another meeting in a couple of days to present options. It seems likely we'll have to file a lawsuit."

Everyone nodded solemnly. All except for two of the board members intended to keep their promise not to tell.

***

SYLVIA AND FRANCISCO

Francisco agreed to meet Sylvia when she called him after her board meeting. He changed his guayabera shirt for one with tiny roses stitched on it and told himself he wouldn't let her get the upper hand.

It reminded him of when they dated, decades ago, and he stopped to put on a little of his Creed cologne before walking out the door.

As he walked to the bistro, he realized how hungry he was. The rigorous schedule was hard work. He hoped he and Sylvia could stop jousting long enough for him to get through to her about the garden. It made him sad to think she'd sold out.

Sylvia was already at a table in the back when he got there. As he slipped in the booth he said, "Don't want to be seen with me?"

She gave a half-smile. "It's not that. I needed a moment to take myself away from prying eyes. Let's call a truce."

The server, a twenty something woman, appeared at the table to ask for drink orders.

Sylvia said, "I'll have a Cinnamon Tequila."

He raised an eyebrow. "Ooh, in the middle of the day?"

"You'll need one, too, by the time we're done talking."

"Make it two," Francisco said to the server. He gazed at Sylvia, who looked stunning, and asked sincerely, "Are you okay?"

She flicked her shining black hair back, and he was reminded of her wealth by the subtle gems in her visible earlobe. "I'm more than okay."

"So what's going on? We don't meet often for lunch." He made a little circle on the tabletop with his index finger. "Although I don't know why we don't." He looked up at her in that boyish way that used to make her heart flip-flop.

"Francisco, we've become antagonistic, and that needs to stop. I have some news that I'm not ready to shout from the rooftops. You deserve to know because I know you truly care about the community garden project."

He leaned back and sighed. "Sylvia, don't tell me you're going forward. What—"

She gestured toward the ceiling. "Stop. Just stop. Francisco, you know we had the garden retested by a company that is transparent and above reproach. Do you want to know what they found?"

He paused a moment, then said, "Whatever they found, I have something to tell you too." His eyes challenged her.

"What?" She crossed her arms, red nails on display like talons. He knew this look, and it was often a precursor to an epic argument.

He said quietly, "Dr. Sliwa's students went in after CTI and did their own re-test."

"Then you know that four and three quarters acres of the Community Garden are fine. The problem—"

"Is the sandpit," they said together.

Their drinks came and each took a moment to sip.

"Man," he said, "I haven't had one of these since college." He put the shot glass down and said, "I'm actually starved."

Once they had their order in he said, "It may not be as bad as we thought, but it's still bad."

"The good news is we can safely grow fruits and vegetables on most of the property while the sandpit is remediated."

He whistled. "Who's going to pay for that?"

She took a sip of her water nonchalantly before answering, "We're going to sue Ring Tire."

Francisco reached across the table and took both her hands. "That's the Sylvia I know. What about your friend, Charlotte Windingle?"

"She's an innocent, Frankie. Her company is going to be a defendant, and she's cooperating. We're going after Monte and Boris Hunt, Douglas Harker, and maybe even the mayor."

He smacked his hand on the table. "I knew it. That's awesome. How can I help?"

"Well, a couple of things. I haven't been able to talk to Mitzi Fowler yet. She's on that commission, and we owe it to her to have this conversation before any announcements are made. What we want is to get going on the land we can plant, and let the lawyers fight out the rest."

"You can't expect me to sit on this."

She leaned back. "Apparently, you already knew."

"True. Dr. Sliwa's been burning up my phone. I can go with that. Does this mean you'll support me for mayor?"

She became coy. "I think I'll vote for you on one condition."

"What's that?"

"Stop being so abrasive. If you really want a chance to win, you need to teach those young people that being snarky and disrupting press conferences makes them look immature. No one will turn this city over to a candidate who allows that."

He was about to argue but remembered that back in college her counsel was always sound. After all, she was the one who made it in the corporate world. Maybe it was the tequila on an empty stomach or how pretty she looked, but he said, "How would you like to be my personal consultant?"

She smiled. "Let's go shopping after lunch."

***

A FEW DAYS LATER

Mayor Reed was working at his desk when Monte Hunt called in a panic.

"Tom, I opened the door at my house and got served with a lawsuit over the Ring Tire thing. They named Boris too."

Tom was cool. "I told you that brother of yours was a few bricks shy of a load."

"You don't sound worried," Monte said.

"Why should I be? It wasn't me who frittered away the time Windingle Development had to do their due diligence. Boris waited too long. Tell him to turn it over to their legal department."

"He can't. That Windingle bitch had him fired. Listen, Tom, I asked you about what to do and you said to use the Tillercon Oil guys to write the environmental impact report."

"I said no such thing. And by the way, the only problem is one part of one acre, so it may not be as bad as you think."

"How do you know that?"

"I have my sources. In any event, I won't be playing golf with you or your brother for a while. Please don't take it personally."

Monte's voice choked. "So that's the way you want to play it. Don't forget, I have sources too."

"Oh?" Tom laughed, more of a low growl. "Be careful, Monte. I'll let that last comment go, but remember who you're talking to."

CHAPTER TWENTY-SIX

THE HERCYNIAN GARDEN

Time passed quickly. We'd spent the rest of the previous day touring. Now Mitzi and I had slept well and were ready to go. We had our one bag each packed. Sasha came to get us.

"Please hurry. We have lunch and a message from Twyla."

That did the trick. I picked up both our bags, and we hustled down the hall to the kitchen dining room. Ehren was waiting. Ekk and Shrumm came in right behind us saying, "Just got the message."

Ekk rocked on his heels and said, a coy look on his face, "I guess Twyla did receive her package."

Ehren must have been told how she left it behind. His face was dark like a thundercloud. "By the gods, if Frederick didn't dote on her so much…" He let the sentence trail off as Ekk's dagger began to whirl and jump.

I was thinking I wouldn't want to be Twyla right now. Soon, I saw Twyla and hologram images of Juniper and Valerie standing behind her. I thought I saw someone else but couldn't be sure. This was a live message.

Twyla said brightly, "Greetings, Ehrenhardt. We got your message." I had to admire her positivity in the face of what was coming.

"We? Who is with you, Twyla?" Ehren spoke through clenched teeth.

It was hard to distinguish colors with this method of communication, but I would swear Twyla blushed. She was wearing jeans and looked so young. "Er, ah, my people I protect and, um, Valerie's mother Etsi Chipta." She said brightly. "It means White Singing Bird."

Ekk spoke before Ehren could explode. "Sir, Valerie Gooden and her indigenous family were the ones who suggested the sweat lodge and provided the earth magic that healed Panda."

Ehren didn't get to be leader by letting his emotions cloud his fine mind. He swallowed and said, "I would like to meet Etsi."

She stepped forward into the hologram's visual area. She was thin and wore beads in her hair, a fringed shirt, faded jeans, and boots. Her smile was wide. "You are the tribal leader?" She pointed at Ehren but looked off to the side. I heard Valerie whisper the word yes.

Ehren made a face that suggested his leadership was obvious, but said, "So you have helped my guardians heal my daughter-in-law." It was one of the few times he referred to me, and I wondered if I was on his bad side. I rubbed my ankle, still grateful the pain was now gone.

Etsi stood straight. "Yes, we have the wisdom of our ancestors to thank. We ran with the wolves once."

"Where is Twyla?"

Twyla had a supplicating, wincing grin that almost made me laugh out loud. He spoke directly to her. Instead of the bombast we all expected, he said, "We have fixed the communication so that cell phones and this method are safe to use, as long as you don't lose them."

She winced. "It won't happen again. Actually, it wasn't lost. I just—"

A hard look from him stopped her from explaining further, even across the distance and through the holographic messaging. "You should all be safe to return to Merryville. Any questions?"

These were the times I both admired Ehren and resented him. I ran my life. Mitzi and I made our own decisions. Here, he was ordering us and our friends around like pieces on a chessboard. Well, Mitzi technically was his daughter, Twyla his stepdaughter, but I was a free agent. Mitzi took my hand and squeezed it. She knew me so well.

Juniper stepped forward. "We're glad you sent Twyla to us." She had her arm around Valerie.

He grunted. "I am too."

I had the sense to simply say, "No questions."

***

To hear Puddle tell it, she was getting used to navigating without being stoned. She missed the international terminal and had to go around again. Then she got stuck in the far lane and couldn't get back over. She told us it was like learning to drive all over again. Mitzi and I were already on the curb with our bags when she pulled up.

"Sorry I'm late." Mitzi and I found ourselves enveloped in patchouli-saturated hugs, which made Mitzi sneeze.

"Puddle, it's only been a minute in your time," Mitzi said. "Thank you for getting us."

"Hey, sis." I gave her a half hug while hauling the bags to the van. I gave the huge white van the once over. "Is this yours?"

"No, it's Ali's. He's going to have it wrapped soon with Taggart's on the side. Wait until you see the store."

Mitzi shook her head as if in a dream. "So much to catch up on." She opened the sliding side door and climbed in.

"What did we miss? Any more snow?" This was a silly question, as the California sun shone brightly.

Puddle laughed. She put the column shift in gear and pulled away from the curb, "I don't know how Florida nabbed The Sunshine State. Should have gone to us." I loved that she was starting to think of California as home. "Tell me about, you know, the Hercynian Garden." She chanced a quick glance at me, curiosity lighting her blue eyes.

Mitzi answered. "It's…fantastic. Let's talk about that when we get home."

"Is it okay to talk about our new community garden?" Puddle asked as she expertly guided us onto the freeway toward Merryville.

Mitzi looked surprised. "Of course. What happened? Did the testing get done?"

"The *Merryville Bee* is in the back," Puddle said. "I saved it for you." I handed it to Mitzi, who spent the rest of the trip to Thistle Drive reading intently.

She burst out, "My own life has been so full of wonder, I'd barely even thought about this. Francisco Gonzalez is collaborating with Sylvia?"

Puddle looked sly. "If collaboration is the same as snogging. Looks like they're a thing to me. You know I don't care about politics, but Ali and I are going to the last debate between him and the mayor. It should be fun." She grinned mischievously.

I smiled. "You and Ali? Are you two *collaborating* too?" I loved this ordinary banter and was glad to be home, smiling at Puddle as she navigated the van onto the 105 freeway. I had lots of time to figure out the ravens. That was a worry for later.

✶✶✶

It was Sunday at noon. That evening, the museum would be hosting the last candidate panel before election day. Juniper arrived early to inspect the preparations. She walked the space outdoors and saw that her staff had set up a stage, and it reminded her of a certain exhibition called *Floodlight* that she put on at the beginning of the year. That event was a doozy that nearly cost her this job.

Her assistant curator, Maribel, walked over from behind the stage, arms open. "Juniper. I'm so glad you're back." Her hair was a mass of soft curls, but for once it wasn't colored in any of the bright hues she usually sported. As an artsy woman, she often used her hair to make a statement.

Juniper touched it lightly. "Your hair. I don't think I ever realized it's light brown."

"They used to call it dishwater blond. Not flattering, but this is a serious event." Maribel saluted. She wore a red, white, and blue modern version of a 1960s dress with cat glasses.

"Are you channeling the Kennedy era?"

"How'd you know?" She looked pretty and would have looked at home on the *Madmen* set. "I'm getting in the mood for the panel today. We're expecting quite a crowd."

"I'm so proud of you," Juniper said. "The museum was in good hands while I was away."

Staff began setting up chairs. Maribel asked, "How is Valerie's family? Everything okay?"

"Yes, we decided to get out of Dodge with that crazy snow, that's all. And," she waved at the car, "we brought back some amazing items from the reservation." She arranged her fingers like a director making a frame. "Raven, weasel, and coyote. I feel a show coming on."

"Oh good. We need something for November to really make waves. It's been pretty calm."

Juniper laughed. "As long as they're talking about us. So for today I understand Lucus Windingle and Linda Chicolet are the moderators?"

"Yes, one conservative, Linda obviously, one not so conservative, very balanced. We also have a couple of pinners in the audience who will listen carefully and let them know if the candidates don't fully answer the questions."

"Sounds good. I'm going to catch up on my mail." Juniper walked back to the main building where her office was located.

***

By six p.m., the parking lot was full. Local organizations had been invited, and the Merryville Horticultural Society had a table near other nonprofits. Janet Bruce-Pippin and Sally Johnson sat behind the table on folding chairs, answering questions as people milled around. Merryville Mavenettes handed out flyers, seeking donations for the community garden opening. Sweet and savory items from a new downtown bakery were displayed on the table next to them. Mavenettes were crowding the cookie tray until Janet Bruce-Pippin chased them off.

Mitzi, who arrived with Puddle, stopped by to say hello. Janet hugged her. "I didn't know you were back. It's been wild." Sally waved at them.

"I'm caught up. Sylvia called me."

"Where's Panda?"

"Doing laundry. She's not as into this political thing. But you know, since I'm on a commission now…" She let that die off. "Hey, I heard about the test results on the community garden."

"I'm so glad we can at least go forward with the four acres. Hopefully, that's what the mayor will say." Sally looked at the stage as Hortense walked by.

"Hi, Hortense. Where are you off to?" Mitzi asked.

"Mitzi. I didn't see you. When did you get back, dear?"

"Late last night." They walked together toward the stage area. Microphones were being adjusted, and a local camera crew was setting up. Sally drifted off, as she was wont to do.

Hortense said, "I've been thinking about what happened at the memory care. Sit with me a moment."

Mitzi and Hortense sat on two folding chairs while people walked by holding lemonade or cups of coffee. "Ever since the hospital shooting and the, you know, she motioned to Mitzi's shoulders, I've been wondering—what is going on in this town?"

Mitzi asked, "What do you mean?"

"The mayor, Tom, specifically asked me to take on that sandlot. Sylvia assigned me the same area and challenged me to make it a succulent garden. Now we find out that's the one piece of land that is polluted."

"That is weird. You probably could have done a cactus garden. No one would have ever known what lay beneath. Do you think he knew something?"

"I'm going to find out. In the meantime, when are you going to tell me about your wings?"

Mitzi's head shook no. "I can't, Hortense. Please believe me when I say we're on the same side if that side is to find the truth." She put a beaded braid behind her ear. "Why don't we go confront the mayor together. I feel a bit used as well after the press conference."

Hortense smiled a dangerous smile. "Let's."

The two women walked behind the stage to where a VIP section was roped off. Maribel stood at the entrance and greeted the women. Tom had already seen Hortense and waved her and Mitzi over. He had just finished talking to Lucas Windingle.

Hortense went right for the jugular. "Giving Lucas your condolences for the lawsuit?"

"What? No. He's a fine young man. They have insurance." He turned to Mitzi. "I heard you were back in town. You must know the results are in." He lowered his voice confidentially. "That was a brilliant speech you gave at the presser. The 'pause' language was inspired."

He started to turn away, but Mitzi said, "When's our next meeting?"

Tom said, "What? Oh, the commission? I think we're going to pause that too. Er, ah, Monte Hunt is stepping down, maybe Doug Harker too."

"Great. I have suggestions for their replacements."

He puffed out his chest. "Now see here. You were invited on the commission by me and have been to one official meeting that you had to leave early—I'll appoint new members if needed."

"And after that one half a meeting you still saw fit to have me deliver a speech about the community garden to the entire city," Mitzi said. "It's just lucky for me that the reports came out like they did. If I'm not mistaken, you were going to go with the EIR that Tillercon Oil threw together to cover your ass."

A couple of notables nearby raised eyebrows, listening.

Tom's face darkened. "How dare you talk to me like that. I'm the one who championed a community garden. Hortense knows how this works." He turned to her. "But obviously you should pick your board members more carefully."

"Oh?" Hortense said. "You called me about adding her to the commission, remember? And by the way, Tom, what did you know about that sandy area on the land? You specifically told me to claim it. Then surprise, surprise, it was assigned to me. Were you hoping I would cover up any improprieties for you?"

Now he looked shocked. During this minor kerfuffle, no one noticed Phillip Pen lurking with a camera. The man had a sixth sense for sniffing out drama.

Red in the face, Tom said, "I'm not going to dignify that with a response other than to say it was the new president of the club who assigned you to the sand, not me."

"So you've been talking to Sylvia? How else would you know that?" Hortense asked. "And another thing. Didn't you tell me that the clubhouse was going to be used as an immigrant welcome center if Francisco Gonzalez won the election?" Her British voice carried. "Apparently that was a lie."

Now a small crowd started to gather. "I said no such thing. What he might do is entirely speculation, especially since he doesn't have a snowball's chance in hell of winning."

"Interesting choice of words," Mitzi said.

"Now the snow is my fault? You two deserve each other. If you'll excuse me." He tried to leave, but there was nowhere to go in the small roped-off area. Furious, he hissed at Hortense, "How soon they forget. I helped Bill avoid a jail sentence."

Hortense slapped him hard. A flash from somewhere made Tom Reed turn to look at its source.

"Did you now?" Phillip said from behind the VIP rope. The flashes kept coming.

The mayor took two aggressive steps toward him, and Phillip snapped what was to become an iconic photo that was later named "Raging Bull" by local pundits. Finally, it appeared the Teflon mayor might be facing something that would stick.

Francisco Gonzalez arrived at that moment, looking quite corporate and handsome in a suit, and asked innocently, "Did I miss something?"

The debate that followed was a surprise to many Merryvillians. Tom Reed, not used to confrontation or exposure, was off his game. He stumbled a bit and shuffled his papers, showing uncharacteristic nerves, while with Sylvia's guidance, Francisco kept on message and cut out the childish digs at the incumbent. This was going to be a tight race after all. From the crowd's response, a person could almost hear the tide turning toward Tom's opponent, at least for now.

***

EKK AND ELSA

Ekk and Elsa walked together on Ekk's favorite path by a lake outside the keep. It was rare downtime for the two of them, the magical sky blue and cloudless and a soft wind blowing. Ekk asked, "What are you thinking about, Elsa?"

She looked out on the lake and sighed. "This is so beautiful, but I'm ready to go back to Merryville."

"This is the first time we've had alone time together. Don't you like that?" Ekk rarely showed insecurity, but he had a tender side.

"It's not that at all, Ekk." She put her head on his shoulder. "I have a feeling it's time for me to check on the girls, and I finally have a kitchen that's the right height and all mine."

"The girls let us decorate it in a Black Forest theme," Ekk said. "Well, this is the actual Black Forest. Isn't that even better?"

"Honestly? No. Can we go home?"

He smiled tenderly. "As long as we're being honest, I miss our treehouse too."

"What does Ehren say?"

He sighed. "Before we can go, we need to have a handle on what's happening from the seers. So far, the only name we have for *Lupus Imperium's* leader is "The Master.""

"Have you heard from Panda? I'm worried about the pressure on her."

Ekk looked at the sky. "She kept asking for magic. Ehren is the type that will throw you in the lake to teach you to swim."

Elsa frowned. "I know they have magic, but Panda needs nurturing, not shock therapy. She's also wounded herself, you know."

"We cured that. The sweat lodge—"

Elsa explained as if to a child, "The sweat lodge cured her physical wound, but she carries another wound inside." Elsa's motherly impulse was strong.

Realizing there would be no peace until they spoke to Panda, Ekk pulled out his dagger and began a call to Twyla.

***

Once alone, the realization that so many counted on me to save the world with "my ravens" when I had no idea how to do that brought me down and I cried. Twyla surprised me when she burst into the laundry room, dagger in hand.

"It's Ekk and Elsa," she announced. In spite of my red eyes, I laughed.

"Hello, Panda. We'll be home soon. How are you doing? Where's Mitzi?" It was as if a friend walked in with a cell phone, only this call was from another world. The holographs of Ekk and Elsa moved with the device, something new to ponder. They stood by a lake with the sun shining.

"Oh yeah. Mitzi's at a debate and I'm doing laundry." I tried to smile.

After a beat, Elsa asked, "Twyla, could you leave us please?"

"Sure, but Ehren said to never let the dagger out of my sight."

"This will be our little secret. We need to speak with Panda, okay?" Ekk said this sweetly.

"Ooooh. Secrets." She winked in an exaggerated manner. "Bye." With a twinkle she was gone.

I wondered why they called. "What are you up to?"

"Good magic, like what you're working on," Elsa said.

"I know time in the Hercynian Garden moves more quickly, but we've only been here a day. Honestly, I don't even know where to begin." I sat down hard on a small bench and threw the wet items into the dryer. "I don't know how to call the ravens. I might never learn how. It might all be a big mistake, and then the whole world is going to suffer." Tears burst out again, and I started sobbing.

Elsa said to Ekk, "I was afraid of this."

"Panda. Panda," Elsa called. I looked up and wiped snot off my nose. "We're coming home and will help you. Listen, you asked me to teach you magic, and I will. It's not an overnight process. This could take months or even years. Okay?"

I pressed my lips together and nodded. "I'm sorry, didn't know all that was in there. I'm glad you're coming home." And I meant it, but my insecurity still hung heavy around me.

"We'll send you our itinerary. Put the ravens out of your mind for now," Ekk said.

"Remember: one foot in front of the other," Elsa chimed in, "and Panda, don't put that red thing in with the whites."
This made me bark a laugh. "Thanks, guys. I need normal right now." At this point, even Elsa's know-it-all cleaning advice was welcome. "See you soon, friends."

"Bye, Panda," they both said.

After we disconnected, I picked up the basket of white laundry and plucked out the red washcloth. Then I returned the dagger to Twyla, who had waited right outside the door.

"I actually came over to help tear down the sweat lodge, unless you want to turn it into an air BnB." This thought was so absurd I laughed again, realizing how much I loved my controlling, ditzy, magical family.

After the call from Ekk and Elsa, I felt a little better. I couldn't wait to take Elsa up on her promise to help me with my magic. I wasn't quite sure what that would entail, but at least it was a start.

The alarm on my phone sounded to notify me it was about time for the debate to end. I patted my pocket to make sure I had my keys, then left to pick up my wife.

Mitzi was surrounded by what appeared to be the entire Horticultural Society board when I pulled into the parking lot. She waved at me, said her goodbyes, and joined me in the car. She was all abuzz with news of how she and Hortense cornered Tom.

"Wow, I can't wait to read about it in the paper." We drove down Main Street and was about to turn toward home when Mitzi pointed the other way.

"Stop at Taggart's on the way home."

"Why? What do you need?"

"Just humor me."

"Okay." Two minutes later, I pulled up to the store and parked at the green curb.

Mitzi was excited. "Remember what a mess all this was?" she asked. "Check this out." She fairly jumped out of the car.

"When did you see it?"

"I stopped by on the way to the debate. Come on."

My Mitzi was full of surprises. The inside of Taggart's was completely renovated from the dusty place it was before the Winter Stone. She wanted to show me everything. After circling the ground floor, she took me upstairs, and I saw the well-lit area had been transformed.

"Is that Bonnie Bruce-Pippin?" Mitzi didn't answer, as it was clear Janet's daughter was stocking shelves. She turned around, stuck her bottom lip out, and blew a wispy blond piece of hair out of her eyes. She wore an apron and had lost some weight since I saw her last.

"Hey, Panda and Mitzi."

"Hi, Bonnie. Wow, do you work here?"

"Yes, and I love it. This is my favorite section too." She was stacking board games on a shelf. "Ralph says I can put a puzzle on the table by the potbelly stove for people to work on."

"Nice." I looked around.

Mitzi pointed to the new lights above. "You can actually see all the cool stuff now."

"Oh yeah, this is great. So many changes." Before, one of the long fluorescent tubes had gone out and not been replaced, making it dim. "How is Ralph?" I asked, as we continued our tour by going back downstairs.

"He's healing nicely. Puddle said he brings Aurora here in the afternoons. I'm sure once Ekk and Elsa get back, they'll work on getting her to the Garden." We reached the bottom floor, which was noisy with customers. Ali was in the corner at a table, handing out samples in little cups.

Upon seeing me he said, "Excuse me" and came over to give me a hug. "My rescuer. Welcome back. Would you like a little of Dr. Badawi's jet-lag potion?" I saw he had reinvented himself as an apothecary.

"Well, sure. But I could actually use a *nap*." I looked at my wife.

"We'll go in a minute," she said to me, then turned back to Ali. "What do you have for me?" Her smile was infectious.

It was then I noticed the music. It had played in the background, but suddenly the volume increased to a screeching level while the lights flickered.

Ali looked worried. "Excuse me." He left for the backroom. Patrons put their hands over their ears, and some made for the exit. The music abruptly stopped. After a pause, things went back to normal. Ali returned and stood behind his table.

"That was weird," I said to Mitzi, who looked startled. Ali handed me a concoction. "For you, I have lavender extract."

I smelled my little dixie cup. "Nice, thank you."

He handed one to Mitzi as well. "Mine smells like lavender too.'"

We started toward the door. I stopped to speak briefly with Puddle, who was finally alone, minding the till. "The place looks great, but has this kind of thing been happening?" I swirled my hand indicating the store, "With the music and stuff?"

She nodded. "But it's mostly awesome, so don't be negative, sis. Look at this crowd." A group of teenage girls approached with cards they'd chosen from a new section. "Now that you're back, we need you and Ekk doing your bookkeeping thing."

I groaned. "I haven't even unpacked."

"Love you." She air-kissed me and addressed the new customers. "Hi. Are these all together or one for each?"

I left her to it, impressed she was embracing her responsibility. It had to be because of Ali. Or maybe Ralph. Or maybe because she was clean and sober. Who knew? I was seeing a new Puddle.

Mitzi steered me through the crowd. "Isn't this amazing?"

I looked longingly at the full chairs near the potbelly stove. That had been my spot when the store was so quiet that it was a place to meditate with coffee in hand. Now the place could only be described as bustling.

I hoped the success would continue for Ralph and Aurora's sake. Ekk warned me the books indicated it would take a lot of cash to really get Taggart's on firm financial ground. "I can see why you wanted to show me," I said to Mitzi. "Take that, Big Box Store." We left and climbed back into the car.

"Oh, the big box thing has been delayed," Mitzi said. "So for now, Taggart's is the only game in town."

"Awesome. Good thing people don't know the Winter Stone came from their storeroom."

"Seriously. People can turn on you so quickly."

CHAPTER TWENTY-SEVEN

THE BIG REVEAL

It was nearing the end of the Merryville Horticultural Society meeting, and time for old business. The mood in the room was party-like, now that the final report was out about the state of the community garden.

Lidia, from the old board, had followed Hortense back and was speaking. "I, for one, would like to meet in our regular clubhouse. It's not easy for me as a senior to walk on this uneven land."

"I understand. We just completed the renovations for the mansion. Charlotte? How long do we have the trailer?"

She smiled. "As part of our commitment to making this land a success, the Windingle board has voted to donate this trailer permanently. It can be our on-site office for this project," Charlotte announced.

The women clapped.

"That will help so much, Charlotte," Sylvia said. "May I add, the club thanks you and your company for the way you've handled this whole affair?"

"Well, they kind of had to." Hortense saying this was so inappropriate that it was actually funny. Denise couldn't help herself and uncharacteristically burst out laughing. Soon, they were all in tears once they could see Charlotte saw the humor too.

Charlotte had a good sense of humor, and made "come on, more" gestures with her hands. It was a good way to call out the elephant in the room. "You're right, Hortense."

Hortense didn't completely understand why everyone laughed at her, but she was affected positively by her fellow board members. Laughing with the group felt better than the triumph of having a barb land.

Charlotte, as if doing penance, wasn't wearing rhinestones this day and, in a plain purple dress, was toned down. After the laughter petered out, she said, "We always wanted good things for this area of town. We fired Boris Hunt and will make sure this remediation is done right." She looked at Hortense. "This is our penance for Windingle Development's part in the soil problem. We've made a lot of money in Merryville, and it's okay to give some back."

Sally said, "Jack and I'll be here coordinating the volunteers. We need to have someone every Saturday."

A discussion followed about how to schedule that. Finally, Sylvia said, "Mitzi, even though you joined us only weeks ago, it feels like longer."

Mitzi said, "You have no idea."

"In a short time, you have become integral to this club. After joining as a volunteer—"

"On my committee," Hortense commented, poking at Denise, who frowned at her.

"And now," Sylvia said, "I'd like to announce our newest official board member, Mitzi Fowler. That is, if you'll accept."

"I am honored," Mitzi said.

Janet began texting. A moment later someone knocked on the door. Sally opened it to let Bonnie in with a cake. Sylvia said, "Meeting closed. Let's party."

***

"Jeremy," Tom Reed said, "how are the polls? And where is Bradley?"

"You're in a statistical dead heat, and Brad went up north to see his uncle."

"Hell of a time to be on vacation. It's that damn Mitzi Fowler. And Hortense. I've been sabotaged. Did you see the paper? Get me that Mona Martin. Isn't that new home center about done? I need a ribbon cutting, something."

"As a matter of fact, the big box store is waffling on the letter of intent. They're talking about moving to nearby Long Beach."

"What? And who's helping my opponent? All the sudden he's walking around in a suit from Brooks Brothers instead of that stupid Cholo outfit he was wearing." Tom drummed his fingers on his desk. "Margaret."

Tom's long-suffering secretary put her head through the open doorway.

"Get Ben Dunning and David Smith in here. They're all I have left on the planning commission."

"What happened to Doug Harker?" Jeremy asked.

"He's ah, taking some time. Wife filed for divorce."

"Oh. What about Mitzi Fowler?"

"She's not invited."

Margaret timidly said. "Sir, according to the city charter, you can't have a meeting without inviting all the members."

Jeremy nodded. "It's a Brown Act violation."

Tom was red in the face. "Then tell them we're playing golf. Tell them I'll meet them at the club in Palos Verdes."

"Yes, sir." Margaret disappeared.

"Do you think it's a good idea to be seen playing golf right now?" Jeremy asked.

"I don't care. I need to let off some steam."

"As long as I have your ear for a moment, I need to talk to you about Brad."

"I'm not interested unless you have golf cleats."

***

Ekk and Elsa had only been back for a week, and we'd made the most of it. Lots of celebration and preparation. We were all tired, that was for sure. Tonight, I'd ordered take out from Chens, the Chinese restaurant down the street. Ralph and his wife took theirs upstairs, and Puddle had moved to the couch. Mitzi was trying to capture a wonton with chopsticks. The news was on in the background and cycled around to the death of Techlife's primary stockholder, Viktor Molotov in a "spectacular explosion that rocked the entire upscale neighborhood."

"I think that's where Sylvia used to work," Mitzi said and successfully got the wonton to her mouth.

"That's giving me a headache," I said to Mitzi. "Can we turn it off now?"

She punched the remote and the screen went dark. We tucked into our dumplings, soup, and Chow Mein. Now that the TV was off, I could concentrate.

Mitzi asked Elsa, "So you're leaving us again?"

I jumped in. "But it's temporary, right? You're our family."

"We can't foretell the future, Panda," Elsa said, "but that's the plan."

Ekk said, motioning with chopsticks, "Elsa and I are taking Ralph and Aurora back to the Garden. Ralph's never visited, but Aurora spent time there as a child. They'll be safe until this thing is over."

Mitzi brightened. "You mean it might be over some day?"

"*Liebchen*, we may get lucky enough to have a long stretch of peace. That does happen from time to time." Elsa pushed her plate away. This cuisine wasn't her favorite.

Ali stood and stretched. "I'm going back to the store. Gotta feed Selket and Ratter."

"You're staying there?" This surprised me.

"Only until Ekk and Elsa take Ralph and Aurora back to the Garden. Ralph had a little space in the back you could barely see with all the junk. "Puddle made me a little nest. I'll be staying at their house after that."

Puddle looked at Ali, then at me. "Once we got the storage room well-lit, you wouldn't believe the things we found."

"Jimmy Hoffa?" I asked, and everyone groaned. "Sorry."

"It's comfortable, and I can keep an eye on the store. But I'm happy to watch their house, mow the lawn. You know how time in the Garden is. They could be away for a while." Ali hugged us and walked toward the door. My sister's chair scraped back, and she hastily wiped her face.

"Looks like somebody has a new boyfriend," I said in a sing-song voice.

"It's nice," Mitzi said. "Leave her alone."

Brutus came and rubbed against my leg. I Looked down at him. My heart was happy. "I missed you, too, my boy."

***

Elsa was in her hallowed spot at the stove, making breakfast. Aurora and Ralph sat at the kitchen table, dressed for travel. "Good morning," I said, rubbed my eyes, and made a beeline for coffee. "How did you sleep?"

Ralph patted his wife. "Best ever."

Mitzi followed right behind me. "Are you nervous?"

Aurora answered, "No, I want to show Ralph where I'm from."

"I thought you were from England?" Elsa shot me a look. "Oh okay, yeah, the Hercynian Garden is pretty awesome."

Elsa said, "Sit." She had already set out plates.

"Where's Puddle?" I asked.

"Taggart's," Elsa said, "helping Ali. Ekk ran over to the store too. He'll be back soon."

"I thought we were all going to the airport together," I said, once we all sat, waffles, bacon and orange juice in front of us. My eyes got misty.

"This is the last time we'll have breakfast together for a while." Everyone else was quiet.

Mitzi said, "Yeah, and two days before my birthday. Did you have to leave today?"

Elsa put her hand over Mitzi's. "It would have been hard any day, honey. We have to get Aurora out of here as soon as possible."

"We would have left sooner," Ralph said, "but I had to get the house secured. Ali's moving in while we're gone."

"Do you have any questions about our treehouse?" Elsa asked.

Brutus strutted in and plopped in his bed. He looked so much better than he had before the sweat. He was actually getting fat with all the treats people were giving him.

"No, I don't think so. You said leave it alone, right?"

Elsa chuckled and looked at me. "It's going to be hard to keep Panda out."

"Are you calling me nosy?"

"It's okay," Elsa said. "I put a protective spell on it, so most people will ignore it."

Ralph shook his head. "A spell for this, a floating fairy for that. I'm not sure I'm ready for all this."

Aurora looked at him squarely, "Wait until we find a marsh. You'll see what I can do."

My coffee cup froze halfway to my lips, and I couldn't help but look at Mitzi with wide eyes. I mouthed "marsh"?

The expression on Ralph's face was priceless.

***

After helping clean up, we left for our polling station. I was a little irritated at everyone for missing our final breakfast. Puddle especially. She wasn't sentimental, I guess. Ekk needed to organize his work, so I understood this was part of his preparation. Ali was still so new to us, I didn't blame him at all. I was glad Ekk's focus seemed to reassure Ralph and Aurora they would have an open business when they returned.

I mentioned all this to Mitzi as we drove to the polls, and she said, "It's okay. Everybody's different."

We had to park down the street, as turnout for the mayor's race was high. The kids at Merida University had done a good job knocking on doors, and Tom Reed's incumbency and name recognition brought out his supporters. We walked past people holding signs and wearing T-shirts with slogans. So much passion. It was hard for me to care, however, when somewhere in Africa, the Summer Stone was waiting for us to find it. Then I reminded myself that voting was the privilege of living in a democracy.

Hortense sat at a table and took my ballot. "Thank you, dear." She spied a Merida student wearing a bright yellow and blue "Vote Francisco Gonzalez" T-shirt and boomed, "No electioneering. Out! Out!"

It made me chuckle. That was the old Hortense we knew.

After voting, we were headed home when Mitzi's phone rang. She answered, and it came over the car speaker. "Hi, Ekk."

"Hey, girls, can you swing by and pick me up at Taggart's?"

"Uh, we're in the Miata. You better get ready. We've got to get you to the airport."

"Oh. Well, come by anyway." He hung up.

"That was odd," I said, and wondered if all was well.

Mitzi didn't say anything but made a quick left, detouring to the store. The closed sign was displayed, and it didn't appear any lights were on. We looked at each other and approached with caution.

I went first and opened the front door, which was unlocked. The bell over the door tinkled and all the lights came on. Several loud voices yelled, "Surprise!"

Mitzi was right behind me and put both hands over her mouth. A "Happy Birthday Banner" was stretched over the entire space, and all the people we loved stood smiling. Ekk, Elsa, Ali, Ralph, Aurora, Puddle, Juniper, Valerie, and even our neighbors Scott and Mary. Scott said, "Are you surprised?"

I socked him. "How come you didn't tell me? I can keep a secret."

Ekk and Mitzi belly-laughed at that.

He said, "Speaking of which…" I ignored the invitation to respond about past events.

Mary and Puddle disappeared and soon returned from the back, pushing a cart which usually carried heavy parts. In the middle was a giant cake with "HAPPY BIRTHDAY MITZI!" on the top and "BON VOYAGE TO RALPH & AURORA" on the bottom.

I grabbed Mitzi's hand, and she blew out the candles. Puddle was teary, and Scott poured us all glasses of sparkling cider.

"When did you have time to do this?" I asked Elsa.

"I had a little help from next door," she said and grinned at Mary.

"Well done." I was impressed that Elsa was learning to ask for help. Her experience with Valerie must have shown her it was okay.

She went on. "We hated missing Mitzi's birthday."

Ekk said, "Come on, let's eat before the customers come in and wonder what the heck this is about."

Ali said, in his deep voice, "I'll tell them it's our grand opening celebration. There's enough here for half of Merryville."

"You are good at promotion, son." Ralph patted him on the arm.

Scott came up to me and gave me a big hug. "You finally going to show me that treehouse?"

I smiled. "Yes, you have full privileges, at least until Elsa locks us out."

Mitzi was happily overwhelmed, talking with Valerie, Juniper, and Ralph in turns. We all enjoyed Mary's baking, but soon it was time to leave.

I cried a little seeing Elsa and Ekk at the airport help the elderly Ralph and Aurora into wheelchairs for their long trip. They waved one more time before being swallowed up by the international terminal crowd. I kept staring out the airport window and felt their loss. "I wish they didn't have to go."

"They'll be safer in the Garden than anywhere else." Mitzi took my hand and said, "I love these people."

EPILOGUE

Francisco walked into his new office with wonder. Sylvia stood next to him and together they soaked in the power. It was a squeaker, but he'd won. He turned and kissed her. "This is how I pictured winning. Always with you at my side." She walked to the window and looked down at Merryville's busy street below.

Slender, fashionable, a perfect political mate, Sylvia turned back to him. "So much to accomplish. And I'm just getting started."

He cleared his throat theatrically. "You mean we."

She smiled, and he marveled again at how pretty she was.

With an unreadable expression under thick lashes she said, "Of course."

The End.

To be continued in

Search for the Summer
Stone

Book Five
of the
Hercynian Forest Series

Acknowledgments

So much has happened since book three! The pandemic, and a new publisher. Let's see if I can get through the acknowledgements without any further exclamation points. I have a new/old publisher, Launch Point Press. First, I want to thank Lori L. Lake for being there for me, as founder of the press, and believing in my little stories. She is still a beloved mentor and friend.

Second, my new "owners" haha, Jodi and Peggy Zeramby, challenge me and make me sit down and do my work, thank you. The result is in this book, the first under their auspices. They laugh a lot, and are wonderfully talented people. Thank you.⦙ (oops) [editor's note: you've reached your quota for exclamation point usage.]

Okay let's just get rid of categorizing first, second, and third. I love all these people: Verda Foster, who edits and painstakingly teaches me about that and which. Since I love fairy tales and myth, she even gives me little rhymes: "Commas that cut out the fat, go with which and not that." I love you, Verda.⦙ Suzan Twilley Gridley, my line editor, is a gift from the universe. She is so fun to talk to about politics as well as proper use of a semicolon. Suzan is patient and always the encouraging teacher. Thank you to beta readers Renae Standen, and my wife and biggest supporter, Stephanie Loftin. People need to know that even good storytellers need a team to make a good book.

About the Author

Biography. Reba Birmingham, born June 27, 1958, is an American fiction writer and attorney. She is best known for her Hercynian Forest Series, which intersects a modern lesbian couple in Merryville, California, with a parallel world of magic in the Black Forest.

Note to Readers

Thank you for reading a book from Launch Point Press. We have made every effort to edit this book. However, typos do slip in. If you find an error in the text, please email publisher@launchpointpress.com so the issue can be corrected.

We appreciate you as a reader and want to ensure you enjoy the reading process. We would like you to consider posting a review on your preferred media sites and/or your blog or website.

For more information on upcoming releases, author interviews, contests, giveaways and more, please sign up for our newsletter and visit us as at Launch Point Press: www.launchpointpress.com and "Like" us on Facebook: Launch Point Press.

Bright Blessings

www.ingramcontent.com/pod-product-compliance
Lightning Source LLC
Chambersburg PA
CBHW060249100726
47907CB00003B/823